METAL GEAR SOLID®

Raymond Benson

METAL GEAR SOLID®

Original story by Hideo Kojima

Ballantine Books DEL REY New York

A Del Rey Books Trade Paperback Original

Published in the United States by Del Rey Books,
an imprint of The Random House Publishing Group,
a division of Random House, Inc., New York.

Del Rey is a registered trademark and the Del Rey colophon
is a trademark of Random House, Inc.

LIBRARY OF CONGRESS CATALOGING-IN-PUBLICATION DATA
Benson, Raymond.
Metal gear solid / Raymond Benson.
p. cm.
"A Del Rey Books trade paperback original"—T.p. verso.
ISBN-13: 978-0-345-50328-2 (pbk.)
I. Title.
PS8552.E547666M475 2008
813'.54—dc22   2008003021

Printed in the United States of America

www.delreybooks.com

2 4 6 8 9 7 5 3 1

ACKNOWLEDGMENTS

For their help and support, the author wishes to thank Hideo Kojima, Ryan Payton, Dallas Middaugh, Jonathan E. Quist, Eric Cherry, Peter Miller, and—of course—Randi and Max.

METAL GEAR SOLID®

1

Dr. Clark quietly reentered the Visiting Chamber, stood still behind the U.S. president and General Jim Houseman, and listened to them whisper. The two men were transfixed in front of the observation window that overlooked the operating theater.

"Is she in pain?" the president asked.

"I thought she was supposed to be sedated," the general replied. "Now they're blocking our view, damn it."

"What's happening?" the president asked. "Can you see?"

"Do not be alarmed, Mister President." Dr. Clark's seductive and eloquent voice echoed in the chamber, startling the president.

"Oh! You gave me a start, Doctor," the gray-haired politician said. It always had struck Clark that the president was a very nervous type when he wasn't in front of a camera. She rather enjoyed scaring the poor man; that was ironic because she *was* a woman, albeit a woman with a commanding presence and powerful charisma.

Clark stepped closer, out of the shadows, and addressed them. "I apologize, Mister President. I thought you were aware I was behind you."

The president laughed nervously. "It must be because we're down here so far underground. I guess I'm a little claustrophobic."

General Houseman said, "We'll get you back up to the surface as soon as you want to go, Mister President." Clark noted that the general didn't look too pleased to be there either.

"Is she giving birth?" the president asked.

"She's been in labor for a long time," Clark answered. "It'll be very soon, I'm sure."

The president squeamishly turned away from the window and waved his hand around the chamber, indicating the hundreds of stalactites on the limestone ceiling. "Do any of those things ever fall?"

"They're thousands of years old, Mister President," Clark replied. "They won't fall on their own, I can assure you of that. And the likelihood of an earthquake occurring in the southeastern corner of New Mexico is quite remote." Her voice reverberated with upper-class sophistication and the timbre of a Shakespearean actress.

The president nodded. "I know. It's just amazing to think that on the other side of that cavern wall is one of America's most popular national parks. Hundreds of tourists pour through it every day."

"The Carlsbad area was perfect for the project. I'm in debt to your predecessor for backing it."

The president tilted his head and said, "You know, Doctor, I inherited this project. Tell me how you got established in this facility."

Clark smiled. "Ever since the caverns were discovered,

there were many caves not open to the public. Caves just sitting here, available to the government. I believe the first time this cavern was used by the government was during World War II. The Roosevelt administration built a safe house here in case America was attacked. Since then, it's been used for a number of research projects." Clark glanced at the general. "Most of them military in nature."

"I see."

"We took it over in the mid-sixties."

The president turned back to the window. "Well, is the project finally going to succeed?" he asked. "This is, what, the ninth try?"

"Have faith, Mister President," Dr. Clark said. "I corrected the genetic code in the last batch. I also made sure that the surrogate mother possessed certain genetic *latches*, if you will, that could connect with those of Big Boss."

The president shook his head in amazement. "I still can't believe you have so many samples of his cells. What did he think you were going to do with them?"

"The man knew only that he was sterile and couldn't produce children. He was unaware of our undertaking here," Dr. Clark said.

"The *Les Enfants Terribles* project."

"Correct. We extracted the cells when Big Boss was in surgery, when he was wounded in the last war. The Pentagon gave strict orders that he was not to know about the project's outcome—whether or not we succeeded. Although, knowing Big Boss, I wouldn't be surprised if he has learned about it by now. The security surrounding our activities has not always been ideal."

"The security has been the best the U.S. government can supply," Houseman countered. "You know that, Doctor."

Dr. Clark went on without acknowledging the military man's defensive remark. "We reproduced the cells through analog cloning and the Super Baby Method, fertilized them into an ovum, as you know, and then implanted the fetuses into the mother."

"Does she know she's going to give birth to *eight* babies?" the president asked.

Dr. Clark corrected him. "She's not giving birth to all eight. Only two. Six of the fetuses were aborted months ago so that we could encourage the growth of the other two."

"So she's going to give birth to just twins; is that it?"

"That's precisely it. But not *exactly.*"

"What do you mean?"

"There will be certain genetic differences in the two children. It was the only way we could succeed, as you know."

"So does that mean one's going to be better than the other? I thought they were supposed to be exactly the same."

Clark shook her head. "Mister President, one will not be *better* than the other. But it's entirely possible that one will possess more dominant genes than his brother. But it's nothing to worry about."

Some new activity behind the glass drew their attention back to the operating arena. All of a sudden, the sterility of the bright room intensified. It was as if the shine on the stainless-steel surgical equipment had imbued the space with artificial energy as the doctors and nurses surrounded the table containing the writhing female patient.

The steel door behind the observers slid open. A nurse entered and announced, "Doctor, they're ready for you."

Clark acknowledged her. "Thanks. I'll be right there."

"Is she giving birth?" the president asked.

"Mister President, I must go deliver two strong baby boys."

The president stuck out his hand. "Look, Doctor Clark, this

isn't something I particularly want to watch. I need to get back to Washington. It's good to see you."

Clark feigned surprise, but she had expected the president's prudish behavior. She shook the man's hand and asked, "Are you certain? We could have a meal later before you depart."

"Thanks, Doctor, but I must decline. To tell you the truth, this place gives me the creeps. Thank you for making us aware of the imminent, uhm, births. By the way—do I get the pick of the litter?"

"I beg your pardon, Mister President."

"You know one of those . . . *things* . . . she's giving birth to will belong to us. I'd like to pick which kid belongs to us, that's all."

"You have that right." Clark held up her hands and laughed good-naturedly. "I have nothing to do whatsoever with the politics behind the project."

The president nodded, satisfied. "All right, then I want the one you said has dominant genes. It's got to have an advantage over the other one."

Clark was astounded by the man's ignorance. She reminded him, "There's no guarantee. But I shall do as you ask, Mister President. Now I must get inside before . . ."

The president of the United States said, "Good-bye, Doctor. And good luck. Please keep me informed." He looked at General Houseman and said, "Let's go."

As the president and his escort walked away from the observation window and toward the cavern's reinforced steel door, Dr. Clark rushed back to join the drama that was unfolding in the operating theater.

It was terribly exciting. Finally, after several attempts, her efforts would bear fruit in the form of two live babies cloned from the genetic makeup of the most powerful fighting man the world had ever known, the legendary soldier Big Boss.

As Clark washed her hands, snapped on gloves, and entered the operating theater, she wondered what would become of the remaining supply of Big Boss's cells. Only a few trusted assistants had access to them. Would the president and his military cronies forget that there were some left?

Dr. Clark was thrilled by the possibilities. Perhaps there could be another birthing procedure—should the need arise.

2

THE SWIMMER DELIVERY VEHICLE shot out of the Ohio-class submarine's torpedo tube and sliced its way through the subzero salt water toward the dock. With no propulsion system, the device was silent and stealthy as it made its way within range of the destination.

It didn't feel as cold as he had expected.

The figure that clung to the SDV was dressed in a polythermal bodysuit, goggles, and scuba gear. The so-called sneaking suit protected him from the extreme temperature, but Dr. Hunter had told him that the shot she'd given him also was contributing to his comfort. Something about the hypodermic containing an antifreezing peptide to keep the blood and other body fluids from turning to ice, which could easily happen in the waters of Alaska's Fox Archipelago.

The Fox Islands were clustered in the Aleutian chain, just east of Samalga Pass and the Islands of Four Mountains group. They were notorious for being difficult to navigate because of recurring adverse weather conditions and an abundance of reefs. As a result, the submarine had to remain a significant distance out to sea; thus the need for what Campbell had called a surgical insemination.

The man rode the SDV for nearly a nautical mile, at which point the missile's forward thrust began to decline. The trick was to guide the thing to make a soft landing on the rocky, icy ocean floor. Allowing the device to tilt slightly to the right or left not only could cause a dangerous collision but also could alert the enemy's sonar to its location.

The rider used both hands to keep the steering mechanism steady as the SDV slowed, drifted lower, and eventually speared over the icy bottom with a smooth thud. When it came to a stop, Solid Snake checked the Codec and verified his GPS position, pushed away from the device, and swam toward the dock.

Snake might have questioned the wisdom of keeping fit after he supposedly had retired. If he had only gained a few pounds and done nothing but sit and watch television, Campbell might have had second thoughts about his taking the job. The fact that Snake was in superb shape gave Campbell another excuse to think that his man was ready to come back to work, even though Snake had fled to the middle of nowhere trying to escape the life.

But he was suddenly thankful that he *was* in excellent shape, for Snake encountered powerful currents that were preventing him from reaching ground. He struggled hard against them, staying focused, concentrating on the breathing and appropriate muscle groups he needed to get through this, the first of many hurdles he would have to overcome before accomplishing his goals. Eventually he arrived at the dock several seconds ahead of schedule. He was glad to use them to rest and get his bearings.

Shadow Moses Island. I made it.

Slowly and quietly, the man with the code name Solid Snake surfaced to his nose and peered at the platform. Floodlights illuminated the area, but the icy wind obscured much of the visibility in all directions. The cargo dock was empty, and so Snake took hold of a support and grasped it tightly. Like a salamander slipping across a stone, he climbed the support, slid onto the platform, and darted to the shadows at the side of the water filtration tank. He was out of sight there, so he removed the tank and flippers and laid them against the wall.

That's it. Just a few moments to recharge. Wish I had a cigarette.

Snake closed his eyes and began his relaxation exercises. In sixty seconds he'd be like new.

As part of the meditation, Snake sometimes allowed his mind to drift over the events of earlier hours. That helped put the mission in focus.

TWO DAYS EARLIER

HE HAD BEEN dreaming about gathering blueberries and salmonberries with a mind toward feeding the huskies he'd been training for the Great Iditarod Trail Sled Dog Race when his internal alarm jolted Snake awake.

He listened for a repetition of the sound that had infiltrated his sleep.

There. A footstep crunching something outside the cabin.

How come the huskies didn't bark?

Snake leaped out of bed, grabbed the 9-mm Heckler & Koch P7 from his gun clipboard, and snapped a magazine into it. He then carefully peered out of the frost-covered window to see three figures darting through the trees behind the cabin.

Black ops. Armed. With assault rifles.

"Who the hell are these guys?" Snake muttered aloud. He quickly took the bulletproof vest from the table and threw it around himself. He had just finished snapping the last strap when he heard the men in the other room, on the other side of the bedroom door. Snake quickly assumed a firing stance at the side of the door, ready for their intrusion.

"Combat operative Solid Snake!" called a voice. "We are your friends! Please throw down your weapon! We're under orders from Colonel Roy Campbell! I repeat, throw down your weapon! We're here from Colonel Roy Campbell!"

Campbell? What the hell?

Snake figured the soldiers were using thermal imaging to determine that he was standing in the other room with a pistol in hand. And since Campbell was the only person who knew that Snake lived like a hermit in a remote cabin near Twin Lakes in the Alaskan wilderness, he reluctantly placed the handgun on the table.

"We're entering your room. Please raise your hands and do not move!"

Snake did as he was told.

Two combat soldiers burst into the room, faced Snake, and pointed their rifles at him.

"Uhm, the door was unlocked, boys," Snake said. "You didn't have to break it down."

"Get dressed, please," one of the men ordered. "The colonel is waiting."

Snake sighed heavily. "He'd better have one hell of a good reason for this."

Five minutes later Snake and six soldiers were trudging through the newly fallen snow to a transport helicopter that had landed a hundred meters away. Snake figured he hadn't heard the chopper because the wind was strong that morning. A major storm was about to come through.

The next hour went by in a blur as the helicopter flew out to sea and made a rendezvous with the SSBN-732 *Discovery*, Colonel Campbell's mobile headquarters, a submarine currently floating in the Bering Sea. The men escorted Snake through the bowels of the boat until he was placed in what appeared to be the medic's examination room. Snake was told to strip to his underwear, as he needed to undergo some tests.

"The hell I will," Snake grumbled.

"You don't have a choice, soldier," one of the men replied. "Just do it." When they left him alone, Snake decided to play along. Perhaps they'd send in a pretty nurse to take care of him. It had been a while since he'd *seen* a female, much less touched one.

After he had been sitting in his shorts for fifteen minutes—he'd kept his beloved bandana on his head—one of the few men Snake called a friend entered the room. Since the officer had been the commander of FOXHOUND while Snake had been a member, the two men had forged a bond that had endured beyond Snake's self-imposed retirement.

"Snake. You look well."

Snake didn't want to say that the colonel appeared older. After all, the man was in his sixties. Colonel Campbell was dressed, as usual, in his old Green Beret uniform, even though he was no longer part of that elite outfit.

"Thanks, Colonel. You look . . . stressed."

Campbell shrugged. "Comes with the job."

"You interrupted a very pleasant dream I was having about berries. This had better be good."

"Sorry if the boys were a little rough. Snake, we need you. This isn't *good*, but it's big."

"Colonel . . ."

"Snake, we've got a serious situation, and you're the only man who can get us out of it."

"You know I'm retired from FOXHOUND, Colonel. I don't take orders anymore."

"Let me tell you what's up and you'll change your mind. You know FOXHOUND splintered and many of the Next Generation Special Forces banded together and became a renegade group of terrorists—for lack of a better word—hell-bent on taking whatever they want and doing whatever they deem necessary to accomplish their goals."

"I heard something about it."

"Well, about five hours ago, our nuclear weapons disposal facility on Shadow Moses Island was attacked and captured by those renegades, led by members of FOXHOUND. They're holding hostages and demanding that the government turn over the remains of Big Boss. They say that if their demands are not met within twenty-four hours, they'll launch a nuke."

A shadow passed over Snake's face at the mention of the name. "Big Boss . . . my—"

"Your father. Yes."

Snake frowned in confusion. "Why do they want . . . a corpse?"

A woman dressed in a white lab coat came into the room. She carried a hypodermic and was smiling. Snake found her attractive and guessed that she was in her late twenties.

At last!

"Who's she?" he asked.

"This is Doctor Naomi Hunter, the unit's chief medic. She's also an expert in gene therapy."

She pointed the needle at him and said, "This won't hurt a bit."

"What's that?"

"I'll tell you in a minute." She proceeded to sterilize his arm and give him the shot before he could protest.

"Damn it, Colonel. I haven't agreed—"

"Shut up and let me finish, Snake."

When she was done, Dr. Hunter stepped back but remained in the room. The colonel continued. "They don't necessarily want Big Boss's corpse; they want cell specimens that contain his genetic information."

"What for?"

"Gene therapy. So they can better themselves."

Dr. Hunter spoke in a cultured accent that was not quite British but certainly Ivy League. "They can enhance their Next Gen forces with the cells. The military has been working toward identifying the genes that make what they hope to be perfect soldiers. Once the genes are identified, we can splice them into regular troops and then—"

"Turn them into supermen."

"Yes. So far we've discovered about sixty of these 'soldier genes' in Big Boss."

Snake shook his head in disbelief. "So his body was recovered after all."

Campbell said, "Yeah. His cells have remained frozen in a cryochamber. His genomic information is, well, priceless."

"Priceless for the military, you mean."

"Snake, you can understand why we can't simply hand over his body. It's more valuable as a weapon than any WMD our enemies could threaten us with."

Dr. Hunter added, "His body was severely burned, but it was possible to restore his DNA profile from just a single strand of hair."

"Who are these terrorists?" Snake asked.

Dr. Hunter replied, "Uhm, they're calling themselves the Sons of Big Boss."

Campbell continued. "There are six hardened members of FOXHOUND, and they're some pretty rough characters. The guy in charge is FOXHOUND's squad leader." Campbell opened a large envelope marked CLASSIFIED and handed him photographs one by one as he mentioned the names.

Snake blinked. "Liquid Snake?"

Campbell nodded grimly. "I'm afraid so. A man with the same code name as you."

"He . . . he looks just *like* me!"

"Pretty shocking, huh? His skin tone is different, his hair is blond and not black, but otherwise you two do look alike, I must admit." Campbell turned away, not looking Snake in the eye. "That's why we really need you for this mission. We believe you're the only person who can stand against him."

Snake rubbed his eyes and tried to digest the information. "Tell me what you know about him."

"He fought in the Gulf War as a teenager, the youngest person in the SAS. His job was to track down and destroy mobile Scud missile launching platforms. You were there, Snake. Didn't you infiltrate western Iraq with a platoon of Green Berets?"

"I was just a kid myself back then."

"The details are classified, but it seems that originally Liquid Snake penetrated the Middle East as a sleeper for the SIS."

"You mean he was a spy for the Brits?"

"He never once showed his face in Century House, though. He was taken prisoner in Iraq, and after that there was no trace of him for several years. After you retired, he was rescued and became a member of FOXHOUND."

"I thought by that time they were no longer using code names."

"I don't know his real name," Campbell said. "That information is so highly classified that even I can't look at it."

Snake rubbed the stubble on his chin. He suddenly felt much older than his thirty-three years. He indicated the other photographs. "Who else?"

"Psycho Mantis, a Russian with allegedly powerful psychic

abilities. I'm sure they use him for brainwashing and psychological warfare. Then there's Sniper Wolf, a Kurdish woman from Iraq who they say is one of the best shots on the planet. Gorgeous and deadly. From Mexico, there's Decoy Octopus, a master of disguise. He speaks a dozen languages and is an expert in transforming his appearance."

"Talented fellow." There were two photos left.

"Vulcan Raven comes from Alaska; he's half Alaskan Indian, half Inuit Eskimo. The guy's a powerful soldier, and not just because he's a giant."

"A *giant*?"

"Two hundred and ten centimeters tall."

"Sounds like these guys could open their own circus sideshow."

"He's also an Indian shaman, practices some kind of voodoo that allows him to control what he calls spirits of the wilderness."

Snake nodded. "I know about those guys in Alaska. They can command animals to do things. Birds, dogs, you name it. Pretty spooky."

"Finally, there's Revolver Ocelot. A Russian, he's an interrogation specialist and formidable gunfighter. Strange guy; he dresses in one of those dusters from the cowboy days and wields a six-shooter. They say the Russians trained him to be quite the proficient torturer. You don't want to get caught alive by him."

"And Liquid Snake is the head honcho? They don't look so tough."

Dr. Hunter spoke up. "Don't forget about their army of genome soldiers."

"I'm afraid to ask."

"They're a combination of brute strength, intelligence, and DNA sampling. Next Generation Special Forces. We believe they're all under control of this Psycho Mantis, which is how they were able to accomplish the coup and overtake the Shadow Moses facility."

"They started out as an antiterrorist special ops unit made up of former members of biochem units, technical escort units, and the Nuclear Emergency Search Team," Campbell explained. "Their purpose was to respond to threats involving next-generation weapons of mass destruction, including NBC weapons."

"Until they were added," Dr. Hunter said.

"Who's 'they'?"

"Mercenaries," Campbell answered. "And it gets worse. Most of them were from a merc agency that I think you're familiar with. They were part of Big Boss's private guard, and after he went down, the military just bought out all their contracts."

Snake winced. "Outer Heaven . . ." He had a sudden flash of memory. One of his first FOXHOUND missions had been to infiltrate the small, self-proclaimed country in South Africa known as Outer Heaven. The powerful military leader Big Boss had turned coat and organized his own "nation" of mercenaries and renegade soldiers there. Big Boss had been wounded severely after Snake's encounter with him, but the man had survived, and he went on several years later to mastermind another military state called Zanzibarland. Snake's second encounter with Big Boss had proved to be the ultimate soldier's final undoing.

Campbell continued. "After that they were merged with our own VR unit, Force 21, and retrained. If you ask me, these so-called Next Generation Special Forces should be called simulated soldiers because they have no real battle experience."

"But don't forget, they've all been strengthened with gene therapy," Dr. Hunter warned. "Don't get careless just because they don't have much experience."

Snake handed the photographs back to Campbell. "I

thought using genetically modified soldiers was prohibited by international law."

"Those are declarations," Dr. Hunter countered, "not actual treaties."

"The interesting thing is that nearly every member of the unit conspired in this attack," Campbell said.

"But how could an entire unit be subverted to rebellion?"

"They're calling it a revolution," Dr. Hunter said. "Like I said, we think Psycho Mantis had something to do with it."

"Since they all went through the same gene therapy, they probably felt closer than brothers. They see the unit as their only family. They'll be the usual types of forces: arctic warfare squads, light infantry, NBC warfare squads, and heavily armed troopers."

Snake shook his head. NBC warfare soldiers handled nuclear, biological, and chemical weapons.

Terrific.

"And then there's the cream of the crop," Campbell added. "The Genome Combat Veterans. They'll be dressed in spec-ops black owl Kevlar-armored fatigues. They call themselves Space Seals."

"Why?" Snake asked. "Do they sit up, clap their flippers, and bark for treats?" No one laughed. "The Sons of Big Boss. But if they were regular army, they must have been interviewed periodically by army counselors."

"According to their files, they all got straight A's on their psychological tests. They all seemed like fine, upstanding patriotic soldiers."

"But they all took part in the uprising?"

"No; several people didn't show up on the day of the exercises. That's why there was a resupply of troops."

"There must have been a sign that something was wrong."

Dr. Hunter said, "There was a report a month ago that they

were acting strangely. Apparently, they consulted classified information about the soldier genes and performed their own gene therapy experiments."

"Listen," Campbell said. "Even the existence of this genome army is a national secret of the highest order. We had been hoping to investigate this thing quietly and deal with it behind closed doors."

Snake sighed and said, "Okay. How many genome soldiers do they have with them?"

"Dozens," Campbell answered.

"Don't tell me," Snake said. "I'm going in alone."

Campbell allowed himself a smile. "Is there any other way?"

Snake turned to Dr. Hunter. "What the hell was in that shot?"

"An antifreezing peptide to protect you from the cold. It also contains nanomachines to replenish adrenaline, nutrition, and sugars. And to top it off, there are nootropics—a class of drugs that will help improve your mental functioning." The woman's eyes sparkled; she seemed pleased with herself.

"Aren't you jumping the gun? I haven't said yes yet." Snake nodded at Campbell. "Why are you involved in this, Colonel? I thought you'd retired, too."

Snake detected a slight hesitation when Campbell replied. "Not too many people know FOXHOUND as well as I do."

"Yeah? And what's the real reason?"

"Okay, I'll be frank. A person very dear to me is one of the hostages. My niece, Meryl. Meryl Silverburgh."

"What was she doing there?"

"She's one of us, an operative, although a very young and inexperienced one. She was assigned to the Shadow Moses Facility as an intern, so to speak. When several of the base soldiers were reported missing, she was called in as an emergency replacement. No sooner had she arrived than the revolt occurred."

"Has she been in contact with you?"

"No. We believe that either she's in hiding or she's a prisoner along with other civilian employees there. I don't dare think of the, uhm, other possibility."

Snake narrowed his eyes at Campbell. "Why would you allow someone so green to be sent there?"

"It was her choice. She was my little brother's girl. He and Meryl's mother never married, so Meryl uses her mother's last name. My brother died in the Gulf War when she was ten years old, and since then I've been watching after her. She's old enough to make her own decisions, although she's not even twenty yet. She's a good soldier, Snake. She's quite adept at hand weapons, and I think you'll find she's quite good at stealth. She knows her way around computers and electric circuitry as well. If you can find her, she could be a valuable ally once you're inside."

Snake didn't particularly want a teenage girl as an ally, no matter how good she was at repairing burned-out wall outlets.

He sighed again and asked, "What do I have to do?"

Campbell almost couldn't contain his joy that his most trusted operative had more or less agreed to the mission. "You'll have two objectives. First, you need to infiltrate the facility and rescue two VIP hostages."

"Your niece and who else?"

"Not my niece. She's not the objective. If you can find her, great." Campbell looked down. "But if you can't, then—"

"I'll find her. Who are the two VIPs?"

"DARPA chief Donald Anderson, and the president of Arms-Tech, Kenneth Baker."

Snake nodded. He knew that DARPA was the Defense Advanced Research Projects Agency. ArmsTech was *the* corporation that supplied weapons and arms research for the U.S. military. Heavy-duty hostages.

"What business did those guys have at a nuclear weapons disposal facility?"

"The truth is that secret exercises were being conducted at the time the terrorist group attacked."

"Huh. Must've been pretty important exercises if those two were involved. What were they doing, testing some new kind of weapon?"

"I'm not privy to that information."

"Well, who's in charge of this operation, Colonel?"

"The president of the United States, Snake."

"So if the terrorists have a nuke, shouldn't the president and his cronies issue a COG?"

"Not yet. Jim Houseman has operational control and is fully aware of the situation. After you infiltrate, if you determine they possess nuclear launch capabilities, a COG will be issued."

Then it was clear. Houseman was the U.S. secretary of defense and a member of the mysterious OSI, an FBI-like organization that conducted criminal investigations among military employees, soldiers, and related civilians. His service record dated back to the Vietnam days. Snake nodded and said, "I *see*. And what's the second objective?"

"It's what I just said. You need to investigate whether the terrorists really have the ability to launch a nuclear strike—and stop them if they do. They've already told us they have a warhead, and they gave us the serial number. It was confirmed as authentic."

"Isn't there some kind of safety device to prevent this type of terrorism?"

"Uh-huh. Every missile and warhead in our arsenal is equipped with a PAL that uses a discrete detonation code."

"PAL?"

"Permissive Action Link. That's the safety control built into all nuclear weapons systems. But even so, we can't rest easy. The DARPA chief knows the detonation code."

"Sheesh. That means it'll be on the front page of the *National Enquirer* tomorrow. But even if they have a nuclear warhead, it must have been removed from its missile. All the missiles on these disposal sites are supposed to be dismantled, right? It's not that easy to get your hands on an ICBM. *Right?*"

"That used to be true, Snake, but since the end of the Cold War, you can get anything if you have enough money and the right connections. Do you understand the seriousness of the situation now?"

Snake stood and stretched. "Okay, I guess you have me, Colonel. But you owe me. Big time."

"Your country won't forget it, Snake. By the way, I'm not a colonel anymore. I'm just a retired old warhorse."

"Sure . . . *Colonel*. I assume this is a weapons and equipment OSP."

"On Site Procurement is the norm; you know that. We'll outfit you with a SOCOM going in, though."

"A handgun? Damn, Colonel . . . Hope that doesn't put you over budget."

"Cut the sarcasm, Snake. Remember, this is top-secret black ops. Don't expect any official support. We'll be in constant contact through your Codec, you know, provide you with maps and tactical advice—you know the drill."

"Tell me more about the facility."

"Unfortunately, it's primarily a hardened underground base. Even with our most advanced intelligence-gathering equipment, we can't tell what's happening on the inside."

"Peachy. Who else is on the team?"

"Let's go in the control room. I'll introduce you. Oh, uhm, after you're dressed."

The colonel and Dr. Hunter left the room while Snake donned the special skintight suit that had been in the room when he'd arrived. Ten minutes later, he emerged, looking more like the Solid Snake combat operative Colonel Campbell had known.

The control room was the hotbed of mission activity. Workstations were arranged in a circle, with each member of the team positioned at a designated station responsible for a single aspect of the mission. As commander, Campbell usually remained in the center of the circle, having easy access to each workstation.

First, Campbell introduced Snake to a very young Chinese girl who sat at a bank of computers. Snake thought she was definitely a babe but way too young for him.

"This is Mei Ling. She's our communications officer, specializes in image and data processing. Besides mine, you'll hear her voice a lot through the Codec's in-ear transmitter."

"Hello," she said with a smile.

The Codec, he reflected, was an ingenious invention. The Codifying Satellite Communication System incorporated antiwiring coding, digital real-time burst communication, sonar utilization, and radar. Normal communication was instantly codified, compressed, and transmitted in a burst one microsecond in length. However, Snake could receive it in real time, unscrambled and decoded. Special earplugs received the transmission and stimulated the small bones of his ear so that no one but him would hear the sound. And he could contact any member of the team with a speed-dial button corresponding to his or her code frequency.

Snake thought Mei Ling resembled a *manga* character come to life. He shook her hand. "I didn't expect a designer of world-class military technology to be so cute."

She gave him a sideways glance. "You're just flattering me."

"I'm serious! Now I know I won't be bored for the next twenty-four, er, *eighteen* hours."

"Hmm, I can't believe I'm being hit on by the famous Solid Snake."

Campbell led Snake to another computer bank, switched on a monitor, and fiddled with a knob until the image of a woman in her thirties appeared on the screen. She had short blond hair and an East European appearance.

"This is Nastasha Romanenko, our nuclear weapons expert. She analyzes military hardware and ordnance. She's your tech guru via Codec, Snake."

"I am so very glad to meet you, Snake," the woman said.

Snake pinpointed the dialect. "Ukrainian," he said.

"How did you know?"

"I guessed. Is that where you are? Ukraine?"

"No, I'm in sunny southern California. LA."

"Lucky you."

Campbell continued. "Dr. Hunter you've already met. She'll be the medical officer on the mission. Did you know her grandfather was Hoover's assistant secretary in the FBI?"

"Is that so?" Snake asked. "And that gives you the qualifications to be chief medical officer?"

"No, but remember, I've already seen you naked."

"Do I get a prize for that?"

Dr. Hunter gave him a wicked smile and retorted, "Well, if you make it back in one piece, maybe I'll let you see *me* naked."

"Whoa! Colonel, when do I start?"

"Settle down, Snake. Do you have any questions? Real ones, that is?"

"No, but I wish you'd rustle Master Miller out of retirement. I miss his cranky pep talks."

Snake had hoped that his former FOXHOUND trainer and mentor, whose real name was McDonnel Benedict Miller, would be present. Miller also had retired to the Alaskan wilderness, but Snake had not crossed paths with him in years.

Campbell chuckled. "Snake, you'll be happy to know that Master Miller has agreed to support you with aid via the Codec."

"You found him?"

"Not exactly. But we're in touch. Don't be surprised if you suddenly hear his voice when you're surrounded by a dozen genome soldiers."

A navy serviceman entered the room and saluted. "Colonel, we're approaching the launch site."

"Thank you, Ensign," Campbell said. He returned the salute and addressed Snake. "Get the rest of your gear on. We don't have much time."

TODAY

AND HERE HE WAS. Less than twelve hours earlier, he had been dreaming of huskies and berries. Now he crouched behind a filtration tank, ready to make his move.

Snake heard boots on metal somewhere above him. He carefully peered around the side and saw two soldiers at the other end of the cargo dock. A man wearing a brown trench coat was with them as they approached the freight elevator.

"I'm going to swat down a couple of bothersome flies," the man told the soldier, speaking with polished elocution. "Stay alert. He'll be through here; I know it."

"I see someone wearing a duster," Snake whispered, the Codec picking up his words. "I think it might be Revolver Ocelot."

"Can you get a positive ID?" Campbell asked, his voice somewhere in the recesses of Snake's ears.

The man in the trench coat stepped into the elevator and turned around, facing Snake.

"Negative. Wait. He turned this way. Colonel, it's not Ocelot."

It was the leader himself—Liquid Snake.

3

THE MAN KNOWN AS Master Miller rolled his fists against the
punching bag and produced a pounding, steady rhythm that
might have come from an African tribe or a Latino rock band.
Working out in his makeshift gym three hours a day not only
kept his aging body fit, it gave his reclusive life focus and purpose. After all, separating himself from the hustle and bustle of
the "real world" did have a few drawbacks. Miller would never
admit it, but there were times when he felt utterly alone. Most
days that was a good thing . . . and others, not so good. For his
money, exercise was the cure-all.

With a distinguished career serving in the SAS, the Green
Berets, the Marine Corps, and FOXHOUND, Miller was one of
those soldiers whom you could take out of the military, but you
couldn't take the military out of the man. It was why he was
FOXHOUND's authority on survival training. The fact that he
was of third-generation American-Japanese ancestry made no
difference to the top brass. The guy was a patriot and an American through and through. He·had a reputation of being an

ornery SOB and the epitome of the loud, aggressive drill instructor, but each and every one of his recruits would forever utter his name with respect.

As Miller continued to pound the bag, he heard one of his huskies howl. That wasn't unusual. There were wolves in the wilderness where Miller had chosen to build a house, and his huskies often did their duty by scaring the beasts away. But suddenly the howl cut off sharply, as if something had silenced the dog with finality.

Miller grabbed the punching bag to still its rapid pulsation. He listened carefully but heard only the wind, which had picked up considerably in the last few hours. Never one to ignore a premonitory warning, Miller moved fluidly across the gym floor and to a clipboard where he kept a couple of handguns. His main arsenal was in another part of the house, but he liked to keep some kind of weapon in every room. He unclipped a Glock 9-mm from the board, checked that it contained a full magazine, and racked the slide. He then climbed the stairs to the ground floor and sprinted to the central alarm system control box.

It was dead. Miller punched buttons on the monitors, but each of the six screens was blank. There was no way he could see what was outside the house.

Someone had to be damned good to find him, he thought. Like Solid Snake, he had built a home in the far eastern Alaskan wilderness, near the Canadian border. There was no easy way to reach the place, and the one and only road leading to the structure was covered in several feet of snow. Besides, his security cameras would have picked up any vehicle traversing the path a mile away.

Miller turned and leaped over the couch in his living room. He lay prone on the wooden floor, listening and waiting for the sound of intruders. By hiding behind the piece of furniture, perhaps he would have the element of surprise in his favor.

But after five minutes there was nothing. Could he have imagined it? Should he go check on his dogs? But if it was a false alarm, why would his security system be on the blink?

No, something was definitely wrong. Call it Zen, call it a sixth sense, call it bullshit—Master Miller knew someone was in the house.

Then he noticed the sweet-smelling odor. It reminded him of a dentist's office. Laughing gas? No, this was different. But whatever it was, it couldn't be good. He had to get out of the house, and fast. Unfortunately, he was wearing gym shorts, tennis shoes, and a tank top. Outside it was minus thirty or forty degrees Fahrenheit.

Miller rose and attempted to jump back over the couch but immediately felt the effects of the gas. His reaction time was much slower, and his head felt like a helium balloon, ready to float to the ceiling without his body. He stumbled and fell onto the couch but got right back up. Determined to get to his closet, don something warm, and jump through the escape hatch to the ice cave beneath the basement, Miller struggled to run across the room.

The smell was much stronger now. Miller thought it was probably sevoflurane, one of the most powerful and popular gases used in modern anesthesia.

Miller's feet felt like lead bricks as he tried to lift them. With a rapidity that surprised him, a wave of confusion enveloped his brain, and the horizon tilted. There was a sensation of falling, but it seemed to take forever. He didn't feel the crash as his face smacked into the floor.

With one final effort, Miller crawled a foot or two before the darkness overcame him.

4

Snake eyed his surroundings and double-checked them with the map grid that appeared on the Codec, which was strapped around his wrist. The cargo dock was in a hollowed-out cavern that was supported by metal latticework. There was an empty berth at which government supply ships could dock. The approximately seventy-five-foot platform was dotted with large shipping crates, which were scattered across the space all the way to the freight elevator. The rest of the facility probably was built into the ground as well as in structures above the surface. Liquid had disappeared into the elevator, so that was obviously the only access to the surface level.

Snake drew the Mark 23 Model 0 SOCOM from its holster and checked the chamber. Locked and loaded. In Snake's opinion, there was no pistol with better accuracy and resilience than the .45-caliber SOCOM. The laser-aiming module was particularly nice. Ironically, in a perfect world Snake would never have to draw the thing. If everything went as smoothly as possible, not a single shot would be fired.

Fat chance.

Snake holstered the gun. It was time to make his move. He slipped around the water filtration tank and crawled under the large pipe running along the wall of the cavern. Some kind of vermin droppings lined the perimeter, and Snake frowned.

"Colonel, I see animal feces. Are there rats here?" he asked.

"Negative, Snake," Campbell replied. "We already checked with vermin control; those are droppings from brown mice. They're harmless; they won't bite. Apparently, everyone who works in the facility is used to them. Be alert. We're picking up three—no, four guards patrolling the cargo dock. Where did Liquid go?"

"He popped into the elevator. It's amazing. Other than the difference in skin tone, the guy could be my twin."

"Snake, he's going to be a formidable enemy. His code name is the same as yours, so you'll be evenly matched, more or less."

Yeah, but it will be the solid *versus the* liquid.

"Right," Snake said. He continued to study the Codec ground plan when he heard the sound of boots nearby. He froze and peered over the pipe to see one of the guards. The man was wearing a white snow-camouflage uniform with a balaclava mask and was armed with a FAMAS assault rifle. The guard moved to the edge of the dock, looked across the water, and sneezed. Snake crept behind him, said "Gesundheit," and executed a silent stranglehold. The guard's neck snapped, and his weight drooped limply into Snake's arms. Snake dragged the body behind the filtration tank and left it there. He heard more footsteps, so he slid under the metal unit, squeezing into the small space between the tank's outside lip and the platform. A soldier must have heard something, for he was walking carefully toward the edge of the dock. Snake rolled out from under the tank on the opposite side, stood, and stealthily inched his way around so that he was behind the guard.

Another stranglehold, another dead guard.

Snake dragged the corpse behind the tank, searched the man, and found a pack of commercially made American cigarettes.

Yuck.

Snake preferred a nicotine-based mix of chemicals and plant leaves that he had made especially for him. They were also somewhat smokeless, which was an asset on a mission. He'd been tempted to swallow a pack before leaving the submarine but hadn't relished the thought of regurgitating them upon arrival. No, for smokes he would have to depend on the usual On Site Procurement, no matter how awful the brand that he found was.

He took the cigarettes and slung the rifle over his arm.

"Snake? Naomi Hunter here."

"Yes, Doctor?"

"Just reminding you that the genome soldiers have highly developed senses of hearing and vision. They'll come running at the slightest noise. I suspect they're equipped with the same antifreezing peptide I gave you."

"That's not going to stop me from putting them on ice."

The colonel interrupted. "Snake, five minutes ago we launched a diversion to keep them from paying too much attention to what's happening at sea. Two F-16's took off from Galena and are headed your way. The terrorists' radar should have already picked them up."

Could that have been what Liquid Snake meant about swatting down flies?

Time to move forward. Snake moved to the edge of the tank and then darted to the nearest crate. He stopped, listened, moved to the opposite edge, and dashed once again to the next closest crate. He continued in that way, sprinting from container to container, gaining yardage toward the end of the platform. When he was at the penultimate crate, he dropped to the ground and peered around the edge at floor level.

The elevator had just descended and opened. The third and fourth guards were patrolling from left to right directly in front of it, on a path some six feet away from the last crate. There was no way to sneak up behind the men, so Snake waited until they turned and began walking away from him. He bolted across the floor to the crate closest to the elevator door. There he waited a few seconds for the guards to turn again and walk slowly toward him. Snake could hear them muttering something about a storm. He surprised them by stepping out from behind the crate and standing directly in front of them.

"Merry Christmas," Snake said as he delivered two powerhouse punches, left and then right, into the guards' faces. The soldiers plopped to the floor. "I forgot to tell you—Christmas is early this year."

Snake took hold of one man's arms and dragged his body around the crate. He repeated the process with the other guard. As soon as the limp figures were stuffed tidily into a corner, a siren sounded throughout the complex.

"Great," Snake said. "Either they know I'm here, or something else is going on. Colonel, I'm taking the elevator."

He stepped into the open cubicle and pressed the button for the surface level. The ride took less than ten seconds. The doors opened to a massive space, the focal point being a Mi-24D Hind-D gunship residing in the middle of a landing pad. Snake looked up and saw that the roof—a sliding slab of reinforced metal—was retracting so that the helicopter could take off. Blocks of snow fell in from above; Snake could see that it was snowing heavily outside.

He moved out of the elevator and slipped along the wall and into the shadows, avoiding the sight lines of two guards at the end of the platform. He crouched in the shadows as a female voice he didn't recognize spoke. "Snake, weather conditions are bad. A blizzard is hitting your position just about now."

"Who's that?"

"Oh, sorry. Mei Ling here. I'll be monitoring the weather as well as your communications devices."

The roof had retracted completely, and the entire room lit up like Times Square. Guards moved out of the way as the rotor on the Hind began to rotate, building to speed in seconds.

"Colonel, there's a Russian gunship here in a state-of-the-art heliport. And someone's crazy enough to fly the thing in this weather."

A good pilot could handle a Hind-D in a blizzard. The machine was known for its agility and speed. Snake had heard that it was the most difficult combat helicopter to shoot down. Its offensive capabilities were formidable as well, as it possessed a Phalanga-P antitank missile complex and machine guns.

The landing lights around the helicopter rotated in place and pointed upward, creating a tunnel of beams to guide the pilot off the helipad. Even though the beast was large for an assault chopper, it gently lifted into the air as if it weighed nothing. It wavered slightly as the pilot fought the strong wind, but whoever was flying the vehicle knew what he was doing. After a moment, the chopper was up, had moved out of the open roof, and was gone.

Snake took a moment to light one of the cigarettes. As expected, the commercial stuff was horrible and nearly made him cough. But bad tobacco was better than no tobacco, so . . .

Campbell said, "Snake?"

"Yeah?"

"Liquid Snake fancies himself an expert pilot. He has a big

ego and probably would insist on flying it in lieu of anyone else. I suspect he's after our fighters. That means the diversion is working."

Mei Ling commented, "I'm surprised *our* pilots can fly in that storm."

Campbell answered, "The Air Force in Alaska is trained to fly in these conditions. They're some of the best of the best, so to speak."

"Hey, guys, I don't mean to interrupt this lively discussion, but does someone want to tell me where I'm supposed to go?"

Dr. Hunter spoke. "Snake, the DARPA chief, Anderson, was injected with the same GPS-transmitting nanomachines as you, so you should be able to track his signal with the Codec. We're not picking him up yet, but you should be able to once you're farther inside the complex."

He checked the device around his wrist and noted a faint signal.

"He's on a different level," Snake said. "And he's a *lot* farther inland. I've got to get into the *bowels* of this place."

Mei Ling said, "Then you'll have to cross the heliport, Snake. We see there's a lot of genome soldier activity in the place so watch your a—, uhm, your back."

Snake grinned.

"There's another large space north of you. Looks like some type of hangar. You'll have to cross that as well to get into the main facility. It's crawling with guards, too."

Great.

"Piece of cake," Snake said.

5

IT WAS A STRAIGHT shot across the heliport to the other side except for two things. First, Snake counted three roaming guards, again wearing the white camouflage uniforms.

Second, lights on the ceiling had flicked on and produced a searchlight effect, with beams zigzagging haphazardly across the floor. As Snake studied the spotlights' patterns, he noticed an object on the helipad close to where the Hind-D had sat. The light passed over it again, and Snake could discern that the object was a box. Was it worth the risk to see what it contained?

Sure, it'll be fun.

He counted the sweeps of the light beams' crisscross pattern and determined that the cycle was repeated every thirty seconds. To get to the box on the helipad without being hit by a searchlight, he had to dart to the edge of the helipad and wait for the crisscross cycle to begin again. The drawback to that was that he would be in full view of the entire helipad. Then, at precisely ten seconds into the cycle, most of the helipad would be in darkness long enough for him to dash to the box, pick it up, and run left, toward the western wall of the structure.

But where were the guards? Two of them had moved out of sight. Snake could still see one standing at the north end of the space, next to a truck—some kind of cargo carrier. Okay, Snake wouldn't have to deal with him until the very end. The other two . . . ? Since he didn't spot them, Snake moved to a group of petroleum barrels, crouched, and scanned the room from a different perspective.

There.

A guard was standing in front of a double doorway on the left side of the room. That was the point to which Snake would have to run after grabbing the box on the helipad. Fine, he would deal with him when the time came. So where was the third guy? Snake waited a few seconds longer, but the man never appeared. Was getting the box still worth the risk? He could be anywhere.

The light beams moved away from the edges of the helipad. It was now or never—or wait for the next cycle, which would take up too much time. Snake bolted across the floor and reached the helipad corner in two seconds. He crouched and willed himself to be invisible. Luckily, the dark sneaking suit blended into the shadows surprisingly well.

You don't see me, you bastards.

He remained perfectly still and counted the seconds as the cycle started over.

Voices. Two men. The third soldier had joined the other man over to the left, where Snake needed to go. That stop was going to be a little more challenging than he originally had thought.

The searchlights swung across the floor.

Snake could still see the guard by the truck, smoking a cigarette. At least he wasn't moving.

The beams crossed each other and moved away from the center. Snake made his move, sprinted onto the painted H, reached the box, and looked inside.

Grenades. Three chaff grenades.

Snake scooped them up, quickly opened his empty pouch, and dropped them in. Time to move.

He ran off the helipad toward the left, where the two guards stood directly in his path, some twenty feet away. They were talking and smoking cigarettes, and even though they were facing in his direction, so far they hadn't seen him.

Snake picked up his running speed as the men's gazes finally focused on him. They had time only to open their mouths in shock as Snake jumped and collided with them like a bat out of hell. Both soldiers fell backward with Snake's arms locked around their necks, just below the chins. With as much force as he could muster, Snake landed on the floor, using the two guards' heads as cushions. The cracking sound on the concrete floor meant that their conversation was over.

Snake twisted his head around and looked north. The guard by the truck was gone.

Uh oh.

Snake grabbed the two soldiers by their fur-lined hoods and dragged them eight feet to an alcove on the left side of the structure. The open double doors he'd seen earlier apparently led to a storeroom of some kind. That could be worth a peek.

A security camera slowly made an arc as it pivoted back and forth across the entrance.

A surveillance camera?!

Time it just right and he'd have it. Snake watched the camera move across his path. The second it was turned away, he ran forward, dived through the double doors and into the room, performed a body roll, and landed on his feet, his SOCOM in hand.

A *fourth* guard sat draped over a table with his hooded head in his arms.

Snake froze.

Was the man asleep?

As if in answer, the guard snorted on an inhalation, moved his head, mumbled, and settled back into his arms again.

Snake stepped quietly to the side of the storeroom to examine the boxes on display. Much of it was food supplies, nothing that might be of use. It appeared that mice had gotten to some of the boxes of grain; there were holes in some of the lower cartons, and grain had spilled over the floor. He moved to the west wall and hugged it, then slowly stepped around the room. Eventually he was positioned four feet behind the sleeping guard at the table.

The man snored loudly and woke himself up. His head rose to the level where Snake wanted it.

"Sounds like you've got sleep apnea," Snake said. "Better get that checked out."

As the guard turned his head to see who had spoken, Snake reached out, grabbed the man's skull through the hood, and twisted it all the way around.

The snap sounded like a slap.

Snake gently laid the man back down onto the table and arranged the head and arms as they had been when the guard had been asleep. He then moved to the north side of the storeroom and looked at the shelves.

"Colonel, I found a pair of thermal goggles."

It was ArmsTech's Model A, reliable and effective heat-sensing stealth equipment. Snake picked them up and placed them in the pouch.

"Hello, Snake? This is Nastasha Romanenko."

"Oh, yeah. The nuclear specialist. How's sunny California?"

"Just fine except it's night here now. I'm glad you found the thermal goggles. You know, they work by thermal imaging instead of amplifying light like night vision goggles. They'll work just as well in complete darkness. Not only that, they can penetrate optic stealth systems. You should be able to spot Claymore mines, too."

"Well, thanks, Nastasha, but I knew all that."

"Oh. Sorry. I guess maybe I'll just stay quiet unless you have a question about something, *da*?"

"*Da*."

"They asked me to participate in this operation as a supervisor from the Nuclear Emergency Search Team. I was happy to accept. We must not allow terrorists to get their hands on nuclear weapons of any kind. I hope I can help you stop them."

"I'll be sure to give you a buzz if I need you, Nastasha," Snake said, and then ended the transmission.

He quickly scanned the rest of the shelves and boxes and was tempted to take a box of shells for an M9 but decided against it. He had spent enough time in the helipad already.

Snake looked out of the storeroom, kept an eye on the surveillance camera, waited for it to turn away from him, and then bolted out and across the floor to a crate. He flattened his back against it and inched along to the edge. All clear. Snake slipped to the next crate, one that was parallel with the truck. The vehicle was an M548 Full Tracked Cargo Carrier. It would be interesting to take a look under the canopy to see what treasures he might find, but Snake didn't have a fix on the last guard's location. He waited a few precious seconds and listened carefully.

He heard bootsteps on the right side of the room. He crouched and saw the soldier walking around a crate, returning to his position by the truck. Snake opened the pouch, removed a chaff grenade, released the safety pin, and tossed the explosive over the top of the crate so that it would land and roll over to the right wall. Five seconds later, the device exploded, sending microscopic metal shards into the air around it. Chaff grenades were not particularly incendiary, and their damage was slight; the main uses were jamming enemy sensory systems and creating diversions.

The guard, surprised by the noise, turned toward the right wall. He called his colleagues by their names and, when he didn't receive a reply, walked cautiously toward the sound of the explosion with his assault rifle readied. As soon as he was around the crate and not in sight, Snake ran to the cargo carrier and crouched behind its left side. He took the time to lift a corner of the canopy and saw that the truck bed was full of cartons. One was open, and it contained more chaff grenades. Snake reached in, grabbed two, and thrust them into his pouch.

He then turned toward the north wall. Closed steel doors led to the next part of the facility, and Snake doubted that merely waltzing through them would be very safe. There was, however, a ventilation duct on the wall next to the doors. It was covered by a simple mesh grating that he could pry off easily with his fingers. That was his next port of call, he thought, but he didn't want the remaining guard to find his incapacitated buddies.

"Over here!" he called.

The guard acknowledged him, thinking the voice he'd heard was that of one of his colleagues. Snake heard the sound of the man's boots running toward the truck, so he lay prone and rolled under the truck. The man, confused that no one was there, called the names of his comrades. Snake emerged from under the other side of the truck, stood, and casually crept behind him.

This time, Snake reached around the soldier and grabbed the man's assault rifle with both hands. He pulled the weapon laterally into the guard's neck and applied continuous pressure until he went limp. Snake opened the passenger side of the truck and unceremoniously stuffed the body into the seat.

He skirted to the grating and pulled it off with his gloved hands. The duct was big enough for him to worm inside, but it was a tight fit. For illumination, he flicked on a penlight that was built into his shoulder padding. Now it was just a matter of crawling through the channel to its other end.

He dragged himself along the claustrophobic metal tunnel, happy to get out of the cold. Even though the heliport was enclosed with a sliding roof, the temperature in the place was almost as low as it was outdoors. Once he was in the facility proper, the central heat would be on.

"How are you doing, Snake?" Campbell asked.

Snake grunted in reply. "There's mouse shit in here." He heard the women giggle. "It's not funny."

"Snake," Campbell said, "if that's the worst of your problems, then you've got it easy."

Snake continued to crawl until he reached a grating flat on the duct "floor." He peered through the mesh into what appeared to be a large area for storing heavy equipment. In fact, he could discern the back end and treads of an armored tank.

"An Abrams," he said.

"What?"

"Colonel, they've got an Abrams tank in there."

"That's right, Snake; they have two. Our intelligence reports that you're approaching a hangar for Shadow Moses's armored vehicles, tank parts, and—*we think*—ammunition."

"Good to know, Colonel, but at the moment I've got all I— hold it."

Two guards appeared on a catwalk directly beneath him, maybe five feet below the bottom of the duct. Snake caught a bit of their conversation as they walked by.

"—the shaft cleaning. They're gonna spray for mice," one said.

"So what did you do with him?"

"The DARPA guy? He was moved to the cell in the first-floor basement, next to the woman."

"I hear she's feisty. What I wouldn't give to . . ."

And they were gone.

Woman? Meryl Silverburgh, perhaps?

"Colonel, I know where DARPA chief Anderson is," Snake said. "And I think I know where your niece is, too."

Snake continued the lateral journey through the duct until he came to a juncture going down. He wasn't sure how far it went, but there was no place else to go. He straightened his arms and used isometric pressure to lower himself with his back sliding along the side of the duct. The strain on his shoulders and knees was tremendous, but he had practiced this maneuver many times at FOXHOUND's obstacle course.

Eventually he came to another ventilation grate. He used his legs and back to wedge himself against the sides of the duct so that he could rest for a moment and look out. The same two guards apparently had come down a set of stairs and were standing seven feet away from the vent, leaning against a rail.

"—been put on alert."

"Why?"

"I heard something about an intruder. He's already done three sentries, and they say he's using stealth. The security detail's been doubled. Come on."

They moved away and continued along the catwalk out of Snake's sight.

An intruder? Stealth?

"Colonel, there's another intruder here. Unless they're talking about me, then things just got a lot more complicated."

"Did you hide the guards you neutralized?"

"Yes, sir. But that doesn't mean they can't be found."

"Then they may be on to you."

But I've done more than three sentries.

"Somehow, Colonel, I don't think so. I think it's somebody else they're talking about. Never mind. I'm going on."

He lifted his torso off the back of the duct and continued the spider crawl all the way to the blessed bottom, which finally appeared after several minutes of spine-breaking exertion. The vertical duct ended in a T, with passages going off in opposite directions. Which way to go? Heads or tails?

To help answer his question, a scratching, scurrying sound grew near.

What the . . . ?

A small herd of brown mice skittered in from his left, ran around his feet, and continued into the duct to his right. When they were gone, Snake muttered, "Where's the fire, boys?" and figured the rodents knew where they were going. He went right.

"Snake, we've got you tracked very near the hangar," Mei Ling announced. "There should be a vent opening in a few yards."

"I see it."

Snake slowed his crawl and focused on staying silent. It was a safe bet that human beings stood just beyond the grating. They might not take kindly to a stranger caught crawling out of their air duct.

He approached the grating and looked through the dirty mesh. It emptied onto the ground floor of the hangar. Although the place was big enough to house a small airplane, dominating the floor space were the two Abrams tanks. Work lights on the ceiling illuminated the hangar well enough that a figure, even one dressed in black, might be spotted darting across the floor.

There were no guards in sight, but Snake could hear the two men talking not far away. He wasn't sure if they could see the vent; nevertheless, he gently snapped the grille out of its sockets, carefully tilted it, and brought it inside the duct. He then dared to poke his head out of the metal shaft.

The two guards stood on a second-level catwalk to his right. There was no sign of men on the ground floor, but that didn't mean there weren't any. Snake thought it best to play it safe and create a diversion so that he could slip out of the vent unnoticed. He reached into the pouch, removed a single .45-caliber cartridge from his supply of ammunition, and snaked his way out halfway onto the floor. Lying on his back, he flung the bullet into the air, aiming over the nearest Abrams tank. He heard it hit the floor on the other side of the hangar, but the guards didn't notice because of the ambient noise in the space. He hated to use another cartridge, but he had no choice. This time, he aimed for the catwalk on the left side of the hangar, directly opposite the guards. Once again on his back, Snake flung the shell hard and hit the left wall. This time the cartridge bounced onto the catwalk, clanging as it fell. The two guards looked toward the noise, mumbled something, and split up. One proceeded to walk to the western side of the hangar via the north-end catwalk, and the other man went the southern route, which would take him directly over Snake's head. Snake waited until he heard the boots tromping above him and then slipped completely out of the duct. He got to his feet, darted to the center of the floor, and took cover on the right side of the nearest Abrams. From there he could see the freight elevator on the eastern wall. He couldn't risk running for it because it was in plain view of the guards on the catwalk.

Snake cursed to himself and eyed his surroundings for another alternative. Fifteen feet to the southeast was a steel flight of stairs that led to the second-level catwalk. He reached into his pouch, grasped another shell, and threw it as hard as he could toward the north end of the hangar. The bullet clanged against the second Abrams tank. The two guards quickly hurried to investigate, their backs now turned to Snake. He used the opportunity to sprint to the staircase and ascend with the quiet, light touch of the feline species. Up there the lighting was less intense. Shadows were Snake's friends, so he embraced them one by one as he traveled along the catwalk until he was crouched on the same side as the guards. They were standing and looking over the rail, studying the area around the second Abrams.

Snake stooped to all fours once again so that he could crawl silently along the catwalk, a trick Master Miller had taught him. Footsteps on metal latticework made too much noise. Literally becoming a cat was the only way to surprise a target in such a setting. When he was approximately thirty feet away from the men, Snake lay prone on the catwalk, reached into a pocket on the calf of his uniform, and removed the SOCOM's sound suppressor. He screwed it onto the barrel, used both hands to aim the weapon, and fired a round at one of the guards. The recoil felt good; it had been too long since he had used the weapon on assignment. Shooting snowballs at his wilderness cabin was good for practice, but nothing took the place of a living target.

The guard flinched slightly, as if he had just been bitten by a nasty bug, and the other man seemed confused about why his partner was wobbling on his feet. Then, as soon as the wounded man began to drop, Snake was able to get a clear shot at the second man. The gun jerked in his hands again. Simultaneously, the first man crumbled onto the catwalk as the second guard wrenched violently, staggered against the rail, and then careened over it. His body fell thirty feet onto the concrete floor with a hard *ka-plump*.

Snake twisted his head back and forth, eyeing the entire hangar for signs of movement.

No one else was inside.

He stood, ran back to the staircase, and descended to the

floor. He could leave the first corpse on the catwalk since it was out of sight, but he had to get rid of the second guy. Snake crossed the space, picked up the man by his ankles, and dragged him to the side of the room near a set of trash barrels with lids. He removed one lid, heaved the man up and over, and secured the lid on top of him.

The storeroom was directly to the right, but the doors were protected by a security keypad.

"Colonel, do you guys have any security access codes for me?"

"Negative, Snake. You'll have to pick those up from somewhere . . . or someone."

Snake didn't feel like trying to guess a code from infinite mathematical possibilities, so he turned his back on the locked treasure trove and ran to the freight elevator. He pressed the button for B1 and said, "Colonel, I'm on my way to the first-floor basement. The show's just getting started."

6

Snake stood in a Weaver stance with the SOCOM in both hands, facing the elevator doors as they opened at the first-floor basement to an empty hallway that led forward several feet before making a jog to the left. Snake continued to hold the handgun at a readied position as he stepped out of the lift. The first thing that struck him was a damp, musty smell overlying the foul odor of an unclean toilet. He thought that if prisoners were being held on this level, they were either mildewed or asphyxiated by now.

A shut steel door with a security keypad was on his right. Snake quickly examined the contraption and knew it was useless to try to hot-wire it.

"Snake," Mei Ling said, "we're picking up three warm bodies in your area. And check your Codec. We're getting the signal that the DARPA chief is just around the corner from you."

"I see it." Sure enough, a blinking blue light appeared on the level ground plan that automatically appeared on the Codec. Snake went farther down the hallway to another steel door; it too was shut tight with a security keypad. "I'm at the door to the cell block. No luck, guys, unless you have a code for me."

"Not yet. There's got to be another way in. Keep looking."

Snake went to the junction and stopped at the edge. He carefully shot a look around the corner and saw that the rest of the corridor was empty. He moved along, the gun still in hand, but there were no doors; it was a dead end. There was, however, a steel stepladder leaning against the back wall.

And another ventilation duct just below the ceiling.

"I just found my way in. Don't change channels."

He quickly set up the ladder, climbed it to the vent, pried off the grating, laid it inside the duct, and crawled inside. The smell was worse in the shaft. Snake crept forward and after ten feet came to an intersection; the shaft kept going straight, but a leg jogged off to the left. Snake consulted the map on the Codec. It was difficult to distinguish which path was the one that would lead him to the blinking blue light that was Anderson; he tried the left path first.

Snake quietly crept along the metal until he came to another grating in the duct bottom. Looking through it, he had a bird's-eye view of a restroom stall. A guard who appeared to be tall and blond sat on the toilet with a magazine in his lap. The noises the man's body was making were nearly inhuman. The guard grumbled to himself, belched, and muttered something about last night's curry.

"We hear him, Snake. We're analyzing the voice algorithms just in case he's somebody important," Mei Ling announced.

Snake checked the indicator light on the Codec. It was now apparent that DARPA chief Anderson was not situated along the duct path he had taken. Still, it would be useful to know the layout of the level in case he ever had to return. Snake moved on past the restroom grating and came to another one twenty feet beyond. Looking down, he could see a messy office containing a desk overflowing with papers and junk food wrappers, a few dirty magazines, and three computer monitors. What particularly caught Snake's eye were the boxes of ammunition and grenades that were on the floor against the wall. He wagered that the office belonged to the man on the toilet.

"He's a low-level guard, Snake, a rookie," Mei Ling said. "He's known as simply Johnny. According to the Shadow Moses personnel records, he's the lead computer technician on base."

"I'd like to get down into his office and poke around."

Campbell spoke up. "Remember your first priority, Snake."

"Don't worry, Colonel. I'm on my way to the other fork."

Snake managed to turn around inside the duct and make his way back to the junction. He took the other path, crawled along for twenty feet, and came to another jog to the left. Just beyond that was a grating in the duct floor. Snake moved to it and peered into the cell below.

A young woman dressed in what appeared to be military trousers and a workout bra was busy doing sit-ups on the floor. She had red hair, was thin and lean, and obviously took her exercising very seriously.

Meryl Silverburgh, in the flesh.

Snake wondered if he should let her know he was there but decided against it. First things first. His orders were to find Anderson before he did anything else. Besides, the girl didn't appear to be in any distress. He'd come back for her.

He moved on to another grating ten feet beyond Meryl's. It, too, was directly over a cell, and Snake could see an African-American man with his head in his hands sitting on the decrepit bunk that was fastened to the wall. Snake checked the Codec and saw that he was right on target. He pried off the grating, pulled it inside the duct, and dropped down into the cell.

DARPA chief Anderson looked up and gasped.

"I'm a friend!" Snake said quietly. "I'm here to get you out."

"Who are you?" The man looked haggard, much older than his fifty-something years. He was dressed in what once had been a nice suit. Bloodstains covered patches of his formerly white shirt.

"My name's not important. You're Anderson, right?"

The man nodded. He stood, a little unsteady on his feet.

"Are you all right?"

"I think so. They tortured me."

"Okay, we're leaving this place, but first I need some information. Sit down for a second."

Anderson hesitated and then returned to the bunk. "What do you want to know?"

"These terrorists, they're threatening a nuclear strike. Are they capable of it?"

"Terrorists . . . ?"

"The guys that took over the base and their little army. They've threatened the White House with a nuclear strike unless some demands are met. Can they do it?"

Anderson closed his eyes and nodded. "I think so. They could launch a nuclear weapon if they really wanted to."

Snake crouched in front of the man so that they could speak softly. "But I thought Shadow Moses Island was just a nuclear waste facility where you dismantle warheads. How could the terrorists get access to a live one?"

"You're not very informed, are you?" Anderson said with a smirk. "That's just a cover story. A nuclear disposal outfit? Yeah, Shadow Moses does that, too, but for years this has really been a government-run arms research and development facility. We've been building a new type of experimental weapon. A damned *important* weapon, if I say so myself."

Snake could see that the man still had his pride, if not his dignity. "What do you mean?"

"It's a walking battle tank. It has the ability to launch a nuclear strike from anywhere on earth. It's *mobile*."

Snake felt a chill run up his back. "Metal Gear? It can't be!"

Anderson registered surprise. "You've heard of Metal Gear? It's our most classified black project! How could you know about it?"

"Let's just say I've had Metal Gear business in the past." In fact, Metal Gears had been involved in the Outer Heaven and Zanzibarland incidents in which Snake previously had encountered Big Boss. "But I thought the project was scrapped—too dangerous."

"Nope. ArmsTech and DARPA joined forces to perfect the thing. We've been working on it for three years, and now it's done." The man sighed heavily. "But now the revolutionaries have it."

Revolutionaries? "You mean terrorists?"

"Er, yeah, terrorists. They have REX."

"REX?"

"Metal Gear REX. That's the new code name. And it's probably already been armed with a warhead. These guys are pros. They're all experienced in handling and equipping nuclear weapons."

A voice at the cell window startled them both. "Hey!"

Snake retreated and hugged the wall next to the door. Johnny, the guard from the toilet, appeared at the window. "Are you talking to yourself again? Shut up!"

Anderson muttered "Sorry," and looked at the floor. After a moment, Johnny moved away. Snake waited a moment more and then slinked around the cell until he was at the edge of the bunk. They continued the conversation in whispers.

"Are there launch safety measures?" Snake asked. "Detonation codes? Fail-safe codes?"

"Yeah, you mean PAL. There are two different passwords to

launch. I know one of the passwords. Baker—the president of ArmsTech—he knows the other password." Anderson bowed his head sheepishly. "But they know my password."

"You talked?"

"I said I was tortured. That one with the gas mask—Psycho Mantis. He can read your *mind*. You can't resist it no matter how hard you try. And believe me, I tried! It's probably a matter of time before they get Baker's password, too. They may already have it."

"Where is Baker?"

"We *were* together, but they separated us. They moved him somewhere in the second-floor basement. I heard the guard say they put him in an area that has a lot of electronic jamming."

"Any other clues?"

"I think they cemented all the entrances, but that was yesterday. I doubt they've painted them yet."

Snake cursed to himself. "That's great. They probably have both passwords."

"But there's another way to stop the launch."

"Yeah?"

"With card keys. There's . . . there's three of them. Even without the passwords, you can insert the keys and engage the safety lock."

"Terrific. Three card keys. Now where are they?"

"Baker has them."

"Then we've got to go get him. Come on, let's get you out of here. Can you walk okay?"

"Oh, I just thought of something." Anderson stood, reached into his pocket, and removed his wallet. He took out what looked like a credit card and handed it to Snake. "This is my ID; it's a PAN card. It'll open any Security Level One door."

"I know how it works. Personal Area Network. Thanks."

"Hey. You haven't heard of any other way to disarm the PAL, have you?"

"What do you mean? I didn't even know there was a Metal Gear here."

"Is the White House going to meet the terrorists' demands?"

"Hell if I know. That's their problem. I have my orders and—"

"What about the Pentagon?"

"The Pentagon? What are you talking about?"

"Then you don't know that—uhm . . . I . . ." Anderson's face suddenly conveyed pain. His eyes bulged in fear as he gasped for air and clutched his chest.

"What's wrong? What is it?"

The man screamed loudly, panicked, and lunged for Snake. He grabbed hold of Snake's shoulders and tried to speak but could only fight for breath. Finally, as if an electric shock had gone through his chest, Anderson jerked violently and then collapsed onto the floor.

"What the hell just happened?" Dr. Hunter asked.

"I don't know! It looked to me like the chief just had a heart attack!"

"Check his pulse!"

Snake did so. "*Nada.* He's flatlined. I don't understand it. One minute he was fine—you heard him—and the next—"

"Forget it, Snake," Campbell said. "Better find the Arms-Tech president, and fast."

"Colonel, what did he mean about the Pentagon? Are you keeping information from me?"

"No, Snake. But . . ."

"But what?"

"Snake, this op is level red. You know the drill. You'd need the highest security clearance to be in on the whole story."

"And I don't have that? You send me in here to do the dirty work and I don't know everything I need to survive?"

"Secretary of Defense Houseman is in operational control; I told you that. I report to him. Come on; we don't have time to sit and argue about it!"

"Fine. Wait—"

He heard sounds of a ruckus in Meryl's cell next door. She was fighting with someone! It went on for several seconds, and Snake wondered if he should hurry up into the air duct and help the woman. But then there was a loud *farump!* and the crash of a body falling against the bunk. Then it was quiet. Snake waited a moment and then heard Meryl's cell door open. He started to climb onto the bunk so that he could slip up into the duct again but heard a key card swipe Anderson's door.

"Mister Anderson?" a soft voice whispered.

The door opened. Johnny stood there, wearing a mask and pointing a FAMAS at Snake. No, it wasn't Johnny.

The feminine voice accused him. "You killed the DARPA chief!"

"What?"

"I heard you through the wall. You killed him!"

Snake noticed that the guard's hands were shaking. He lowered his SOCOM. "You ever pointed a gun at anyone before? Your hands are shaking."

"Who are you?" Meryl Silverburgh asked.

Snake almost laughed. "Can you shoot me, rookie?"

"Careful, I'm no rookie."

"You've never had to kill anyone, have you? You haven't even taken the safety off, rookie."

The woman pulled the mask down so that she could get a better look at him. "Liquid?"

"Huh?"

"No. Wait. You're not . . . but you *look* like . . ."

"Yeah, I know. Come on, let's get out of here, all right? I'm on your side. Your uncle Roy sent me. What happened to Johnny?"

She lowered her rifle. "He got fresh. I left him in my cell. How do I look?"

The guard's uniform was a little big on her. "I think you'll pass. I have to get to the second-floor basement. Do you know ArmsTech president Baker?"

"Yeah."

"Then come on."

They stepped out of the cell together, and Snake noticed that Johnny was on the floor of the cell, facedown with his ass sticking up in the air.

Then he heard the entrance to the cell area slide open.

Three heavily armed genome troopers stormed into the cell block. Meryl immediately whirled to fire the FAMAS, but as Snake had noted, her safety was on. Snake thought fast and drew the SOCOM—*thwack, thwack, thwack.* Three head shots and the trio was down.

"So, uhm, nice work, *rookie,*" Snake said.

"Shut up."

The sound of approaching boots gave them no time to jump for cover. Three more troopers poured through the door, and this time Meryl let loose a volley of noisy spray fire, mowing down the men in seconds.

She turned to Snake as if to say, "See there?"

"Nice shooting, but now everyone in the complex will know we're here."

She ran toward the door and said, "Come on; I know my way around this place."

"Meryl! Wait!"

But she was gone.

What the hell? Where's she going?

Snake followed her out of the cell block and saw her at the end of the hallway, headed for the exit. She turned, aimed the FAMAS at him, and fired another volley of rounds. Snake leaped to the side to avoid being hit, rolled, and cursed aloud. When he sprung back to his feet, she had disappeared.

The crazy woman! Why'd she do that?!

Snake started to run after her but suddenly felt disoriented. For a moment he wasn't sure where he was, and then a searing pain knifed through his head. He staggered and leaned against the wall. He was confused but had the presence of mind to wonder why there were no bullet holes from Meryl's blast. The wall was completely smooth.

Am I imagining things?

And then he closed his eyes—

—and saw DARPA chief Anderson strapped in a chair, an interrogation lamp shining brightly over his head. Anderson was dead or had passed out. Snake recognized three figures standing around the poor man: Liquid Snake, Revolver Ocelot, and Psycho Mantis.

"He's dead," Ocelot said.

"You fool!" Liquid grumbled. "I told you to be careful!"

Psycho Mantis replied, "His mental shielding was too strong."

"We'll never get the detonation codes now."

"Wait, sir," Mantis said. "I have an idea."

—and the vision dissipated as Snake opened his eyes. He felt the cold steel of the cell block wall against his face. Consciousness returned, and he found that he was standing, hugging the wall. The headache went away as rapidly as it had appeared, and he no longer felt disoriented.

"Doctor Hunter?"

"Yes, Snake?"

"I just . . . I don't know. Something weird just happened."

"What?"

"I had some kind of hallucination. And a splitting headache for about a minute, but now it's gone."

After a pause, Dr. Hunter replied. "It could be psychometric interference coming from Psycho Mantis. He's probably nearby. What was the hallucination?"

Snake shook his head and flung the cobwebs away. "Never mind. I'm on my way to the second-floor basement. Let's hope Baker's still alive. And Colonel?"

"Yes, Snake?"

"Your niece is one wacky babe."

7

THE FREIGHT ELEVATOR stopped at the second-floor basement, and the doors opened to a large, dimly lit room the size of a gymnasium. Concrete pillboxes were positioned across the floor. Snake figured that each one contained supplies and weapons. He hugged the wall and moved to the corner of the room to survey the situation. It was very quiet . . . *too quiet.*

And what the hell happened to Meryl? Where did she run off to?

"Snake, you're in an armory," Mei Ling said. "Our intelligence reports that each of those concrete blocks is sealed with a Security Level One lock. The ArmsTech president is most likely beyond the armory, in one of the storage rooms on the other side of the pillboxes."

"Thanks. You know, there's something about this place I don't like." Snake reached into his pouch and retrieved the thermal goggles he had snatched. He put them on and immediately noticed the warm outline of a square on the floor in front of him. A trapdoor—what those in the business called a murder door. More often than not, a gruesome death in the form of a long drop, steel spikes, or a drowning pool awaited the unwary soul who fell into one.

Snake made a running start and jumped over the trap. He kept the goggles on in case there were more, but now he understood why there weren't any guards about. Why waste manpower when booby traps could do the work?

By clearing the first murder door, Snake had access to the closest pillbox. He swiped Anderson's PAN card, and the steel door slid open. He stepped inside and was happy to find boxes of SOCOM ammunition, along with extra handguns. He grinned as he envisioned himself as a cowboy with a gun holster on each side of his waist. A two-fisted automatic gunslinger . . . wouldn't it be fun? Unfortunately, he didn't have another holster, so he picked up one of the handguns, loaded it with a full magazine, and put it in his pouch. He then grabbed as much ammunition as he could carry. There were other types of arms and ammo, but there was only so much a guy could do with two hands. Snake left them and exited the pillbox.

The thermal goggles picked up another trap in the floor on the way to the next block. Once again, Snake leaped over it, moved swiftly to the next pillbox door, and used the PAN card to get inside.

Explosives. Lots and lots of C4 explosive. The stuff came in small containers that were attached to a surface by magnets or sticky tape. Remote sensors activated the things, and they were good for demolishing low- to medium-level security doors, wood, some plasters and concrete—depending on the thickness—and cameras. They wouldn't be effective on steel. Nevertheless, Snake picked up three of them and stuffed each one in a separate pocket on his trousers.

He left the block, studied the floor in front of the third pill-box, and discerned another trap. This one he could skirt. The PAN card opened the security door, and he was inside the block.

This one appeared to be stocked with various types of grenades and other explosives. There were some Claymore mines, more chaff grenades, flash-bangs, and some frags—frag-mentation grenades. The Claymores were way too bulky, he al-ready had some chaffs, and the flash-bangs caused too much attention for Snake's comfort, so he grabbed three frags and thrust them into the bulging utility pouch.

"Find anything useful, Snake?" It was Romanenko on the Codec.

"Lots of grenades. Some Claymores. They're too big to carry."

"You should maybe try. Claymores can be set up above ground and are designed to produce maximum damage in a wide fan-shaped area. When they go off, they spray seven one-point-two-millimeter steel pellets in a sixty-degree pattern, much like an oversize shotgun. Traditionally, Claymores use a trip wire to set them off, but the ones you have there are a new type. They are camouflaged using the new stealth technology and are equipped with sophisticated motion detectors."

Snake almost laughed. "You really know your sh—er, your *stuff*, eh, Nastasha?"

"I take pride in my work, if that is what you mean."

"Never mind. Talk to you later."

He exited the pillbox and proceeded to the storage room area where Baker most likely was being held, but he encoun-tered a concrete wall where the map indicated a door should be. And it was unpainted. Was this what Anderson had told him about? He examined the texture and determined that it was a fairly new structure; it had been plastered within the last couple of days. Thus, it was still weak.

Snake *loved* coincidences like this. A C4 canister was just the ticket for the job. He just hoped that the noise of the blast wouldn't alert the entire army of genomes and bring them down on his head but saw no other alternative.

"Colonel, I have to blast my way through a wall." He explained the situation, and Campbell concurred with the strategy. Snake scanned the floors and walls to make sure no cameras were pointed his way and then took one of the C4 containers, exposed the sticky tape, and placed the object in the middle of the freshly painted plaster. He flicked the switch on, moved back behind the pillbox, and held the remote in his hand. The explosive wasn't timed; he could detonate it at any time with the touch of a button. Snake placed his thumb on the trigger, said *"Mazel tov,"* and pushed it.

The blast was loud but not as thunderous as he'd expected. Still, it surely would send *someone* his way.

Light shone behind the thick clouds of smoke and dust that clung to the air around the hole in the wall. Snake waited a moment, his SOCOM in hand and ready. Sure enough, the silhouette of a trooper appeared. The soldier played it safe by staying behind the wall and peering out through the smoke. Then another man joined him.

Too bad that backlighting gives you two away.

The sound-suppressed SOCOM jerked twice, and the troopers dropped like bags of refuse. Snake rushed to the edge of the hole, hugged the wall, and waited for any others to investigate why someone would blow a hole in their nice new wall. But none did. He ducked through the opening, waved away the debris in the air, and moved toward the light. The air cleared a few yards into the storage block, and he saw a man sitting in a chair by a pillar. He was positioned directly beneath a bright interrogation lamp. As Snake moved closer, it was apparent that the man was tied to the chair and had a gag in his mouth. He, too, obviously had been tortured recently.

The explosion must have frightened the man terribly. His eyes darted around in panic. Snake approached him, held up his hands, and said, "I'm a friend. Are you ArmsTech president Baker?"

The man nodded furiously.

Snake reached over and took off the gag. The man coughed violently and spit blood on the floor. Snake started to untie the knots, but Baker cried, "No! Don't touch me!"

Then he saw it. A pack of C4 had been strapped to Baker's back, between his shoulder blades. The ropes were attached to the explosive in such a way that loosening them would set it off. Snake examined the canister and realized it would take some time to neutralize the thing. As for Baker, the man looked as if he was at death's door anyway. He was breathing shallowly and barely could hold up his head.

"I'm going to get you out of here," Snake said. "Somehow."

But a booming voice cut through the cold, concrete room. "So *you're* the one the Boss keeps talking about."

Snaked whirled to see a tall figure wearing a duster and several belts of ammunition around his chest. The man had long yellow-white hair, a beard, and a long mustache. Snake thought Central Casting could use him for the role of General George Custer in a community theater production of the Battle of the Little Big Horn. The man grasped a six-shooter in his right hand, and for a crazy moment Snake was reminded of his recent cowboy daydream. Again, a coincidence.

"And you must be Revolver Ocelot," Snake said. "That's quite a get-up you have on. Didn't they tell you the Sioux surrendered a long time ago and live in peace now?"

"I've been looking forward to meeting you, Solid Snake,"

Ocelot said. "You have quite a reputation to live up to. You know, it really is amazing how much you resemble Big Boss. I met him once."

"Did you?" Snake kept his hand on the SOCOM, ready to blast the guy once he finished reminiscing.

"I first met him in the *sixties*! We had a duel." Ocelot laughed. "Big Boss beat me, too, fair and square. Your daddy was quite the warrior. Do you measure up to him?"

"I don't know. I didn't bring my *ruler*."

Ocelot's eyes narrowed. "Your mission is *over*, Snake!"

The pair stood several paces apart, with the pathetic Mr. Baker in the middle. "Please . . . help me . . ." the wounded man whimpered.

Ocelot slowly held up his gun and pointed the barrel upward, indicating that he wasn't going to shoot. "A Colt single-action Army. An original. Finest six-shooter ever made. Six bullets . . . more than enough to kill anything that moves. I see you use a SOCOM. The handgun chosen by the U.S. Special Operations Command. Hah! Everyone wants to use the newest and latest technology. Back in the old days, when they really knew how to make things, gunsmiths put their souls into their work. As they say, it ain't the wand, it's the magic in it! I can use this gun like it's part of my own body."

He twirled the handgun around his finger with the panache of a Western star and then thrust the barrel into the holster at his side.

The glove had been thrown.

The two men faced each other, their gun hands ready for a quick draw. Snake slowly inched to his right so that Baker would not be in the line of fire. Ocelot mirrored the steps, but Baker was still dangerously close.

Throughout Snake's long career, he had never had to

duel another man face-to-face in such a fashion. The scene prompted him to imagine himself on a stage performing the grand climax of an archetypal opera, with the orchestra building to a crescendo as the principals sang their guts out. Or perhaps he was the protagonist in one of the old Italian Western movies.

Snake felt a trickle of sweat beneath his bandana as the synapses between his brain and trigger hand grew ultrasensitive. In the time it took to *not think* of drawing the weapon, it would be in Snake's hand. It was something Master Miller had taught him: Let the phantom music in his head become a sound track to the situation and then envision each action in the past *before* actually doing it.

He also had learned from Master Miller how to read a person's eyes. "The truth always resides in a man's eyes," his mentor had said. Snake usually could determine if a person was lying, if he was friend or foe, by the eyes. Unfortunately, Ocelot's eyes had squinted into dark slits, and it was difficult to see the whites, much less the soul that lurked behind the pupils. Revolver Ocelot obviously took the gunslinger persona to an extreme.

As if a clock were counting down, Snake felt the seconds tick closer to the final moment when the duelists *had* to draw. Knowing when to act depended on the instinct of a professional; timing was everything.

Ocelot's eyes glinted.

Now.

Ocelot drew his weapon.

Snake saw himself in slow motion as he pulled the SOCOM from its holster and pointed it at the enemy. He simultaneously leaped to·the right to perform a body roll. The trick was pulling the SOCOM's trigger once his feet had left the ground and keeping the weapon properly aimed.

Ocelot's revolver fired, and the bullet soared over Snake's left shoulder. If he hadn't moved, it would have struck him in the face. Snake squeezed the trigger, released three rapid shots, hit the floor with his arm, rolled, and landed on his feet in a crouching position. The three rounds cut the air inches from Baker's head and ricocheted off a metal girder just behind Ocelot's yellow-white locks of hair. He jerked his head out of the way without moving the rest of his body, a sign that he had little fear.

By then, Ocelot had fired two more rounds from the revolver. Snake felt the heat from the bullets as they soared too close to his rib cage for comfort. His momentum in moving sideways never faltered, and he took cover behind a girder. He quickly removed the sound suppressor—he'd have better aim without it—and then swung the SOCOM out from behind the beam and fired. But Ocelot also had hidden.

The man's voice came from behind a concrete pillbox in back of Baker's chair. "The challenge of a duel, for me, is reloading a revolver during battle," Ocelot announced. "It's such a risky thing to do, taking the time, making yourself vulnerable for those few seconds." Snake heard the cylinder snap shut, and then Ocelot spun it. "Hear that, Snake? Such a beautiful sound. The sound of impending death."

Snake considered using one of the frag grenades but quickly nixed that idea because of the stockpiles of explosives around the area. And with the C4 strapped to Baker, Snake couldn't risk it. He would have to depend exclusively on the SOCOM's firepower and his ability to dodge Ocelot's barrage to get through the duel.

"I love the smell of cordite," Ocelot boasted. "The smell of fire, the smell of the devil, the smell from the bowels of the earth . . . it's the smell of victory!"

Snake eyed an area to his right that was full of stacks of

crates. A work light on the ceiling illuminated the space much too well, so Snake took a bead on the bulb and fired. It exploded, plunging the area into shadow. He then ran for the first tower of crates, dodged a round from Ocelot's revolver, and took cover. He crouched low and crawled quickly to another stack. From there he could see Ocelot standing behind Baker, using the ArmsTech president for cover.

The gunslinger had no idea where Snake was, but that didn't stop his bravado. "It won't do you any good to hide back there, Snake! There's no way out. I'm sure our noisy little tête-à-tête will summon a squad of genome troopers in minutes."

Snake needed to force Ocelot away from Baker. A steam pipe stretched down from the ceiling and along a girder that was directly over the terrorist's head. To get a better shot, Snake lay prone and raised his arm at a forty-five-degree angle from the floor. He aimed carefully, squeezed the trigger, and blew a hole in the pipe. A burst of hot steam hit Revolver Ocelot on the side of his face. The man yelped and jumped aside. "Damn you!" he shouted. As the gunslinger moved, Snake let loose a salvo of spray fire and shot a couple of holes in the tail of Ocelot's duster, but the man had slipped behind another pillar for cover.

Baker sniveled in fear as the hot steam from the burst pipe blasted over his head. Although it wasn't burning him, Snake figured it wasn't very comforting either. The sooner he got the ArmsTech president out of harm's way, the better shape he'd be in to talk.

Snake ran to another stack of crates but had no better shot at Ocelot there than before. The battle was destined to be a game of tag until one of them made a serious mistake and exposed himself for the split second it would take for the other to get a clean shot. Perhaps it would be advantageous for Snake to shoot out some more work lights. The thermal goggles would come in handy and could very well be his only hope of defeating the sharpshooter. Snake scanned the ceiling and shot out the nearest bulb, darkening the space around Baker. But that action gave away his position, prompting Ocelot to let loose a volley of rounds that forced the operative to crouch behind the crates.

"It's been so long since I've been in such a rewarding battle!" Ocelot said. "You're not bad, Snake, I must admit. But it's to be expected, I suppose, since you have the same code as the Boss. But I'm just getting warmed up. Very soon I will—"

And then there was an ear-splitting cry of pain.

At first Snake thought it was Baker, but he quickly realized that something had happened to Ocelot. He peered around the crates and saw that Ocelot's trigger hand was *gone*. Blood gushed from the man's severed forearm as he shouted, "*Who?— What?—Aggh!*"

There was someone else in the room. Snake heard swishing sounds, the kind of noise made by a sword as it cut through air. He saw a dark figure pounce as the gunslinger ducked and leaped for safety. The blade crashed into the pillar, breaking off pieces of concrete. As the intruder moved about, his form seemed to appear and disappear, blending with the surroundings like a chameleon's skin. He was *fast*, too.

Stealth. The guy's wearing a stealth suit.

Revolver Ocelot turned and fled, holding his injured arm and leaving his lifeless right hand, still holding on to the Colt, lying in a pool of blood on the floor. Snake stepped out from behind the crates to confront the intruder, but the figure had vanished. Snake rushed to Baker, who had passed out from fear.

"Baker, wake up!" He slapped the man gently on the cheeks, rousing him. But as soon as the ArmsTech president groaned back to life, Snake heard the whooshing sound of the blade. He ducked just in time, for the sword smashed into the pillar behind Baker. Snake performed a lateral roll on the floor to escape another blow from the sword, got to his feet, and faced his new enemy.

The man was dressed as a ninja, completely covered in a sleek armored bodysuit made from stealth material, as Snake had suspected. His face was masked by a helmet that had no holes for the eyes; instead, there was a glowing red sensor in the center, giving him a Cyclops-like appearance. In his right hand he held a replica of an eighth-century sword, but it was equipped with an ultrasonic generator that created a high-frequency blade, allowing the weapon to cut through much denser substances than normally would be possible.

But as the ninja moved, Snake gleaned more about the man's costume. It was one of the latest optic camouflage actuator suits, an "exoskeleton," usually worn by soldiers who had been wounded severely. The suit utilized a supersonic motor that operated with high-frequency voltage; in essence, the electric currents in the man's muscles were detected and operated by the sensors in the suit.

The man was a cyborg—a living human being controlled by machinery that kept him alive.

A cyborg ninja.

"Who are you?" Snake asked. "Are you on the side of the terrorists?"

"I am like you," the ninja said in a metallic, electronic voice. "I have no name."

"Well, take it easy. I have no beef with you."

The ninja suddenly trembled and touched his head with his free hand, as if he was experiencing a major headache. "I . . . am tortured." Snake could hear the pain behind the words. Something was terribly wrong with whoever was inside that exoskeleton.

Then the cyborg straightened, brandished the high-frequency sword, and said, "Only the blaze of battle can wipe away the agony. Prepare yourself."

DR. NAOMI HUNTER twirled her swivel chair around away from her computer monitor and stood.

"I'll be right back," she said to Campbell.

The colonel looked at her and saw that her face was ashen. "Are you all right, Doctor?"

"I'm fine. I just need to go to the ladies' room."

"You look like you've seen a ghost."

She laughed uncertainly and then continued on her way out of the control room. She walked down the hall, pushed open the door to the washroom, and went inside. Once alone, she moved to the sink and held on to the sides to keep herself from collapsing. She looked into the mirror and didn't recognize the shock that was apparent in her eyes.

Could it be . . . ?

It was impossible . . . or was it?

The man in the exoskeleton. As soon as she had heard his voice—filtered through the electronic voice box—the memories of her childhood trauma and subsequent salvation had flooded through her. She wanted to cry out in pain but wouldn't allow herself to do so. For now she had to keep silent. For her sake and for his.

What was he doing on Shadow Moses Island? It broke her heart to see him in that condition—the one he would have to live with for the rest of his life. To have to wear that horrid suit just to stay alive would be a hell beyond her wildest imagination. But that wasn't the worst of it. It was apparent that the man's *mind* was gone. Did he know who he was? Did he know about his former relationship with Solid Snake? Did he remember *her*?

His appearance on the island certainly threw a wrinkle into the mission.

No matter what happened, Dr. Hunter knew she had to remain calm and not give herself away.

For now.

8

THE CYBORG NINJA attacked, with the high-frequency sword spearheading the lunge at Snake as if it had been launched by a powerful bow. Snake barely avoided the blade because the armored soldier moved with the speed of lightning. Despite his evasive action, the sword slashed Snake's suit just beneath the left arm and sliced the skin along his rib cage. The pain caused his adrenaline to pump overtime, which shocked him into overcoming the complacency with which he had been executing the mission thus far.

Whoever this guy is, he's not playing around.

The ninja continued to swing the sword back and forth in blink-of-an-eye strokes, shearing slivers off whatever material happened to be in the way—wood, metal, and plaster. If the cyborg got a fraction of an inch closer, one of Snake's arms, or his *head*, surely would be rolling on the floor. Snake managed to back up and jump onto a four-foot-high platform of stacked forklift pallets. The maneuver surprised and confused the ninja, providing Snake with the moment he needed to fire his weapon.

He squeezed the trigger and bombarded the cyborg with several rounds. But the ninja *knocked the bullets away with his sword*!

Snake had never seen anything like it. The creature obviously could move with a speed far greater than that of any normal man.

He switched to spray fire and emptied the magazine, but the ninja continued to bat away bullets. Even though many of them got through the sword's defenses, the rounds simply bounced off the armored suit as if they were marbles.

"Your weapon does not do you honor," the ninja said. "Too slow."

Snake foresaw the sword swinging at him, jumped, and grabbed hold of a low-hanging girder. He swung his legs up and hugged it as the blade swiped the space where his body had been a split second earlier. The ninja attempted to strike him from the floor, but he wasn't tall enough, so he *jumped six feet into the air from a standing position*. The blade swished toward Snake as he released the girder and fell onto the stack of wooden pallets. The top few split into timbers as his body crashed through them. He tried to wiggle out but was stuck within the broken slats.

The ninja raised the sword to strike. Snake furiously kicked out the sides of the pallets to free himself, sending missiles of wood in the cyborg's direction. The ninja's blade easily shattered them into a hundred pieces. The distraction gave Snake the opportunity to pull back his knees and jackknife out of the pallets, perform a flip in midair, and land on his feet.

The cyborg staggered back and held his head again.

"The pain . . ." he groaned. The man's entire body trembled for a second, and then he shook himself like a dog that had just emerged from a pool of water. The red sensor on his face focused on Snake, and then he brandished the sword. "The pain makes me feel so *alive*!"

And he attacked again.

Snake didn't waste time fighting, because it was futile. He needed a completely different strategy, and to formulate one he had to find some cover for a couple of minutes. He holstered his weapon and performed a somersault out of the way of the sword, which crashed down onto the floor where he'd been standing. Master Miller had taught him to use walls, stationary objects, and the furniture in a room as "springboards"—push-off points to get quickly from one place to another. Thus, Snake became something of a human pinball as he bounced away from the cyborg, leaping and kicking off solid surfaces with the agility of a circus artist. Three seconds later, he was behind one of the concrete pillboxes, his back against the wall, taking deep breaths. Reflexively, he reloaded the SOCOM and said for the benefit of the Codec, "Any suggestions on how to beat this guy would be greatly appreciated."

"Stand by, Snake; we're working on it," the colonel answered.

Stand by? Was he kidding?

Snake closed his eyes and concentrated on the sounds around him. The ninja moved silently and swiftly. Would he be able to hear the creature if he came close? What Snake *could* hear was his own heart beating furiously. It had been too long since he'd seen action such as this. Perhaps he *hadn't* been in the best shape.

Stop it, he willed himself. *Of course I'm in shape. It's that* ninja *who's got the superpowers.*

He remembered more of Master Miller's admonitions. Put an enemy's strengths into perspective. Don't compare him to yourself. Measuring the abilities of one man against those of another was pointless. What mattered was confidence, positive thinking, and envisioning victory over defeat before the battle had begun.

Easier said than done.

Becoming impatient with the dead silence in the room, Snake finally moved to the edge of the pillbox and stole a look back at the storage room. All he could see was Baker, still sitting under the lamp and the leaking steam pipe. The ninja was gone.

Was the creature using his suit's stealth qualities as camouflage? Was the cyborg right in front of his eyes but cleverly blended into the background?

Snake slipped the thermal goggles back on. The heat from Baker's body was clearly visible, but it was weak—the man was dying. He had to get over there and talk to the guy before it was too late.

There was no other heat source.

Snake cautiously slipped out from behind the pillbox and then moved slowly back into the storeroom. He looked up and down the rows between equipment and supplies, but the ninja was nowhere to be seen. The creature must have fled.

He didn't sound like he was all there mentally, either.

Snake set out for Baker but halted in midstride. Something wasn't right. There was definitely another entity nearby. Snake's senses were so finely tuned that he could *feel* when there was danger around the corner. It was an asset of the genetic coding that went into his makeup, but Snake also had become more sensitive as a result of the post-traumatic stress disorder he had suffered from over the last couple of years. His previous mission for FOXHOUND had shaken him to the core, resulting in his early retirement and retreat into the Alaskan wilderness. It had taken months to rid of himself of the hallucinations, paranoia, and mental confusion that accompanied PTSD, but his rehabilitation inexplicably left him with ultra-awareness. He heard better, saw more clearly, reacted faster—and although he didn't believe in a sixth sense, Master Miller had remarked that Snake had developed one.

METAL GEAR SOLID | 77

It was this sixth sense that saved his life. As he stood between the stacks of crates, a mere fifteen feet away from Baker, Snake became conscious of a presence hovering over him. He quickly glanced at the ceiling and reflexively leaped to the side before the exoskeleton fell on top of him.

The cyborg ninja had climbed onto the girders and waited for the moment when he could leap upon his prey. But instead of colliding into Snake, the ninja crashed facedown onto the floor. The creature was slightly stunned.

Snake used the opening to jump into position and kick the ninja in the head. The cyborg's skull jerked backward as he emitted an unearthly cry of pain. Snake spun his body in preparation for another roundhouse kick, but this time the cyborg caught his ankle. Using unimaginable strength, the ninja lifted Snake with one arm and tossed him into a pile of crates as if the operative had the weight of a house cat. Then the cyborg got to his feet, drew the sword from his scabbard, and pointed it at Snake. He moved closer so that the sharp point touched Snake's Adam's apple.

"Are you or are you not my enemy?"

Snake was dazed by the throw. He lay helplessly on his back, looked up at the imposing exoskeleton, and waited for the inevitable skewering. But then he realized that the creature had asked him a question.

"I'm not your enemy," he answered. He took off the thermal goggles so that the creature could see the sincerity in his eyes.

The cyborg hesitated. The red sensor on his face fluctuated in intensity. He then pulled back the sword and straightened his body. Once again, the ninja rubbed his head. "The pain . . . I do not know . . ."

The ninja turned from Snake and started to walk away as if he had just woken up from a dream and didn't know where he was.

"Wait," Snake said. "Let me help you!" But the ninja broke into a run and was gone before Snake could get to his feet. "Damn, he's fast."

Snake didn't chase after the tormented creature. He stood and brushed the splinters from his suit as he considered that there was something familiar about the ninja—but he didn't know what it was. There was no time to think about it, either. Perhaps he'd run into the cyborg again, but for now, Baker was his main priority.

The ArmsTech president appeared to be unconscious, but Snake could see that he was still breathing. "Baker?" He approached and gently rustled the man. "Wake up. Can you hear me?"

Baker groaned and lifted his head. "Who are you?" he asked in a whisper.

Snake took the canteen that was fastened to his utility belt, opened it, and gave the man a few sips of water. "I'm not one of them," he answered.

"Thank you," Baker said. The liquid seemed to give him a little strength. "You're from . . . the Pentagon, aren't you? Jim sent you?"

Snake replaced the canteen. "Anderson said he gave them his detonation code. What about yours?"

Baker winced and looked away. "I . . . I talked."

Damn!

Snake wanted to slug the guy. "So now the terrorists have both codes? Do you realize what this means? They can launch a nuke anytime they want!"

"It was the physical . . . torture . . . But . . . but I resisted Psycho Mantis's mind probe. The surgical implants . . . in my brain. Everyone . . . everyone who knows the codes has them."

"Even the DARPA chief?"

"Yes."

"But Anderson said Psycho Mantis got the code from him. How can that be?"

Baker shook his head in confusion. "I . . . I don't know. Please. I'm . . . dying."

Snake crouched in front of him. "Listen to me. Okay, so the terrorists have both codes. But what about the card keys? The ones that override the detonation code? Do you have them?"

The man shook his head again. "Not . . . anymore. I gave them . . . to the girl . . . There was a soldier, a young girl . . . She arrived at the facility recently . . . I trusted her . . . I gave them to her. They threw her in prison because she didn't join the revolt. I hope she's all right."

Meryl.

"I hope she is, too. She's a bit green but seemed to me to be pretty tough." Snake wondered if the card keys might have been confiscated when she was put into the cell. He had to find her again.

"I see you have . . . a Codec." Baker smiled slightly. "She has one now. She . . . stole one from a guard. Her Codec frequency is . . . two point sixty-three. Or it was. I hope they . . . haven't caught her."

"I think she's running around loose, Mister Baker. I'll find her. What can you tell me about the terrorists? I know Liquid Snake is the leader. Who are his closest lieutenants? Revolver Ocelot?"

Baker coughed. "Ocelot . . . he tortured me. Bad. He is one of the top men . . . but the right-hand man . . . is Decoy Octopus. But I don't know . . . I don't know what happened to him."

"What do you mean?"

"Octopus was near Liquid . . . all the time . . . but he disappeared . . . He must have been . . . sent away on a mission . . . or something. Watch out for the woman . . . the one with the wolves."

"Sniper Wolf."

Baker nodded. He coughed up blood, and it dribbled down his chin.

"Tell me. If the keys don't work, is there another way to prevent a nuclear launch?"

Baker nodded and coughed again. "Otacon. Find Otacon."

"Who?"

"That's his code . . . code name. Hal Emmerich. Doctor Hal . . . Emmerich. He's the team leader . . . chief engineer . . . of the . . . Metal Gear REX project. If anyone can figure out how to . . . stop Metal Gear from launching . . . it's him."

"Where is he? How do I find him?"

"He's . . . he's a prisoner, too."

"Where?"

"I think . . . in the Nuclear Warhead Storage Building."

Snake knew from studying the maps that this was a part of the main complex, where the terrorists most likely were holding down the fort. "Do you know who that was just now? That ninja thing?"

"Ninja? Oh . . ." The man coughed. "That was FOX-HOUND's dark little secret."

"Huh?"

"An experimental genome soldier. Ask . . . Doctor Hunter . . ." A coughing fit overtook Baker. Blood spewed from his mouth and spattered the front of his clothing. It was obvious to Snake that Baker wasn't going to hold up for much more interrogation.

"Okay, take it easy, Mister Baker. Now, let's see what we can do to get this C4 off you." Snake examined the mechanism, but Baker shook his head.

"Don't. Forget . . . it. I'm . . . dying. Don't . . . waste your time."

Snake knew the man was right. "I'm sorry, Baker."

"It's all . . . right. Go."

"Baker, why the hell did you guys revive the Metal Gear project?"

"There is so much . . . nuclear material . . . in the world . . . unaccounted for. Any small country . . . or terrorist group . . . could easily get hold of a nuke. So we . . . the U.S. . . . to maintain our policy of . . . deterrence . . . we needed a weapon . . . of overwhelming power."

"But it's crazy."

"My company . . . ArmsTech . . . we pushed for Metal Gear to be developed . . . as a black project."

"Black project?"

"Secret projects paid for by . . . the Pentagon's black budget. That way . . . the bleeding-heart liberals can't stop them. Anyway . . . the Metal Gear was going to be formally adopted . . . after the results of this exercise."

"Frankly, I don't give a crap about your company."

"Right . . . So here . . . reach into my trouser . . . pocket." Snake did so and found a computer disk. "This is what you . . . what you came for. The optical disk."

"I don't know what—"

"It's what you need to give . . . give to Jim. It is the . . . only remaining copy . . . of the data."

Snake stuck the disk into a pocket on his utility belt. "What data?"

"All the data collected . . . from this exercise. Make sure . . . Jim gets it."

"Jim? Jim Houseman? I take my orders from Colonel Campbell. I don't know anything about—"

"Listen!" Baker coughed, and his breath became shorter. "You must . . . stop them. If it goes . . . public . . . ArmsTech is . . . finished."

"Why? Metal Gear uses existing technology, doesn't it?"

"Sure . . . Metal Gear does . . . but . . ." He coughed more as blood oozed out of his mouth. Then his body jerked and trembled as his eyes rolled up into his head. He groaned in pain.

"What?"

"No! It . . . can't . . . be!"

"What's happening? Mister Baker!"

"Those Pentagon . . . bastards! They went . . . and . . . did it."

"What are you talking about?"

"They're *using* you to . . . to . . ."

Baker's entire body went into spasm for a moment, and then he stiffened. With one final exhalation, he sagged in the chair. Snake reached out and felt for a pulse, but there was none.

"Colonel? Are you listening? Baker's dead."

Dr. Hunter spoke. "The torture must have been too much for him. Was it a heart attack?"

"I think so," Snake said. "Just like Anderson."

"Well, we won't know for sure until there's a postmortem."

"What the hell was that ninja thing? Do you know?"

"I'm afraid I don't have enough information, Snake."

"A member of FOXHOUND?"

"No."

"Are you sure?"

"We have no one like that in our unit."

"Colonel? Are you there?"

"I'm here, Snake."

"Okay, what was Baker talking about? What does the Pentagon have to do with all this?"

"Snake, now is not the time—"

"Damn it, Colonel! It's *my* life on the line here! What are you not telling me?"

"I can't reveal classified information to you, Snake. I'm sorry."

"Well, that's just hunky-dory. What about Decoy Octopus?

Baker said he's gone. Do you have any record of transports leaving the island in the last twenty-four hours?"

"No one has left the island, Snake. Octopus must still be there. Remember, he has the ability to *become* anyone. He is *the* master of disguise."

"Thanks, Colonel. Are there any *more* words of wisdom that you have to offer?"

Campbell hesitated and then answered. "Snake, I want you to find my niece and work together."

With as much sarcasm as he could muster, Snake asked, "And can I trust *her*?"

"Snake, you can probably trust her more than you can trust me."

"That's what I figured. Look, Colonel, I don't know what's going on and I can see that you're not about to tell me. But something *smells* about this mission, and it's not the mouse droppings I keep crawling over."

The colonel's silence spoke volumes.

9

Snake studied the aerial map of the facility on the Codec. The Nuclear Warhead Storage Building was a separate structure. He would have to return to the first level and the tank hangar to access an exit. It appeared that a narrow lengthwise canyon connected the two buildings. There was no telling what kinds of defenses the terrorists had set up outside, but one thing was certain—it would be cold. Snake was thankful for Dr. Hunter's injection and wondered how long its effects would last.

Time for a cigarette. As much as he hated the kind he'd pinched from the soldier, he needed the nicotine fix. Snake lit up, winced at the taste, and then punched in the code to reach Meryl Silverburgh. After a moment she answered, and her masked face appeared on the Codec's small view screen.

"Who is this?"

"You're the colonel's niece, Meryl, right?"

"I asked you a question."

"I'm called Solid Snake."

"You don't say? The legendary Solid Snake?"

"That's right. I'm working for your uncle."

"I figured he'd send someone. I didn't think it would be you. I thought you'd retired."

"I *am* retired. I'm just doing this for fun."

"That was you before? In the cell block?"

"Uh-huh."

"Well, sorry about running out on you. I didn't know *who* the heck you were. I didn't want to take the chance that you were one of the bad guys. You look like—"

"I know. Where are you now?"

"I'm in the belly of the security system. I'm *this* close to figuring out how to hot-wire the hangar's cargo door. It's got a Level Five security lock on it. No one has a Level Five clearance except for the terrorists. I assume you want to get to the other buildings?"

"That's affirmative."

"Then you need my help. You'll never get that door open by yourself."

"I don't know; I'm pretty good with doors. I do windows, too."

"Mister, by the time you've found the security system, they'll have already launched a nuke."

This gave Snake pause. "So tell me, Meryl, what is this place, really? It's not just a nuclear disposal facility."

"Of course not. Didn't my uncle tell you *anything*?"

"Not enough, apparently."

"This place is owned and operated by an ArmsTech dummy corporation. It's a civilian base. For the development of the Metal Gear. Do you know what that is?"

"I'm, uhm, familiar with it."

"This was supposed to be sort of a final test. You know, before a formal adoption of the program by the Pentagon."

"I don't like it. No government has any business fooling

around with these Metal Gear contraptions. They might blow someone up."

Meryl laughed. "You're pretty funny for an ex-FOXHOUND operative."

"So where are all the hostages? The facility's employees?"

"I don't know. They were rounded up and put somewhere. Some of them were interrogated, brainwashed, I don't know . . ."

"Baker told me he gave you the three key cards that stop the REX from launching. Do you have them?"

"Hmm. I have *a* key. He didn't give me three."

"Really? Then what was he talking about?"

"I have no idea. But I still have the one he gave me."

"Then hang on to it. How did you manage to keep it hidden from the guards?"

"Uh, women have more hiding places than men."

Snake almost smiled. "Do you know Doctor Emmerich?"

"Yeah, he designed the new REX. Nice guy."

"Where is he?"

"Probably in the research lab of the Nuclear Warhead Storage Building. That's across the canyon, outside, to the north. Did you bring your snow boots and winter coat?"

"Yes, Mom. I'm going to find him. If we can't override the detonation code in time, maybe he knows how to destroy the damned thing."

"You can't take on REX by yourself, mister."

"I've done it before. I'll check in with you later. Get that door open for me and I'll buy you an ice cream when we get back to civilization."

"Oh, boy, can't wait. Give me a few minutes. Wait for me in the hangar and I'll go with you."

"Nope. No offense, Meryl, but you don't have enough real combat experience. I want you to find a good hiding place and concentrate on not getting caught again until I've sewn this place up. Then we'll meet up and I'll get you out of here."

"Look, I'm sorry about before, you know, with my gun. I don't know what happened; I just couldn't pull the trigger right away. I never had any problems during training. But when I thought of bullets tearing into those soldiers' bodies, I guess I just hesitated."

"Shooting at training targets and shooting at living people are very different."

She sighed. "Ever since I was a little girl, I dreamed about being a soldier. All my life I trained for the day I'd see some real action, and now . . ."

"So you want to quit?"

"I can't quit!"

"Look, Meryl. Everybody feels sick the first time they kill someone. Unfortunately, killing is one of those things that get easier the more you do it. In a war, all of humankind's worst emotions and worst traits come out. It's easy to forget what a sin is in the middle of a battlefield. You're just a little jumpy from the combat high. The adrenaline in your bloodstream is starting to thin out. Just take it easy."

"I learned all about combat high at the academy."

"We'll talk about it later. For now, just think about keeping yourself alive . . . and staying the hell out of my way."

"You're a real bastard. My uncle was right," she said. "Look, I know my way around this place. I could be useful."

"Sorry. I work alone. I wouldn't want anything to happen to you on your uncle's watch."

Snake could *feel* her pouting. She was obviously still young and inexperienced in field operations. She had no idea how dangerous it really was.

She pulled off her mask. "All right, Snake," she said. "I'll be a good little girl. And *maybe* I'll open the hangar cargo door for you."

He was struck by her model's good looks. He'd had *no idea*.

"What?" she asked, aware that he hadn't said anything.

"Nothing. It's just . . . your eyes."

"My eyes?"

"They're not soldier's eyes."

"Oh, right. *Rookie's* eyes, huh?"

"No. They're beautiful, *compassionate* eyes."

"Hmpf. Just what I'd expect from the legendary Solid Snake. You trying to sweep me off my feet?"

Snake gave her a cynical laugh. "Don't worry; you'd land right back on them as soon as you got to know me. The reality is no match for the legend, I'm afraid. Let's link up later. *Stay put.*"

Snake clicked off and moved toward the freight elevator. He took it to Level 1, stood to the side of the car so that he wouldn't be seen when the doors opened, and waited. He heard nothing nearby, so he cautiously slipped out of the lift and hugged the wall.

The tank hangar was as he'd left it except for one significant change. One of the Abrams tanks was gone.

THE GIANT STOOD on a glacier that jutted out over the side of the canyon and eyed the building that housed the tank hangar. So far the door had remained closed.

The canyon was the size of an American football field, approximately a hundred yards between the hangar building and the Nuclear Warhead Storage structure. The snow had continued to fall at a steady pace, covering the canyon floor with a minimum of two feet, but weather reports predicted severe blizzard conditions within hours. At the moment, though, the atmospheric state was nothing out of the ordinary for Shadow Moses Island. For a small island in the Aleutian chain that stretched from Alaska to Russia, adverse climate was par for the course. The giant wondered why the U.S. government would build a facility in such a remote and harsh location. But his was not to question the antics of American politicians and military commanders. Even though he was an American by birth, his allegiance was to Russians, for whom he had worked for years. Since the fall of the Soviet Union, the giant had worked for hire. The "new" FOXHOUND was just as good an employer as anyone. At least he would see some action . . . soon.

A large black bird circled the glacier and eventually landed on the giant's shoulder. Vulcan Raven reached into a pocket and pulled out a handful of dried fruit pieces. He held it to the raven and allowed it to feed. The bird dug in even though it preferred fresh carrion.

"Patience, my friend," the Alaskan said. "The time is near. Very soon we will see the enemy emerge from those doors. Then we will join our comrades in the tank and commence battle. The ancestors will be proud of our victory today."

Vulcan Raven looked down onto the canyon floor, where the M1 Abrams sat. The two gunners were already in position inside the vehicle. They were ordinary genome troopers who had no wish to bear the brunt of the cold weather. The climate didn't bother Vulcan Raven. He could survive for days in subzero temperatures. He wasn't half Alaskan Indian and half Inuit Eskimo for nothing. His immense size also contributed to the way his body generated warmth. He was a walking, breathing energy source.

"I suppose we should climb down the glacier now. What do you think, my friend?" he asked the bird. The raven squawked, finished the sample of dried fruit, and lifted off to hover over its master's head. The giant picked up his Gatling gun, a 20-mm

M61A1 Vulcan that he could wield by hand as if it were a pop-gun, and slung it over his shoulder. Before descending the cliff, he touched the birthmark on his forehead. The elder shamans had taught him from an early age that he had been born with the mark of destiny. Eskimos and Indians worshipped ravens, and Vulcan Raven happened to enter the world with the shape of the bird engraved on his skin. Much of the giant's mystical power derived from the birthmark. Whenever he became excited, such as in the heat of battle, the mark disappeared and his senses were heightened to inhuman levels. But Vulcan Raven's size and birthmark were not the only things about him that intimidated enemies. His imposing body was covered from head to toe in tattoos depicting petroglyphs copied from prehistoric Indian ruins. The markings resembled circuit wiring, which Vulcan found ironic. Even two thousand years ago, the ancient shamans had foreseen the coming of the age of electronics.

"Let's go, friend."

The raven floated alongside him as the giant began his descent.

SNAKE VENTURED FARTHER into the hangar and immediately became aware of a genome guard on the catwalk to his left. He froze, hoping that the man hadn't seen him. In the shadowy lighting, Snake's suit could blend into his surroundings, but movement would give him away. (Snake wished his suit really *could* blend into his surroundings!)

The guard walked along the catwalk, stopped at the rail, and lit a cigarette.

The bozo hasn't seen me. Good.

Snake waited until the guard turned to continue his patrol in the other direction. As soon as the man's back was to him, Snake moved against the wall, out of the guard's sight lines. He then slipped toward the metal staircase. His plan was to get rid of the guard, check to make sure there weren't any others in the hangar, and then be ready for the slatted cargo door to roll up. *If* Meryl was as good as she claimed she was.

The operative crept silently up the stairs and reached the catwalk. The guard was walking slowly toward him, so Snake stayed on the top steps, below the level of the mesh walk. He listened carefully for the sound of the boots approaching. Six feet . . . four feet . . . two feet . . .

Snake reached up and grabbed the man by the ankles and pulled. The soldier fell flat on his back, generating an unwanted loud *clang* on the metal walk. Snake quickly leaped up onto the platform and stomped on the guard's face. A second kick to the side of the head and the man was in dreamland.

He whirled around and surveyed the entire hangar from the advantageous height. There was no other movement. He could see, however, the tracks left by the missing Abrams tank. It had been driven from its position on the floor to the roll-up cargo door. It assuredly was waiting for him outside.

Snake descended the stairs and ran to the egress. He quickly punched in Meryl's frequency code.

"What?"

"I'm waiting."

"Hold your horses. I've just about got it."

The mechanism in the wall clicked on and whirred as the slatted door lifted and rolled up into the ceiling. A blast of cold air wafted into the hangar.

"Do I get a gold star?" Meryl asked.

"I'm impressed. Can you cook, too?"

"I make a mean western omelet."

"I'll take you up on that in another time and another place. Now stay put."

"Right."

She disconnected as Snake peered into the dark tunnel that stretched from the hangar to the outside opening. It was tall and wide enough for a tank to pass through, was about sixty feet long, and emptied onto a snow-covered field. He took a step forward—

"Snake! Don't move!"

It was Mei Ling.

"Why not?"

"Put on your thermals!"

He did so and immediately understood the team's concern. An elaborate mesh of minute lasers, unseen by the naked eye, crossed the tunnel horizontally. They each moved up and down vertically at different speeds. Tripping one or more would certainly set off alarms or worse.

Campbell spoke. "Snake, our intelligence from the Knee Cap reports that the loading ramp to the hangar, where you are now, has been outfitted with nerve gas. You can probably see laser trip beams that—"

"I see them, Colonel."

"Then avoid them at all costs. The tunnel would seal off, the gas would be released, and you'd be dead in minutes."

"You always have such cheery news."

"Just giving you a heads-up, soldier." Snake could hear the attempt in the colonel's voice to lighten the tension that had risen between them earlier. He wasn't having any of it. Snake didn't care for the way Campbell was handling the mission. He liked being told everything there was to know before going in, and the colonel hadn't leveled with him. There were still a lot of things Snake didn't understand about the undertaking. If Jim Houseman really was overseeing the entire operation, it was possible that even the colonel didn't know all the facts. Snake supposed he should give Campbell the benefit of the doubt, but he wasn't going to.

The thermal goggles clearly delineated the laser beams. The first one moved at a fairly slow speed. It was a simple procedure to wait until the line was just over his head and then slip under it. The second one was much quicker and was no more than two feet away from the first. It also had an erratic vertical pattern—it didn't just go up and down; it went up a little ways, then down a bit, up some more, down a lot, up even higher . . . It was unpredictable. Snake had to stand completely straight and pause until the beam was nearly touching the floor. Before the laser rose again, he stepped over it and walked forward out of harm's way.

The mesh configuration continued for another thirty feet. The up-and-down patterns were more complex as he progressed. The intervals between lasers also varied: Some were close together and others a fair distance apart to give an intruder a false sense of safe passage.

Snake punched Meryl's code on the Codec.

"What?" she said, feigning annoyance.

"Sorry to *bother* you, but while you're up in the security system, can you find a way to turn off these stupid lasers?"

"Sorry, Snake, I already checked. There's no way. You really do have to have a Level Five security card, and the only place you can turn them off is there at the door."

"Okay, I was just checking."

"You'll make it through okay?"

"Don't worry about me."

"I won't. I'll meet you at the storage building."

"What?"

"I said I know my way around. See ya!"

"Meryl! I told you to stay put!"

"I changed my mind."

"Don't do something stupid!"

"Sorry, but this is the only way I can find out if I'm cut out to be a soldier. I gotta get my hands dirty! See ya there!" And she was gone.

Great. That's all I need.

If it turned out she knew another way to get to the storage building, he was going to have her hide. But first, the task at hand.

Snake studied the patterns of the next three lasers and determined that he would have to traverse the closest two without stopping in between them. They were only a foot apart, and as much as he watched his weight, he wasn't *that* skinny. The problem was that when one of the lasers was at a height over his head, the other one was at thigh level and moved too quickly for him to slip between the two. He would have to crawl under both, and he had a mere two seconds to do it.

He crouched, studied the pattern for another few moments, and then lay parallel to the beams. As soon as the second laser left the floor, Snake rolled like a log, cleared both beams, quickly jumped to his feet, and then leaped over the third laser.

Two more to go. These crossed each other: One was at the top while the other was at the bottom, and then they met in the middle. Snake waited until they parted, and then he ducked, lifted one leg high, and hurdled over the bottom beam.

He was clear. The icy wind was strong at the opening, and massive drifts of snow covered the field. Maneuvering through the deep stuff would be slow going and ponderous. But he had no alternative.

And somewhere in the blinding weather was a deadly armored tank.

10

SNAKE STEPPED INTO the knee-high snow and moved to the side of the open door, hugging the wall to stay out of sight.

The Codec beeped. Snake glanced at it and was surprised to see that it was a nonburst transmission. That meant it wasn't from Campbell or the others.

"Who is this?" he answered.

"A friend." It was a male voice, deep and controlled.

"Can you be more specific?"

"Snake, you must be careful in the canyon. There are Claymore mines planted at various locations. You have a mine detector?"

"Yes. Who *is* this?"

"Use the mine detector to pinpoint the Claymores. Stay out of their sensor range."

"I know how to use it. Tell me who you are, damn it!"

"Consider me a fan. You can call me . . . Deepthroat."

The transmission clicked off. Snake attempted to bring up

the frequency code of the last incoming call, but the digital readout simply read 0.

What the hell?

Nevertheless, if the fellow was being straight with him, Snake's life might have been saved. He opened a side pocket of the utility belt and removed the ArmsTech Pathtracker 3000, a handy tool that located unexploded mines and bombs by picking up radio waves from buried devices. Once the detector scrambled a mine's signal, the user could disarm or detonate the explosive from a safe distance. Snake held the machine, which was the size of a deck of cards, and flicked it on. He extended the antenna and pointed it at the ground in front of him.

The outlines of three Claymore mines materialized on the screen. One was very close, about ten feet away from the hangar entrance. Two more were ten feet beyond that, nearly side by side. He would have to get farther onto the field to detect any more.

He turned the frequency knob and pointed the antenna at the spot where the first mine was buried. A green indicator light was supposed to brighten when the explosive was disarmed, but nothing happened. Snake wasn't sure if the two feet of snow had had an impact on the unit's functionality; perhaps it had. The best thing to do would be to avoid the area altogether.

Snake moved to the left side of the canyon and trudged to the north along the rock cliff. The wind wasn't as strong and visibility was better next to the wall. Could he cross the entire field by staying on that course?

The answer came when the Pathtracker picked up a series of Claymores blocking his way. Once again he attempted to disarm them, but it was no go. He would have to move back toward the center of the field to go around them, out where he would be a sitting duck.

Snake put on his sun goggles to keep the wind out of his eyes, donned a pair of thermal gloves, and set out.

It took nearly twenty minutes to make the journey to the center of the canyon. Most of the Claymores had been concentrated in the first fifty yards, and now it seemed that the rest of the way was clear. Snake felt like Doctor Zhivago as he fought the harsh, frigid wind and plodded forward. He could have used a wool scarf and a down jacket, but Dr. Hunter's nanomachines were doing a good job of keeping him warm. The worst part was the tedious traipsing through the deep snow. It was harder work than climbing a steep hill.

"This is Raven's territory! Snakes do not belong in Alaska! You will not pass!"

The deep voice resonated through the air, carried by the wind. It came from a loudspeaker somewhere up ahead. Snake squinted through the goggles and made out a dark, bulky shape that was growing larger.

The Abrams tank was coming his way.

Snake took the scope from his utility belt and focused it on the armored monstrosity. A very large man with a bird painted on his forehead sat in the turret. No—it was a tattoo or a birthmark.

Vulcan Raven, the shaman giant, in the flesh.

Before Snake could begin to plan a defensive strategy, the tank's 105-mm M68 rifled gun fired a shell at him. The only thing he could do was leap sideways as hard as he could and burrow himself as deeply into the snow as possible.

The explosion rocked the world around him. He felt his body being lifted and then slapped into the air. He landed with a thud despite the snow's cushion. For a moment Snake saw stars, and there was a tremendously painful ringing in his ears.

Vulcan Raven laughed boisterously. "That's right! You should crawl on the ground like the snake you are!"

The voice reminded him where he was. Snake quickly took
stock of his arms and legs and determined that everything was
still there. He carefully flexed each appendage and was grateful
that nothing had been broken or torn by shrapnel. The ringing
in his ears subsided but remained a steady annoyance.

He had been damned lucky.

The ground trembled below him, and he heard the
Abrams's engine coming closer. This time, the tank's 12.7-mm
machine gun rattled the snow around him. If anything was
going to make him move his ass, that was it.

Snake got up and forced himself to leave the spot where he
had fallen. It was impossible to run; it was like walking through
molasses. What was he going to do?

Yet another lesson from Master Miller came back to him. It
was an appropriate one, too, for it concerned a battle between a
man with few defenses and a powerful giant.

"Do you remember the story of David and Goliath?" Miller
had asked the class of trainees. "David was a young Israelite lad,
strong enough, but no match for the powerful Philistine warrior
Goliath. The giant was armed with a sword and a club and
armor and brute strength. David had nothing but a slingshot.
But he used his wits to defeat Goliath. How did he do that? By
invoking the principle that something *small* can often penetrate
large defenses. So he placed a pebble in his sling, spun it in
order to increase its speed and force, and flung the stone at the
giant's face. The rock struck Goliath between the eyes and
killed him. Of course, it helped that David was a damned good
shot! So let this be a lesson to you—know how to use your
weapons expertly but also know *when* to use them. There is a
time and place for every offense, no matter how small, and no
matter how big the defense."

Snake smiled at the memory. He knew exactly what he had
to do.

The tank roared closer as Vulcan Raven's voice boomed: "We shall toy with you a little longer, Snake. Only when you've had enough will I deliver the killing blow!"

Snake dived into the snow and dug deep until he felt the icy ground. Luckily, the snow was fairly soft, enabling him to tunnel his way toward the tank below the surface on his hands and knees. He could imagine what Vulcan Raven must be thinking as the giant searched the field for a sign of his prey. The snake truly had become a creature close to the earth. But unlike his cold-blooded namesakes, Solid Snake was a warm-blooded mammal who could withstand the frosty temperature below the snow's surface.

When the tank sounded as if it was rolling on its treads a mere few feet from him, Snake reached into the pouch and took out one of the frag grenades. Holding it firmly in hand, he stood, broke through the snow, and faced the oncoming juggernaut. He was at its broadside, about ten feet away. A gunner was in the turret next to Vulcan Raven, operating the smaller machine gun. He clearly heard the giant say, "Is that him? Over there?"

The gunner fired a burst of ammunition at a target perpendicular to and thirty feet away from where Snake was standing. He had fooled them. Snake pulled the grenade's pin with his teeth, counted to five, and tossed the pineapple at the gunner. He then turned and ran—trudged, rather—through the thick snow, moving away from the vehicle. The ensuing blast, which must have occurred in front of the gunner's face, sent the man flying into the air. His lifeless rag doll body plopped into the snow directly in front of Snake.

Snake turned to see that a billow of black smoke now covered the top of the turret. After a moment, the dark cloud dissipated and Vulcan Raven's head jutted out of the turret. He appeared to be unharmed. Snake figured that the giant must have ducked into his compartment inside the tank just as the grenade detonated.

"Damn you!" the shaman called.

Snake turned to the dead gunner and quickly searched inside the man's fur-lined coat. There were two more frag grenades attached to the guard's belt as well as a SIG Sauer handgun. Snake ignored the gun and took the grenades. As an afterthought, he went through the man's pockets and found a key card. It was identical to the one Anderson had given him—a PAN—only this one was marked as a Level 3.

Brilliant!

He stuck the card in his pocket and dived under the snow once again.

"You cannot hide forever! I know where you are!"

Machine-gun bullets strafed the drifts, coming too close for comfort. Snake's ruse had worked the first time, but it wasn't going to deceive the giant any longer. So instead of crawling forward in the snow, Snake retreated into one of the "tunnels" he had created earlier. While the shaman ineffectually shot up the snow close to the Abrams, Snake put distance between them.

Time for a new plan.

He stood and saw that the tank was twenty-five feet away, facing south. A second gunner had joined Vulcan Raven on the turret. The shaman manned the larger machine gun and operated the tank while the trooper blasted the snow with the 7.62-mm gun.

"Where is he?" Raven shouted at the gunner. "Find him! You let him get away!"

Snake had a clear shot at the turret from where he was standing. He drew the SOCOM, stood in a Weaver stance, drew a bead on the gunner, and fired. The man shuddered, cried out, and then slumped over the turret. Raven turned just in time to face an oncoming bullet from the SOCOM, but he eluded it with a subtle shift of his body. Snake's mouth dropped in surprise. The man was unbelievably quick. Snake figured that it must have something to do with his alleged mystical powers.

By then the shaman had swung the 12.7-mm machine gun toward Snake and let loose a volley of hellfire. Snake jumped into the snow, dug deep, and clutched the frozen ground; he knew it was only a matter of seconds before he would be hit. It was all over. He would die there in the snow-covered canyon, the terrorists would launch a nuclear weapon, and the world would never be the same.

But then the machine-gun fire abruptly stopped.

What had happened?

Snake dared to thrust his head up to the surface to look. Vulcan Raven was working frantically on the machine gun. Since both of his gunners were dead, the giant had no one to act as a loader. This was Snake's chance.

Using all the leg strength he could muster, Snake plodded through the thick snow toward the tank. As he ran, he reached into the pouch and retrieved another frag grenade. When he was fifteen feet away, he pulled the pin and tossed the explosive into the tank's treads. He dived sideways into the frost, covered his head with his hands, and endured the repercussion of the blast. This time he felt the heat and a bit of debris fall into the pocket of snow where he lay.

After a moment he hoisted himself up to survey the damage. The Abrams was immobile, one tread completely blown off the wheels.

It was time for the David and Goliath maneuver.

He plucked another grenade from the pouch, slogged through the snow toward the rear of the tank, pulled the pin, and tossed it up at Vulcan Raven, who was too busy struggling with the machine gun to notice that his prey was behind him. The grenade dropped into the compartment—a better bull's-eye Snake couldn't have asked for. Snake turned and trudged as fast as he could away from the Abrams.

The explosion shook the entire canyon.

LIQUID SNAKE SAT in the Shadow Moses director's office and watched his nemesis walk away from the burning tank. He sighed heavily and then glanced over at Revolver Ocelot, who was resting on a couch. The gunslinger's right arm was heavily bandaged. The painkillers had done the trick, and now Ocelot was eager to close the distance between FOXHOUND and Snake.

"He got away, didn't he?" Ocelot remarked. "Let me try again. I'll kill the bastard."

Liquid held up his hand. "Quiet." He gestured to the screen. Vulcan Raven could be seen, miraculously crawling out of the wreck unscathed.

"He's still in range," the giant said. "Shall I destroy him?"

Liquid pressed the button on his communicator to speak. "No. Let him go."

"Are you certain?"

"But keep an eye on him."

"He got the card."

"I know. We'll play with him a little longer."

Ocelot stood and whispered, "Are you mad? The man's dangerous!"

Liquid shot Ocelot a look that gave the gunslinger no choice but to sit down and shut up.

Vulcan Raven said, "You would do best not to underestimate him, Boss."

"What did you think of him?" Liquid asked. "In battle, that is."

"He is just as you said. It's as if he is possessed by a demon.

Much like you. I would expect no less, considering your *relationship*."

"Yes. I told you so. But don't worry. I *will* kill him."

"Is Ocelot with you?"

"Yes."

"Revolver Ocelot!" the giant called. "I understand he took your hand *and* your dignity!"

"Watch your mouth, shaman!" Ocelot called from the couch. "It was that blasted ninja that took my hand, but it was Snake who distracted me. I could outgun you anytime, anywhere—with or without my right hand."

"Let me tell you something about our intruder friend. In the Sioux language, *Sioux* means 'snake.' It is known as an animal to be feared."

Ocelot sneered. "Well, I fear nothing, especially Solid Snake! He is *mine* now. When we next meet, I will take *special* care of him."

Vulcan Raven spit. "The raven on my head thirsts for his blood. Snake and I will battle again. Of that you can be sure."

Liquid switched off the communicator. "He is a formidable enemy. The next several hours are going to be most interesting, eh, Ocelot?"

"What is it you hope to gain from him? He is a pest. Swat him down!"

"Not yet, my friend. I still have plans for him."

"Why do you let him live, Boss?"

The FOXHOUND leader's eyes flared. "I have my reasons."

11

"SNAKE?" IT WAS MERYL, calling him on the Codec.

Snake was just about to enter the Nuclear Warhead Storage Building at the north end of the canyon. His body and suit were soaking wet from being in the snow, and he looked forward to warming up.

He pushed the button to accept the frequency and spoke. "Where are you, Meryl?"

"I'm in the subbasement of the nuke building." There was a hint of one-upmanship in her voice.

"What the . . . ? How did you get there?"

"I *told* you I know my way around this place."

"Well, why didn't you let me in on it? Do you realize what I just went through in that damned canyon?"

"Snake, relax. You couldn't have gone the way I did. I'm dressed as one of *them*, remember? I got into a transport with ten other troopers. They drove the long way around, on a snow-covered road. I kept my mask on and wore a helmet. They didn't have a clue who I was."

"You're mad, Meryl. They could have easily caught you again."

"Well, they didn't. So where are *you*?"

"I'm just entering the nuke building now."

"Yeah? Well, be careful. For heaven's sake, don't use your weapon in there. It's full of decaying nuclear waste and warheads. So no firepower, okay? No bullets, no grenades, no nothing! One spark and *ka-boom!*"

"I got you. Thanks for the heads-up. Now, I want you to stay put somewhere until I can find you."

"I'm on the Basement One level. Just take the elevator, but watch out for guards. They're roaming all over the place up there where you are. Out."

She signed off, and Snake shook his head. *Of course* she was Roy Campbell's niece. She was just as stubborn and full of herself as the colonel had always been. But even though she was green, Snake had to admit she had a lot of balls. He'd never encountered a young woman who was as brave and determined as she.

He was beginning to like her.

Stop that. Concentrate on the task at hand.

Snake wanted to hit himself for allowing his thoughts to roam in that direction. A love life was something he didn't need. He'd had his fair share of romantic disasters, and he wasn't about to get himself involved with a girl more than a decade younger than he. That was the path to catastrophe.

Perhaps.

SNAKE USED THE Level 3 PAN card to open the slatted door, which was similar to the tank hangar exit. Before any guards could notice, he slipped into the building at the corner of the opening and quickly rushed to the left wall, next to a metal ramp ascending to the main floor of the storage facility. Standing in the shadows, he watched as three guards appeared at the door, wondering why it had opened suddenly.

He breathed slowly and deeply. Snake *refused* to be seen.

"Must have malfunctioned," one of the guards said.

"There was some kind of accident out there; did you hear? One of the tanks was destroyed."

A man pushed a button, and the door rolled down, totally secure. "Our new bosses like to play with matches. You play with matches, you start fires."

They began to walk up the ramp to the main floor. "You don't like our new bosses?"

"I didn't say that. Things are a lot more exciting around here since they took over. I was about to die of boredom before."

They laughed and disappeared. Snake relaxed and moved to the end of the ramp, got on his hands and knees, and crawled far enough so that he could lift his head over the edge of the floor and give it a quick reconnaissance.

Meryl was right. The place was littered with troopers. They all wore gas masks along with their standard-issue uniforms. Snake figured the place was booby-trapped with nerve gas, just like the tank hangar exit. The terrorists weren't taking any chances. He couldn't imagine this kind of security in place when the civilians were running the base. Either Liquid was a masochist or he was incredibly paranoid.

One thing he could do was use the chaff grenades. They didn't do incendiary damage and were good for diversionary tactics. Snake glanced at the ceiling and saw several surveillance cameras trained on different areas of the space. The chaffs definitely would jam them. The grenades *did* make noise, so the question was how many guards would come running. Was it worth the risk? Snake couldn't see any other way to get through the storage facility to the other side of the room where the elevator was. He had to take the chance.

He dug a chaff grenade out of the pouch, pulled the pin, and rolled it across the floor. It stopped not quite in the middle of the room, in between insulated tanks marked HAZARDOUS. Five seconds elapsed, and the grenade's blast made all the guards in the place jump out of their skins.

Suddenly it was like a beehive that had been poked with a stick. The men immediately began to run around and shout at one another. They naturally assumed that the grenade had come from the entrance area, so Snake quickly hopped up onto the floor, scooted left, and ran between rows of storage boxes. An empty cardboard container the size of a large television set was among them; he jumped inside and pulled the flaps down over his head. He crouched there in the box and remained still as two guards rushed past him. Once the sound of footsteps had diminished, he opened the flaps and climbed out of the container.

Then he saw them.

Lying in berths on the left side of the room were two dismantled ICBM missiles. They were each a little over six meters long and looked as if they actually had seen some action. The exterior surfaces were beaten and scratched, secondhand relics of Cold War design and development.

Near them, in open containers marked DANGER — RADIATION, were objects that Snake recognized as warheads. They appeared to be weather-beaten as well. Snake reckoned that they were all useless; after all, Shadow Moses was a *disposal* facility. But he supposed the terrorists must have the means to extract the plutonium or make at least one operational.

Not good.

Using his Codec in camera mode, Snake snapped several

shots of the arsenal for posterity and also transmitted them to Nastasha Romanenko. A few seconds later, she appeared on the Codec.

"Thank you for the photographs, Snake," she said. "You do not have to worry about the warheads. They are not functional."

"But if they wanted to dispose of them," Snake asked, "why wouldn't they just dismantle them right away?"

"They cannot do that. You see, when you dismantle a warhead, you still have nuclear materials that must be stored. At this point, all the nuclear material storage facilities are way past capacity. But they could not stop dismantling weapons while at the same time pushing the START-II treaty."

"So you're telling me that this base was built so they could temporarily avoid being in conflict with START-II?"

"Most people think that we live in a safer world now. But with all the dismantled nuclear weapons and waste around, the threat of nuclear terrorism has increased tremendously."

Snake grunted in acknowledgment.

The Ukrainian woman went on. "After the START-II accord was signed in 1993, Russia and the U.S. reduced their strategic nuclear warheads to between three thousand and thirty-five hundred each. They completely dismantled all the ICBMs that contained multiple independently targeted reentry vehicles. As a result of that, there are over fifteen thousand dismantled nuclear warheads waiting to be disposed of. That is why the Shadow Moses facility was built."

"Nastasha, you're a walking encyclopedia," Snake said.

"Uh, I will take that as a compliment, Snake. I think."

She signed off, and Snake moved along the storage boxes, headed for the north side of the room and the elevator—and came face-to-face with a guard who had just turned the corner.

"Hey—" the man managed to say before Snake delivered a

one-two-three punch-punch-kick combination that finished the sentence for the surprised trooper.

Snake pulled the limp body between the boxes and dumped it on the floor. That had been too close. Time for another diversion. He drew another chaff grenade from the pouch, pulled the pin, and threw it high over the storage boxes, toward the center of the room. The thing exploded in midair, causing all kinds of commotion. Snake crept forward, utilizing the dart-and-freeze method of advancing within an enemy-occupied environment.

At the north end of the rows of storage boxes, Snake encountered two troopers standing at the bottom of a flight of metal stairs that led to a catwalk.

"Stay here and kill anything that moves," one said to the other. He left the man alone and then joined his comrades in another part of the space.

The lone trooper was between Snake and the elevator. Snake ducked behind a stack of boxes and pulled two SOCOM cartridges from his pouch. He tossed one across the aisle and hit a different pile of cartons; then it bounced onto the floor with a clatter. The trooper by the elevator turned toward the sound. He wasn't sure what he had heard. Snake tossed the second bullet, repeating the noise. This time the guard had to investigate. He readied his assault rifle and slowly walked to the head of the aisle. Snake remained hidden behind the first stack of boxes, but the guard focused his attention on the second pile, from where the noise had come. The man stepped slowly toward the boxes and eventually turned his back to Snake.

The stranglehold worked like a charm.

Snake left the guard on the floor and ran to the end of the row of cartons. It was a clear path to the elevator. He dashed to the wall, pressed the call button, and withstood the excruciating few seconds it took for the elevator to arrive. The doors opened, and Snake slipped in without any of the other troopers noticing. He pressed the B1 button and waited for the doors to close before contacting Meryl with the Codec.

She didn't answer.

Uh oh.

Had something happened to her? He dared not think about it.

The doors opened to a hallway perpendicular to the elevator. He held them open to check for guards, but all he saw was a surveillance camera on the ceiling, *pointed at the elevator.* He quickly pulled back out of view, let the doors close, and pulled the emergency shutoff button so that the elevator couldn't be called to another floor. Snake fitted the suppressor onto the SOCOM, checked the magazine, and then flicked the elevator switch back on. He assumed a firing stance and hit the open door button with his elbow. The doors opened, and he fired a silenced round at the camera, obliterating it.

He stepped out into the hallway and listened for activity. There was some muffled talking somewhere on the floor, and he heard a toilet flush behind the door marked MEN at the end of the hall to his right. Snake hurried to the bathroom door, pushed it open, and went inside.

A guard had just finished doing his business and was about to exit a stall. Snake rushed into the adjacent stall and waited. As soon as the man walked out, Snake grabbed him, performed his signature choke hold, and pulled the body back into the stall. He sat the man on the toilet and flushed the commode. Then he flushed it a second time for grins.

"It's a long way to Washington," he quipped.

Snake cautiously stepped out of the washroom and was headed for the other end of the hallway when his Codec chirped. His heart filled with joy when he saw the caller's frequency code.

"Master Miller! My, my, it's really great to hear from you."

"Likewise, Snake. It's been a long time. Having any fun yet?" The man's face on the Codec monitor was a sight for sore eyes. He looked pretty much the same; he was even wearing his trademark sunglasses.

"You know I am, sir. The colonel said you might be on hand."

"Indeed I am."

"Well, there's no one I'd rather be in a foxhole with than you."

Miller's transmission started to break up. "Listen . . . after . . . for the FOXHOUND guys to . . ."

"Master Miller? I'm losing you. Can you read me?"

". . . again. I'm sorry. Is that better?"

"Yeah. Where are you?"

"In my cabin in Alaska."

"Right. I heard you *retired*. Like me."

"It's great, isn't it? Just me and my huskies. But listen . . . tell you . . ."

"You're breaking up again. Master Miller?"

". . . in the office on your floor. The subbasement of the . . ."

"What?"

". . . sorry. There. Transmissions aren't very good from the middle of nowhere. That's better. I wanted to tell you that you're going to need a rocket launcher on the Basement Two level, and you can find one on the floor you're on."

"How do you know that?"

"Hey, I'm Master Miller. Remember?"

Snake creased his brow. Something wasn't right. "Go on."

"Anyway, you remember how to operate the remote-controlled minirecon missiles for a Nikita Personal Remote Rocket Launcher?"

"I'm pretty sure I do."

"There's a Nikita in the office marked B4. There's ammo in there, too. Get what you can carry and head down to the next basement level. You should be able to find Doctor Emmerich there."

Master Miller was surprisingly up to speed on what Snake was doing. "Okay. Thanks."

"Good luck, Snake. We'll catch up later."

"Master Mill—" But the transmission ended.

Strange.

Master Miller wasn't particularly the talkative type, but he was usually more specific about his instructions. Nevertheless, Snake thought it best to heed the man's advice and find the rocket launcher. He hugged the wall in the hallway, SOCOM in hand, and turned the corner. A row of office doors lined the corridor, starting with B1. B4 was in the middle of the hall and required the Level 3 PAN card to open the lock. Snake swiped the card and heard the gratifying click. He pushed open the door to see—

A genome trooper working at a desk! The man registered surprise and reflexively reached for a button to sound an alarm.

Snake pointed the SOCOM and fired. The round struck the man squarely in the forehead, and he and his chair fell back onto the floor with a crash.

Snake quickly stepped into the room and shut the door. Sure enough, in an open portable carrying case that sat on a worktable was the Nikita. Alongside it was a box of shells. The Nikita was an ingenious device, a somewhat bulky but manageable rocket launcher shaped like a short, stubby bazooka that was held on one's shoulder and supported with both hands. Snake didn't particularly want to lug the thing around, but if Master Miller said he needed it, that was what he would do. Snake performed a cursory search of the office and also found a gas mask in one of the desk drawers. Figuring it might come in handy, he slung it around his neck but kept it off his face for now.

Armed with his new toys, Snake opened the office door, peered out to an empty hallway, and swiftly moved back to the elevator. Once inside, he pressed the B2 button, slung the Nikita over his shoulder, and readied the SOCOM.

The doors opened to another hallway perpendicular to the elevator. Snake carefully stepped out, made sure there were no patrolling guards, and moved toward the left. A sign on the wall indicated that following the corridor would take one to the laboratory. Snake continued in that direction and soon came to an archway. The hallway continued beyond the arch, but the floor on the other side was made of metal mesh rather than being a carpeted floor.

Odd.

Snake took a step toward the arch, and suddenly the air quality changed. Minute yellow particles blew into the corridor from vents in the ceiling and floated in front of him the way dust is visible in a beam of sunlight. The lack of odor suggested to Snake that the hallway was filling with sarin nerve gas. The only sensible thing to do was to get the hell out of there by running as quickly as possible through the arch and across the metal floor to the far end of the corridor.

Another coincidence—it was Snake's lucky day. He donned the gas mask but decided to take no chances and rush through the hall anyway. He almost stepped through the arch when—

"Snake! Don't move!"

Snake recognized the voice as belonging to the mysterious Deepthroat. "You again?"

"Don't take another step! The floor in front of you is electrified!"

"Terrific. What am I supposed to do?"

"You'll need to turn off the electricity."

"Okay. Want to tell me where the circuit breaker is?"

"Unfortunately, it's at the end of the hallway in front of you."

"Oh, well, that's convenient, isn't it?"

"Look at the corridor. At the end, it jogs to the left. See?"

"Uh-huh."

"It then doubles back, parallel to the wall on your left side. Like the queue for a ride at an amusement park."

"Okay, it's U-shaped."

"The high-voltage switchboard is at the end of that part of the hall."

Snake looked at the wall to his left. "So do I blow a hole in this wall with a grenade? Will that work?"

"No. It's too thick. Even a Claymore mine won't help you. You'll have to use a remote-controlled missile."

Snake nodded to himself. *The Nikita. Master Miller was right.*

He was extremely impressed by the elaborate defenses the FOXHOUND renegades had set up to protect their so-called revolt. Even the training exercises Snake had undergone when he first had become an operative had not been as diabolical as this.

He loaded the portable rocket launcher with one of the recon missiles and turned on the remote radar screen. The Nikita allowed the user to set a flight path for the missile and then guide it with the remote control. Because the missile obviously traveled very fast, it took an experienced eye and nimble fingers to steer the shell accurately to the intended target. Snake had practiced with the Nikita at FOXHOUND headquarters for three months until Master Miller had given him acceptable marks. *It wasn't easy.*

Snake needed to punch a figure for the proposed range. "Uhm, Deepthroat?"

"Yes, Snake?"

"Do you know how many meters it is from me to the switch-board?"

"Sorry, Snake. I don't have a clue."

He did his best to estimate the number. Using the two knobs, he then drew onto the view screen a digital line that represented the missile's planned trajectory. He couldn't afford to miss, as the ensuing explosion surely would alert the bad guys and he'd need a place to run. He didn't particularly want to step onto an electrified walkway.

Snake double-checked the calculations, flipped off the safety, and held the launcher as steady as he could.

"One shot. Here goes," he said.

Snake liked the fact that the Nikita had no kick. The launcher tube rested on his shoulder as the missile shot out of the gun, soared through the arch and down the hall, and then made a ninety-degree left turn at the end. The shell disappeared from his sight, but Snake could hear the thing *whoosh* through the hallway on the other side of the wall.

The explosion rocked the entire floor. Snake supported himself against the right wall, and in a few seconds it was all over. All the fluorescent lights in the hallway ceiling went out, plunging the place into darkness. Two seconds later, emergency lighting kicked in.

Had he succeeded? Snake could see that the gas had stopped pouring out of the vents, but he was reluctant to remove the gas mask just yet. He carefully stepped through the arch and placed a foot on the metal mesh.

Nothing happened.

"Deepthroat? You still there?"

"Yes, Snake."

"How did you know about this? And how the hell did you know what my position was?"

"Sorry, that's on a need-to-know basis. And you don't need to know."

"Damn it, who *are* you?"

"Be careful. It's not over yet."

And the stranger's transmission ended.

Snake punched in Mei Ling's frequency.

"Yes, Snake?"

"Are you aware of these transmissions I'm receiving? From someone named Deepthroat?"

"Yes. We can't determine where they're coming from."

"No clue as to his identity?"

"We're working on it."

"Okay. Out."

Snake set the bulky Nikita on the floor. He hated to abandon it, but there was no way he could carry something that cumbersome and do what he had to do. He continued down the hall, turned the corner, and then saw the damage. The switchboard was a mess; it had been a direct hit.

Master Miller would have been proud.

12

SIX TROOPERS STOOD in the corridor outside the laboratory. The squad leader looked through the bulletproof window to make sure the doctor had not pulled a fast one. He didn't trust the brainy nerds who worked at the Shadow Moses facility. They always had tricks up their sleeves and answers for everything. When the FOXHOUND renegades took over the complex, the squad leader felt personal satisfaction that the tables had been turned on the scientists who made the big money.

"Hey, Sergeant, why are there so many of us guarding this guy?" one of the men asked.

The squad leader replied, "The Boss wants us to take special care of the good doctor. Nothing's supposed to happen to him. The Boss needs him. High-priority asset. Why, I don't know. In my book, the only good *otaku* is a dead *otaku*."

The men laughed. One of them opened a coffee thermos and started to pour cups for everyone in the hallway. "So did the Boss say why the power went out? What was that explosion?"

The sergeant indicated the communicator. "He told us not

to worry but that we might have company. It's probably not a good idea to have a coffee cup in your hand right now."

As soon as the squad leader had said these words, the man dropped the cup and its contents all over the floor.

"You clumsy fool!" the sergeant snapped.

"I—I didn't drop it. Someone . . . *something* knocked it out of my hand!"

"Don't be an idiot. I saw you drop—"

There was a glimpse of a shadow moving across the corridor. No, not a shadow. More like a blur, like when one's glasses are smudged, only this smudge had moved.

"What was that?"

"What?"

"There. Look."

The men turned and followed the sergeant's pointing finger. "I don't see nothin', Sarge."

The squad leader's eyes darted over the room. *There it was again!* "Look, you fools! There!"

"Boss, I think you're seeing th—" But before the man could finish his sentence, the top of his skull slipped off his head on a diagonal split. The bone and brain had been severed by something *invisible*. The man's legs buckled, and he fell to the floor next to the bloody body part that contained half of his mind.

"Oh, my God!"

"What happened?"

"Look out!"

"Shoot anything that moves!"

The men began to fire their FAMAS rifles wildly about the room, spraying the hall with a salvo of bullets but hitting nothing.

Whoosh—swish—flit. An unseen sword sliced the air and flesh-and-blood appendages. Those sounds were followed by screams.

• • •

Outside the hallway, Snake heard the carnage occurring on the other side of the Level 3 security door. The gunfire, the screams of agony, the noise of bodies falling to the ground . . .

What's going on in there?

He quickly swiped the card, and the door opened.

It was as if he had stepped into a slaughterhouse for human beings. At first it was difficult for Snake to count just how many men had been in there, for body parts and blood were spattered all over the hallway. Snake had seen some terrible things in his lifetime, but this gruesome scene nearly made his bile rise.

One man with both arms severed was still alive. A stab wound in the chest was causing him to spit blood as he struggled to breathe. Snake knelt beside him. "Who did this?" he asked.

The man coughed and whispered, ". . . ghost . . . it's . . . a ghost . . ."

And he was dead.

Snake stood, stepped over the puddles of red goo, and made for the laboratory door. He peered through the window and saw a young man wearing a white lab coat sitting on the floor, his back against the wall. He wore glasses, had long hair, was thin, and was trembling so badly that Snake thought he was about to wet his pants.

Dr. Hal Emmerich was scared to death, looking up at something that wasn't there.

Snake swiped the card in the door, but it wouldn't open. It was a Level 4 security lock. Snake cursed to himself and moved to the closest slaughtered body. It was a repugnant task to search the guard's bloody clothes, but he found what he needed: the man's PAN card.

Snake used it on the door, which slid open. Dr. Emmerich

was whimpering as tears ran down his face. He was focused on the space in front of him, but Snake couldn't see anyone else in the room.

Wait. There.

Sure enough, the cyborg ninja was standing in front of the scientist. The stealth suit glimmered in and out of visible mode as the warrior brandished the sword.

"No, please! Don't hurt me!" the engineer cried . . . and wet himself.

"Where is my friend?" the ninja asked. "Tell me where he is now or suffer the same fate as those fools out there."

"I'm . . . I'm sorry! I . . . I don't know what you're talking about! Please don't kill me!"

"DON'T MOVE!" Snake stood with the SOCOM in both hands. The ninja turned slowly and focused the eye sensor on him. "Drop the sword and back away from the nerd. Do it nice and easy."

Even though the helmet covered the warrior's head, Snake could sense that the man was smiling. "Ah, excellent. I've been waiting for you," the thing said in his metallic, electronic voice.

"Just who the hell are you?"

The ninja didn't drop the sword. Instead, he held it in front of him as if he were preparing to do battle. "Neither enemy nor friend. I have returned from a world where such words are meaningless."

Snake squinted at the cyborg. There was definitely *something* familiar about him: the way he carried himself, the speech inflection. Who was he?

"I've removed all obstacles," the warrior said. "The path is clear to me now. You and I must fight to the death."

Snake was taking no chances. He squeezed the SOCOM's trigger—and the ninja batted the bullet away with a lightning-fast flick of the sword.

"Pathetic! There is no honor in that weapon!"

"What do you want?"

"I've waited a long time for this day. Now I want to savor the moment."

Dr. Emmerich continued to shake and whimper as he watched the two gladiators in front of him. "Wha—what's with these guys? It's like . . . a scene out of one of m—my anime movies!"

The cyborg continued to talk in riddles. "I've come from another world to do battle with you."

"What is this about?" Snake asked. "Revenge?"

"It's nothing as trivial as revenge. A fight to the death with you . . . Only in that can my soul find respite. I will kill you or you will kill me. Either way, it makes no difference."

The engineer could take no more. He saw an opening, got to his feet, and bolted from the room. Screaming like a madman, he ran into a sterile procedure room adjacent to the lab. He slammed the door behind him, locked it, and peered at the two fighters through a plate glass window.

"Ah, fine," the ninja said. "Let him watch from his perch."

Snake snarled, "I need that man unharmed. You'd better give up now or this won't be pretty."

"Yes," the ninja hissed. "That's the spirit! Make me *feel* it! Make me feel *alive* again!"

With that, the man in the exoskeleton moved forward . . . and disappeared. Snake fired several rounds at the space in front of him but heard only the *swish-clang* of the ninja's sword knocking away the bullets.

The ninja materialized several feet away from where Snake thought he was. "That weapon is useless against me! Haven't you learned anything?"

"Apparently not." Snake utilized spray fire and emptied the magazine. Watching the ninja was like viewing a sped-up video in which every character moved at ten times the normal alacrity. Not a single round touched his body.

Then the ninja dropped the sword. "This is futile! Let us fight as warriors. Hand to hand. The basis of all combat. Only a fool trusts his life to a weapon such as *that.*"

Snake took a deep breath and holstered his gun. "Whatever." He assumed a fighting stance and forced himself to forget everything else. It was what Master Miller had always taught him: *Concentrate on the task at hand. See the victory before you even begin.*

And the fight commenced.

The ninja attacked with a double-jumping roundhouse kick that knocked Snake to the floor. Slightly stunned, Snake managed to roll out of the way as the cyborg attempted to repeat his maneuver. The warrior missed, allowing Snake to get to his feet and avoid yet another roundhouse kick.

Unarmed combat is a matter of dodging.

It was another of Master Miller's admonishments. Offensive moves were essential in order to win hand-to-hand combat, but the trick to surviving was defense. Snake let his opponent attack again so that he could watch the man's technique. Every fighter relied on tried-and-true moves; if you could anticipate what the enemy was going to do, you could avoid the onslaught and develop a strategy to counteract it.

The ninja performed the double jump again and walloped Snake. The operative crashed backward into an electronic bank of controls, causing an eruption of sparks that lit up the room. He noticed, though, that the cyborg had paused slightly between the two jumps. Snake bounced back from the assault and beckoned the ninja to try again. This time, Snake leaped into the cyborg's personal space during the split-second pause and delivered a punch-punch-kick combination that connected hard and violently. The ninja recoiled, surprised and slightly dazed. Snake refused to let his opponent recover. He took advantage of the opening and performed his signature one-two-three punch-punch-kick maneuver. The cyborg sailed across a workstation and smashed a computer monitor onto the floor.

"Yes! The pain!" the ninja cried. "I've been waiting for this pain!"

The guy's crazy as a loon!

The cyborg rolled off the desk, landed on his feet in a crouching position, and then leaped forward like a grasshopper. He collided into Snake with tremendous force, and the two of them catapulted off the floor, defying gravity for two seconds. They slammed into another bank of electronic controls. They rolled onto the floor, fists flying and knees lunging. Snake pounded the ninja's helmeted face as hard as he could, ignoring the agony he felt in his knuckles.

"Yes! Hurt me more!" the ninja cried. "More! More!" The cyborg managed to swing himself on top of Snake, who took the opportunity to grab the warrior's arms and employ the ancient judo principle of turning an opponent's weight into an asset. Snake placed the sole of his foot against the exoskeleton's chest for leverage and flipped the man over his head. The ninja hit the wall with a crash that shook the room.

Snake got to his feet and delivered double roundhouse kicks to the cyborg's head before the man could get up. The warrior was definitely stunned. But when Snake tried it a second time, the ninja grabbed his ankle, twisted it, and forced Snake to spin in midair. He landed on the floor with a thud.

"I know that move, Snake. I felt it." The ninja stood. "Do you remember? The feel of battle?"

Snake shook the stars away and looked up at the exoskeleton.

"Do you, Snake? Do you remember me now?"

And then something snapped inside the dark recesses of Snake's memory banks. The ninja's stance, his speech pattern, his use of Snake's name . . .

No! It can't be!

"You!" Snake spat. "You were killed! In Zanzibarland!"

The words seemed to confuse the ninja. "Killed? Zanzibarland? I . . . don't . . ."

Suddenly the cyborg began to shake uncontrollably. His suit sparked and made noises akin to an electrical discharge. The ninja screamed in pain, held his head, and fell to his knees.

It's like what happened to him before!

"What's happening?" Snake yelled.

The ninja screamed, "The *medicine!*"

"Not again," Snake muttered.

The cyborg's suit emitted an energy field that grew into a ball of bright light. Snake retreated and held his arm in front of his eyes. It was as if the ninja himself were short-circuiting and frying on the inside of the stealth suit.

"I'm . . . losing . . . myself!" he cried.

And then Snake knew the identity of the cyborg. There was no doubt.

"Oh, my God. Gray Fox," he whispered.

After a few moments, the energy field dissipated and left a broken man on the floor, barely keeping upright on his hands and knees. His breathing was coarse and measured.

"Are you all right?" Snake asked. He started to approach the man, but the ninja let loose with a heart-wrenching cry of anguish and pain. The cyborg shook his fists at the heavens, stood, and ran for the laboratory door. The suit's stealth function kicked in, and he disappeared in front of Snake's eyes. The door opened for a second and then slammed shut.

The tortured soul was gone again.

Dr. Emmerich called from the procedure room. "Is it over?"

"I don't believe it," Snake said, trying to catch his breath. "Gray Fox . . . it can't be . . ."

13

DR. NAOMI HUNTER sat at her computer terminal and avoided looking at Campbell when Snake transmitted a message.

"Colonel! That ninja is Gray Fox. No doubt about it."

The erstwhile colonel replied, "That's ridiculous, Snake. You of all people know he died in Zanzibarland."

"No," Dr. Hunter whispered. "No, he didn't."

"Did you say something, Doctor Hunter?" Campbell asked.

"He didn't die," she repeated. "He should have died. But he didn't."

Campbell blinked. "What?" He left his finger on the transmit button so that Snake could hear.

She swiveled in her chair and faced him. "It happened before I joined FOXHOUND's medical staff. They . . . they were using a soldier for their gene therapy experiments."

"I never heard that, Doctor Hunter."

"It happened right after you retired. My predecessor . . . Doctor Clark . . . was in charge and started the gene therapy project."

Over the Codec, Snake's voice sounded strained. "And where is he now?"

"You mean 'she.' Two years ago she was killed in an explosion in her lab."

"So what about this soldier they used?" Snake asked.

The doctor turned the chair again so that the colonel could not see how upset she was. "Apparently, for their test subject, they decided to use the body of a soldier who was recovered after the fall of Zanzibarland."

"And that was Gray Fox? Frank Jaegar?"

Campbell interrupted, "But he was already dead!"

Naomi Hunter barely could contain her anger. "Yes, but they *revived* him. They fitted him with a prototype exoskeleton and kept him drugged for four years while they experimented on him like a plaything. Today's genome soldiers were born from those experiments."

Campbell took a seat for the first time since Snake had left the submarine. "That's the sickest thing I've ever heard!"

"They used him to test all sorts of gene therapy techniques." Her eyes filled with tears, but she refused to let them fall onto her cheeks.

"Naomi," Snake said, "why didn't you tell us about this sooner?"

"Because it's confidential information."

"Is that the only reason?"

When she didn't answer, Campbell asked, "Naomi, what happened to Gray Fox after that?"

She shrugged. "The record says he died in the explosion along with Doctor Clark."

Campbell rubbed his chin. "Hmm. I see. But even if that ninja is Gray Fox, the question is why: Why is he there?"

"From what I could tell, he didn't know who he was," Snake remarked.

"Are you saying he's just a mindless robot?" Campbell inquired.

"I'm not sure, but he seems intent on fighting me to the death. We'll meet again; I know it."

"So you'll fight again?" Naomi asked. "Until you kill him?"

"I'd rather not, but maybe that's what he *wants*."

SNAKE SIGNED OFF and entered the procedure room. Dr. Emmerich had not done a very good job of hiding inside a cabinet, for the tail end of the engineer's white lab coat stuck out from under the door.

Snake knocked. "How long are you gonna stay in there?"

Emmerich's voice sounded muffled and frightened. "Are . . . are you one of them?"

"No, I'm not. I always work alone."

"Alone? Are you an *otaku*, too?"

Snake didn't know what the hell the man was talking about. "Come on, get out of there. We can't stay here forever."

The door opened. Dr. Emmerich was sitting on the floor of the cabinet, his knees to his chest. His glasses were askew, and his eyes were wide with fear. "Your . . . uniform's different from theirs."

"You're the Metal Gear chief engineer, right? Hal Emmerich?"

"You know me?"

"I heard about you from Meryl."

"Oh! So you're here to rescue me?" For the first time, Emmerich smiled. He got up and came out of the cabinet, bringing with him the pungent smell of urine, but the scientist didn't appear to be concerned about his wet pants.

"Sorry, but no. There's something I've got to do first."

Emmerich brushed off his coat and shrugged. "Oh, well. At

least you're not one of them." He walked across the room with a noticeable limp and sat in a chair.

"Are you hurt?"

"I'm okay. I just twisted my ankle a little trying to get away."

"Well, if that's all, then it's nothing to worry about. Listen, I need information about Metal Gear."

Emmerich lifted his head in surprise. "Huh? Metal Gear?"

"Yeah. What's Metal Gear really designed for?"

"It's a mobile TMD, you know, Theater Missile Defense system. It's designed to shoot down nuclear missiles . . . for defensive purposes, of course."

Snake grabbed the man by his coat lapels. "Liar! I already know that Metal Gear is nothing but a nuclear-equipped walking deathmobile!"

Emmerich flinched, expecting to be hit. "Nuclear? What . . . what are you talking about?"

"The terrorists are planning to use Metal Gear to launch a nuclear missile. You telling me you didn't know?"

"What? How can they do that?"

"You tell me!"

"Uh, the only way would be to put a dismantled warhead into Metal Gear's TMD missile module."

"Wrong." Snake released him, and the engineer fell back into the chair. "From the beginning, the purpose of this exercise was to test Metal Gear's nuclear launch capability using a dummy nuclear warhead. The terrorists are just continuing the work you started!"

"No, no, you're wrong."

"I heard it directly from your boss. Baker."

"No . . . a nuclear missile on REX . . ." He shook his head, first in denial and then in apprehension.

Snake studied the man. He was a pretty good judge in determining whether someone was telling the truth. "So you really didn't know?"

"No. All the armament was built by a separate department. And the ArmsTech president personally supervised the final assembly with the main unit."

"President Baker?"

"Yeah. I was never told exactly what they armed REX with. I only know it's equipped with a Vulcan cannon, a laser, and a Rail Gun."

"A Rail Gun?"

"Yeah. It uses magnets to fire bullets at extremely high velocities. The technology originally was developed for the SDI system and later scrapped. We were successful in miniaturizing it in a joint venture between ArmsTech and Rivermore National Labs. The Rail Gun is on REX's right arm."

"Metal Gear's main function is to launch nuclear missiles. You sure you're not forgetting something?"

"Well, it's true that Metal Gear has a missile module on his back that can carry up to eight missiles. But . . . are you saying it was originally meant to carry nuclear weapons?"

"Yeah," Snake answered. He sat on a workstation and noticed for the first time the posters on the walls featuring Japanese anime and video game characters. He then faced the engineer and added, "But that's not all I think. If Metal Gear fired only standard nuclear missiles, then they should already have all the practical data they need."

Emmerich rubbed his brow. "No, could it be?" He snapped his fingers and looked at Snake. "Rivermore National Labs was working on a new type of nuclear weapon. They were using NOVA and NIF laser nuclear fusion testing equipment and supercomputers!" He stood and limped to a bank of machines in the main laboratory, and Snake followed him. "These are some of the supercomputers. You can't use virtual data on a battle-field; they would need actual launch data. If you link these computers, you can test everything in a virtual environment. But it's all just *theoretical!*"

Snake knew it was true. "This exercise was designed to test the real thing."

Emmerich leaned against the computer bank, removed his glasses, and rubbed his eyes. "Oh, man. What did our president do? If the terrorists launch that thing . . . damn! Damn!" He dropped to his knees and began to bang his head on the floor. "I'm such a fool! It's all my fault!"

Snake didn't enjoy watching a grown man cry. He turned away and sat in another chair.

"My grandfather."

"What?"

Emmerich wiped the tears off his face. "My grandfather was part of the Manhattan Project—you know, where they created the atom bomb. He suffered with the guilt for the rest of his life. And my father . . . *he* was born on August 6, 1945!"

Snake understood. "The day of the Hiroshima bomb. God's got a sense of humor, all right."

"Three generations of Emmerich men. We must have the curse of the nuclear weapons written into our DNA." He started crying again. "I used to think I could use science to help mankind, but the one that wound up getting used was *me*. Using science to help mankind—that's just in the stupid *movies!*"

Snake leaned forward and snapped, "That's enough crying. Pull yourself together!"

The engineer took a few deep breaths and then sat cross-legged on the floor. He wiped his face again and after a moment seemed to be better.

"Where is Metal Gear?" Snake asked. "Where on this base are they keeping it?"

"REX is in the underground maintenance base."

"Where's that?"

"North of the communication tower. It's a long way there."

"The emergency override system for the detonation code is there, too?"

"Yeah, in the base's control and observation room." He quickly got to his feet. "Gee, you'd better hurry! If they were planning a launch from the start, then their ballistic program is probably finished. And since they haven't called me in a few hours, they must not need me anymore. They must be ready to launch!"

Snake stood. "Meryl's got the detonation code override key. We'll link up with her."

"If we can't override the launch, we'll have to destroy REX." He started to limp toward the door. "I'll show you the way."

"On that leg of yours? No way. You'll just slow me down."

"But you'll need me if you're gonna destroy REX."

"I don't need you. I just need your *brain*."

"I created REX. It's my right . . . and my duty to destroy it."

"You'll help me remotely. That's the best I can do for you."

Emmerich was about to protest more, but the scruffy man in the dark uniform intimidated him. "All right. I wish EE were here to help us. She's *great* at computer programming."

"Who's EE?"

"My sister Emma. Emma Emmerich. Well, her full name is Emma Emmerich-Danziger. She works for the government, too. Systems analyst for the NSA. Oh, well. She and I don't get along too well, anyway. We haven't spoken in a long time."

Snake couldn't help oozing sarcasm. "Then I guess she won't be much help to us, huh?" He walked to the lab door and looked into the hallway. "If you get a chance, try to escape. When the coast is clear, I'll contact you by Codec. I see you have one."

Emmerich nodded but then asked, "How am I supposed to escape from an island?"

Snake exhaled heavily. "Okay. Good point."

"So what, then?"

"I want you to hide somewhere and keep me informed. You know this place well, don't you?"

"'Course I do. And don't worry; I've got *this*." Emmerich manipulated something on his lab coat and suddenly *vanished*. "It's the same stealth technology as the ninja. FOXHOUND was going to use them, but . . . with this I'll be fine, bad leg and all." He reappeared and grinned.

Snake was impressed. But then he said, "So why didn't you activate the stealth when the ninja was after you? Why did you hide in the closet?"

Emmerich's mouth dropped open. "Oh, uh, gee . . . I guess I was so scared, I didn't think about it. Hmm. You're right."

"Yeah. So don't forget about it next time. And I want Meryl to watch after you, too." He punched in her code. "Meryl?"

"Yeah?"

"Where were you earlier?"

"Uh, I had company, but it's okay now."

"Meryl, the engineer's all right."

"Oh, that's a relief!"

"I want you to look after him. Where are you now?"

"Very close. In fact, I—oh, no! Gotta go; they've spotted me!"

"Meryl? What happened?" But she had switched off. "Damn, something's wrong. I gotta go find her. When did you last see her?"

"I dunno . . . earlier today?"

"What was she wearing?"

"She was dressed in the same green uniform as the terrorists." He moved his eyebrows up and down. "She has a cute way of walking. She kinda wiggles her behind."

"Oh, so you were really looking?"

"Well, she has a cute behind! If she's disguised as the enemy, then you'll have to contact her when she's alone. There's only one place where we can be sure she's by herself."

"Where's that?"

Emmerich made a face. "Don't be so dense!" He fished something out of his pocket and handed it to him. "Here, use this security card. It's a Level Five."

As soon as Snake took the card, he remembered what had happened to the last two men who had given him PAN keys. "You feel okay? Nothing bothering you?" He approached Emmerich and looked closely into the man's eyes.

"Uh, what's wrong? Getting friendly all of a sudden?"

"Oh, nothing." He stepped back, embarrassed. "I—uh, I'm glad you're okay."

Emmerich laughed a little. He said, "You're strange . . . but in a *good* way!"

"I'm a little nervous. Everyone else I've saved suddenly dies."

"You're bad luck, I guess."

"Forget it, Doctor."

"Call me Otacon."

"Huh?"

"Otacon. It stands for Otaku Convention. An *otaku* is a guy like me who likes Japanimation. Anime. Japan was the first country to successfully make bipedal robots. They're still the best in the field of robotics."

Snake figured he now knew why Emmerich seemed like such a nerd. "And Japanese cartoons played some part in that?"

"They did! I didn't get into science to make nuclear weapons, you know."

"That's what all the scientists say."

"I became a scientist because I wanted to make robots like the ones in Japanese anime. Really, it's true!"

"It just sounds like a childish excuse to me."

Otacon shrugged. "You're right. We have to take responsibility. Science has always thrived on war. The greatest weapons of mass destruction were created by scientists who wanted to be famous. But that's all over. I won't take part in murder anymore."

"Whatever. All I'll want from you is information when I ask for it."

"I'll be there for you, Mister, er, what *is* your name, by the way?"

"Solid Snake."

"Snake? Gee, the terrorist boss is named Snake, too."

"I know. Coincidence, huh?"

"Yeah. You kinda look like him, too. I guess you'd better get going."

"Stay put and keep safe, Otacon," Snake said.

"Don't worry," the engineer said. He flicked on the stealth apparatus and disappeared. Snake heard his voice move away, across the room. "They'll never find me now. You be careful, too."

Snake left the room and headed back through the hall of dead soldiers to the elevator. The next step was to find Meryl. And when he found her, he didn't know if he wanted to spank her for disobeying him or kiss her if she was alive and unhurt.

Maybe he'd do both.

14

THE ELEVATOR OPENED on the First Basement Level, and Snake immediately heard voices. He held the doors open with his foot, carefully peered into the hallway, and saw the backs of two guards turn a corner and disappear. He slipped out, let the doors close, and glanced at the surveillance camera he had destroyed earlier. Either they hadn't noticed it was out of order or they were ignoring it. Hugging the wall, he moved to the corner and watched the two guards pass through a doorway. Creeping as silently as possible, he went to the door and saw that the lock was marked with the number 5.

Snake smiled. He took the Level 5 PAN card Otacon had given him, swiped it, and opened the door.

The room was full of computer terminals. The two guards still had their backs to him. One of them sat at a terminal and was busy punching the keyboard. The other stood idly by, watching. Both guards wore the standard green uniforms with head coverings. Time once again for the Snake Stranglehold.

Snake moved slowly and stealthily to the guard who was

standing. Suddenly, though, the soldier moved and walked to the other side of the room . . . with a wiggle in the rear end.

As Snake eyed the guard more carefully, he could see a decidedly thinner and curvier posterior underneath the trousers. He wanted to laugh but thought it best to take care of the other guard first.

He quickly walked up behind the guard at the terminal, wrapped his arm around the man's neck, and strangled him to death.

Meryl—or the guard he *thought* was Meryl—turned to see what was happening and gasped. She ran for the door before Snake could call out, "Wait!" Snake let the dead man fall to the floor and chased the feminine soldier out of the room and down the hall. She turned a corner, rushed to a door marked WOMEN, and went inside.

"Hey!" a man's voice called behind him.

Snake turned to see another soldier at the far end of the hall. With reflexes that rivaled those of his namesake, Snake drew the SOCOM and fired at the man. The shot reverberated in the hallway, surely loud enough to attract more troopers. To head them off, Snake ran toward the fallen man, hugged the corner, and fitted the SOCOM with the suppressor. As he'd predicted, he heard the sound of running boots a few seconds later. He lunged sideways, landed prone beside the dead soldier, and fired at the three men coming at him while using the corpse as cover.

Three shots—three cadavers.

Snake decided to take a small amount of time to drag the bodies into an open office. He did so, shut the door, and rushed to the first guard he'd shot. There was a grouping of potted plants in a corner of the hallway, so Snake picked up the corpse and deposited it behind the pots. Not great, but it would do. He then rushed back to the women's washroom and pushed open the door.

Meryl Silverburgh stood in front of him with a FAMAS aimed at his head. What surprised Snake more than that was the fact that she had stripped off her uniform and was dressed only in a bra and panties. The sight nearly took his breath away.

"Don't move!" she spat.

Snake froze and then slowly raised his hands. "Take it easy."

"That's not why I'm aiming this at you."

"Then why are you?"

"Because men aren't allowed in here, pervert." She held the stance for a couple more seconds and then laughed. She put down her weapon and said, "That's the second time I've had the jump on the legendary Solid Snake."

"You know, there's no way you can pass as a man for long. I had no idea you were so . . . feminine."

"This is no time to try to hit on me, Snake."

"You're the one in your underwear."

She laughed. "Besides, it's a waste of time. When I joined up, they gave me psychotherapy to destroy my interest in men."

"If you say so. What's the matter? Are you hurt?"

"No."

"What happened a while ago? When you stopped transmitting."

"Oh, there were a bunch of guards. I had to blend in, so to speak." She opened a stall and picked up some clothes that were lying on the floor. The trousers were military issue, and the black tank top was most likely from a high-end fashion shop.

As she started to put them on, Snake asked, "Why are you changing? You'd be a lot better off disguised as one of them."

"I'm tired of that." She slipped the tank top over her head. "The truth is the uniform smelled like blood."

For the first time he saw the FOXHOUND tattoo on her left arm. "Hey." He pointed. "What's that?"

"Oh, this? It's not a real tattoo; it's painted. I've been a fan of

FOXHOUND from way back. When guys like you and my uncle were in it. None of that gene therapy bullshit like there is today. You guys were real heroes."

"There are no heroes in war. All the heroes I know are either dead or in prison. One or the other."

"Snake, you're a hero. Aren't you?"

"I'm just a man who's good at what he does. Killing. There's no winning or losing for a mercenary. The only winners in war are the people—if they're on the winning side."

"Yeah, right, so you fight for the people."

"I've never fought for anyone but myself. I've got no purpose in life. No ultimate goal."

"Oh, come on . . ."

He moved away from her, stood over the sink, and examined his scarred face in the mirror. As he adjusted his bandana, he continued. "It's only when I'm cheating death on the battlefield. That's the only time I feel truly alive."

Now dressed, Meryl leaned back against the wall and pulled on boots, one foot at a time. "Seeing other people die makes you feel alive, huh? You love war and don't want it to stop. Is it the same with all great soldiers throughout history?"

He was annoyed at the direction the conversation was taking. "Why didn't you stay where I told you?"

She shrugged. "You could use my help. How'd you recognize me in disguise?"

"I never forget . . . a lady."

"So there's something about me you like?"

"Yeah, you've got a great ass."

She raised her eyebrows. "Ass? Oh I see . . . First it's my eyes, and now it's my ass. What's next?"

"On the battlefield you never think about what's next."

She made a face and then jumped on the counter to sit. "So,

how are things going? Is the president gonna give in to their demands?"

"Not if I can help it."

"It's all up to you, is it?"

"Somebody's got to stop them from launching a nuclear missile."

"You know, there are two ways. Either we destroy Metal Gear or—"

"Or we override the detonation code. I know. You got the card key from Baker?"

"Yeah."

"I still don't understand why he told me there were three of them."

"This is all he gave me."

"Where could the other two be?"

"Hey, if we can't find them, then we'll have no choice but to destroy Metal Gear."

Snake took a sip of water from his canteen and handed it to Meryl. She chugged it longer than he wished. "I'm going on. I heard REX is in an underground maintenance base to the north of here."

She gave him back the canteen. "Take me, too! I know this place better than you."

"You'll just slow me down. You don't have enough battle experience. One person's blunder can compromise the entire mission."

"I won't slow you down, I promise!"

"And what if you do?"

"Then you can shoot me!" She almost sounded serious.

He shook his head. "I don't like to waste bullets."

"Look, the overland way is blocked by glaciers. I know a secret way to get there."

"You do?"

"Uh-huh."

Snake pounded his right fist into his left palm. "Damn it. I don't suppose you can just tell me about that secret way?"

"Nope."

He pointed a finger at her. "You stay by me. You don't do anything stupid. You follow my orders."

"Got it. I'll be careful." She saluted him, smirked, and went to the discarded clothing, where she'd left her weapon. As she passed the mirror, she stopped and examined a blemish on her cheek. "You know, I don't use makeup the way other women do. I hardly ever look at myself in the mirror. I always dreamed of becoming a soldier. No, that's not right. It wasn't really my dream. My father—he was killed in action when I was young."

"You wanted to follow in your father's footsteps?"

"Not really. I thought that if I became a soldier, then I could understand him better."

"So are you a soldier yet?" Snake noticed that the young woman had dropped her bravado. Whether it was intentional, he wasn't sure.

"I thought I was until today. But now I understand. The truth is I was just afraid of looking at myself. Afraid of having to make my own decisions in life. But I'm not going to lie to myself anymore. It's time I took a long hard look at myself." She picked up a large handgun and a holster belt. As she strapped it around her waist, she continued. "I want to know who I am, what I'm capable of. I want to know why I've lived the way I've lived until now. I want to know—"

Sheesh, the girl really is still a teenager.

"Hurry up; we need to go."

She grimaced at him and exhaled. "Yeah."

"This *isn't* a training exercise. Our lives are riding on this.

There are no heroes or heroines. If you lose, you're worm food."
He picked up the FAMAS. "Is this functional?"

"Unfortunately, it's out of ammo."

"You pointed it at me and there were no bullets in it?"

She grinned and raised her eyebrows again.

There was a pile of grenades on the floor as well. "What all
do you have here? Flash-bang grenades? Frag grenades?"

"Yeah."

"Can I have some?"

"Take what you want."

He stuck a couple of each in his pouch and then gestured to
the handgun at her waist. "Where'd you get the Desert Eagle?"

"I found it in the armory. It's a fifty-caliber Action Express."
She acknowledged his weapon and added, "There was a
SOCOM, too, but I chose this."

"Isn't that gun a little big for a girl?"

"Don't worry, I can handle it."

"You can use—"

She interrupted him by drawing the Desert Eagle quickly,
removing the magazine, snapping it back in, and racking the
slide with smooth, professional finesse. "Listen, I've used a gun
like this since I was eight years old. I'm more comfortable with it
than I am with a bra." She was ready. "Come on. If we're gonna
go north, we'll have to go through the Commander's Room on
this floor. My Level Five PAN card will open the door."

"I've got one now, too." There was one more piece of equipment on the floor. She picked it up and slung it over her shoulder.

"Whoa!" Snake said. "A PSG-1. What a fine piece of
weaponry. Where'd you get it?"

"I stole it from a guard when he set it down and wasn't looking. I figured you never know when a sniper rifle might come in
handy."

"It's probably the most accurate semiautomatic rifle in the world. You've got experience with that?"

"Uh-huh. And I have plenty of ammo, too." She tossed him a box of cartridges. "Hold on to these for me, will you? I've run out of room in my pack."

"I'm loaded down, too, but I'll take 'em." He opened the bathroom door a crack, looked out, and said, "Coast is clear."

She pushed past him. "I'll lead the way to the Commander's Room."

Snake hoped he wouldn't regret it, but he followed her. He noted, though, that she was adept at moving with stealth. She hugged the walls, traveled lightly on her feet, and kept to the shadows. Perhaps it wouldn't be so bad, after all.

They passed the office where Snake had found the Nikita. He paused to listen at the door, was satisfied the room hadn't been disturbed since he'd left it, and moved on. Meryl took a turn, and they entered a long corridor that led to a single door at the end. The hall was lined with paintings, and the floor was carpeted. They obviously were entering a portion of the complex that normally was occupied by upper management.

"That's funny; there's no guard," she said, indicating the door at the end.

"That's the Commander's Room?"

"Yeah."

"I've got a bad feeling about this. Earlier I made a hell of a lot of noise on this floor. I don't understand why there aren't more troopers."

"Maybe they're busy fighting off all the other mercenaries trying to get in on the Shadow Moses Island action."

"You're not funny."

She shrugged and whispered, "*You* are." She approached the door and listened. "It's quiet in there." With the PAN card in hand, she started to swipe it in the lock, but she dropped it on the carpet and held both hands to her head. "Owww!"

"What's wrong?"

"My head! Ooooh, it *hurts!*" She dropped to her knees. Snake started to go to her, but she snapped, "Don't touch me! Don't come here!"

Snake didn't know what to do. She was obviously in a great deal of pain. Was she having a heart attack like Baker and Anderson? No, this was her head. It was something else.

Then, just as quickly as it had begun, Meryl's severe headache went away. She shook her hair, wiped her forehead, picked up the PAN card, and then stood. "I'm fine now," she said flatly.

"What happened?"

"I said I'm fine." She stared straight ahead at the door and mechanically swiped the card. "Come on, Mister FOX-HOUND; the commander is waiting." She opened the door and stepped inside. Snake was bewildered by her sudden change in demeanor. Then he remembered that he, too, had been struck with a severe headache that had lasted a few seconds and then subsided.

As he entered the room, Snake felt a strange disturbance in the place, as if it gave off an ominous vibe. The Commander's Room looked more like the library of a country manor than an office. It was opulently furnished with an antique mahogany desk, a sofa, three comfy chairs, and shelves lined with books. More paintings adorned the walls, and several busts and urns sat on marble pedestals. The busts were distinguished in that they were covered by black leather S&M bondage masks and gear.

Weird.

A holographic reproduction of the Shadow Moses facility sat on a large table at the side of the room. Snake moved to it so that he could study the layout. It was an impressive structure with its two communication towers standing like sentinels at the northern end of the base.

Meryl stood by the door; she hadn't moved. She watched him curiously and then made sure the door was shut and locked behind her. Then she drew the Desert Eagle, pointed it at Snake, and began to advance toward him.

"Snake, do you . . . like me?" she purred.

He looked up. "Meryl, what the hell?"

"Do you like me?" She came closer, batted her eyes, and moved her body in a way that accentuated her curves.

For a split second, Snake was certain that someone else was behind Meryl. But he blinked, and the apparition was gone.

"What's wrong with you?" he asked.

Breathing heavily, she said, "Snake, hold me!" She was now very close, but the Desert Eagle was still pointed at his face. Should he risk disarming her?

"Meryl! Stop that!"

"Make love to me, Snake! Hurry!" Her breathing increased as if she were in a kind of sexual frenzy.

The image of a figure—*floating a few feet above the carpeted floor*—flashed behind Meryl again. This time Snake knew that something bad was happening.

"Snake! I want you!"

Again the floating figure. There and gone in an instant.

"Who are you?" Snake yelled.

"What's wrong?" Meryl asked with a come-hither voice. "Don't you like girls?"

Snake had no choice. He pulled back his arm and slugged Meryl in the jaw as hard as he could. She didn't have time to cry out. She plummeted to the floor, dropping the gun and losing consciousness.

"Sorry, Meryl," he said.

And then the figure appeared and remained in view. Still floating three feet above the floor, the man looked like something from another world. He was dressed in a skintight uniform that resembled the leather bondage costumes worn by S&M sexual slaves. Even more bizarre was the gas mask helmet that covered his head.

Psycho Mantis!

"Useless woman," he said with a high, almost shrill voice. It hurt Snake's ears to listen to the man.

"You!" Snake shouted. "You were the one manipulating her!"

"Of course I am, you idiotic buffoon. I am beyond your pitiful intellect. I can destroy your *mind.* I will make you break down and cry like a baby!"

"All smoke and mirrors, I'll bet, just like that optic camouflage you have on. I hope that's not your only trick," Snake challenged.

"You doubt my power? Now I will show you why I am the most powerful practitioner of psychokinesis and telepathy in the world! I can read your every thought and anticipate your every move." The terrorist laughed and said, "You *like* the girl, don't you, Snake? Even though that goes against what your head is telling you to do, your *heart* is falling for her. Isn't that right?"

"You don't know what the hell you're talking about."

"Oh, and let's see, you've made friends with Doctor Emmerich! But where is he now? I do believe he's making the acquaintance of a very beautiful woman at this very moment. A seductive and . . . *frightening* . . . woman."

"Why don't you come down and fight like a man?" Snake demanded, but his own headache was returning. It had the same intensity as the one he had experienced earlier. Dr. Hunter had said that it was due to Psycho Mantis and his mental weaponry.

Snake tried to draw his SOCOM, but the thing was stuck in his holster. Someone had plastered it with cement!

No, it's a hallucination!

But try as he might, Snake was unable to pull the gun out of its holster. In fact, the grip was *hot*—hot as fire! He had to release it and blow on his hand.

Psycho Mantis laughed maniacally. "Having a little trouble with your armaments, Snake?"

Snake retreated by moving behind the ornate desk. There had to be some kind of defense he could use against this *thing*. He grabbed a letter opener off the desk and flung it at Psycho Mantis, but the sharp instrument stopped spinning in midair and simply dropped to the floor.

"Pitiful, Snake!" The man laughed. "Can't you do better than that?"

Snake jumped onto the top of the desk and then leaped at the floating man's legs in an attempt to pull him down to the ground. But Psycho Mantis vanished, and Snake fell to the floor next to Meryl. He picked up her Desert Eagle, but it, too, was blazing hot. He had to drop it before the thing seared his hand.

It's not really hot! It's an illusion!

He tried to pick it up again, but the villain's power over Snake's perception was too strong. No matter how much he fought against the thought, the gun's grip was still too hot for him to touch. In fact, the metal glowed red as if it had been sitting in a blast furnace.

"Damn you!" Snake shouted, but Psycho Mantis merely laughed in his sickening way.

"Snake!"

The voice was familiar. He turned to see a lean, fit man in his fifties standing near the wall. He wore sunglasses that Snake knew all too well.

"Master Miller!" Snake cried. "How did you get here?"

"No time to chat, Snake. We have to run and get away from this clown." Miller held out his hand to help his former trainee off the floor.

Totally confused, Snake looked around the room. Psycho Mantis was nowhere to be seen. Meryl still lay on the floor, unconscious. When he made a move toward her, Miller said, "Forget her, Snake. She'll only slow you down, just as you told her."

"But she's Campbell's niece."

"Forget her, soldier! That's an order."

Resigned, Snake followed Master Miller out of the Commander's Room and into—

An outdoor amusement park.

"What the . . . ?" Snake was completely overwhelmed by the sights and sound and smells of the very familiar midway.

I've been here before . . .

"Recognize it, Snake?" Miller asked. "You used to come here when you were little."

It was true. They were standing on the midway of Kiddieland, a small, privately owned theme park in the small town in Oregon where he had lived the first ten years of his life. He had visited Kiddieland at least once a week during the summer months, when the place was always open. When he wasn't *training*.

"How did we get here? Master Miller, what the hell is going on?" It took a great deal to frighten Snake, but at the moment he was filled with a trepidation the likes of which he hadn't felt in years.

This isn't happening!

But it seemed so real. It was night, and the park was full of people: parents with their small children, teenagers running back and forth, barkers in front of the "games of chance" and the rides—the wonderful rides. Snake had loved fast rides, especially the Mad Mouse roller coaster. There were no huge, modern high-tech coasters at Kiddieland. The amusement park was "old school"; the rides consisted of traditional favorites such as the Tilt-A-Whirl, the Octopus, and the Zipper. Piped-in carnival music blasted through loudspeakers throughout the grounds, mixing with kids' joyful screams. Colorful lights brightened the place. The sensory overload made Snake feel eight years old again.

"Why are we here?" he asked Master Miller.

But his trainer was no longer by his side. In fact, Snake was *entirely* alone in the park. The crowds had vanished suddenly. The lights were extinguished, and everything went dark. The music and happy shouts and screams continued to fill the air, but *no one was around*. It was as if he were standing in a ghost park. The rides and arcades were long closed down, but the spirits of ancient guests still played there under a night sky that was a blanket of deep, dark dread.

Snake closed his eyes and tried to concentrate. It was one of Psycho Mantis's tricks. It had to be. But try as he might, Snake couldn't shake the powerful illusion. The only thing he could do was walk through the midway and look at this relic from his past.

Near the end of the main drag was the Fun House. He had always loved the Fun House. It wasn't particularly scary, but it contained all the usual trappings: curved mirrors, slides, jack-in-the-box clowns that popped up when you least expected them, rocking floors, and a mirror maze.

A woman was standing at the entrance. She had red hair and a nice . . .

Meryl!

She waved and beckoned him to come inside the Fun House. He wanted to shout and warn her not to go in. It had to be a trap. Besides, the park was closed; there was no one running the rides or taking tickets. But Snake couldn't get the words out of his mouth. It was similar to what happened in dreams in which your legs were too heavy to run or your voice came out in a whisper.

Meryl disappeared into the building, leaving Snake with no choice but to follow her. He bounded up the steps, went through the turnstile, and entered the dark, foreboding attraction. With the lights off, the place was much more sinister than usual. But all the mechanisms were working, including the very first "obstacle," a floor that rocked back and forth. The trick was to maintain your balance as you walked to the other side. Many kids would fall and slide on the tilting floor—often on purpose—laughing like crazy. Snake had always played by the rules and really tried to get across without falling. He'd never failed.

This time, however, as soon as he stepped on the platform, it tilted so high that he couldn't help but fall and slide to the edge. He managed to brake and stop his body from plummeting off the platform—

But there used to be a wall there to stop kids from falling off . . . !

—which emptied into a vast crevice of nothingness. In fact, it was a sky full of stars! It was as if Snake were holding on to the edge of the known universe, and if he let go, he would be lost in the infinite chasm of outer space.

Don't look!

He forced himself to focus on the arch at the other side of the tilting platform, the one that led out of the room. Meryl was standing there waiting for him. She was pointing and laughing at him.

"Look at the legendary Solid Snake!" she cackled. "He can't even stand on his own two feet!"

There were grooves in the tilted wooden floor that were deep enough for Snake to grip with his fingertips. Using all the strength he could muster and ignoring the pain in his fingers, he slowly inched up the platform. It seemed to take forever, but after a few minutes he had done it. He rolled off the tilted floor onto the metal mesh walkway by the arch. Meryl was no longer there. Snake stood, went through the arch, and found himself in the room lined with curved mirrors.

He remembered laughing at his body's funny shapes when he stood in front of the mirrors. One mirror made him short and fat, another tall and skinny with a big head, and one gave him a very wide torso but with tiny legs and feet. This time, however, when Snake stepped up to the first mirror, he saw Meryl. She seemed to be trapped inside. There was an expression of terror on her face as she banged on her side of the mirror.

"Help me, Snake! Get me out!"

Snake examined the sides of the mirror, but it was fastened firmly to the wall. There was nothing he could do. He moved along to the next mirror and saw Otacon in the same predicament. The young man was trembling with fear.

"Snake! Can you get me out of here?" Otacon shouted. "They're going to kill me! Help me!"

Feeling increasingly helpless, Snake moved on to the third mirror. Inside of it was a uniformed man he hadn't seen in many, many years. Unlike the other two prisoners, he stood silently, resigned to being trapped and knowing there was nothing that could be done about it.

"Big Boss?" Snake whispered. "Is that you?"

The soldier smiled at him. "Yes, my son. Have you missed me?"

Snake banged on the glass mirror, but it proved to be too strong to break. "Why are you here? What's going on?"

"Son, they're going to kill me unless you tell me the deactivation codes."

"But . . . you're already *dead*!" In fact, Snake had killed the man with his own hands. His own father. Big Boss. Yet here he was, alive and breathing.

"Please, Son," he pleaded. "Give me the codes. If you don't, I will die a horrible death."

No. *This isn't real. This IS NOT HAPPENING!*

Then blood began to pour from Big Boss's nose and mouth.

"Yes, it is painful, Snake!" He clenched his eyes shut.

"Big Boss!" Snake shouted. "I don't know the codes! They already have them! Baker and Anderson talked! They already have the damned codes!"

The man behind the mirror screamed bloody murder as his head began to *split apart*! Brains and goo dribbled out of the cracks in one of the most grotesque displays of horror Snake had ever seen.

The operative fell to his knees and shouted, "NO! THIS . . . IS . . . NOT . . . REAL!!"

—and found himself on the carpeted floor of the Commander's Room once again. Meryl was still lying beside him. And Psycho Mantis floated in the air a few feet away, laughing.

It was a hallucination! And I broke it!

"You are a strong warrior, Solid Snake," Mantis said. "You have a healthy mind and a tough heart. You resisted my little mind games. Very admirable! But you are still no match for my powers!"

Before Snake had a chance to recover from the "trip" he had just experienced, the three antique chairs in the room floated into the air, and then were hurled at him with ferocity. Snake flattened himself to the floor to avoid being struck by them.

"Psychokinesis!" the villain gloated. "The weapon of the gods!"

The chairs were followed by the two metal urns. They levitated and then soared at Snake as if they had been projected from cannons. He managed to dodge one, but the second one grazed his left shoulder and bounced off. The pain was intense but not nearly as bad as it would have been if it had struck full-on.

An antlered deer-head trophy attached to the wall split away from its plaque and zoomed toward Snake. The sharp antler points certainly would do far more damage than the chairs or urns. Without thinking, Snake's hand went to the SOCOM in its holster, and he drew it. He let off three rapid-succession shots and blew the deer head to bits, knocking it out of the air.

I have my gun in hand! It is no longer stuck!

Psycho Mantis wasn't laughing anymore. Instead, the villain concentrated on creating the illusion that the gun's grip was hot again. This time, though, Snake was able to hold on to it.

"It won't work this time, Mantis," Snake said through gritted teeth. He forced himself to clutch the SOCOM no matter what his pain receptors were telling his brain. He lifted the handgun and pointed it at Psycho Mantis, but it suddenly became extremely heavy. Snake held it with two hands, but it was as if it had gained five hundred pounds in weight. He had no choice but to drop it.

As Mantis laughed uncontrollably once more, books flew off the shelves at Snake. They bombarded him like stones, forcing him back against the desk. He held his arms over his face to protect himself and then rolled his body into a ball on the floor.

Why had he been able to draw the SOCOM before? The answer had to be that Psycho Mantis could do only so many telekinetic tasks at a time. If Snake could keep his adversary busy throwing objects, perhaps he could pick up the gun and get off a shot.

With that in mind, Snake abruptly and boldly stood and ran

for the door. One of the leather-mask-clad busts careened off of its pedestal and soared at Snake to block his path. The operative ducked and immediately turned back toward the desk. The other bust lifted off and joined its counterpart to become guided missiles, following Snake around the room. No matter where he went, the marble busts tailed him as Psycho Mantis waited for the perfect opportunity to smash one over Snake's head. The result surely would be death.

"Do your worst, you circus freak!" Snake shouted as he zigzagged through the room. "Did they leave your cage in the sideshow unlocked, Mantis? Don't you miss living with the geeks?"

Obviously, Psycho Mantis did not care for taunting. The villain summoned all his potency to unleash every object in the room that wasn't fixed. The busts, the urns, the chairs, the books, even the heavy mahogany desk and comfy sofa—they all lifted into the air, ready to tumble down on Snake. But at the crucial moment when everything was above the ground, Snake performed a forward roll on the floor, picked up the SOCOM in one hand, spun out to a crouching position, and fired two rounds at Psycho Mantis.

The man screamed and dropped to the floor, along with all the objects. Snake was bombarded by dozens of books but was spared from being hit by the heavy stuff. Both bullets had punctured Mantis's chest. Blood poured from the wounds as the man feebly attempted to crawl to safety.

Snake stood with the SOCOM leveled at Mantis's head and said, "Game over, freak."

The man wheezed as he breathed, apparently struggling to take in oxygen. "You are . . . powerful . . . indeed . . . but I know . . . your weak point!"

"Shut up and say your prayers."

"Meryl," Mantis commanded, "stand right where he can . . . see you . . . and blow your brains out!"

On cue, Meryl shook herself awake, got up from the floor, picked up her Desert Eagle, and held it to her temple. Snake could see that she was struggling with the psychic command, for she attempted to pull away her gun hand with her left.

The Desert Eagle fired!

But Meryl had managed to move her head in time. A trickle of blood dribbled down her forehead; the bullet must have scraped her scalp.

"Shoot . . . yourself!" Mantis demanded.

"Stop! Meryl!"

Snake fired a round into Psycho Mantis's kneecap. The villain screamed in agony; at the same time Meryl was able to pull the gun away from her face. Snake then dropped the SOCOM, stepped in, grabbed Meryl by the gun arm, and threw her over his shoulder. She dropped the handgun and crashed into the mahogany desk, unconscious once more.

Snake picked up his weapon and walked over to where Psycho Mantis lay. The man's breathing was now very shallow and forced.

"I . . . wasn't able . . . to read your . . . future," Mantis gasped.

"A strong man doesn't need to read the future. He makes his own."

Mantis coughed. "Perhaps . . . but let me try . . . Please . . . remove my mask."

Snake didn't think it could hurt. He knelt by the dying man and removed the gas mask. Underneath was a hideously scarred creature with a face that Darth Vader or Frankenstein's monster wouldn't have wanted to possess.

"To get to the Metal Gear's . . . underground maintenance base . . . you must go through . . . the hidden door. Behind the bookcase."

"Go on."

"Travel past . . . the communication towers. Use the tower's walkway."

"Why are you telling me this?"

"I can read people's minds. In my lifetime . . . I have read the pasts . . . presents . . . and futures of thousands of men and women . . ."

Meryl began to stir. Snake glanced over at her to make sure she was all right. After a moment, she stood, shook her head, and slowly walked over to them. When she saw Mantis's face, she said, "Eww, gross . . ."

Mantis strained to continue. "Each mind that I peered into . . . was stuffed with the same . . . single object of obsession. That selfish . . . and atavistic . . . desire . . . to pass on one's seed. It was enough . . . to make me sick. Every living thing . . . on this planet . . . exists to mindlessly pass on . . . their DNA. We're designed that way. And that's why . . . there is war. But you . . . are different. You're the same . . . as us. We have no past. No future. We live . . . in the moment. That's our only purpose. Humans weren't designed . . . to bring each other . . . happiness. From the moment we're thrown into this world . . . we're fated to bring each other nothing . . . but pain and misery."

Snake and Meryl gave each other a look. The man was as mad as all the inhabitants of an asylum combined.

"The first person whose mind . . . I read . . . was my father. I saw nothing but . . . disgust and hatred for me . . . in his heart. My mother died . . . in childbirth, and he despised me . . . for it. I thought my father was going to . . . kill me. That's when my future . . . disappeared. I lost my past as well. When I came to, the village . . . was engulfed in flames."

"Are you saying that you burned your village down to bury your past?" Snake asked.

"I see you have suffered the same . . . trauma." Mantis

laughed as best as he could, but it was a dark, evil laugh. "We are truly the same . . . you and I . . . The world is a more interesting place . . . with people like you in it . . ."

"He's insane," Meryl whispered, stating the obvious.

"I never agreed . . . with the Boss's revolution . . . His dreams of world conquest . . . do not interest me. I just wanted an excuse . . . to kill as many people as I could."

"You monster!" she shouted.

"Let him talk," Snake snapped. "He doesn't have much time left."

"I've seen . . . true evil. You, Snake. You're just like . . . the Boss. No, you're worse. Compared to you, I'm not so bad. Wait . . . I see you . . . Must be decades from now . . . You are *old* . . . with a gun in your mouth . . ." Mantis glanced at Meryl. "I read . . . her future, too. You occupy a large place . . . in her heart."

Meryl emitted a small gasp.

"But I don't . . . know . . . if your futures . . . lie together. I have a request."

"What?"

"Please . . . put my mask back on."

Snake obliged. The man's breathing was barely audible.

"Before I die . . ." Mantis coughed, "I want to be myself. I want to be left alone . . . in my own world. I will . . . open the door for you."

There was a click in the back of one of the bookshelves behind the fallen desk. The entire bookcase slid to the side, revealing a dark passage.

Now very weak, Mantis said, "This is the first time . . . I've ever used my power . . . to help someone. It's strange . . . It feels kind of . . . nice."

The exhalation of breath was final and absolute. Snake and Meryl stood there for a moment, trying to comprehend what they had just witnessed. After a moment, she turned to Snake and said, "I'm so sorry."

"What for?"

"How could I let him control my mind like that?"

"If you're going to doubt yourself, I'll leave you here," Snake answered.

She nodded and took a deep breath. "You're right."

"Never doubt yourself. Just let it make you stronger. Learn something from it."

"You're right. I won't let it happen again."

Snake moved toward the open bookcase. "Is this the way out? Like he said? Was this what you were going to show me in this place?"

"Snake . . . I didn't know anything about this room. Something was telling me to lead you here. It was *him*. I'm sorry. Snake? Can I ask you something?"

"What?"

"About what he said . . . about us."

"What is it now? What's the problem?" He sounded annoyed.

"Oh, nothing. Never mind. Hey, what's your real name?"

He sighed. "A name means nothing on the battlefield. The only thing that matters is surviving."

"How old are you?"

"Old enough to know what death looks like."

"Any family?"

"No, but I was raised by many people."

Then, she asked softly, almost inaudibly, "Is there anyone you like?"

"I've never been interested in anyone else's life."

"So you're all alone? Just like Mantis said?"

He stood in the open doorway, his back to her. "Other people just complicate my life. I don't like to get involved."

"You're . . . you're a sad, lonely man."

He was not about to disagree. "Come on, let's go."

BACK AT THE CONTROL ROOM in the *Discovery* submarine, Dr. Hunter turned to Campbell and said, "It looks like your niece is going to be okay."

"The brainwashing will wear off, right?" the colonel asked her.

"Yes. But why did Snake go so far out of his way to save her? For your sake? Or does he like her?"

Campbell felt sobered by everything that had just transpired. "Naomi, it's true that Snake has killed a lot of people, but that doesn't mean he doesn't have a heart."

15

A STONE STAIRCASE led from the open bookcase into a dark, damp passageway. It reminded Snake of the dungeons in the medieval Scottish castles he had toured many years earlier. Meryl rubbed her arms and shivered.

"It's cold down here."

"Yeah. You should have worn a sweater."

"Sorry, *Dad*. I left it at home."

They followed the passage for several feet until the stone-work ended. From that point forward, the walls, ground, and ceiling became a tunnel of natural rock.

"It's an underground cavern," Meryl observed.

The light was minimal. Snake flicked on the penlight on the shoulder of his suit, and it provided adequate illumination for them to see where they were going. The passageway twisted and turned and at one point branched in two directions. The left tunnel was decidedly smaller.

"Which way do we go?" she asked.

As if in answer, several howls filtered through the tunnels.

"Wolves?"

Snake listened and answered, "No. Wolf-dogs. Half wolf, half husky."

"How do you know so much?"

"I ride dogsleds. I'm a musher."

"Are wolf-dogs dangerous?"

"They can be. They're not *tame*, if that's what you mean."

She took a deep breath. "Okay. Why don't I take the right fork? You take the left. If it turns out one of these is a dead end, we'll contact each other by Codec and meet back here. How's that?"

"Sounds like a plan."

Snake wasn't comfortable letting her go alone, but she had handled herself fairly well so far. He couldn't worry about her. He had a job to do, and no matter how much he was beginning to like the girl, he wasn't about to let her interfere with the mission.

He ducked his head and moved into the tunnel with the lowest ceiling. It was a pain having to bend at the waist and walk at the same time, but he could take it. The tunnel continued in a maze of twisty passages, all alike, and for a moment Snake feared he might get lost or stuck. To add to his anxiety, after a hundred feet or so, the passageway grew narrower and the ceiling dropped. He would have to crawl.

The built-in knee pads in his suit were helpful. He moved along the cold wet rock for nearly ten minutes until finally the tunnel began to expand. A few more feet and he could stand once again. Eventually, the passageway opened into a large cave with a very high ceiling. Stalactites dripped cold water, and there were puddles all over the cavern floor. In some portions, the ice on the walls had melted and there was soft mud mixed with rock on the ground. He'd have to watch his step.

Another wolf howl was much closer than before. Snake figured the animal was probably somewhere in the cave.

He punched Meryl's frequency on the Codec. "Meryl?"

"Yeah?"

"How are you doing?"

"I'm in a large cavern."

"Me, too. It's probably the same one. Let's see if we can meet up at the north end. Careful. There may be wolf-dogs in here."

"Okay."

He signed off and continued moving forward. At one point he came to a large boulder that at one time had been a part of the ceiling. He skirted it and came upon not one wolf-dog but a pack of four.

Jesus!

The animals growled, and their eyes glowed red in the dark cave. The two in front bared their fangs. One barked.

"Easy, doggies."

He held out his hands, palms up, the way one was supposed to do. Of course, that usually worked only when dogs were somewhat domesticated. These animals were wild and huge, weighing 120 pounds or more each. They could tear the flesh off a man in seconds.

The two in front crept forward, their growls intensifying.

Snake didn't want to kill them but would if he had to. But there was another alternative. He slowly opened the pouch and removed a flash-bang grenade, which was another name for a stun grenade. Moving with the speed of a snail and keeping his legs perfectly still, he brought the grenade to his mouth, pulled the pin with his teeth, and counted to four. He then tossed the explosive at the pack and immediately crouched and covered his head.

162 | RAYMOND BENSON

The grenade's highly charged magnesium exploded, causing a flash that would knock out most animals and humans. Snake waited a few seconds and then looked to see what damage he had caused.

All four wolf-dogs were lying on the ground. He approached them cautiously, put a hand on the leader's pelt, and felt him breathing. They were all still alive. Satisfied, Snake moved on.

"Hey!" It was Meryl up ahead. "What happened?" She was holding something in her arms.

"Had to put some wolf-dogs to beddie-bye." Snake noted that she was carrying a live wolf-dog puppy.

"Are you hurt?" Meryl asked.

"No. Where did you find that?"

"He was wandering around over there, looking for his mommy. Isn't he cute?"

"I think I just put his mommy to sleep. Put him over there with the rest of them. We don't have time to rescue animals."

"I thought you liked dogs."

"I *do*. When I'm at home and not in the middle of a mission!"

"Okay, okay." She ran over to the sleeping pack of animals and let the puppy loose. He quickly ran to one of the wolf-dogs, sat down beside her, and began to lick his mom's pelt.

"He'll be fine. Come on. Look, I see a way out of here, I think." Snake pointed to a large opening in the cave's northern wall.

"Sounds good to me."

When they emerged from the cavern, the pair found themselves in a man-made underground passage with a high ceiling and a floor made of steel. There were shallow alcoves in the walls every ten feet. Snake figured the tunnel was about fifty yards long. At the end was the base of the first communication tower. They could see the lower two stories of what appeared to be a slender but massive structure that protruded up through the ceiling and extended above the surface. It was made of steel latticework with crisscross patterns. Snake had studied a little architecture in his lifetime—it was an essential subject for anyone who wanted to be adept at infiltrating buildings—and the design of the tower reminded him of the work of the Chinese architect I. M. Pei.

"How tall are the towers?" Snake asked.

"I'm not sure. Twenty, thirty stories?"

"I hope their elevators work."

She started to move forward, but he grabbed her arm. "Wait! Let me check something." He pulled out the mine detector and switched it on.

Three Claymores lay under the steel directly in front of them.

"I think I just saved your life again," he said.

Meryl's eyes widened. "Thanks. Is that all there is? Just three?"

"Looks that way."

She studied the layout on the detector's monitor. "Okay, I'll lead." With the delicate poise that only a female could possess, Meryl lightly moved between the mines' locations and stood on the other side. "What are you waiting for?"

He'd been enjoying watching her form but simply grinned in response.

She made a face and put her hands on her hips, but Snake knew she didn't mind the attention. He quickly followed in her footsteps and sidestepped the danger.

They continued walking forward through the tunnel. The silence was eerie, but they instinctually stopped talking because the echo effect was strong within the passage. Even their footsteps, as lightly as they attempted to step, tended to reverberate. When they made it to the halfway mark, Snake thought he saw the flash of a red light. He blinked and looked at Meryl. Sure enough, there was a red dot on her chest between her breasts.

It was a laser sight.

"Meryl!"

"What is it?"

"Get down!"

He pushed her out of the way, but it was too late. The shot resounded throughout the passage, and a red flower of blood spurted on her left shoulder. She screamed in pain but didn't realize she'd been shot. Snake started to tackle her, but the sniper fired another round, hitting her in the side just above the waist. This time she went down for the count. Another bullet hit the metal floor between Snake and his fallen companion, forcing him to retreat and take cover in one of the alcoves on the side.

"Meryl!" His companion lay behind him about twenty feet away—in plain view of the sniper. She had dropped her Desert Eagle a few feet from her, and the PSG-1 sniper rifle also lay at her side. Meryl attempted to pick up the rifle but couldn't manage it. Instead, she reached for the handgun with her good arm, but it was about a foot too far away. She gritted her teeth and stretched for the piece, but another shot from the sniper dented the metal floor inches from her fingers.

"Snake! Leave me and run!"

"Meryl!"

Snake heard more disappointment than pain in her voice. "I guess . . . I'm a rookie after all . . . !"

"Don't worry, Meryl. It's me they want!"

"I know . . . It's the oldest trick in the book . . . The sniper's using me for bait to lure you out."

Snake cursed to himself. He'd been afraid this would happen.

"Shoot me, Snake!" she cried.

"No!"

"I promised . . . I wouldn't slow you down!"

"Don't move!"

"I can still help . . . I want to help you . . ."

"Quiet down! Save your strength!"

She was crying now. "I was a fool! I wanted to be a sol-dier . . . Snake, please! Save yourself! Go on living . . . and don't give up on people!"

He knew she was right. There was nothing he could do for her. If he even attempted to drag her to cover, the sniper would pick him off.

"Get out of here!" she screamed. "Just . . . don't forget me . . ."

Snake eyed the sniper rifle at Meryl's side. If he could get hold of it, he might have a fighting chance.

"Snake?" It was Campbell on the Codec.

"Yeah?"

"It's a trap! A sniper's trick to lure you out. If you go help Meryl, you'll be picked off. Don't do it!"

Snake could hear the pain in the colonel's voice. This was his *niece* he was talking about.

"I know that, Colonel. But I can't just leave her there." So much for not worrying about her and not letting her interfere with the mission.

Dr. Hunter spoke up. "It must be Sniper Wolf, FOX-HOUND's best shooter."

"Don't snipers usually work in pairs?"

"Yes, but not her. I know her. She can wait for hours, days, or weeks. It doesn't matter to her. She's just watching and wait-ing for you to expose yourself."

"Maybe so, but Meryl can't hold out that long."

"Snake, can you see Wolf from where you are?" Naomi asked.

"I think she's on the second floor of the tower. Between here and there, there's no place to hide."

Campbell's voice shook. "If Wolf's in the communication tower, then she can see you perfectly! It's the classic sniper's position. At this distance you won't be able to hit her with a standard weapon!"

"Colonel, take it easy," Snake said. "Meryl's got a sniper rifle. I'm going to save her, no matter what it takes."

The former FOXHOUND leader was breathing hard, but Snake's words seemed to calm him down a little. "Okay. Thanks."

Snake heard Naomi Hunter make a noise. "Naomi? Did you say something?"

"Nothing," the doctor replied. "I'm just surprised you're willing to sacrifice yourself. You've got the genes of a soldier, not a savior."

"You trying to say I'm only interested in saving my own skin?"

"I wouldn't go that far, but . . ."

"I don't know what the hell my genes look like, and I don't care. I operate on instinct. I'll save Meryl. I don't need an excuse. And I'm not doing it for someone else, either. I'll save Meryl for myself. Colonel, don't worry!"

"Snake, I didn't mean . . . I'm sorry," Dr. Hunter said. "I understand."

He signed off and studied the distance between himself and the rifle. The old cliché "so near yet so far" certainly applied. Snake thought about what he had in his inventory that could help.

The flash-bang! He had one left in his pouch. The blast it created just might be enough to mask what he was doing temporarily. The sniper wouldn't be able to target him through a brief, bright blaze. It was his only hope.

He retrieved the grenade and calculated where the best place would be to throw it. As long as it covered the area in front of Meryl, he should be okay. Without wasting another second, he pulled the pin, tossed it twenty feet into the passageway, and prepared to make his move. He anticipated the explosion and emerged from behind his cover. He hoped Sniper Wolf would attempt to shoot him but then be blinded by the flash.

The flash-bang went off as desired, thrusting a wave of hot breath at Snake as he ran for Meryl's position. The blast knocked him over, but he was careful not to look at the brightness of the momentary blaze. If he hadn't been expecting the detonation, he would have been stunned. As it was, he had to crawl to Meryl.

He took a second to examine her face. She was unconscious. Snake squeezed her hand, grabbed the PSG-1, stood and ran to the opposite side of the passageway, and took cover in an alcove. He checked that the magazine was full with six rounds in the chamber, lay prone on the ground, and carefully exposed the rifle, his arms, and his head.

"Snake, this is Nastasha."

Snake glanced at the monitor on his Codec. "Can't chat right now, Nastasha. I'm kind of busy."

"The colonel asked me to advise you. You have a PSG-1. Is that correct?"

"Yeah. It was Meryl's."

"Excellent. It's one of the best sniper rifles in the world. It is accurate enough to shoot cleanly through a two-point-five-centimeter square from a distance of one hundred meters. And it is semiautomatic, unlike other sniper rifles. Just remember, Snake, the slightest tremble can make you miss your target by inches. Try to keep your hands as still as possible."

"Thanks, Nastasha. You just reminded me. I have some diazepam with me. That'll steady the nerves."

Dr. Hunter interrupted, "I was going to suggest that, too."

Snake found the pillbox in his belt and took the fast-acting drug that produced a calming effect on subjects. Normally it would take at least twenty minutes to be effective, but FOX-HOUND's medical department had come up with a sublingual tablet that dissolved and acted in seconds.

A minute later, he was ready.

Come on, bitch. Show me where you are!

Sniper Wolf's laser sight pinpointed his forehead. Snake saw the tiny red dot originating on the tower's second floor, just as he had suspected. Before the woman had a chance to fire, he squeezed the PSG-1's trigger. The empty casing ejected hard and high, landing nearly ten feet from him. This was considered an advantage because it lessened the enemy's ability to locate the shooter's position.

Through the telescopic sight, which was accurate up to six hundred meters, Snake spotted a figure moving from one metal support to another. He caught her in the crosshairs and fired again. The woman jerked, but he wasn't sure if he had hit her. Nevertheless, this gave him time to jump up and run closer.

Snake darted into the passageway and ran in an erratic pattern. The sniper fired twice, hitting the floor at his feet. He took refuge in another alcove, but now he was at least twenty yards closer to the tower. Although it made him an easier target for Sniper Wolf, it also made *her* a less difficult shot for him.

Three rounds battered the wall at the edge of the alcove, reminding him that he couldn't be careless when peering out to shoot. He needed another diversion, so he pulled out a chaff grenade. It wouldn't do much except perhaps make her blink a couple of times, but that might be enough for him to get in a shot or two. Snake pulled the pin and tossed it into the air in the middle of the passageway.

It went off in its singular way without creating much of a blast; however, Snake simultaneously leaned out of the alcove, picked up the figure in the crosshairs, and squeezed the trigger.

He could have sworn he heard the woman shout in pain!

Snake returned to the alcove and waited a few seconds before attempting to take a look. He scanned the visible floors on the tower with the rifle's telescopic sight and didn't see a soul. It would be best to make sure by securing the area at the base of the tower and then deal with getting Meryl some medical attention. He slung the rifle over his shoulder and ran to the structure. With the SOCOM in hand, he checked the perimeter of the base and the metal stairs that led to the second-floor balcony.

There were a few drops of fresh blood on the steps. Snake looked up and saw that there was a direct line from the balcony rail to where he was standing. Obviously, he hadn't killed Sniper Wolf, but he'd certainly winged her.

Snake turned around with the intention of running back to Meryl, but his path was blocked by the sudden appearance of a dozen troopers fast-roping down lines from the second floor, ninja style! Each man had a FAMAS assault rifle pointed at him.

"Don't move!" one of the men shouted.

Snake could see that these guys were the elite. The Space Seals. The cream of the crop of genome soldiers. And they had him surrounded.

"Drop your weapon! Now!"

He had no choice. Snake tossed the SOCOM to the ground.

"Kick it over here!"

He did so.

A steel door slid open at the base, and a tall woman with an extraordinary body emerged. Her uniform fit tightly and was open at the neck to reveal magnificent cleavage. She had short blond hair and green eyes. It was too bad she was one of the enemy—the woman was definitely a babe.

The only good thing about the situation was that Sniper

Wolf's left arm was in a makeshift sling and the fabric around her shoulder was soaked in blood.

"You were a fool to come here, stupid man," she said with an accent. Snake placed it as Middle Eastern and then remembered Campbell's briefing: The woman was a Kurd from Iraq.

"A lady sniper," Snake said. "Who woulda thought?"

"Didn't you know that two-thirds of the world's greatest assassins are women?"

"What happened to your shoulder? Hurt yourself?"

"It's just a scratch." She licked her lips. "Do you want to die now? Or after your female friend? Which will it be?"

"I'll die after I kill you."

She laughed, mocking him. "Is that right? Well, at least you've got spirit. I am Sniper Wolf, and I always kill what I aim at. You're my special prey." She stepped closer to him. Snake was aware of her strong scent—certainly feminine but decidedly the stuff of animalistic menace.

Sniper Wolf swiftly reached out and scratched Snake's left cheek with her long, sharp nails. Blood trickled out of the wounds, but Snake didn't flinch.

"I've left my mark on you," she said. "I won't forget it. Until I kill you, you're all I'll think about." She licked her lips again, and Snake felt her hot breath on his neck. She held the gaze between them for a moment longer and then abruptly broke away.

"Take him away!" she commanded the troopers.

Before Snake could protest, something hard and heavy struck him on the back of the head—and everything went black.

16

VOICES FILTERED IN through the haze. He wasn't sure who they were at first, but he thought they were familiar.

A female asked, "Do you need his DNA, too?"

"Yes," a man with a familiar, polished voice replied. "I want a sample while he's still alive. We need it to correct the genome soldiers' mutations."

"Then we'll be able to cure them?"

"No. We still have to get our hands on Big Boss's DNA."

The woman seemed perturbed. "Have they given in to our demands yet?"

"Not yet."

"They won't give in. They're all hypocrites, every one of them."

"Is that your opinion? As a Kurd?"

"They always put politics first."

"That's right," the man said. "That's why they want to avoid any leak about their precious new nuclear weapon."

"Hey, Boss," a new voice remarked. "It looks like our friend is awake."

"Can you hear me, Solid Snake?" The voice had a British accent.

When Snake opened his eyes, he saw three blurry figures standing in front of him. One was definitely a woman; he could tell that much. The others? One seemed recognizable, but everything was so cloudy. His head hurt. And when he tried to move—

"It's no use, Snake," the third man said. "Your body is strapped down tight."

It was true. Snake's arms and legs were spread apart and tightly bound onto a flat surface, but he was in a semistanding position. All his gear was gone, but he was still wearing his suit and, oddly, his bandana.

"Can you hear me, Snake?"

"He's tougher than I thought," the woman said.

"Do you know who I am? I always knew that one day I would meet you."

Snake attempted to focus on the man with long golden-white hair. Slowly the cobwebs melted away and the world became clearer. He was in a room much like the outer cell area where he initially had found DARPA chief Anderson and Meryl, but it was full of what appeared to be medical equipment, machinery, and laboratory paraphernalia. The room might have been a hospital operating theater if it had not been for the slightly sinister characteristics of the apparatus.

That's because it's a torture chamber . . .

Not only were his arms and legs securely fastened, there was a strange belt around his chest with wires leading out of it and ominous nozzles attached to the sides of his chair/table, pointed directly at him.

"There definitely is a resemblance. Don't you think, little brother?"

Finally, Snake's vision was clear. The man known as Liquid Snake stood in front of him. When Snake first had glimpsed him upon his arrival at Shadow Moses Island, he had known that Liquid looked like him. But now, seeing the man face-to-face, it was as if he were staring into a mirror. The only difference was the hair color and length and a darker complexion.

"Or should I say *big* brother? I'm not sure. Anyway, it doesn't matter."

What was the guy talking about? Little brother? Big brother?

"Are you figuring it out, Solid? Is it clear to you now?"

Snake groaned.

Liquid chuckled. "That's right. You and I are the last surviving sons of Big Boss."

A device on Liquid's belt chirped. He took it off, punched a button, and put it to his ear. "It's me." He listened to the caller and then reacted strongly. It wasn't good news. "What? Really? Then what? Those idiots! All right, Raven. I'll be right there." He hung up the phone and replaced it on his belt. He then addressed the other two, whom Snake recognized as Revolver Ocelot and Sniper Wolf. Ocelot's right hand had been replaced by some kind of mechanical prosthetic. Wolf's sling was gone, and she had changed out of her bloody tunic—Snake figured he hadn't wounded her as badly as he'd thought—but she was still dressed provocatively. "They're not responding to our demands. We'll launch the first one in ten hours as planned."

"Damned Americans!" Wolf spat.

"Looks like you read them wrong," Ocelot added.

Liquid shook his head. "Something's not right. Normally the Americans are the first ones to the negotiating table. They must think they've got something up their sleeves."

"So it's come down to it?" Ocelot asked. "We're gonna launch that nuke and ride it all the way into history?"

The call Liquid had received from Raven had disturbed him. "I've got to go take care of some launch preparations. You're in charge here, Ocelot."

"What about you? Wanna stay for the show?" Ocelot asked Wolf.

"I'm not interested." She started to leave the room but stopped to take a couple of pills from a plastic case in her pocket. She popped them into her mouth and swallowed. "It's time to feed the family."

"So you prefer your wolves to my show, huh?"

"Ocelot," Liquid said, "don't screw up like you did with the chief."

"I know. That was an accident. I didn't think a pencil pusher like him would be so tough."

"Well, his mental defenses were reinforced by hypnotherapy."

"Boss, what about that ninja?"

Liquid made a face that indicated it was one more problem he had to deal with. "He's killed twelve men. Whoever he is, he's some kind of lunatic."

"Bastard took my hand. How could he have gotten in here?"

"Perhaps," Liquid said, glancing back at Snake, "there's a spy among us." He addressed Ocelot and Wolf. "Mantis is dead. We've also got to find out what killed Baker and Octopus. We're shorthanded, so make this little torture show of yours as short as possible."

"Torture?" Ocelot protested. "This is an interrogation!"

"Whatever." Liquid turned back to Snake. "See you later, brother." With that, he left the room in a hurry.

Sniper Wolf also reversed direction and came back to the torture table. She leaned in close to Snake and whispered in his ear, "Your *woman* is still in this world."

A hoarse, scratchy voice emerged from Snake's dry throat. "Meryl . . ."

"Catch you later . . . handsome."

The woman licked Snake's ear, smiled, and then walked out of the room.

Ocelot laughed. "Once she picks a target, she doesn't think about anything else. Sometimes she even falls in love with them before she kills them." He moved closer to Snake. "So. Finally, just the two of us. How are you feeling?"

Snake glared at the gunslinger. "Not bad. I caught a nice nap on this comfortable contraption of yours. Too bad I was sleeping alone."

"Glad to hear that. This is some bed, all right. I'm about to show you some of its nicer features."

"Where are my clothes? My gear?"

"Oh, don't worry. They're all here." Ocelot jerked his head, indicating that they were nearby, perhaps in the next room. "Washington was taking quite a chance sending you here. Someone must have a lot of faith in your skills, huh, carrier boy?"

Snake ignored the taunt. "So Metal Gear is armed with a new type of nuclear warhead, huh?"

"*Tsk, tsk, tsk.* Why don't you ask Campbell for the full story?"

"The colonel?"

"By the way, you got an optical disk from President Baker, didn't you?"

"What if I did?"

"Is that the only disk? There's no other data?"

"What do you mean?"

"There's no copy? If not, that's fine. We don't care."

Ocelot moved back to a control panel that was positioned a few feet away from the torture table.

"Is Meryl okay?" Snake asked.

"She's not dead yet. Wolf must have been feeling generous. The bullets were removed, and she is recovering. But if you want her to stay that way, you better start answering my questions right now. You were holding one card key. Where are the other two? What's the trick behind that key?"

"Trick?"

"That weasel of a president said there's some kind of trick to using the key."

"Hell if I know."

"I see. No problem, then. We're going to play a game, Snake. And we'll find out what kind of man you really are. When the pain becomes too great to bear, just give up and your suffering will end. But if you do, the girl's life is mine. I'm going to run a high-voltage electric current through your body. If it's just for a short time, it won't kill you. Did you know it was the French who first thought of using electrical shocks as a means of torture?"

"That figures. They also like Jerry Lewis."

Ocelot laughed. "You're a tough guy, Snake. But I got some bad news for you. You're no POW. You're a hostage. There's no Geneva Convention here. No one is coming to save you." He laughed some more. "Starting to feel a little scared? Good! You should be. Okay, let's get started."

Snake braced himself. He had undergone various levels of pain in his lifetime, but being rendered helpless and made to withstand pure torture was not something in his realm of experience. Could he stand it? Would he survive? Or would he ultimately submit and surrender?

No. *Surrendering is not an option!*

Revolver Ocelot threw a switch on the control panel. The nozzles on the sides of the table suddenly came to life and discharged bolts of current directed at the belt around Snake's chest. The belt somehow absorbed the electricity and distributed it into his body.

It was as if he had been struck by lightning. Every nerve erupted with a thousand screams. Every muscle exploded in agony. Every cell in his skin, his blood, his organs, and his brain ignited with the heat and intensity of a million suns. All his senses—sight, smell, hearing, taste, touch—shut off and focused on one thing only: extreme and unimaginable *pain*.

And then it stopped as abruptly as it had begun.

It took a moment for Snake to remember where he was. He had been lost in a universe of misery for what seemed like eons, but it had been only a couple of seconds.

"How did you like that?" Ocelot asked. "Fun, huh? It's amazing, isn't it? It transports you to another dimension, and not a very nice one. Perhaps it's hell. Is it hell, Snake? Or are you not sure? Here, let's give you another glimpse into Satan's abode."

He flicked the switch again. This time the shock seemed even more intense. Snake's nerves had been traumatized by the first dose and were now overly sensitive. The collision of electricity and human flesh produced an anguish that Snake never knew was possible.

After a third jolt, Ocelot said, "Now, let's see. What was I supposed to ask you? I think I'm supposed to be interrogating you, but I can't remember what it is we want to know. I don't think it matters. We have the PAL passwords. The key cards would be nice, but they *stop* the launch, so we don't really need them. I guess I'll just have to keep this up until I hear you beg me to stop. Yes, that's what I want, Snake. I want to hear you cry for mercy. I want to hear you say that you surrender and give up. I want to hear you say that the girl is mine to do with whatever I wish!"

And he threw the switch again.

• • •

SNAKE LOST COUNT of how many times Ocelot applied the electricity. It was probably only five or six administrations, but it seemed like a hundred. He was certain that he had lost consciousness for a moment. Now he was aware of the straps on his arms and legs being unbuckled.

"You're a strong man, Snake," Ocelot said. "Well, that's enough for now, I think. The Boss said not to kill you. We'll resume our game after you have a short rest."

Two guards had appeared and were standing at the sides of the table. They caught Snake and kept him from collapsing onto the floor once he had been freed.

Ocelot patted Snake's face. "See you in a little while."

HE PASSED OUT for a few seconds as the troopers escorted him out of the medical room and came to as they threw him onto a cold concrete floor. Snake heard the men leave, shut an iron door, and lock it with a key card.

Weak and sore, he lifted himself into a sitting position with his back against a wall. It was a cell that was equipped with a bunk bed, a toilet, and a sink, just like the one in which he'd found the DARPA chief. The door had a barred window. And over in the corner lay a corpse.

As soon as he saw the dead man, Snake was aware of the stench.

Christ, how long has that guy been dead?

He forced himself to stand and approach the body. Snake was no expert in forensics, but from the look of the cadaver, he'd say that the man had been dead at least three days. His flesh was still intact and soft, but there were a few maggots already crawling in and out of his ears and nose. Even more peculiar was the lack of color. The blood had been drained from the body.

Wait a minute . . . that guy looks familiar . . .

It was DARPA chief Anderson! But how did he get in the cell, and why did he look so . . . *dead*? The man had died only a few hours earlier. He couldn't possibly have decomposed that much so quickly.

Snake retreated to the bunk bed and sat. He wished he could sleep for a month, but that pipe dream was shattered quickly by the more urgent determination to escape. He evaluated his body's condition and made sure there was no external damage; it was his insides that had been scrambled by the electricity. And as he examined his arms and legs, he found that his captors had been careless.

The PAL card key was still in the hidden pocket inside his suit, and he still had his Codec.

Colonel Campbell answered quickly. "Snake! Are you okay?"

"I've been better."

"We've been trying to contact you."

"I've been a little busy."

Dr. Hunter asked, "How's Meryl?"

Snake sighed. "They've got her."

"Damn!" Campbell's deflation and worry were evident in his voice. There was silence for a moment, and then the colonel spoke again, this time all business. "Okay. Snake, the government has decided not to give in to their demands. We're trying to buy some more time."

"Come on, Colonel. Why don't you stop playing dumb? I'm sorry about Meryl, I really am, but I want the lies to end now."

"What are you talking about?"

"Metal Gear was designed to launch a new type of nuclear warhead, wasn't it?" When Campbell didn't answer, Snake knew he was right. "You knew all along, didn't you? Why did you try to hide it?"

"I'm sorry."

"Can't tell the grunts anything, huh? You've sure changed a lot. Does the White House know about this? How deep does it go?"

Campbell answered, "Snake, as far as I know, as of yesterday, the president had not been briefed about the REX project."

"One of those need-to-know-basis things? Is that the idea?"

"These are sensitive times, Snake. Even subcritical nuclear tests are causing quite a stir."

"Plausible deniability, huh?"

"Yes. And tomorrow, the president and his Russian counterpart are scheduled to sign the START-III accord."

"I get it. That's the reason for the deadline."

"That's right, Snake," Dr. Hunter said. "And that's why we can't let this terrorist attack go public."

"We still haven't even ratified START-II or dealt with the issue of TMDs," Campbell continued. "This has to do with the president's reputation and America's place as the dominant superpower."

"So patriotism is your excuse for circumventing the Constitution?"

"Please, Snake. Just stop them."

"Why should I?"

"Because you're the only one who can."

"In that case, tell me the truth about this new type of nuclear warhead."

"I told you before. I don't know the details."

"I don't believe you. If the situation is so serious, why don't you give in to their demands? Let them have Big Boss's remains."

"You see—"

"Or is there some reason that you can't do that? Something you haven't told me about?"

Campbell didn't answer that one. Dr. Hunter butted in and said, "Publicly, the president has been very vocal in his opposition to eugenics experiments. We don't want the media to know about the existence of the genome army."

"And that's the only reason? Huh. The hell with you!"

Campbell said, "I'm sorry, Snake."

Snake sat on the bunk for a long while without saying anything. He felt like removing the Codec and throwing it against the concrete wall.

"Snake? Are you there?" Dr. Hunter asked.

"Yeah."

"Let's try to assess the situation you're in now, okay?"

Snake grunted.

"Where are you? We can see from the nanomachines in your blood that you're back in the first building complex."

"They've got me in a cell. They fried my brains and threw me in here with a corpse. Oh, yeah; the corpse of the DARPA chief is lying right here next to me."

"Anderson?"

"But it's strange. He looks and smells like he's been dead for days. All his blood's been drained, too."

"Drained?" Campbell asked.

Dr. Hunter ventured, "Maybe to slow down decomposition?"

"I have no idea."

"But the DARPA chief died only a few hours ago, right?"

"Right. But he's already throwing a party for maggots."

"What does it mean?"

Snake didn't much care. "Something in his blood they wanted?"

"I doubt it. Just the nanomachines and the transmitter."

Campbell asked, "Anderson told them his detonation code, right?"

"Yeah. It looks like they've got both codes and are nearly ready to launch."

"Is there any way to prevent it?"

"There's some type of emergency override device that can cancel out the detonation code. It's a countermeasure that Arms-Tech installed secretly. You have to unlock it with three special card keys."

"Where are the keys?"

"I've got one of them hidden in my suit. I don't know where the other two are. Besides, I'm locked up here."

"We've got no choice," Campbell said. "Forget about the keys. Your top priority is to destroy Metal Gear itself. I'm sorry to have to lay it all in your lap, but you're all I've got. Bust out of there!"

"Sure, Colonel, no problem!"

"Also . . ."

"What?"

"I know it's asking a lot . . ."

"Meryl, right?"

"Yeah."

"I'll save her."

"Thanks."

Snake heard footsteps approaching. "I've got to go." He signed off as a trooper unlocked and opened the door. Four armed guards entered and gestured for him to stand. One of them was none other than Johnny, the soldier Meryl had clobbered.

"Let's go," he said. "Showtime."

REVOLVER OCELOT was in a talkative mood once again during the second round of torture. While Snake battled the demons from hell on the electrical table, the gunslinger spoke as if his victim were a barroom buddy.

"You're a soldier. You should understand. You and I can't continue to live in a world like this. We need tension . . . conflict. The world today has become too soft. We're living in an age where true feelings are suppressed." He yawned in between throwing the switch the third and fourth times. "So we're going to shake things up a bit. We'll create a world dripping with tension. A world filled with greed and suspicion, bravery and cowardice. You want the same things we do."

Snake answered by screaming.

"Liquid is the one. He's an incredible man, the true successor. He's the man who can really make it happen. Liquid has a close friend high up in the Russian government who's currently the head of the Spetsnaz. He's agreed to purchase this new nuclear weapons system. The Hind was just a down payment. You saw our Hind, didn't you? I will personally receive gratification when the sale is made. I want Russia to be reborn to lead a brave new world order."

Snake grunted unintelligibly.

"I was trained by the Russian GRU, you know. I've fought wars in Afghanistan, Mozambique, Eritrea, and Chad. Among the mujahideen guerrillas, I was known and feared as 'Shalashaska.' But I'm not like one of those KGB slugs. To me, this isn't torture . . . it's a sport."

Snake lost consciousness.

"Oh, dear. Our time is up. I'll see you at our next session."

JOHNNY BANGED ON the cell bars with a metal cup. "You alive in there?"

Snake opened one eye. He lay on the bunk bed, broken and exhausted. He was too sore and shaken to sleep.

I'm wired—*ha ha.*

Johnny banged the cup again. "Hey! I asked you a question! Do I have to come in there?"

"What do you want?" Snake managed to ask.

"Oh, it talks! Pretty soon we can teach it to do tricks!" The guard laughed at his own cleverness and then said, "I'm just supposed to make sure you're still alive. The Boss wants you for another round in a few minutes, so be ready!" He laughed loudly and walked away.

Snake cursed the man under his breath but didn't move. They would have to carry him back into that room. There was no way he was going to walk in there voluntarily, guard or no guard.

"Snake?" It was Naomi Hunter on the Codec.

"Yeah."

"Are you all right?"

"Yeah. Nothing new to report."

"I'm increasing the level of painkillers in your blood. You know, the nanomachines."

"Thanks."

"That should help. Some."

Snake wasn't sure what he felt. His body was one big live wire, on the one hand ultrasensitive to the slightest touch and on the other hand completely numb from the trauma. "Talk to me," he said. "Say something to take my mind off the pain."

"What can I say?"

"Anything."

"I'm . . . I'm not a very good talker."

"Just . . . I don't know. Tell me about yourself."

"Myself? That's a tough one."

He figured he'd have to ask questions to get her to open up. "Any family?"

"Uhm, that's not a happy topic for me."

"Your grandfather worked for Hoover in the FBI."

Dr. Hunter shrugged. "Big deal. He did more as an under-cover agent investigating the Mafia in New York during the post-war years. And you?"

"I don't have any family. Well, there was a man who said he was my father. But he's dead. By my own hand."

Campbell jumped into the conversation. "Big Boss."

"What? *You* killed Big Boss?" Dr. Hunter was genuinely sur-prised. "I had no idea!"

"There was no way you could," the colonel explained. "It happened in Zanzibarland six years ago. Only Snake and I know the real truth of what happened there."

"So it's true, then?" she asked. "Big Boss is really your fa-ther?"

"That's what he said," Snake replied. "That's all I know. I never knew my mother."

"And you were able to kill him even though he was your fa-ther?"

"Yup."

"How?"

"He wanted it. Besides, some people just need killing."

"That's patricide!"

"Yup." Snake sighed. "That's the trauma Psycho Mantis was talking about. The one we share in common."

"Is that why you left FOXHOUND?"

"Let's just say I needed to be alone for a while and Alaska was the perfect place."

There was silence for a moment, and then Dr. Hunter spoke again. "I didn't have a real family, either. Just a big brother who put me through school. We weren't even blood related, and he was much older than me."

"Where is he?"

There was a hint of anger embedded in her sadness. "He's . . . dead."

"I'm sorry."

"Yeah." She paused again and then asked, "Snake, is there a woman in your life?"

"Nah. After you've been through as many wars as I have, it's hard to trust anyone."

"Friends?"

Snake grinned, anticipating the reaction. "Roy Campbell."

The colonel gave a self-deprecating laugh. "Ha! You're still calling me a friend?"

Dr. Hunter asked, "Is that it? Just him?"

"No, there was another . . . Frank Jaegar."

"Really?"

Campbell continued, "He was Big Boss's most trusted lieutenant and the only member of FOXHOUND ever to receive the code name Fox—Gray Fox."

"I actually learned a lot from him," Snake said.

"But . . . but didn't you try to kill each other?" Naomi asked.

"It's true. We did. In Zanzibarland. But it was nothing personal. We were just professionals on opposite sides at the time. During the Outer Heaven operation we were on the same side. That was no longer true when it came to Zanzibarland. That's all."

"And you still call him your friend?"

"Hard to believe? War is no reason to end a friendship."

"That's kinda crazy."

"I first met him on the battlefield. He was being held prisoner by Outer Heaven. But he didn't look like a prisoner to me. He was always so cool and precise. I was still green, and he showed me the ropes."

"Did you know him well?"

"No. We never talked about our personal lives. Sort of an unwritten rule. The next time I saw him on the battlefield, we were enemies. We were fighting bare-handed in a minefield. I know it sounds strange to most people, but we were just two soldiers doing our jobs."

The loathing in her voice was apparent. "Men and their games! You're like wild animals!"

"You're absolutely right, Naomi. We *are* animals."

"So if you were friends, then how do you explain the ninja's behavior?"

"I don't know. His mind is . . . not the same."

"It's your *genes*. They make you predisposed toward violence."

Snake almost chuckled, but it hurt too much. "You really like talking about genes, Naomi. Why did you get into genetic research?"

"Oh, I don't know. I never knew who my parents were or even what they looked like. I guess I studied DNA, genetic structure to . . . you know, I thought maybe I'd find out who I really am. I had a theory that if I could analyze a person's genetic information, I could fill in the blank spots in that person's memory."

"Memory is stored in DNA?"

"We're not sure. But we know that a person's genetic fate is determined just by the sequence of the four bases in their DNA."

"So what about *my* fate?" Snake asked drily. "You know *my* DNA sequence, don't you?"

"Your *fate*?" Dr. Hunter sounded somewhat distressed, perhaps even a little guilty. "I'm sorry . . . I have no idea."

"Of course you don't. You're a scientist, not a fortune-teller."

188 | RAYMOND BENSON

A whispered "Psst!" interrupted the conversation. It came from the barred window in the door. Snake eyed it but didn't see anything.

"Snake! It's me, Otacon!"

He deactivated his stealth control and appeared outside the cell. Snake suddenly felt energized. He shut off the Codec transmission, leaped off the bed, and moved to the door. "Boy, am I glad to see you!"

"It took me a while to find you," Otacon said. "I knew they'd captured you, but I ran into some trouble of my own. There's this woman who's part of the terrorist team, and she has all these *dogs*—"

Snake reached through the bars and grabbed the programmer's lab coat by the lapels. "Never mind that! Get me out of here!"

"Hey, lemme go!"

"Hurry up!"

"Whoa, take it easy!" He broke away from Snake's grasp. "Geez, is that how you ask a guy a favor? Come on!"

"Sorry. I just . . . I gotta get out of here."

Otacon stepped forward again and looked through the bars. "Yuck, it's like an animal's cage. It stinks!"

Snake moved out of the way so that his friend could see. "It's because of him."

"*Eeeyaah!* It's the DARPA chief!"

"If you don't hurry and find a way to get me out of here, I'll be lying right next to him."

"Those bastards!" He examined the lock on the door. "This won't open with a security card. You need a key like the soldiers carry. But here." He handed a PAN card to Snake through the bars. "It's a Level Six. It'll get you out of that medical room where they're questioning you."

"Thanks, but I wouldn't say they're *questioning* me exactly."

"Are you all right?"

"I'll live. Is that idiot guard out there?"

"Johnny? He used to be the head computer technician here at Shadow Moses. I guess the terrorists brainwashed him or something to work for them."

"Is he *out* there?"

"I saw him go into the bathroom. That's when I moved past his station and got in here. I think he's got the runs. He's holding his stomach and—"

"I don't give a damn if he's having his gallbladder removed! Find a way to get me out!"

"Okay, gee." Otacon scratched his head. "Let me think." He removed a brightly colored handkerchief from his lab coat and wiped his forehead. Snake thought it was decidedly feminine.

"Where did you get that?"

"Oh, it belongs to Sniper Wolf."

"Why do you have it?"

"She gave it to me. I don't know why, but she's nice to me."

Snake studied him and then asked, "You know what Stockholm syndrome is?"

Otacon became defensive. "You don't understand. See, I used to take care of the dogs here. But then, after the terrorists took over, they were going to *shoot* all the dogs. But Sniper Wolf stopped 'em. She likes dogs. She told me I could keep taking care of the animals. She must be a good person. Don't hurt *her*, okay?"

"Wake up, you fool! She's the one who shot Meryl!"

"She did?"

"Yes! She's as bad as they come! *Hitler* liked dogs, too!"

Otacon's face betrayed his puzzlement.

"They're planning to launch a nuke! I've got to stop them!"

"Then you'll have to take out the guard. Johnny's got a key."

Snake nodded at the handkerchief. "Give me that."

"What?"

"Give me the damn handkerchief! I've got an idea."

Otacon reluctantly handed it over. Once the cloth was in his hands, Snake could smell Wolf's distinctive scent on it.

"Oh, jeez . . . he's coming back! See ya later!" The programmer flipped the switch on his coat, and the stealth feature kicked in. At that moment, Johnny strutted into the outer cell area. He belched loudly, shook his head, and approached the door.

"Something in that food . . ." Johnny mumbled. He clanged on the bars with the metal cup. "Okay, bud, it's showtime again. Places for act three!"

But Snake wasn't on the bed. In fact, he wasn't anywhere, but there was a brightly colored handkerchief lying on the cell floor in the middle of the room. What the hell was that?

Johnny grumbled and unlocked the door with his card key. He pulled a FAMAS from around his shoulder, readied it, and then opened the door.

It was true—Snake wasn't in the room.

Baffled beyond belief, Johnny slowly stepped into the cell. The DARPA chief was still there. But where was the other prisoner?

That handkerchief. It's a clue, the guard thought. He moved to the middle of the room and stooped to pick it up.

That was when the prisoner dropped from the sky and knocked Johnny out of the ballpark.

Snake had been using isometrics to wedge himself in the corner formed by the ceiling and two of the walls. It was a simple thing to do, provided that one had the strength to maintain the position for several seconds. He relieved Johnny of his weapon, took the key card, and left the cell.

"Otacon?"

There was no answer. Snake figured he'd slipped out when Johnny came in. Snake left the outer area, gazed quickly up and down the hall, and opened the medical room door with the Level 6 card. With the FAMAS ready to blast away anything that moved, Snake entered the horrid place, but it was empty.

He had a good mind to empty the FAMAS's magazine into Ocelot's torture table and power source. But it was best, of course, to keep quiet and get the hell out of there unnoticed. Snake found his belongings on a table, and surprisingly, everything was there: the SOCOM and ammunition, his utility belt, the pouch containing what was left of his grenade supply, and his cigarettes. He quickly equipped himself and then lit up.

The rancid commercial tobacco actually tasted good this time. And he didn't cough.

Things are definitely looking up . . . !

17

SNAKE LEFT THE medical room and found himself in familiar surroundings. He was in the First Basement of the original building, near the prison cells where he had seen Anderson and Meryl. He decided to search the outer area, where Johnny's office was located; maybe he could find some SOCOM ammunition and more grenades. Snake fitted the sound suppressor onto the handgun and edged around the corner to look. A lone guard sat at a desk, reading a newspaper.

The kid gloves were off now. No fooling around.

Snake shot the man in the head. He then aimed the SOCOM at the brand-new security camera that someone had installed during the last couple of hours and blew it to bits. He moved into the room and found the cell where Anderson had been. Using Johnny's cell door key, he swiped it in the lock and opened it.

What the hell . . . ?

Anderson's corpse was still lying on the floor where he'd had a heart attack and died. He still looked fresh, too.

Then who was the other guy . . . ?

He didn't have time to ponder the mystery. Snake left the cell and went straight to Johnny's office. He shot the lock off a steel cabinet, opened the doors, and found what he was looking for: plenty of ammunition for both the SOCOM and the PSG-1; some frag, stun, and chaff grenades; C4 explosive; and a splendid commando knife that looked like it was a Fairbairn-Sykes, U.S. Marine issue. Snake took as much as he could carry, made sure the weapons were fully loaded, and then strapped the knife's sheath to his right calf.

He was curious about a large flat box on one of the cabinet shelves. He pulled it out, set it on Johnny's desk, and opened it. He almost laughed aloud.

You don't find many of these in Cracker Jack boxes!

It was what they called a tank torso: a Kevlar-coated M1-11 combat vest. In other words, body armor.

He pulled it out of the box and was surprised by its light weight. Nevertheless, he put it on and strapped it tight. It wouldn't stop a Nikita rocket shell, but it might protect him from a bullet or two. Couldn't hurt to keep it.

"Snake?"

He glanced at the Codec. It was Master Miller's frequency. "Hey," he answered.

"I heard you had a little trouble."

"Nothing a good massage and a bottle of vodka wouldn't cure."

"You know, I was tortured in 'Nam. The Vietcong were vicious little bastards. But I had the satisfaction of blowing the brains out of the chief interrogator when I escaped."

"I plan on doing the same thing to Revolver Ocelot. What's up?"

"Snake, I need you to change brands. Those cigarettes you like are going out of style."

Snake understood. That was code that meant he should switch to a secure frequency.

"Do you have a suggestion?" Snake asked him.

"I like the ones with the gold band, twenty-three percent nicotine and seven percent tar."

"I'll keep that in mind. Thanks." He signed off and configured the Codec to receive messages from the frequency 23.7, which was unusual since Codec frequencies normally began with the number 1.

Master Miller's voice returned a few seconds later. "You there, Snake?"

"I'm here."

"I didn't want the colonel or anyone else hearing this."

"What?"

"I've heard some very disturbing chatter in the intelligence community."

"What do you mean?"

"I think you should be very wary of your internal contacts, and that includes our friend Roy and that doctor. Even the secretary of defense."

"Houseman?"

"I know it's hard to believe, but there's a traitor in your midst. Watch your back."

"Wait. How do you know that?"

But Miller already had signed off. Snake grumbled and tuned the Codec back to receive his normal channels.

"Colonel?"

"Yes, Snake?" Campbell sounded tired.

"I'm on my way back to the communication tower. I've got a long way to go."

"We know. Mei Ling, what kind of intel do you have on enemy activity between Snake's position and the comm tower?"

The woman reported, "We're still having satellite interference because of the storm, and the underground shielding doesn't help. But I think you can bet that most of the genome soldiers are now located in the other buildings, closer to the two towers and the building north of that—the underground maintenance base."

"Nevertheless, exercise extreme caution, Snake."

"I always do, Colonel. Thanks, Mei Ling."

He signed off and made his way to the Tank Hangar, where he first had seen the Abrams he had destroyed. The huge room was devoid of humans, and it seemed that all the power was off; not only that, the cargo door was still open. The wind had blown snowdrifts several yards into the hangar.

Mei Ling was right. They were all in the other buildings. Except for the lone guard in the cell area, the terrorists had abandoned this facility. But what had happened to Revolver Ocelot? Surely he was still around somewhere. The bastard hadn't finished with the torture sessions. Knowing him, the one-handed sadist would have kept it up for days until Snake had broken. Then they would have killed him.

It was too easy . . .

It was as if the terrorists *wanted* him to escape.

Fine, he thought. *I'll play into their hands.*

He'd trudge through the snow-covered canyon back to the Nuke Building. If they had a reception waiting for him there, he'd be ready for it.

THE BLIZZARD HAD let up. It was still snowing in the canyon, but it was the kind of slow-falling snow that reminded Snake of one of those decorative glass globes that one shook to make the "snow" fall. The sky above had a dull, dark blue tint to it, but the

stars were visible through the clouds. It was a beautiful yet un-
nerving effect, similar to those odd times when it rained while
the sun shone.

Snake checked the location of the Claymore mines with the
detector and noted that they were still there. He skirted them
and hugged the icy rock wall as he headed for the structure at
the other end of the chasm. The Abrams tank sat in a heap
where it had been hit, blackened and charred from the explosion. The dead gunners had been covered completely by the
snow, buried in cold, lonely graves.

The loading door to the Nuke Building was wide open.
Again, Snake had the uneasy feeling that they *wanted* him to
continue his mission. He kept to the edge of the wide doorway,
peered inside, and saw three NBC troopers carrying items from
one side of the storage facility to the cargo carrier that still sat on
the ramp. Snake couldn't imagine how the truck was going to
move anywhere with the snow so deep. Perhaps they were simply loading it to be ready sometime in the near future.

He crept up the incline, removed a stun grenade from his
pouch, pulled the pin, and tossed it at the truck. The bright
flash lit the warehouse with searing intensity as the three men
hollered in surprise. Two went down for the count, but the third
stumbled blindly away from the truck. He pulled the FAMAS
from his shoulder and began to shoot indiscriminately in
Snake's direction. Snake hit the floor and crawled forward on
his belly until he had a good angle and then took the man out
with one shot from the SOCOM.

It was a quick elevator ride to the First Basement level. The
floor was quiet and empty, too. Snake wondered how many people the Shadow Moses facility employed. Where were all the civilian hostages? Had they all become brainwashed slaves of the
terrorists? Or were they all lying dead somewhere, a pile of corpses
resembling the horrid death pits in Nazi concentration camps?

Psycho Mantis's body lay on the floor of the Commander's Room, exactly where he had fallen.

They don't care much for collecting their wounded or dead, do they?

Snake experienced a fleeting moment of remembrance as he made his way to the secret passage. The image of Meryl holding a gun to her head, ready to blow out her brains, was not something he was likely to forget soon.

The cavern passages were as damp and cold as before, but the wolf-dogs no longer howled. The animals probably were sleeping, although Snake had no concept of what time it might be. It was the type of mission in which he merely kept track of how many hours had elapsed since his arrival and how long until the deadline. Day and night were immaterial. Snake figured it had been at least twelve hours since he had climbed onto the Shadow Moses dock from the sea.

He emerged from the cave into the underground passage leading to the tower base. A blood patch remained on the spot where Meryl had been shot. The sights and sounds of those terrible moments came flooding back to Snake. He wished he had made her stay behind. If only she had listened to him, if only he hadn't let her talk him into allowing her to accompany him. If only, if only . . .

"There is no such thing as 'if only' or 'but' in this business!" It was another of Master Miller's philosophical axioms.

Before moving closer to the tower, Snake swung the sniper rifle off his shoulder, looked through the scope, and spotted two troopers patrolling the second-floor balcony from which Sniper Wolf had taken potshots at him. The two men symmetrically marched back and forth, coming together in the middle of the balcony and then moving to opposite ends before turning and repeating the pattern in reverse.

Snake centered the crosshairs on one man's head and

steadily followed him as he approached his colleague. As soon as the two men were side by side, Snake fired. The round entered the temple of the man closest to Snake, exited, and then penetrated the second man's temple. Blood and gray matter from both soldiers spattered onto the tower wall.

Two birds with one shot.

Snake was particularly cautious when he approached the tower base. He didn't want a repeat of what had happened the last time. But no soldiers fast-roped from above, and there was no opposition awaiting him. The door from which Sniper Wolf had emerged was shut and required a Level 6 PAN card to open. Snake swiped the card Otacon had given him, and the panel slid to the side, revealing a dimly lit corridor. He edged around the opening, immediately saw a security camera mounted on the far wall, and blasted it with his SOCOM.

"Snake!"

It was that guy again. Deepthroat.

"Snake! Are you there?"

"Yeah."

"The tower is crawling with guards. Be careful."

"I don't see any yet."

"They're all on the inside. I suggest taking the stairs to the roof and then crossing the sky bridge to the second tower."

"How do you know all this? *Who are you?*"

"Oh, and there's a gun camera just inside the first-floor stairwell. You'll have to take it out as soon as you open the door."

"Thanks."

"One other thing. If you make it into the second tower, go to the third floor. There's a portable Stinger missile launcher in the conference room there. The terrorists were inspecting it earlier, and I'm pretty sure they left it in the room."

"Why would I want to carry around a Stinger missile launcher?"

"It might come in handy."

"Look, Deepthroat or whatever your name really is, I have to rely on stealth to get around. A missile launcher is heavy and cumbersome."

"It was just a suggestion. By the way, have you looked inside your pouch for anything that doesn't belong?"

"What are you talking about?"

"It might be a good idea."

"Are we ever gonna meet face-to-face?" Snake asked.

"I don't know. Perhaps. Maybe we already have."

The transmission broke off. Snake cursed to himself and grudgingly looked inside the pouch. There were grenades, the C4 device, a couple of boxes of ammunition, his rations, and . . . something else. It was the size of a grenade, but it was something he'd never seen. It was definitely electronic, for a tiny LED indicator blinked down in seconds.

He had been carrying a goddamn *bomb*!

Snake tossed it back into the passage and ducked. The thing exploded with the strength of two sticks of dynamite. Snake held his position for several seconds and listened for any evidence of nearby guards.

How did Deepthroat know?

Snake breathed a sigh of relief and continued to the end of the hallway. There was a coiled rope hanging on the wall. He didn't know why, but he had an inclination to take it. If he was going to climb twenty-something flights of stairs, a rope just might be useful. He grabbed it and put the coil around his neck. Now he *really* felt like a mule with both the rope and the sniper rifle hanging from his shoulders.

Snake readied the SOCOM, stood to the side of the stairwell door, and opened it. The gun camera—a surveillance device with a weapon attached to it—had turned automatically toward the open door, ready to register whether the person entering the stairwell was friend or foe. Snake reached around with one hand and, without looking, fired at the mechanism. It was disabled with finality. Snake then entered the stairwell, closed the door behind him, and proceeded in a vertical direction. It was going to be a long climb. He was reminded of his days at boot camp, when he had to carry heavy loads up and down a hill to build his stamina. Here he was again, encumbered with a sniper rifle, a rope, a handgun, a knife, a pouch full of explosives and ammunition, and body armor.

At least he felt invincible.

As soon as he got to the fifth-floor landing, an alarm sounded throughout the building. Snake figured his destruction of the gun camera had triggered it, or perhaps they'd found the two dead troopers on the second-floor balcony. Whatever the reason, he knew he was about to have company. Snake drew the SOCOM, made sure it had a full magazine, and continued the ascent.

The seventh-floor stairwell door burst open, and two troopers appeared on the landing. Before they had time to register Snake's presence, the operative had shot them both. One man careened over the stair rail and fell several stories before colliding with a flight of steps.

Snake was well aware that he had been doing an awful lot of killing since escaping from the cell. For a brief moment, he wondered if he might be overreacting to being tortured and Meryl being hurt.

No, that's not it, he told himself. Time is running out. The stakes are higher. I have good reason to resort to extreme methods.

Snake increased the speed of his climb, jumped over the remaining corpse, and pushed onward to the eighth floor. By the time he reached the twentieth floor, he was out of breath and his legs were aching. Keeping in mind that there were only seven more levels, he forced himself to press on. But on the twenty-second floor, he encountered three more guards. They spotted him, shouted, and aimed their FAMAS rifles at him. The bullets chipped off pieces of concrete from the wall behind Snake. The operative dived for the landing below him, removed a stun grenade from the pouch, pulled the pin, and tossed it onto the stairs just as the troopers descended toward him.

The blast demolished several steps, and the guards fell through the hole, plummeted a story, and rolled down several more flights. When they eventually stopped moving, it was obvious from their inelegant body positions that their necks or backs were broken.

Snake got up and navigated his way around the huge hole in the staircase, careful not to step on insecure pieces of concrete. By hugging the wall and edging around the hole, he was just able to do so. He stopped on the twenty-first floor's landing to drink from his canteen and eat one of the ration bars he kept in the pouch. He hadn't realized how hungry he was until then, but he knew he had to conserve the food.

When he reached the roof, he was met with blistering cold high winds. There were no guards outside, thank goodness, and it appeared that Snake had a clear path to the other tower via the bridge. Dominating the roof of the second tower was a gigantic satellite dish, the complex's communications relay system. That, along with the view of the landscape, was spectacular. Looking behind him toward the sea, Snake could see the roof of the original building in the distance, the canyon separating it from the Nuke Building, and the snow-covered ground that blanketed the passage to the tower base. He had come a long way.

Snake proceeded to move across the icy skywalk but stopped when he heard the sound of approaching rotor blades.

Oh, my God . . . !

The Hind-D rose from behind the roof of the second tower

and unleashed half a dozen 57-mm unguided rockets at the satellite dish, causing a magnificent explosion that knocked Snake from his feet. He covered his head and shielded his eyes as the entire tower shook. Daring to peek through his arms, he watched the dish topple onto the bridge connecting the towers, smashing it to pieces.

His only route to the second tower had been destroyed.

A cackle came from the Hind-D's loudspeaker system. "That road is closed, Solid! Detour! Detour!"

Liquid Snake. The villain was piloting the attack chopper again.

The helicopter swung over to the first tower, placing Snake in an extremely vulnerable position. The operative got to his feet and ran back to the stairwell entrance, but Liquid let loose a Phalanga-P radio-guided antitank missile and destroyed the only possible escape route from the roof.

When the smoke cleared, Snake found himself lying on the concrete, covered by debris. Again he heard the maniacal laughing coming from the chopper's loudspeaker. Snake felt the helicopter hover above him and knew he was a sitting duck. He rolled onto his back and fired the SOCOM at the Hind-D, knowing full well it was akin to trying to kill a rhinoceros with a rubber band.

More laughter from Liquid. "You've got to be kidding, brother! Your puny weapons are no match for one of Russia's best pieces of warfare technology!"

Snake had the foresight to get to his feet and run just as Liquid fired the chopper's machine guns at the roof. The bullets followed Snake to the edge of the tower, cornering him. There was no other way off the tower—except down.

The rope!

Snake tied an end to a girder, threw the other end over the side of the tower, and immediately began a long, difficult rappel down the building. It was something he was adept at doing, but he'd never had to rappel from a height of twenty-seven stories and avoid gunfire from a Hind-D at the same time!

He got to what he thought was the eighteenth or nineteenth floor when the Hind swirled around the tower and pointed its nose at him.

"Look at that fly on the wall!" Liquid taunted. "I just *love* swatting flies!"

Another barrage of machine-gun fire made a line of holes just below Snake's feet. He stopped rappelling and waited until the attack ended and then continued the descent. Liquid was playing with him. The pilot could shoot him down easily enough, but it appeared that the terrorist leader just wanted to scare the crap out of him.

Snake reached a ledge halfway down the tower and stopped to rest. He landed on his feet and crouched there as the helicopter came around the tower to shoot again. As the chopper appeared, Snake lay prone on the ledge to avoid the gunfire, but this time Liquid fired another rocket directly at the side of the ledge. The building rocked as the platform exploded into bits, flinging Snake into the air. If he hadn't been clutching the rope, he'd have fallen to his death.

The rope broke his rapid descent, but the impact jerked the life out of his arms. He screamed aloud at the pain but refused to let go. Miraculously, the rope had not been split by the blast. He hung there for what seemed like an eternity, swinging like a pendulum as the Hind circled the tower again.

Move, damn it! Move your ass!

He forced himself to continue the rappel. Hand over hand, a few feet at a time, lower and lower . . . He would make it . . . He *had* to make it . . . It was that or die there!

Liquid's laugh filled the air as the chopper buzzed around the building's edge. The machine-gun bullets dotted the build-

204 | RAYMOND BENSON

ing around Snake, but not one of them touched him. This convinced him that Liquid didn't really want to kill him . . . yet. And that would be the terrorist leader's mistake. Snake wasn't going to let the guy have another chance if he could help it.

Snake was six floors above the ground when the helicopter appeared again. This time Liquid indiscriminately shot rockets at various areas on the tower, creating fireballs that expanded from the building like small suns. The intense heat seared the exposed skin on Snake's face and arms, but he maintained his grip on the rope.

Lower . . . lower . . . not much farther . . . !

He touched the snow on the ground before he realized he'd made it. He dropped and fell into the blessed cold stuff, picked up a handful and rubbed it on his face, and thanked his lucky stars. The snow felt like heaven on his burned skin.

But Liquid hadn't given up. The Hind hovered lower and aimed at the spot where Snake lay.

"Try to get to the second tower, brother! Go ahead! Give it your best shot!" the terrorist mocked.

Just to spite the guy, Snake pulled himself to his feet, made sure he had all his stuff, and ran for the second tower base.

Two Phalanga-P missiles soared out of the chopper and created a hell on earth in front of Snake. He leaped for cover and buried himself in the snow as a wave of fire and brick thundered over him. There was a tremendous rumbling as the ground shook. Debris fell on top of him, and he braced himself for the weight of something heavy and deadly. But it never came. The tremor dissipated until there was only a crackling noise that filled the air.

Snake lifted his head out of the snow and saw that much of the lower two floors of the second tower was in ruins and on fire. Whatever was holding up the building must have been awfully strong, for the tower remained standing. Nevertheless, Liquid had presented a new problem for Snake: how to get through the tower to the other side so that he could get to the underground maintenance base, where Metal Gear was housed.

The helicopter had disappeared. Perhaps Liquid had decided to end his game of cat and mouse for the time being.

Snake made his way around the burning rubble and found a route inside the wreckage. The stairwell was unharmed, but the main entrance and lower floors were impossible to traverse. He would have to climb the stairs *again*.

There was no gun camera awaiting him this time. He ran quickly to the third-floor landing, which was just above the blaze, and carefully opened the door. There were screams coming from somewhere on the level, but they were far away. Snake wasn't too concerned about them, and so he slipped into the hallway and looked for the conference room. Sure enough, he found it after a couple of jogs in the corridor. He listened at the door and heard nothing, and so he threw caution to the wind and went inside.

Just as Deepthroat had said, a Stinger missile launcher lay on the table, already armed with a missile. Its open case was on the floor.

Snake grinned and contacted Nastasha.

"Hey, I got me a Stinger. I just wanted to brag."

"Congratulations, Snake. I hope it's not too cumbersome for you. It utilizes a two-color infrared ultraviolet detector with fire-and-forget technology, correct?"

"Looks like it. I trained with one very similar."

"Then I assume you need no instruction in how to use it."

"No, ma'am. But thanks for asking."

Nastasha laughed. "*Da*, no problem."

After signing off, Snake picked up the launcher and decided that it wasn't much more cumbersome than the Nikita had been.

Now he knew how to get rid of the Hind.

Snake made his way back to the stairwell and continued the ascent to the second tower's roof. He knew it was a dangerous venture; there was no telling if the fire below eventually would weaken the supports that held up the building. The images of what had happened to the World Trade Center towers on 9/11 flashed through his mind, and he hoped that the fires would not be that intense. Those towers had been undone by the tons of burning fuel from the airplanes that had crashed into them, and that was not the case here. He felt relatively secure.

Nearly fifteen minutes later, he arrived on the twenty-seventh floor, once again out of breath and feeling the strain in his leg muscles. He stopped to rest for a minute, drink some more water, and eat another energy bar.

There was the sound of footsteps to his right.

Snake drew the SOCOM with lightning-fast speed.

"Don't shoot! It's me! Don't shoot!"

But Snake didn't see anything.

"Snake, it's me!" Otacon deactivated the stealth control and appeared, standing a few feet away.

"Otacon!" Snake lowered the gun and thrust it into the holster. "How did you get here?"

"The elevator!"

"But the first floor was destroyed."

"That's why I took the elevator."

"It's *working*?"

"Uh-huh. Gosh, you're incredible! Like a movie hero or something."

Snake relaxed and leaned against the wall. The fatigue was catching up to him. "No, you're wrong. In the movies, the hero always saves the girl."

"Oh. You mean Meryl? Sorry. Uhm, forget I said anything."

Dr. Emmerich opened the stairwell door and looked down. "No one followed you. I think you can relax."

Snake didn't say anything.

"Listen, there's something I want to ask you," Otacon said. "It's why I followed you up this far."

"What."

"Have you ever . . . loved someone?"

"*That's* what you came to ask?"

"No, I mean . . . I was . . . I was wondering if even soldiers fall in love."

The guy was a bigger nerd than he'd originally thought. "What the hell are you trying to say?"

"Do you think love can bloom on a battlefield?"

"That's really a stupid question, Otacon, but to give you an answer, yeah, I do. I think at any time, any place . . . people can fall in love with each other. But if you love someone, you have to be able to protect them."

Otacon nodded happily. "I think so, too!"

Snake rolled his eyes and moved toward the elevator. He pushed the button, but the lift was stuck on one of the lower floors. "I thought you said this was working."

"That's weird. It was working before." Otacon took over pushing the button, but nothing happened. "I'll go down and see. Leave it to me. I can fix it."

"Get it working for me, will you?" Snake gazed toward the roof. "Now *I* have to go and swat a fly."

"Okay. I'll hold down the fort. Good luck. Oh, there's something I forgot to tell you."

"What."

"There were five stealth camouflage prototypes in my lab. You know, where I got the one I'm wearing."

"Yeah, so?"

"If you take out the one I have, that leaves four."

"This isn't first-grade math class, Otacon. What's your point?"

"I thought I'd get one for you, so I went back to the lab and . . . well, the four suits were missing. Just thought you'd want to know that."

Snake frowned and eyed his new friend who looked as if he'd been through the wringer and had emerged only half-intact. "You really look like hell. You okay?"

"Don't worry. I just turn the switch and it doesn't matter. I just pretend like I'm not here. Then I'm not scared." He flicked on the stealth control and vanished.

Snake shook his head. "Strange logic. I'm counting on you. See you later." He then strode to the stairwell, went inside, and climbed the last flight of stairs to the roof. Once again a blast of cold wind struck him in the face. The roof was a mishmash of burned rubble from the earlier destruction of the satellite dish. Black smoke from the burning lower floors filtered up into the sky, creating an ominous backdrop for the battle that was about to occur.

"All right, you bastard," Snake muttered. "Show yourself."

As if on cue, the *chop-chop* sound of the rotor blades grew louder until the giant insect-like Hind-D rose over the side of the roof.

"So, the snake has finally come up out of his hole," the loud-speaker boomed over the noise of the chopper. "Are you ready now, brother?"

"Why are you calling me brother?" Snake shouted. "Who the hell are you?"

"I'm you! I'm your shadow!"

"What?"

"Ask father! I'll send you to hell to meet him!" With that, two S-5's shot out of the pods toward the spot where Snake was standing. The operative ran sideways and leaped onto the ice that covered the roof. Like a baseball player sliding into home plate, Snake held the Stinger launcher against his chest and glided on his back across the only unobstructed strip of surface. The deafening explosion behind him jolted the building, and for a moment he was afraid the roof might cave in. He stopped himself from sliding off the edge of the building by slamming his legs against a large piece of rubble that once had been part of the dish. Then, using the wreckage as cover, Snake crouched and readied the Stinger launcher. He rested the launching tube on his shoulder, focused the sights on the Hind, and switched on the guidance system.

Liquid Snake must have seen what his enemy was about to do, for he pulled back on the chopper's joystick to elevate the aircraft. But the missile launcher was made to follow the target; the missile was locked on to it.

"Who's going to hell now, Liquid?" Snake said as he pulled the trigger.

The heat-sensitive Stinger burst out of the launcher, giving Snake a satisfying kick. Even as the Hind rose higher, the missile stayed on track until it plunged into the bottom of the aircraft.

It took only a couple of seconds, and it was better than the Fourth of July.

The back end of the Hind disintegrated into a fireball, sending pieces of metal and burning debris in all directions. The blazing hulk wavered in midair as if it were trying to decide what to do, and then it buckled and began spiraling to the earth. A trail of flaming junk followed it down.

"That takes care of the cremation," Snake said.

He went back to the stairwell—the door had been blown by Liquid's rockets—and stepped inside. He punched Emmerich's frequency on the Codec.

"Otacon?"

"Hey, Snake! I saw the whole thing from a window! That was fantastic!"

"I'm glad you liked it."

"But Snake, I think I saw something come out of the cockpit. Looked like a person."

"You mean he ejected?"

"I couldn't tell for sure. Maybe."

"Damn. Then it ain't over."

"Well, come on down. The elevator's working."

"You fixed it?"

"No, that's the weird thing. It just moved by itself. It's headed your way now."

"So I can get to where Metal Gear's being stored from the bottom of this building?"

"Yeah. The entrance to the underground maintenance base is toward the back of the snowfield behind the tower. Just remember to take the elevator to the third floor, because below that it's an inferno! You'll have to take the stairs from the third floor down to the ground."

"Okay. Find a safe place to hide."

"Right. The elevator should be at the top by now."

"Thanks. Out."

"Out."

Snake descended to the twenty-seventh floor and pushed the elevator button. The doors opened, and sure enough, the empty car was there. He stepped inside and pressed the number 3.

But he wasn't alone.

18

As the elevator began to move, Snake's uncanny sixth sense
kicked in. Perhaps it was that inexplicable nagging feeling that
someone was nearby. Or maybe it was the fact that the elevator
seemed heavier than it looked. But the biggest giveaway was
most likely the diminutive, subtle sound of breathing that wasn't
Snake's.

He went for the holstered SOCOM, but it was too late. Several invisible hands grabbed his arms and shoved him to the
back of the elevator car. Then a powerful fist slugged him hard
in the stomach, but the Kevlar body vest absorbed the blow.

"YAAAOOOOWWWW!" cried the unseen foe. Whoever it
was, the bones in his right hand were broken.

It was clear now. The four missing stealth camouflage suits.
They were in the elevator with him. Worn by four Space Seal
guards.

Snake broke away from the soldiers' grip and lashed out
blindly, attempting to gauge where in the car the four men
might be standing. He kicked and punched with the speed of a

whirling dervish, but the closeness of the car was a significant hindrance. There was simply no room to maneuver with the kind of agility he would have liked to display. Nevertheless, his fists and feet struck solid human body parts, although Snake wasn't sure what he was hitting. In contrast, the soldiers knew exactly where their fists were landing; after all, they could *see* him.

Snake tried something different to break the monotony of the brawl by applying a twirling technique that Master Miller had taught him. It utilized the same principle that an ice skater employed when performing a spin on point. This required a command of balance and the ability to stay on the toes of one foot while slugging large, heavy objects with outstretched arms. The faster one could spin, the more effective the maneuver was.

It seemed to work, for Snake felt fewer blows connecting with him and heard his opponents slam against the walls of the car. Then one of them crashed against the elevator control panel, causing the car to lurch and stop between floors. It also extinguished the lights.

That evens up the odds, Snake thought. He couldn't see them, but they also couldn't see *him.*

Snake concentrated on imagining the shape and form of the four men, mentally drawing their pictures in the darkness in front of him. He could see in his mind's eye their height, weight, and bulk. It was an instinct he had honed with experience, something that had saved his life more times than he could recall. And for some odd reason, it was easier to do in the dark than it had been earlier, when the lights were on.

A face must be *there,* so he hit it! The guard cried out in surprise and went down.

This man's stomach was *there,* and a roundhouse kick forced the guy to double over, allowing Snake to clobber him on the back of the head. He was down, too.

The third guard was to Snake's left. The operative visualized the man's neck and spear-handed it, bursting the Adam's apple. The soldier cried in pain and fell to the floor, unable to breathe. He was dead within a minute.

That left the fourth man, the one with the broken hand.

"Where are you?" Snake asked.

The whimpering came from the corner of the elevator. The guard was huddled there, trying his best to remain silent.

Snake's foot lashed out and connected with the man's nose. The whimpering ceased.

Snake flicked on his penlight and examined the control panel. It was completely busted. The only thing he could do was pry open the doors with his fingers. They were heavy, but he got them to part enough so that he could slip out and onto the floor, which was three feet above the bottom of the elevator.

At least the lights on this floor were on. The number 8 was printed on the wall. That wasn't too bad. At least he didn't have to descend a zillion flights of stairs to get to the bottom.

He followed the corridor to the stairwell.

BLIZZARD CONDITIONS HAD returned to the outdoors.

A vast snowfield lay between the second communication tower's base and a building to the north. Pine trees dotted the landscape, but visibility was at an all-time low. With the wind howling and the night sky covered with dark clouds, it was an effort for Snake to see anything at all. He decided to step back inside the tower structure and enjoy a smoke before venturing further. After lighting one of the awful cigarettes he had filched, Snake dug the standard-issue Mode B night vision goggles out of his pouch. He wished he'd had them on in the darkened elevator.

As he inhaled the foul-tasting but refreshing smoke, Snake

thought about the events of the last several hours and wondered how much more there was to go before he was finished with the blasted mission. He appreciated the importance of succeeding— he didn't want the FOXHOUND terrorists to launch a nuke any more than the suits in Washington did—but he also had mixed feelings about the way everything had been handled. Master Miller's warning played heavily on his mind. If there was a traitor in their midst, who was it? Colonel Campbell obviously had withheld vital information from him, and that was unlike his old friend. But Snake found it difficult to believe that Campbell could do something unethical. Dr. Hunter was an enigma. Snake hadn't known her before the mission. Was it possible that she was against them? Mei Ling seemed harmless enough, but who knew? Then there was the Russian nuke expert, Romanenko, who had more smarts than a Mensa debate team. And what about Emmerich, the hapless but affable fellow known as Otacon? What was his story? Could Snake really depend on him?

And then there was Meryl, the woman he had let down. The question wasn't whether he could trust *her*; it was more like, would she ever again be able to trust *him*? That is, if he found her . . . alive.

Snake stubbed out the cigarette butt and stepped into the freezing cold. Dr. Hunter's injection apparently was still working. He barely felt the temperature, but the wind was sharp and the air was simply wet.

The goggles improved the visibility a great deal. If it wasn't for the thick snowfall, he'd be able to see all the way across the field to the building. But something caught his eye to the left, on a line of pine trees. It was white and was blowing in the wind. Snake plodded through the snow toward the trees to get a closer look. When he was thirty feet away, he recognized it for what it was.

An opened parachute, hanging in the branches.

Could it have belonged to Liquid? Had Otacon been correct about seeing something eject from the burning Hind-D?

Snake couldn't worry about it. He had to move on. The clock was ticking.

He trudged toward the maintenance building, when a shot rang out and a single bullet missed his foot by an inch. Snake leaped to the side and crawled behind a tree. Another shot, and pieces of bark violently scattered in all directions.

There's only one person who can shoot like that . . .

But he couldn't see a soul.

"Snake?"

He looked at the Codec and accepted Otacon's transmission. "What?"

"Are you okay?" Emmerich asked.

"Otacon! Were there any other stealth prototypes?"

"No. Only five."

"So . . . this isn't stealth camouflage, then . . ."

"What are you talking about?"

"Someone's shooting at me. In the middle of this blizzard."

"It's her!" Otacon sounded thrilled.

"Wolf? Sniper Wolf?"

"Yes, it's her! It's definitely her!"

"Otacon, you sound like you're happy about it."

"No. I'm not."

"So, then what is it?"

"Snake. Please don't kill her!"

"Are you insane?"

Emmerich sounded as if he might cry. "Please. She's a good person! You'd know that if you talked to her."

"Listen to me, kid. She's a merciless killer."

A burst of static garbled the transmission for a moment. Then a female voice with a Middle Eastern accent came through. "I can see you perfectly from here. I told you I'd never quit the hunt. Now you're mine."

How the hell did she get hold of a Codec? Could it be Meryl's?

Otacon pleaded with her. "Wolf! No, you can't!"

"Don't get between a wolf and its prey!"

Snake challenged, "You're pretty good if you can hit me in this storm."

"Wolf!" Otacon continued. "Don't do this!"

"Snake," the woman purred. "I am near. Can't you sense me near you?"

Snake scanned the entire field from his position behind the tree. Granted, he couldn't see everything, but he was certain he'd be able to spot the woman if she was as close as she intimated. "Not yet, but if you reveal your location . . ." he said.

"I'm going to send you a love letter, my dear. Do you know what that is? It's a bullet straight from my gun to your heart."

"Wolf! Snake! No!"

"Quiet, Hal!" the woman commanded. "Don't get in our way!"

Snake snarled, "I'm going to pay you back for Meryl."

"You men are so weak. You can never finish what you start."

And then a bullet splintered the tree just above Snake's head. He hit the ground and lay flat as another round roughed up the snow near his face. He had to move, and quickly!

Snake jumped to his feet and ran away from the trees. Sniper Wolf's targeting laser followed him, and she fired again. This time he determined where she was perched: somewhere in a clump of trees in the middle of the field. Snake was willing to bet she had climbed one and was using the height to her advantage.

The operative zigzagged to a protrusion of rocks that was twenty yards away. The woman continued to shoot at him, but he successfully evaded her until he reached cover. Once he was safe, Snake was able to scrutinize the trees carefully, and he saw her. Sure enough, she was lying across a tree branch, rifle in hand. The woman was dressed in a white snowsuit, which accounted for her camouflage.

Snake removed the PSG-1 from his shoulder, leveled it at the sniper, aimed with as much precision as he could muster, and squeezed the trigger.

A splotch of red appeared on the woman's suit.

He watched as she dropped to the ground and ran for cover behind a different tree. Snake fired again, splitting the bark where she hid. Then—nothing. Had he hit her? There was no movement, so Snake kept perfectly still, the rifle aimed for the trees, his eye to the scope. Then he saw her rifle barrel appear at the side of the tree and ducked just in time. A bullet hit the rocky surface in front of him, splintered it, and sprayed jagged shards at his face. If he hadn't been wearing the goggles, he'd have been blinded for sure.

Snake wiped the blood off his nose and cheeks and gazed at the trees again. Sniper Wolf was on the move. She was running toward the maintenance building, obviously headed for a group of trees around the front entrance. Snake stood and aimed the PSG-1, but she disappeared behind a row of snow-covered shrubs. He waited until he could see the pinpoint of her laser sight searching for him. Then he aimed the rifle and fired. He wasn't sure if he struck his target because nothing happened. Once again, she had hidden effectively.

He had to get closer.

Time for another diversion. He reached into the pouch and removed a stun grenade. He wouldn't be able to throw it as far as he'd like, but perhaps the blast would provide enough cover for him to reach the group of trees where she had been earlier. Snake pulled the pin, stood, and threw it like a football. The

218 I RAYMOND BENSON

thing exploded in the air, creating a bizarre lighting effect in the snowstorm. He immediately ran forward, kicking up the snow as he did so, and headed for the trees.

Sniper Wolf got off two shots, one dangerously close. Snake dived for cover behind the first tree just as another round sliced the air near his neck. He lay flat for a moment so that he could catch his breath, but now he felt more confident. The woman was good, but she was no match for him now. He had winged her—he knew that—and she also had been wounded during their first encounter. She wasn't on her best game, and he was.

Snake crouched behind the tree, leveled the rifle, and searched for his prey through the scope.

There. She was moving from tree to tree, trying to find the best position from which to shoot.

He gritted his teeth and fired.

Sniper Wolf's chest burst into an inkblot of red, and she fell to the ground.

"No!" It was Otacon. He ran from the communication tower and struggled across the snow to reach the woman. Snake stood and followed him, but he knew there was nothing the young man could do. Something obviously had happened between Otacon and the female assassin, and now Otacon would pay an emotional price.

When Snake reached the fallen woman, Emmerich was kneeling beside her. She was breathing heavily as blood dripped from her mouth.

"I've . . . I've waited for this moment," she gasped. "I am a sniper. Waiting is . . . my job . . . never moving a muscle . . . concentrating . . ." She looked at Snake and said, "Please. Finish me quickly."

Otacon was crying. "No, please, no."

"I am . . . a Kurd. I've always dreamed . . . of a peaceful place like this." She was referring to the snowfield; it did have a certain beauty despite being a scene of bloodshed. "I was born on a battlefield. Raised on a battlefield. Gunfire . . . sirens . . . screams . . . they were my lullabies. Hunted like dogs day after day . . . driven from our ragged shelters . . . that was my life. Each morning . . . I'd find a few more of my family or friends dead beside me. I'd stare at the morning sun . . . and pray to make it through the day. The governments of the world . . . turned a blind eye to our misery. But then . . . he appeared . . . my hero . . . Saladin . . . He took me away from all that."

"Saladin?" Snake asked. "You mean . . . Big Boss?"

She nodded. "I became a sniper . . . hidden, watching everything . . . through a rifle's scope. Now I could see war not from the inside . . . but from the outside, as an observer . . . I watched the brutality, the stupidity of mankind . . . through the scope of my rifle. I joined this group of revolutionaries to take my revenge on the world."

She coughed and gasped. More blood dribbled out of her mouth as her breathing became even shallower. "But . . . I have shamed myself and my people. I'm no longer . . . the wolf I was born to be . . . In the name of vengeance, I sold my body and my soul. Now . . . I'm nothing more than . . . a dog."

Snake felt a compassion for her that he hadn't expected. "Wolves are noble animals," he said. "They're not like dogs. In Yupik, the word for 'wolf' is *kegluneq*, and the Aleuts revere them as honorable cousins. They call mercenaries like us 'dogs of war.' It's true; we're all for sale for some price or other. But you're different. You're untamed. Solitary. You're no dog. You're a wolf."

The woman squinted at Snake. "Who are you? Are you Saladin?" She was losing her sense of reality.

"Wolf," Snake whispered. "You spared Meryl's life."

"She . . . was never my real target . . . I don't kill for sport."

"Rest easy. You'll die as the proud wolf you are."

She closed her eyes. "I understand now. I wasn't wait-
ing . . . to kill people. I was waiting . . . for someone . . . to kill
me. A man like you . . . a hero . . . Please . . . set me free."

Otacon grabbed her hand. "No, no!" Then, quietly, he said,
"I loved you."

Sniper Wolf gestured with her other hand. "My gun . . . give
it to me . . . She's a part of me . . ."

Snake didn't think it could hurt. He picked up her rifle and
rested it in her arms. She was in no condition to fire it.

"Everyone's here now," she managed to say. "Set . . . me . . .
free . . . now . . ."

Otacon looked at Snake, who nodded, indicating that he
would grant her wish. Emmerich stood and turned away. It was
something he couldn't watch.

Snake drew the SOCOM and pointed it at the woman's
forehead. The gun recoiled once, and it was over.

Otacon walked a few steps away, his head bowed. Snake approached him and put a hand on his shoulder. "What happened
between you two, anyway?"

"Snake," Emmerich said through tears, "you said that love
could bloom on a battlefield . . . but I couldn't save her."

Snake squeezed the young man's shoulder. "Whatever it
was with you and her, it wasn't real. Do you hear me? You were
under her spell. I know you're unable to hear that now or don't
want to hear it, but in time you'll understand. I'm sorry."

Otacon sighed heavily and pulled a brightly colored handkerchief from his lab coat pocket. It was just like the one he'd
given Snake in the cell. The programmer walked back to Sniper
Wolf and laid the cloth over her face.

Snake was losing patience. "Otacon, I don't have any more
tears to shed. I'm going to the underground base. We're out of
time."

"I know."

"You'll have to protect yourself now. Don't trust anyone."

"Yeah."

"If I can't stop Metal Gear, this whole place will probably be bombed to hell."

"Yeah."

"We might not meet again."

"I'll hang on to my Codec. I want to keep helping." He handed Snake another Codec. "Here. She had this. I think it was Meryl's."

Snake took it. "Probably so." He stuck it in the pouch and walked toward the building to the north. "You can leave anytime. Get a head start, a head start on your new life."

"Snake!" But the operative didn't turn. "Snake, what was she fighting for? What am I fighting for?" Then he had to shout for Snake to hear him. "What are *you* fighting for?"

Snake turned and yelled, "If we make it through this, I'll tell you!" He continued toward the building.

Otacon kicked the snow and muttered to himself, "Okay. I'll be searching, too."

19

THE LEVEL 6 PAN card opened the door to the maintenance building. Snake stepped inside, SOCOM ready, and was met by a wave of heat. It was as if he had just stepped into a sauna, although there was no steam in the air. The place was noisy, too, with the industrial rumbling of heavy machinery echoing throughout a vast area. The room was as large as some of the other gymnasium-size spaces in the Shadow Moses facility, but in this case Snake was at the top looking down at a cacophony of metal that was bathed in a warm orange glow. He stood on a grid platform from which catwalks extended in different directions. One led to a metal staircase on the left side of the room; the stairs descended to another level of catwalks, and so on, for what appeared to be four floors. The bottom of the expanse was a smelting pit full of yellow-hot molten steel. Snake spotted two genome soldiers in the northeastern corner of the lowest floor; behind them was a large door that led to what appeared to be a cargo elevator. That was where he needed to go.

Unfortunately, there were surveillance cameras and at least two, sometimes three, guards standing on every landing, all the way down. Given the angles involved, there was no surreptitious way to descend the stairs without being seen. He would have to find another way to the bottom, and that presented a challenge. There were at least two large lead pipes running vertically on every wall, and the western wall appeared to have narrow ledges at each level. Snake could visualize a route along one of the ledges, but it would be extremely hazardous. One slip, one misstep, and he would fall to a molten death. Not only that, but the gigantic smelting arm—a mechanized lever that clutched, lifted, and moved heavy, hot objects—was rotating around the room. On each orbit, the "claw" came extremely close to the western wall. Snake counted the seconds of a single rotation and came up with the number 35.

It's doable, but . . .

After quickly studying the rest of the room, he came to the conclusion that it was his only course. Still carrying the sniper rifle on his back, he darted across the platform to the catwalk that led closest to the western wall. To leap from the landing to the ledge on the wall, he needed a diversion. He dug into the pouch, removed a frag grenade, pulled the pin, and dropped the explosive. It detonated a few feet above the smelting pit. Snake was thankful that genome soldiers weren't very bright: They all stopped what they were doing to gaze at the blast, scratch their heads, and give one another questioning glances. By then, Snake had jumped to the ledge, but he struggled to keep his balance. There was nothing to hold on to, and the ledge was no more than a foot wide. It was a feat more suited to a circus performer accustomed to acrobatics and aerial derring-do.

Once his weight was stabilized, Snake took a deep breath and dared to look down at the soldiers. They hadn't noticed

224 | RAYMOND BENSON

him. He heard one man mutter that the molten ore in the smelting pit had bubbled up and popped. They went about their business, and so did Snake.

Step by step . . . Snake felt as if he were walking a tightrope without a safety net. The only difference was that he was navigating the ledge while standing against a flat wall, which made it all the more difficult.

He hadn't moved ten feet when he heard a loud, cranking noise approaching.

The smelting arm!

He squatted in place, almost losing his balance again. The huge mechanical limb swerved over his shoulder and continued its orbit around the room. Snake took another deep breath, slowly stood upright, and resumed the crossing. It was a dizzying sensation. He never had encountered symptoms resembling vertigo, but for some reason the heat, the noise, and the dangerous height all contributed to an onset of light-headedness.

What do you expect? he asked himself. After all, he'd been on the move for well over twelve hours, had had very little rest, had undergone severe torture that literally had given a shock to his system, had eaten only the rations he'd brought with him, and had been a human punching bag several times over. It was a miracle he was alive, much less still standing.

Those thoughts might have demoralized an ordinary person, but for Snake they were incentives to stay the course. Master Miller had a saying, "When the going gets tough, the tough beat the shit out of everyone else." Snake lived by that adage, and he hated to lose. He would finish the mission—successfully—or there would be no use returning to his home in the Alaskan wilderness.

The mechanical arm came around again. This time, Snake ducked without thinking; after having been through the cycle once, he had no trouble adapting to it and building into his rhythm the anticipation of the machine's approach.

Before he knew it, he was on the other side of the pit. His target all along was one of the thick pipes that ran vertically from the ceiling to the floor. It was roughly a foot in diameter and was made of lead. The surface was hot, so Snake quickly slipped on his gloves, grasped the pipe with his legs and hands, and began to descend as if the pipe were a rope.

He was halfway down when an alarm blared throughout the steelworks. The guards on the various platforms jumped to attention and ran down the stairs to the bottom, gathered in a huddle, and then spread out around the smelting pit. They obviously were searching for something . . . or someone. But in separating, the guards left the space around the bottom of the pipe clear. Snake slid down without being seen, hugged the wall, and crept closer to the cargo elevator.

But they were waiting for him just beyond the other side of the pit. Four guards ambushed him, taking Snake completely by surprise. Two men grabbed him by the arms, and another forced him toward the side of the smelting pit. Snake struggled against them but was overpowered and outmatched. The soldiers pushed and dragged him closer to the pit with the intent to throw him into the molten-hot liquid.

It was time to fight dirty. Only in cases of extreme emergency did Snake resort to unethical techniques, but he figured that all was fair when you were fighting for your life.

Snake twisted his body to the right and kneed the man holding his arm directly in the groin. The soldier let go of him, cried out in pain, and dropped to the floor. The freeing of his right arm allowed Snake to swing it hard at the man to his left, crushing the soldier's Adam's apple. Then, in the time it took to blink, Snake elbowed the man directly behind him in the sternum, crushing the bone and stopping the guard's heart. Now unrestricted by the grasp of the ambushers, Snake turned and kicked the fourth genome trooper between the legs. The soldier froze in shock and pain long enough for Snake to pick him up by the arms and calmly toss him into the smelting pit. The guard's scream quickly was extinguished by the lava-hot metal.

All that had taken approximately 4.8 seconds.

Snake considered disposing of the three other men in the same fashion, but he didn't bother. He'd wasted enough time as it was, so he simply kicked the two conscious men in the head to send them to dreamland.

Thankfully, the cargo elevator was empty when the doors opened. Snake stepped inside and pushed the button to descend to the lower level.

"Snake!"

Master Miller was on the Codec. Snake answered and said, "Hey, you know what you once said about—"

"Never mind that, Snake. I have something to tell you."

"What?"

"Is this conversation secure?"

"Don't worry. The monitor's off. And we're on the frequency you picked before."

"Okay."

"What's up?"

"It's about Naomi Hunter."

Snake felt a shiver of dread. "What about her?"

"I was in the FBI, too, you know."

"I didn't know that," Snake said, "but what's your point?"

"Doctor Hunter's story about her background . . . about her grandfather being an assistant secretary to Hoover in the FBI and then going undercover to investigate the Mafia in New York . . . ?"

"Yeah? What about it?"

"It's all a big lie."

"How do you know?"

"J. Edgar Hoover was a racist, Snake. Doctor Hunter's father was Japanese."

"So?"

"Back then there wasn't a single Asian investigator. Also, the undercover Mafia sting operations hadn't started at the time she claims. And they started in Chicago, not New York."

"But—"

"You better check it out. The DARPA chief and the Arms-Tech president dying like they did, and that ninja . . . too many strange things are happening."

"Are you saying that Naomi might be behind it?"

"I don't know. Either that or she's working with the terrorists."

"I can't believe it!" Snake rubbed his brow and shook his head. "Could it be?"

"If I find out any more, I'll call. In the meantime, be careful!"

Miller signed off, leaving a weary and mistrustful Snake alone just as the cargo elevator came to a stop.

20

SNAKE FELT THE sudden dip in temperature deeply in his bones, especially compared with the heat of the blast furnace area. The elevator doors opened to a dimly lit massive space with a ceiling fifty feet high. The room was filled with shipping containers and crates, but it felt like the frozen meat section in the supermarket. Snake thought that it was so cold in the place that he might as well have been outside in the blizzard.

"Colonel? Naomi?"

The Codec sparked to life, and Dr. Hunter answered. "Yes, Snake?"

At first Snake was reluctant to talk to her. If what Master Miller had told him was true, he could be assisting the traitor in some way. He decided to limit the conversation to his basic question. "I'm in some kind of underground warehouse. They keep it really cold. It's probably below freezing in here. Any idea why?"

"I'm following you on the map, Snake, and our intel doesn't provide us with the purpose of particular areas in the complex. I can only guess that they have materials stored there that can't be exposed to heat. Mei Ling, do you read this?"

The woman answered, "Yes. I see you, Snake. Your body heat resonates as a big red dot on my screen. I think you're all alone in there. I don't see . . . wait. I don't understand."

"What?"

"There's a larger than normal source of body heat in the room with you. I can't tell if it's three or more people bunched together or what. Unless it's an animal of some kind."

"Is it moving?" Snake asked.

"Negative. Hold on. I see more heat sources. Several. *Tiny* ones. They're moving toward you, Snake."

"What do you mean by 'tiny'?"

"Smaller than cats. But definitely alive."

What the hell? Snake scanned the cavernous room in front of him but saw nothing but the large containers sitting on the floor in rows. And then . . . a black bird flew over a crate and circled his head.

"It's a crow. Or a raven," Snake said. "Wait. There are more of them."

The single bird was joined by a large unkindness of ravens numbering in the dozens. They formed a dark, black mass above Snake's head and flew as one, squawking loudly and menacingly.

Ravens. That meant only one thing.

"Welcome, *Kasack*!" the voice boomed. Snake drew the SOCOM and stepped forward and around a container to see the giant sitting on a crate with the Gatling Vulcan in his lap. "This is the end of the road for you. Right, my friends?" He addressed the birds, and they circled back through the air to their master. Most of them landed on the various containers and crates. A few alit on Vulcan Raven's shoulders. They cawed in answer. "Listen, Snake. They agree with me."

Snake gritted his teeth and spat on the floor. "I would have thought our last meeting might have convinced you to run for the hills."

The giant laughed. "That was no true battle! The ravens and I were testing you to see what kind of man you are. The judgment is decided. The birds say that you are a true warrior." With those words, the raven-shaped birthmark on the shaman's forehead seemed to animate, grow in size, and separate from the man's huge skull. It began to *fly* toward Snake.

Reflexively, Snake ducked. "Whoa! Am I hallucinating?"

The apparition disintegrated into nothingness over Snake, and then one of the live ravens flew toward him. It descended slowly and landed gently on Snake's shoulder. Snake tried to swat it away but found that he was unable to move. No matter how hard he tried, his muscles would not respond to his brain's commands!

"I can't move!" he managed to say. The shaman had cast some kind of black magic spell on him.

Vulcan Raven smiled. "Blood from the East flows within your veins. Your ancestors, too, were raised on the barren plains of Mongolia. Inuit and Japanese are cousins to each other. We share many ancestors, you and I."

"There are no crows in *my* family tree," Snake answered through clenched teeth.

"You jest, but indeed ravens and snakes are not the best of friends. Nevertheless, you will make a worthy adversary. You live in Alaska, too. You know of the World Eskimo-Indian Olympics?" The giant snapped his fingers, and the raven on Snake's shoulder spread its wings and lifted off. As the bird flew back toward its master, Snake's mobility returned. It was as if it hadn't happened.

"Yeah, I know it," he said. "You must be a real threat in the Muktuk Eating Contest."

"Ha ha ha! Yes, you are right. But there is another event that I excel at. It is called the Ear Pull. It's an event where two opponents pull each other's ears while enduring the harsh cold, as it is in this warehouse. It tests spiritual as well as physical strength."

Snake couldn't help allowing sarcasm to seep into his words. "You want to pull each other's ears?"

Vulcan Raven shrugged. "The form is different, but the spirit is the same. Rejoice, Snake! Ours will be a glorious battle!"

Snake took a step forward. "This isn't glorious. It's just plain killing. Violence isn't a sport!"

"Well, we will see if there is iron in your words!"

With that, Vulcan Raven swung the M61A1 at Snake and let loose with a barrage of 20-mm shells. It was only Snake's anticipation of the attack and his years of training that got him the jump—literally—on his nemesis, for Snake executed a perfect sideways cartwheel just before the bullets struck him. He landed on his feet behind the cover of a shipping container.

Raven stopped firing and laughed. "Excellent, Snake! That is something I could never do! But you will need more than tumbling skills to escape your defeat!"

Snake quickly reached into the pouch and removed a flashbang. He pulled the pin and flung it over the container. The stun grenade exploded before hitting the ground, causing several of the ravens to caw madly. Snake heard their feathered bodies drop to the floor, but had it done any damage to their master? Snake listened and waited for a sign that he had succeeded.

"You have hurt my family," the giant said. "Your puny stun grenades cannot harm *me*, though. I will admit I was blinded for

232 I RAYMOND BENSON

a moment, and yes, the burns are painful. But you will not get away with that again, Snake. And for the damage you have caused my beloved ravens, I will *annihilate* you!"

The behemoth charged around the container like a bull elephant. Snake shot several rounds from the SOCOM at the man, but the shaman simply blocked the bullets with the Gatling gun. Not only was the damned weapon the size of a Buick, it must have been custom made from a superresilient, bulletproof metal. And despite the giant's size, Vulcan Raven was *fast*.

Snake turned and ran.

"That's right! Run like the coward you are!"

To hell with that bastard! Snake thought. He wasn't running because of cowardice; he was retreating to formulate a plan of attack. The situation called for something drastic, and Snake had no idea what to do. He wished he still had the Nikita or the Stinger launcher, but he had left those bulky weapons behind long before. Retracing his steps to retrieve one of them would be impossible at this point.

He still had the sniper rifle. Snake swung it off his shoulder and checked the magazine. He then climbed on top of a shipping container and lay prone. He could see Vulcan Raven's massive form moving down a row between crates, searching for his prey. Snake aimed the PSG-1 at the man's head, steadied the crosshairs, and pulled the trigger, but a raven swooped from nowhere and jarred the rifle with its claws. The bullet seared the giant's ear, causing it to bleed severely, but it was definitely a miss. In response, Vulcan Raven swung the Gatling gun around and strafed the area where Snake lay. The operative flattened himself as much as possible as the bullets tore up the container and the air around him. The giant walked toward him, leaving Snake with no choice but to roll off the container, land on his feet, and run again.

But several bullets struck him in the back. It was as if he'd been clobbered by three or four sledgehammers; Snake's body was propelled forward, and he fell hard on his face. For perhaps a second he lost consciousness, but he regained awareness just as he heard the shaman's heavy footfalls approaching. The pain in his back was severe, but the body armor had prevented penetration. He was alive.

Move your ass!

Snake scrambled to his feet and slipped around the corner of another container.

Oh, my God! he cried to himself. His back felt as if it were on fire. The Kevlar-coated vest might have saved his life, but it did nothing to ease the discomfort of being shot. Snake wouldn't have been surprised if a rib or two had been cracked by the impact.

More rounds from the Vulcan strafed the container on the other side from where Snake was standing.

"You can't hide, Snake! Next time it will be a head shot, where you're not protected by armor!"

Snake slipped away, darted between lines of crates, and crouched behind a steel barrel near the back wall of the warehouse. Although he knew it wouldn't do much good, he removed another flash-bang, pulled the pin, and rolled it like a bowling ball down the aisle. It detonated just as Vulcan Raven appeared at the end of the row. This time the man yelled in pain, but he stormed through the smoke, even angrier than before. The Gatling gun roared again and perforated the back wall just as Snake fled from behind the barrel to another container. He then circled back to the point where Raven had been struck by the grenade. A large hole had been blown out of the container there, revealing stacks of *Claymore mines!*

Snake reached inside and removed two. Before the giant could spot him, he charged away and headed for the other side of the warehouse. He made a couple of turns, went down different aisles, and finally stopped at a large container near the cargo elevator. He quickly attached the Claymores to the side of the container at the height of his own head. He then found the C4 plastic explosive in his pouch and attached it to one of the Claymores. With the touch of a button, he set the C4 to detonate by remote and quickly programmed the radio frequency on his Codec.

Now he had to lure the big lug to him. Snake heard a familiar squawk above his head and saw one of the ravens hovering. With no remorse, he drew the SOCOM, aimed, and shot the bird out of the air.

"Snake!" The giant was furious. "You dare to kill my pets!"

He heard the heavy footsteps lumber closer. Snake backed away from the mines, jogged around the container, and moved closer to the cargo elevator. He then dropped to his knees, bent over as if he were experiencing tremendous pain, and held one hand over the Codec.

A few seconds later, the shaman appeared at the corner of the booby-trapped container. The blood from the wound on Vulcan Raven's ear had covered his upper body, creating a sight that was frightening and surreal.

"Ahh," he said. "My bullets have finally weakened you, despite your armor. Say your prayers, Snake. This is the finish. You fought valiantly but, alas, not well enough. Good-bye, fellow warrior!"

Vulcan Raven raised the M61A1 for one last salvo, and Snake pushed the button on his Codec.

The C4 detonated, causing both Claymores to explode in the giant's face. The entire warehouse shook from the blast, and the noise reverberated in the cavernous space for several seconds.

The remaining birds cawed in horror and sadness, flew in

concentric circles, and finally settled onto the large man lying in the aisle.

Snake stood and walked to the giant. Miraculously, Vulcan Raven was still alive, but barely.

"Just . . . just as the Boss said," the giant managed to say, "it is my existence . . , which is no longer needed . . . in this world. But my body will not remain . . . in this place. My spirit and my flesh . . . will become one . . . with the ravens."

The birds squawked in unison.

"In that way . . . I will return to Mother Earth . . . who bore me." The giant slowly lifted his heavy arm and pulled something from his pocket. He held it out to Snake. "Here. Take this. It will open the back door and lead you . . . to where you want to go."

Snake took it. It was a Level 7 PAN card. "Why?" he asked.

"You are a snake not created by nature. You and the Boss . . . You are from another world . . . a world that I do not wish to know . . . Go and do battle with *him* . . . I will be watching from above."

Snake said, "You are an honorable man. I won't forget you."

The giant looked at the operative with bloodshot resigned eyes. Vulcan Raven coughed and winced in pain. Only then did Snake see the horrible wound the size of a tire in the giant's side. The man's rib cage and internal organs were clearly visible. He would not live much longer.

"The man you saw die before your eyes . . . That was not the DARPA chief."

"What?"

"He was Decoy Octopus. A member of FOXHOUND."

Snake's jaw dropped. Suddenly the mystery of the two corpses was clear.

"He was . . . a master of disguise . . . He copied his subjects down to the blood. So he drained Anderson's blood and took it . . . into himself. But he wasn't able to deceive . . . the Angel of Death."

"The Angel of Death?" Snake figured the man was becoming delirious. "But why go to so much trouble? Why impersonate the chief?"

Vulcan Raven attempted to smile but couldn't. "You must solve the rest of the riddle . . . yourself. Snake . . . in the natural world, there is no such thing as . . . boundless slaughter. There is always an end to it. But you are different."

"What are you trying to say?"

"The path you walk on has no end. Each step . . . you take . . . is paved with the corpses of your enemies."

Snake didn't want to hear this. He turned his back on the dying man and strode toward the warehouse exit.

"Their souls will haunt you . . . forever!" the giant called, cursing his enemy. "You shall have no peace! Hear me, Snake? My spirit will be watching you!"

At that moment, the unkindness of ravens swarmed over their master, completely covering him. Snake stopped, turned, and watched in amazement as the birds did something he had never witnessed before.

After several seconds of cawing in grief, the birds suddenly took off in flight. There was nothing left of Vulcan Raven—his body had vanished completely. The ravens circled the spot where the shaman had fallen and then flew away into the darkness of the warehouse.

"What the . . . ?"

Snake rubbed his eyes and looked again. He exhaled loudly and turned back toward his goal. Even though personally he was skeptical, he knew that the Eskimo-Indian people believed in magic. That certainly had been one hell of a trick.

"Snake?"

The Codec. Master Miller again.

"Yeah?"

"Turn your monitor off. It's about Naomi Hunter."

But before Snake was able to do so, Colonel Campbell cut in. "What about Naomi?"

"Damn!" Miller muttered.

Snake sighed. The jig was up. "Colonel, is Naomi there?"

"No, she's away. She's taking a short nap. Master Miller, we've been trying to contact you for hours. Where have you been?"

"I've, uhm, been dealing only with Snake, Colonel."

"That wasn't our arrangement. We're all in this together."

Master Miller cleared his throat and said, "Fine, Colonel." Snake found that odd. Usually his former trainer got along well with Campbell.

"So what is this about Naomi?"

Miller answered, "Okay. Maybe we'd better let the colonel hear this, too."

"Yeah," Snake agreed. "Go on, Master."

"Well, basically, Doctor Naomi Hunter is not Doctor Naomi Hunter at all."

"What? Come on!"

"I thought the story of her background sounded kind of fishy, so I checked it out."

Campbell sounded skeptical but was willing to hear the man out. "And . . . ?"

"There is an actual Doctor Naomi Hunter, or I should say there was one. But she's not the woman we know. The real Naomi Hunter disappeared somewhere in the Middle East. Our Naomi must have somehow obtained her identification papers."

"So, then who is she really?"

"She must be some kind of . . . spy. Maybe sent to sabotage this operation."

"Are you saying she's with the terrorists?"

Snake jumped in. "I don't want to believe it, either. But I think she's working for FOXHOUND."

"You think she had a part in the uprising?"

Miller answered, "Or she could be working for some different group altogether."

"A different group? It couldn't be . . ."

"Place her under arrest, Colonel," Miller suggested.

"What? I—"

"She's betrayed us. She needs to be arrested and interrogated to find out who she's with."

"If she's one of their spies, then we're in big trouble . . ."

Snake detected something in the colonel's voice that indicated that his thoughts weren't exactly on the doctor. The man was worried about another problem that hadn't been mentioned. "What do you mean, Colonel?" he asked.

"Nothing."

"Uh, Colonel," Miller inquired, "have you let her in on some kind of vital secret or something?"

Campbell didn't answer.

"Does this have anything to do with the mysterious deaths of the DARPA chief and the ArmsTech president?" Miller demanded.

"I . . . I have no idea," the colonel replied, but he didn't sound convincing.

After a beat of silence, Miller said, "Anyway, we can't allow her to participate any further in this mission."

"Wait, wait," Campbell argued. "Without her, we can't complete this mission."

"I knew it," Snake said. "You're hiding something."

"No, no, it's not that . . . I'll try to get it out of her."

Miller said, "Hurry, then. We've got to figure out who she is and what she's doing here."

"I understand," the colonel answered. "Snake, give me some time."

Snake grumbled, "I don't have any time left for you, Colonel." He switched off the Codec, strode toward the warehouse door, slid the PAN card into the lock, and opened the door.

21

DR. NAOMI HUNTER gave up her attempt to take a nap and resumed her position at the computer terminal. Trying to forget the pain and guilt was a futile exercise. Her mind had raced over the events of the last several hours, and she couldn't relax if her life depended on it. She knew that things were going to come to a head sooner rather than later. The inevitable disaster was at hand.

She would have liked to have a strong drink, preferably a gin and tonic with a slice of lemon. The thought sounded so good that she salivated. Not only would the taste satisfy the craving, the alcohol would dull the senses. It wouldn't be long before she was in a world of pain, and there was no way she could escape it.

Colonel Campbell entered the control room and stood behind her.

"Naomi."

She didn't swivel in her chair to face him. Instead, she focused on the computer monitor, tracking Snake's position as he moved from the cold storage warehouse to the underground maintenance base where the Metal Gear was stored.

"Yes, Colonel?"

"You're wanted in the conference room." His voice was stern and direct. This was an order.

"Sir?"

"Now, Naomi. There are . . . some men . . . who want to question you."

Only then did she turn the chair. She hadn't realized that an MP had followed Campbell into the room and was standing at attention behind him. "Why? Who are they?"

"They're part of our security force here on the sub. They work for the Defense Department. You know that."

"Why do they want to question me?"

"Now, Naomi." The colonel nodded to the MP, who stepped forward. "This man will accompany you."

So it had happened much sooner than she'd expected. Dr. Hunter looked into Campbell's eyes and saw disappointment and anger. With resignation, she nodded, stood, and walked out of the room with the soldier.

SNAKE USED THE Level 7 PAN card to open the warehouse's back door, which revealed yet another underground tunnel built on an incline heading deeper into the earth. The Shadow Moses facility had more secret passages than the Magic Castle in Los Angeles, and this convinced Snake more than ever that it hadn't been constructed solely to store and dispose of nuclear throwaways. The mission had been straightforward enough, but Snake had discovered an unpleasant subtext to everything that didn't feel right. As the clues added up, Snake was convinced that the operation was a smoke-and-mirrors job, a cover for

242 I RAYMOND BENSON

something else entirely. Master Miller had given him a couple
of hints, and the dying FOXHOUND renegades had intimated
that all was not as it seemed.

Screw it, he thought. *Just finish the goddamn job.*

As he came to the end of the tunnel, he noticed a gun camera mounted above the door. It sensed him, too, for it suddenly
jerked out of a dormant position and pointed in his direction.
The lens and gun barrel scanned the tunnel for any sign of
movement, but Snake had slipped into the shadows and pressed
himself against the wall. He slowly reached into the pouch and
removed a chaff grenade. It would circumvent the camera's
ability to sense him but wouldn't disable the gun. But first things
first. Snake pulled the pin, tossed it, and watched the grenade
explode in front of the door. He then stepped out to the middle
of the tunnel and noted that the gun camera didn't track him.
He drew the SOCOM, aimed, and blasted the gun off its
mount.

The PAN card opened the door, and he stepped onto a long
metal bridge that led into a room that took his breath away. It
was the largest space he'd been in so far, and it looked as if it belonged in a *Star Wars* movie or a Japanese *manga.* It might have
been a cathedral built in reverence to the gods of mechaniza-
tion and high-tech wizardry. But the room was nothing compared to the monstrosity that stood before him on a large metal
platform. The thing inspired the kind of awe that one experienced when gazing at Mount Rushmore, the Taj Mahal, or the
Grand Canyon.

Metal Gear REX was a gigantic mech that resembled
some kind of reptilian beast. Snake estimated it to be at least
twelve meters tall and six meters wide. It was very broad-
shouldered with massive strong "legs" that let it walk like a
man. Its right arm was a long cannon, and the left was a short
barrel-shaped housing for various types of weapons. There was

no head per se, but the top of the Metal Gear was flat, and the middle of the shoulders extended forward to a cockpit where its pilots could sit.

It was nearly impossible to determine exactly what kinds of armaments were built into the machine. Snake could see machine guns in the nose, probably 30-mm. Guided antitroop TOW missile launchers also were built into the cockpit area. If the tank was anything like the other Metal Gears Snake had seen, somewhere on the behemoth was a laser powerful enough to slice and dice anything in REX's path. He guessed that it might be an ArmsTech International V17 Vulcan Cannon Searing LaserStorm High-Energy Cutter, which was the state of the art in laser weaponry. Finally, the right arm was equipped with an 18.5-m Rail Gun, a type known as a Widowmaker. And attached to it was a fully armed nuclear missile, ready to launch.

If that wasn't intimidating enough, REX's platform was surrounded by a moat containing what appeared to be murky, discolored sludge. The source of the liquid was a small waterfall flowing out of a machine on the left side of the room; the stuff was obviously waste material. The Codec had a Geiger counter feature, so Snake took the liberty of crossing the bridge and standing on the outer perimeter of the moat. There, he knelt at the edge and activated the Codec. The Geiger reading indicated that the water was contaminated with radioactivity. It was probably safe to be in the room, but taking a swim would not be wise. The sludge was like quicksand, a prescription for a distasteful death that could not be swift enough.

He stood and then realized how odd it was that the place was completely empty of genome soldiers. Snake was all alone with REX, and that didn't make sense. Where was everybody? He looked up and saw a large observation window high on the back wall. The lights were on behind the window, and he thought he glimpsed a figure moving away from the glass, out of sight. Snake figured that was the control room, the brain center for the entire operation. If his instincts were correct, plenty of secrets were stored there. A catwalk ran along the wall beneath the window, and there appeared to be an open door next to the window—the way in to the control room.

"Snake, it's me," the Codec chirped, revealing Otacon's frequency.

"Did you find a good place to hide?" Snake asked.

"Yeah, thanks to the stealth gear. It looks like they've finished getting Metal Gear ready."

"How do you know that?"

"I overheard them talking. Where are you now?"

"I'm standing right in front of it! But it's strange."

"What is?"

"There's nobody here. No guards, nobody patrolling. It's too quiet."

"Maybe 'cause they're all ready. They said they even inputted the PAL codes."

"What should I do?"

"All we can do is use the override system that President Baker told you about."

Snake cursed silently. "But I've only got *one* of the three keys. And besides that, like Ocelot said, there's some trick in using them."

"Okay, leave it to me."

"You got some kind of plan?"

"Well, I'm in the main computer room right now. I'll try to access Baker's private files."

"Baker's files? Don't you need a password?"

"Of course. But there are ways . . ."

The man's list of abilities continued to surprise Snake. "Are you a hacker, too?"

"Sure am. That describes me pretty well."

"Does it look like you can do it?"

"I won't know until I try!"

"Hop to it, then. I'm counting on you."

Snake signed off and studied the room's layout. Obviously, the best way to get up to the control room was by climbing Metal Gear. At the side of the base there was a movable stairway similar to what was used in small airports to receive passengers. He could wheel it next to REX's right leg and climb, giving himself access to the mech's knee. From there it would simply be a matter of making his way up the waist and torso, onto the cannon arm, and over the shoulder, finishing on the shoulder level. He looked around the room one more time to make sure he was still alone and then darted to the rolling stairs. The unit moved easily, and he was thankful that the wheels didn't squeak; the slightest noise echoed heavily in the church-like chamber. Once it was in place, Snake ascended the twenty steps, grasped the side of the mech's leg, and hoisted himself onto the knee.

Although REX's exterior obviously was made of a durable bulletproof steel, the texture was smooth to the touch. But it didn't have a sleek finish like an automobile. Metal Gear's design resembled the hardware appearance of Transformer toys or spaceships in post–*Star Wars* science fiction movies. This was a heavy walking tank that didn't try to hide the fact that it was completely mechanized.

Snake spent the next few minutes navigating his way up onto the chest and then onto the long right arm, and then it was a trivial matter to climb onto the shoulder platform. As soon as he was in place, Otacon called back on the Codec.

"Snake, it's me again."

"How's it going?"

"Not bad. I just got past Baker's third security level. He was a pretty careful guy."

"Do you think you can break in soon?"

"I never met a system I couldn't bust into."

"Okay, keep trying. I'm sitting on Metal Gear's head."

Otacon sighed. "I must admit I'm proud of it. Pretty impressive, isn't it?"

"Yeah, except for the fact that it could wipe out a city with the touch of a button."

"Oh, uh, yeah, I guess it can. It's armed, isn't it?"

"Looks that way."

"Then I'd better get to work. Give me a few more minutes."

Snake eyed the catwalk that ran beneath the observation window and the open door. The lights were still on, and he definitely could see movement. There was no easy way to get from REX's head to the catwalk other than by jumping. It was a good eight feet—a piece of cake in normal circumstances, but Snake didn't take any chances. He moved to the far end of REX's nose—the cockpit—and got a running start. He dashed across the platform and leaped as if he were performing an Olympic broad jump. His hands slapped the metal bottom of the catwalk, and he gripped it as tightly as possible. Snake hung there for a moment and didn't dare look down, for the radioactive sludge was only a fifteen-meter drop. He breathed deeply and then flexed his arm muscles to pull himself up and over onto the catwalk. He'd made it.

"Snake, I did it!"

Snake crawled to the edge of the catwalk closest to the wall just in case whoever was in the control room happened to look out. He punched the Codec receiver and whispered, "You got past security?"

"Bingo!"

"Great! So whaddaya got?"

"I accessed the confidential Metal Gear file."

"You see anything about the PAL override system that Baker talked about?"

"Haven't found it yet."

"That's what I need to know!"

"But Snake, I found something else!"

"What?"

"The secret behind the nuclear weapon! It's just as I thought. The nuclear warhead is designed to be fired from the Rail Gun like a projectile. It doesn't use fuel, so it isn't considered a missile. That way it can get around all sorts of international treaties."

"Pretty sneaky."

"But effective. And that's not even the scariest thing about this weapon."

"I can't wait to hear this."

Otacon whispered with urgency, "It's a *stealth* weapon!"

"You mean it won't show up on radar?"

"Yeah! The truth is, they've been working on a stealth missile since the late seventies. But they couldn't ever develop one because of the missile's rocket propulsion system. It would be picked up by enemy satellites. But unlike a missile, the Rail Gun doesn't burn any propellant. It can't be detected by any current ballistic missile detection systems."

"So it's an invisible nuclear warhead."

"Yeah. Totally impossible to intercept. On top of that, it's got a surface-piercing warhead designed to penetrate hardened underground bases. This thing could mean the end of the world!"

Snake rubbed his brow and looked down at the thing. "It's the ultimate weapon. And from a political point of view, it avoids the problem of nuclear reduction and nuclear inspections. Colonel? Are you listening to this? Are you there?"

Campbell cut in. "I'm here. I heard it."

"If word of this got out, it could delay the signing of the START-III treaty and cause a huge international incident."

Otacon agreed, saying, "Yeah, it'd be nasty. The United States would be denounced by the UN. It could even bring down the president."

"Did you know this, Colonel?"

Campbell hesitated before answering, "I'm sorry."

Snake felt a sudden pain in his chest, as if he'd been stabbed. Sometimes the worst wounds were caused by the knowledge that a friend hadn't been honest. "Colonel, you've changed," was all Snake could say.

"I won't make any excuses," Campbell replied.

"Snake, listen to me," Otacon interrupted. "This new nuclear weapon; it's never actually been tested. Only simulated."

"You mean they ran a computer model?"

"Yeah, that's why they were conducting this exercise. They needed to get actual experimental data to back up the simulation."

"What were the results of the exercise? Do you know?"

"It looks like it went better than they hoped for. But I can't find the data anywhere on this network. You'd think data as important as that would be carefully recorded."

Then Snake remembered. "It was. President Baker gave me an optical disk with all the test data."

Campbell spoke up. "What? Do you still have it?"

"No. Ocelot took it from me."

"Damn!"

Otacon continued, "The terrorists replaced the dummy warhead with a real one. Once they input the detonation codes, they should be ready to launch."

"You think they can do it?" Snake asked.

"Well, the dummy warhead was designed to be identical to the real thing, so I think so, yeah."

"Did you find out how to override it yet?"

"Not yet. It must be in a separate file. Right now I'm looking through all of Baker's personal files. Snake, I think I found Baker's ulterior motive."

"I'll bet he was just looking to get rich."

"Well, that's part of it. ArmsTech is in much worse financial trouble than I thought. You know they lost their bid to make the next-generation fighter jet? That, plus the reduction in SDI spending . . . Anyway, it looks like there was some talk of a hostile takeover."

"Then everything was riding on this project."

"And it looks like we were paying a lot of bribe money to the DARPA chief."

"Why am I not surprised?"

"Yeah, and Baker was a big proponent of the nuclear deterrent theory."

"I see." Snake shook his head. "Colonel? Tell me you didn't know about any of this."

"Not all of it, Snake. But yeah, I knew about the hostile takeover and Baker's attempts to prevent it. I knew he and Anderson were in this thing together."

"Okay. Otacon?"

"Yeah?"

"Find out about the override!"

"Yes, sir!"

Snake signed off. Right then he could have wrung Campbell's neck. What else had the man kept from him? Had this entire mission been about saving ArmsTech's face? It was degrading. If there hadn't been a viable threat involving a possible nuclear weapon launch, Snake would have turned around and gone home then and there.

But that was unthinkable now. He had come too far to give up. He *couldn't* give up. Even though his sympathy for the so-called human race was at an all-time low, he wasn't about to let the terrorists bring about doomsday.

Snake got to his feet and crept to the side of the observation window. The control room was full of computer banks and several workstations . . . and two immediately recognizable men—Liquid Snake and Revolver Ocelot. They stood over three separate laptop computers that sat on a single workstation in the middle of the room. Their voices were faint, so Snake risked moving next to the open door. From there, he could hear everything the terrorists said.

"—me know when you're done," Liquid was saying.

"Okay. I've entered the PAL codes and disengaged the safety device," Ocelot replied as he punched one of the laptop keyboards with his only good hand. The right hand, now a prosthetic, hung at his side. "We can launch anytime."

Liquid paced away from the workstation. "There's still no response from Washington. It looks like we'll have to show them we mean business."

"Should I set it for Chernoton, Russia?"

"No, there's been a change. The new target is Lop Nur, China."

"Why, Boss?"

"I'm sure neither you nor Mister Gurlukovich would really like to see a nuclear bomb dropped on your motherland, right?"

Ocelot shrugged. "But why? There's nothing there."

"Wrong. It's a nuclear test site. If we nuke a major population center, the game's over. But a nuclear explosion at a test site can still be concealed from the public. Meanwhile, Washington will be worried about the retaliatory strike from China."

Ocelot grinned. "That'll probably mean top-secret talks between both countries' leaders."

"Of course. And in the process, the president will be forced to divulge the existence of a new and highly destabilizing nuclear weapon to the Chinese. What do you think that will do to the U.S.'s reputation? Or the president's?"

"And with the CTBT, that means that China and India . . . I see!" Ocelot leaned back against the desk and folded his arms in admiration of his boss.

"Yes. When the other countries hear about the new weapon, they'll all want to contact us. Washington won't be very happy when we start selling their own system to the highest bidders. The president will surely break. He'll give in to our demands."

"Big Boss's DNA and one billion dollars . . ."

A *billion dollars!* Snake closed his eyes, unable to fathom what kinds of minds could dream up such a scheme.

"That money will be used to cure our genome soldiers as well," Liquid continued. "I'm also including the FoxDie vaccine in our demands."

Ocelot grumbled. "FoxDie. It killed Octopus and the Arms-Tech president. So it's true that it affects older people first. Mantis might not have been affected because he wore a mask."

"Wolf wasn't infected, either. Perhaps due to those tranquilizers she always took."

"Or something to do with the adrenaline level in the blood? Or maybe it's just because this FoxDie is still experimental and they haven't worked out all the bugs yet."

What the hell is FoxDie? Snake wondered.

Liquid made a gesture indicating that he wanted to change the subject. "In any case, have you heard from your friend at the Spetsnaz yet? What does Colonel Sergei Gurlukovich have to say?"

"He still has doubts about the ability of Metal Gear. He said we can talk after Metal Gear's test launch is successful."

"He's such a *prudent* man," Liquid said with sarcasm.

"There's nothing to worry about. The colonel wants Metal Gear and the new nuclear weapon so bad, he can taste it. If Russia wants to regain its position as a military superpower, they need to reinforce their nuclear arsenal. They need a nuclear weapon that can't be intercepted. Metal Gear will allow them to gain first-strike capability over the rest of the world."

"Their regular army is in shambles, and they think they can restore their country's military power with nuclear weapons? That Gurlukovich—he's no warrior, he's a politician!"

"Maybe so, but he's the one who gave us the Hind and most of our other heavy firepower."

"He's also got over a thousand soldiers under his command. If we joined forces, we could put up quite a resistance here. We could use the extra manpower—since Mantis died, the genome soldiers' brainwashing has started to wear off. I'm worried about the men's morale. An alliance with the Russians could serve us well."

Ocelot frowned. "What are you saying?"

"We're not going anywhere. We're going to dig in here. It's going to be a long war."

"We could still escape . . ."

Liquid shook his head. "We've got the most powerful weapon ever made, and we're about to ally with Gurlukovich's forces."

"What, are you going to fight the whole world?"

"And what's wrong with that? From here, we can launch a nuclear warhead at any target on the planet . . . a nuclear warhead invisible to radar and totally immune to interception! And on top of that, this base is full of spare nuclear warheads. Once we get the DNA and the money, the world will be ours!"

"But Boss, what about your promise to Colonel Gurlukovich?"

Liquid turned away from Ocelot and walked toward the observation window. Snake had to duck out of sight. "I have no interest in the revival of Mother Russia."

"You're not thinking of reviving Big Boss's dream?"

"Ocelot, you read my mind. From today, you can start calling this place Outer Heaven."

Snake winced. It sounded all too familiar. The ghosts of the past were rearing their ugly heads.

Outer Heaven . . . Big Boss's dream . . . Oh, my God . . . !

"Boss," Ocelot asked, "you're not worried about the PAL being overridden? If the code is entered again, it'll be deactivated."

"No need to worry. The DARPA chief and the ArmsTech president are both dead."

"Does Snake know how the override system works?"

"You interrogated him. Don't you know?"

"He didn't have any keys on him."

"Good. Then no one can stop Metal Gear now." Liquid went back to join Ocelot at the three laptop computers.

"By the way," Ocelot said, "what should we do with the woman? Want me to kill her?"

"Let her live. She's Campbell's niece, and Snake cares for her. We'll keep her as our ace in the hole."

Meryl! She's alive!

Snake suddenly was filled with an overwhelming desire to run into the room, confront the two FOXHOUND terrorists, and demand to know where they were holding Meryl. He wanted to strangle them both and throw their bodies into the radioactive sludge below the Metal Gear. But before he could do anything rash, the Codec beeped.

"Snake, I found it! Baker's top-secret files!"

"Great job, Otacon!"

"Where are you?"

"I'm looking into the control room. They've finished inputting the PAL codes. So how do we deactivate them?"

"Okay. You see the override system that the president was

talking about? It can also be used to input the detonation codes."

"There are three laptop computers," Snake said. "Is that the override system?"

"Yes! Now, if you insert the keys when the warhead is active, you deactivate it. And if you insert them when it's inactive, it becomes activated. You'd better get started; we don't have much time."

"But it takes three keys, right? I've only got one of them!"

"Hold on a minute! You see, that's the trick! You already have all three keys!"

Snake was losing patience quickly. "What the hell are you talking about?"

"The card key is made of a shape memory alloy. You know, it's a material that changes shape at different temperatures. The key is made out of it!"

Snake took it out of his utility belt and examined it. The card didn't appear to have any special properties. "This card key?"

"Yeah. It changes shape at different temperatures. It's actually three keys in one!"

"Clever. So what do I need to do?"

"Can you see the input terminals in the center of the control room?"

"Yeah. I see them."

"Those three laptop terminals are for the emergency input. There should be a symbol on each screen. Each symbol corresponds to a different key."

Snake removed his binoculars from the pouch and carefully edged in front of the window. Ocelot and Liquid had their backs to him, so Snake was able to zoom in on the laptops.

"You input the keys in order from left to right," Otacon continued. "The left one's for the room temperature key. See the symbol?"

Snake focused on a key icon that was colored black and white. "Yeah."

"Next to that goes the low-temperature key. The one on the right is the high-temperature key." Sure enough, the second terminal displayed a blue key icon and the third had a red one.

Snake put away the binoculars and said, "Okay, I got it. First I change the shape of the card and then I input them in order, right?"

"That's right. All you do is insert the card keys. After you insert the key into the module, a hard disk reads the information contained on it. Once you've finished with all three terminals, the code input process is complete. But you can only use the key three times—once on each terminal."

Campbell cut in, "The world is riding on that key, Snake!"

"Okay, I—"

But an alarm resounded throughout the maintenance base. A light beam shot down from the ceiling, quickly moved along the catwalk, and focused on Snake. Somehow he had been spotted by a hidden surveillance camera inside the control room!

Ocelot shouted, "Who's that?" and instinctually drew his revolver with his left hand. He fired at Snake, whose shoulder could be seen through the open door. Reflexively, Snake jerked out of the way and attempted to draw the SOCOM at the same time, but in doing so, he *dropped the key card*! He watched with horror as the thing flitted down past Metal Gear and into the radioactive sludge.

"Damn! The key fell into the drainage ditch!"

Behind him, the door to the control room slid shut. Snake turned to see Liquid gloating on the other side of the glass. "Well, well, Snake!" Snake swung and pointed the SOCOM at his nemesis. "This is bulletproof glass! There's no way in! I'm going to enjoy watching you die!"

Campbell shouted over the Codec, "Snake, you've got to get that key!"

Snake continued to point the SOCOM at Liquid but knew it was hopeless. But he had to unleash his rage and frustration. He jerked the handgun to the ceiling, aimed at the spotlight, and pulled the trigger. He then ran to the end of the catwalk to look for a way down.

He would have to take a swim after all.

22

THERE WAS NO way down from the end of the catwalk. The walk-way was simply a balcony of sorts for anyone who wanted to step out of the observation/control room and watch the proceedings in the maintenance lab below. From there, Snake heard the running footfalls of heavy boots behind a closed metal door. He grasped the SOCOM with both hands, knelt on the grid, and aimed. As the door slid open, he squeezed the trigger and spray-fired at the incoming guards. Three of them went down before someone had the sense to shut the door. Before reinforcements could arrive, Snake hurried back to the middle of the catwalk and leaped onto the top of Metal Gear. He scurried down the mech's chest and then jumped from the knee to the platform, dreading what he was about to do.

He pressed the Codec's transmit button. "Nastasha? Are you there?"

"Yes, Snake."

"What do you know about radioactive water? How dangerous is it? I would ask Doctor Hunter, but she's, uhm, indisposed."

"Well, Snake, it depends on how much radioactivity is in the water. You have a Geiger on your Codec, right?"

"Yeah. The reading is in the red zone."

"Then it is very dangerous."

Damn. "How long can I stay in the water without doing permanent damage?"

"Difficult to say. Is it absolutely necessary?"

"Yes!"

"Then don't stay more than ten seconds. Fifteen or twenty at the most. Beyond that and you could be in serious trouble."

"That's all I need to know. Thanks."

Snake set the Codec's timer at twenty seconds, put on the night vision goggles, snapped on the SOCOM's holster cover, and then, without a second thought, took a deep breath, held it, and dived into the sludge at approximately the same spot where the key card had fallen in. At first his vision was poor because of the murkiness, so he flipped on the penlight. This, combined with the goggles' infrared capability, allowed him to see a decent six feet ahead of him. The sludge was full of indescribable crud that appeared to be pieces of scrap metal, other garbage, and slime. Snake imagined that it couldn't have been grosser if he had been swimming in a sewer.

He hoped that the viscosity of the moat would be to his advantage. There was no current, so the key card would not have been carried to another part of the sludge; in all likelihood it simply had sunk slowly to the bottom. That was where Snake concentrated his search. It took him four full seconds to reach the dregs-filled floor, for it was a struggle to swim in the stuff, although Snake wouldn't exactly call it swimming.

Where is it? Come on, find it!

It was like trying to find the correct item in a-what-doesn't belong picture puzzle. Scattered among larger discarded objects were dozens of pieces of metal that looked like key cards. Only after picking up a couple of them did Snake discover that they weren't the exact shape.

He glanced at the timer. Nine seconds had elapsed.

Snake didn't know if the radioactivity was affecting him. He didn't feel any different—not yet, anyway.

Hurry! Focus!

He rummaged through the junk as he crawled over it, now desperate to finish the awful task and get out of there. At one point his heart leaped with joy when he found what appeared to be the key card, but it was only a useless Level 3 PAN security card.

Only seven seconds left. It was now or never.

He felt like an ocean-floor bottom-feeder as he crept along the grimy debris, picking up pieces and discarding them when he saw that they weren't what he wanted. Then—at three seconds remaining—he saw it. Snake grasped the key card, examined it to make sure it was the right one, and then worked as hard as he could to ascend to the surface.

He broke out and gasped for air at exactly negative one second. He scrambled out of the moat, lay on the platform, and took stock of his body. He didn't *feel* any different. He figured there was no way to be sure if the radiation had hurt him until he was examined by a medical team. He hoped that Nastasha Romanenko's time limit estimate was off by at least five seconds.

The guard reinforcements hadn't shown up. The lab was still empty, and REX stood silent and still above him. Snake removed the goggles, stuck the key in his belt, and proceeded to scale the mech again to get to the observation/control room. The climb was much easier and quicker now that he had done it once before, even though he had just exerted himself in the muck. As soon as he reached the catwalk, Snake peered through the observation window and saw that Liquid and Ocelot had left. He opened his pouch, removed a frag grenade, pulled the pin, and tossed it at the sealed door. He then dashed out of harm's way to the end of the catwalk. The blast did the trick by knocking the door out of the frame, although a portion of the catwalk was blown away as well. Snake carefully approached the entrance, straddled the hole in the walkway, pulled the door out, and let it fall to the platform below.

The control room was quiet and cool. Snake approached the three laptops on the workstation, removed the key card from his belt, and inserted it into the computer on the left. An automated female voice announced through the laptop's speaker: "PAL code number one confirmed. Awaiting PAL code number two."

Okay, that takes care of the first part.

Now he had to freeze the key. Snake looked around the room to see if there might be something he could use, but the place didn't even have an employee refrigerator. He punched Otacon's frequency on the Codec.

"Snake?"

"How the hell do I freeze this key card?" he asked.

"You got it? Great!"

"I've already put it in the first laptop. Now I gotta freeze it. How do I do that?"

"Gee, I guess you need to find someplace cold to put it for a few minutes. Is there something close by that's cold? Can you take it outside in the snow?"

Snake rubbed his chin. It wouldn't be long before the place was crawling with more guards or maybe even Liquid and Ocelot. "I don't know. But the warehouse I was in earlier—it was freezing in there. It's not too far, I guess." Then he remembered what the third phase of the deactivation process entailed. "So I have to heat the key on the third go-round?"

"That's right."

Snake winced. "How hot do I have to get the key to make it change shape?"

"Pretty darned hot. Not hot enough to melt it, but pretty close!"

Snake cursed when he realized he would have to make a trip back to the blast furnace room as well.

"Snake, if the warehouse is the only place you can think of, then you'd better get going! Hurry!"

He was afraid Otacon would say that. "Right. I'm on my way," he grumbled.

SNAKE HUGGED THE underground tunnel wall and carefully approached the back door of the warehouse. It was wide open, and he heard voices inside the cold storage room. Using extreme caution, he peered around the edge of the doorway and saw three guards dressed in snow uniforms with black insignia that identified them as Space Seals. Two of the men carried a large rectangular box, and the other one had his hands full with a bulky square container. Fortuitously, they were close enough for Snake to hear their conversation.

"Where do you want this?"

"Set it down over there. The Boss says he's coming to get it in a few minutes."

"What happened to the other one?"

"The intruder stole it. We don't know what he did with it."

"Seems like all we do is move stuff around. I'm getting tired of it."

"Me, too."

"I don't know about you, but I don't feel as enthusiastic about our new bosses as I did two days ago."

"Me, neither."

"I heard some of the guys left."

"In this weather? How?"

"They took some of the snowmobiles."

"Come on, let's get back. Boss says the intruder is where he wants the guy. The fireworks are gonna begin soon."

"Too bad the hostages won't see it."

Hostages? Snake's ears pricked up.

One man laughed. "We could always give 'em a closed-circuit TV. Let 'em watch like it was on CNN or something."

"I wouldn't be surprised if it *is* on CNN!"

"They wouldn't have very good reception in that underground bunker."

"I was *kidding*, numbnuts. We're not gonna let the hostages have *televisions*, for Christ's sake. What's next? Gourmet meals?"

The other two laughed, and they walked away, out of earshot. Snake waited a few moments longer to ensure that they were really gone and then slipped inside the freezing warehouse.

Underground bunker. Wonder where it is . . .

Snake punched the Codec. "Otacon?"

"Yeah?"

"Where are you?"

"I'm still in the computer room in case you need more help."

"Good thinking. Hey, do you know anything about an underground bunker where they're keeping the rest of the hostages?"

"Is that where they are? I was wondering about them."

"Do you know where it is?"

"I think so. If it's what I think it is, the entrance to the underground bunker is outside, near the entrance to the tunnel road that leads to the parking garage. But that's always sealed tight. There's another entrance underground, but I'm not sure where it is."

"Find it, will you? I suppose it wouldn't be a bad idea to free those people after I stop World War III."

Otacon laughed. "That's mighty thoughtful of you, Snake. Where are you now?"

"I'm in the warehouse. I'm cooling off the key card as we speak."

Snake pulled the card out of his belt and placed it on top of a container. He was amazed to watch the thing slowly change shape before his eyes. "How long does this take to change, Otacon?"

"Shouldn't be more than a minute or two in that kind of temperature."

"Right. I'll let you know when I get back to the observation room."

"Okay."

Snake signed off and then lit a cigarette. Why not enjoy the short break while he had one?

As he inhaled the ungodly tobacco—and again repeated the mantra that beggars can't be choosers—he eyed the two boxes the guards had brought in. They were sealed tightly, but the Fairbairn-Sykes knife came in handy for prying off the lids. The square container held a supply of explosives: C4, Claymores, frag grenades, and flash-bangs. Snake figured this was as good a time as any to replenish his stock. He filled the supply pouch with as many devices as would fit and then turned his attention to the rectangular box.

Lo and behold, it contained another ArmsTech portable Stinger launching system with three missiles. Snake grinned, stubbed out the cigarette, and closed the box. Somehow he knew that the weapon would come in handy, but he had to hide it so that Liquid wouldn't get his hands on it. The case was heavy, but Snake reckoned he could carry it as far as the maintenance lab.

The key card had finished morphing into a slightly different shape and now glowed with a cool blue tint. Snake stuck it back in his belt and then heaved the Stinger case onto his back.

UPON ENTERING THE maintenance lab, Snake surveyed the room for a suitable place to stash the case. He decided to store it next to a grouping of machine parts containers stacked against the lab's western wall. At first glance, the Stinger case appeared to be just another box among several. Unless someone was looking for it actively, he doubted anyone would notice the weapon.

The lab was still devoid of guards. From the gist of the conversation he'd heard in the warehouse, it seemed that Liquid had been correct: Psycho Mantis's brainwashing hold over the genome soldiers was wearing off. Some of them were deserting. With any luck, more would come to their senses and maybe even rebel against the renegade FOXHOUND operatives. But Snake couldn't count on it any more than he could expect Liquid and Ocelot to surrender. No, he had to see the mission through to the end alone.

After the climb up the Metal Gear, Snake found himself in the observation/control room once again. The key card was still cold, and it slipped right into the second laptop's slot.

The automated female voice intoned, "PAL code number two confirmed. Awaiting PAL code number three."

Snake punched the Codec and dialed Otacon's frequency.

"How's it going, Snake?"

"Okay. The second PAL code's been inserted. I'm on my way back to the blast furnace to heat this baby up. It's a little farther, so it's gonna take longer. Have you found the entrance to the underground bunker yet?"

"Not yet. I'm searching through tons of computer files that show diagrams of the facility's layout. Don't worry. I'll find it."

Snake signed off and headed out the door. He was all the way down Metal Gear and into the tunnel when the Codec beeped again. The frequency indicator registered as Master Miller's.

"Master? What's up?" Snake asked.

"Snake, it's about Naomi Hunter."

"Then you should just talk to the colonel. He's looking into it."

"Turn your monitor off, Snake."

He did so. "Okay. No one else can hear us. Go ahead."

"Sorry, but I didn't want Campbell to hear."

"Okay. What's up?"

"I've got a good friend in the Pentagon. He's the one who told me about it. It looks like the DIA recently developed a new type of assassination weapon."

"An assassination weapon? What do you mean?"

"Snake, have you ever heard of something called FoxDie?"

"Just a little while ago. I heard Liquid and Ocelot talking about it."

"Well, it's some kind of virus that targets specific people. I don't know all the details, but—"

"Look, Master, I don't have time for beating around the bush. What are you trying to say?"

"It's too similar."

"What is?"

"The cause of death. Didn't the ArmsTech president and the DARPA chief, er, I mean Decoy Octopus—didn't they die of something that looked like a heart attack?"

"Yeah?"

"Well, apparently FoxDie kills its victims by simulating a heart attack."

Snake stopped moving and leaned against the tunnel wall just before reentering the warehouse. "Are you telling me that Naomi is behind it?"

"Snake, try to remember. Did Naomi give you some kind of injection?"

Shit. The nanomachines.

"She was in the best position to have done it, but I don't know what her motive was," Miller said.

"Does the colonel know?"

"I'm not sure."

"Okay. I'll ask him myself." Snake switched the frequency. "Colonel?"

"Yes, Snake?" Campbell's voice sounded tired and tense.

"What's new with the Naomi situation?"

"She's in deep trouble. She was sending coded messages toward the Alaskan base. I didn't want to believe it, but she must be working with the terrorists."

"Are you sure?"

"I'm afraid so. She's being interrogated now."

"What kind of interrogation?"

"Well . . ." Campbell sighed. "I'd like to avoid the rough stuff, but we don't even have any sodium pentothal here on the sub."

"Call me if you find out anything." Snake switched the frequency back to Master Miller. "Master, it's not good."

"So it's true, isn't it?" the old trainer asked.

"Naomi . . . I can't believe it. You think she's the one that made this virus?"

"Who else? It's supposed to attack people on a *genetic* level. For example, anyone possessing, say, FOXHOUND genomes in their blood could be a target."

"My God . . ."

"But doesn't that mean there would be a vaccine?"

"You'd think so."

"So, I bet she has a FoxDie vaccine around somewhere. We have to find it."

"Listen, I've got bigger things to worry about right now. Why do you care so much?"

"Snake, you might be infected, too!"

I can't do anything about it, can I? Snake stopped himself from shouting it. "Sorry. Look, all I can do is let the colonel handle it. I gotta go."

He clicked off and entered the warehouse.

NAOMI HUNTER SPLASHED warm water on her face and looked in the bathroom mirror. They had put her through the wringer, but the ordeal hadn't been as bad as she'd feared. The interrogators hadn't been easy on her, but then again, she hadn't been tortured or anything. After all, she was aboard a military submarine in the Bering Sea. There wasn't a lot they could do at this point. She had managed to stall them for a little while.

The doctor dried her face, straightened her business suit, and walked out of the washroom. She went down the hall to the control room and peeked inside. Colonel Campbell was busy with some of the technicians and probably wasn't aware that the interrogation was finished.

This was her chance.

Dr. Hunter went straight to her quarters, where she kept a spare Codec.

SNAKE STEPPED OUT of the blast furnace room's cargo elevator and immediately broke into a sweat. The rise in temperature was a shock after the cold warehouse. The corpses of the guards he had dispatched earlier no longer were lying beside the smelting pit, so Snake exercised extreme caution before moving into the area. As he stood out of sight within the elevator alcove, he scanned the upper catwalks and staircases for any sign of movement and noticed that the surveillance cameras seemed to be functioning again. He drew the SOCOM, aimed at the closest camera, and fired, blasting the device into a hundred pieces. Two higher-mounted cameras were more difficult shots, so he swung the sniper rifle off his shoulder and drew a bead on one. He knocked the camera off its mount and then quickly repeated the action on the third.

The sound of running footfalls approached the elevator. A lone guard must have been alerted by the shots, for Snake heard the man speaking into a transmitter and calling for backup. Snake waited in the alcove for the trooper, but the man slowed his gait and advanced with vigilance.

"Who's there?" the soldier demanded. "Show yourself! Throw down your weapon!"

Snake kept perfectly still. So far the man hadn't seen him. But with a few steps more . . .

At precisely the right moment, Snake stepped into view, kicked the assault rifle out of the guard's hand, spun around, and delivered a second kick to the trooper's abdomen. Without pausing, he clobbered the soldier in the face with powerful one-two punches. The man went down like a slab of beef.

Snake gave the place a cursory look to make sure he was alone and then removed the PAN card from his belt. He set it on the lip of the smelting pit and waited as the thing changed its shape much more quickly than had happened in the cold warehouse. In a minute it was complete, glowing with a red tint.

He quickly took the "new" key card and dashed to the cargo elevator.

SNAKE WAS SPRINTING through the warehouse when the Codec beeped. The LED indicated an incoming call from an unknown frequency.

"Snake? Can you hear me? It's Naomi."

He stopped in his tracks and punched the button to transmit. "Naomi! What the hell?"

She spoke softly and urgently. "Colonel Campbell and the others are busy right now. I'm on a different Codec."

"Naomi, is what the colonel says true?"

The doctor hesitated before answering. "Yes . . . but not everything I said was a lie."

Snake's eyes narrowed. "Who are you?"

"I don't know."

"Come on."

"No, really, I don't know. I don't know my real name or even what my parents looked like. I bought all my identification. But my reason for getting into genetics was true."

"Oh, I *see*. Because you want to *know* yourself, right?"

She ignored the sarcasm. "That's right. I want to know where I came from. My age, my race . . . anything."

"Naomi . . ."

"I was found in Rhodesia sometime in the eighties . . . I was a dirty little orphan."

"Rhodesia? You mean Zimbabwe?"

"Yes. Rhodesia was owned by England until 1965, and there were lots of Indian laborers around. That's probably where I got my skin color from, but I'm not even sure about that."

Snake decided to continue the journey back to the maintenance lab as he talked. He moved quickly but kept the Codec transmitter on. "Naomi, you're too worried about the past. Isn't it enough to understand who you are now?"

"Understand who I am now? Why should I? No one else tries to understand me!" She took a breath to control the outburst and then spoke evenly again. "I was alone for so long . . . until I met my big brother . . . and *him*."

"Your big brother?"

"Yes. Frank Jaegar."

"*What?*"

"He was a young soldier . . . He picked me up near the Zambezi River. I was half-dead from starvation, and he shared his rations with me. Yes, Frank Jaegar, the man you destroyed. He was my brother and my only family."

"*Gray Fox?*" The revelation created a nauseating sensation in Snake's stomach.

"We survived that hell together, Frank and I. He protected me. He's my one connection . . . the only connection that I have to my past."

"And he brought you back to America?"

"No. I was in Mozambique when *he* came."

"Who is *he*? You mean Big Boss?"

"Yes. He brought us to this 'land of freedom' — to America."

Snake made it through the warehouse and entered the underground tunnel as she continued the story.

"But then he and my brother went back to Africa to continue the war. And that's when it happened. You killed my benefactor and sent my brother home a cripple. I vowed revenge and joined FOXHOUND. I knew it was my best chance to meet you, and I prayed for the day that I would. I waited two long years."

"To kill me? Is that all you cared about?"

"Yes. That's right. Two years. You were all I thought about for two long years. Like some kind of twisted obsession."

For some strange reason, the words hurt Snake deeply. He had felt some kind of connection to the doctor, and now everything had changed. "Do you still hate me?"

"Not exactly. I was . . . I was partly wrong about you."

"What about Liquid and the others?"

"I'll have my revenge on them, too!"

A thought struck Snake. "Naomi . . . you didn't kill that doctor, too, did you? The one who used Gray Fox for his genome experiments?"

"Doctor Clark? No. That was Frank. Afterward I covered it up and helped him hide from the authorities."

After a pause, Snake asked, "So that ninja—I mean Gray Fox—he's come here to kill me?"

"I don't think so. I think he just came here to fight you. I wasn't sure before, but now I think I understand. A final battle with you . . . that's all he lives for. I'm sure of it."

Snake stopped moving and leaned against the tunnel wall. "Fox . . . no . . ." Memories of his old friend flashed through his mind, but they were overtaken quickly by images of the man in the strange exoskeleton—the cyborg ninja. "Naomi, tell me something."

"You want to know about FoxDie?"

"Yeah."

"FoxDie is a type of retrovirus that targets and kills only specific people. First, it infects the macrophages in the victim's body. FoxDie contains 'smart' enzymes, created through protein engineering. They're programmed to respond to specific genetic patterns in the cells."

"Those enzymes recognize the target's DNA?"

"Right. They respond by becoming active. Using the macrophages, they begin creating TNF-epsilon."

"Huh?"

"It stands for tumor necrosis factor, a type of cytokine, a peptide that causes cells to die. The TNF-epsilon is carried along the bloodstream to the heart, where it attaches to the TNF receptors in the heart cells."

"And then . . . it causes a heart attack?"

"The heart cells suffer a shock and undergo extreme apoptosis. Then the victim dies."

"Apoptosis. You mean the heart cells commit suicide. Naomi, you programmed that thing to kill me, too, right?"

She didn't answer. Snake thought he heard a sniffle.

"How long do I have?" he asked. When she didn't respond, he said, "Naomi, I don't blame you for wanting me dead. But I can't go yet. I still have a job to do."

"Listen, Snake . . . I'm not the one who made the decision to use FoxDie."

"You weren't?"

"No. You were injected with FoxDie as part of this operation. I just wanted to let you know that. No, that's not the whole truth . . . The real thing I wanted to tell you was—"

But she was interrupted by a man's voice. *"Hey! What are you doing?"*

Naomi shrieked, and then Snake heard the sound of a scuffle. Her Codec fell to the floor, and the tiny screen on Snake's Codec filled with snow and static.

"Naomi? What's happening? Naomi!"

And then Colonel Campbell came on the line. The transmission was crystal-clear once again. "Snake, I can't allow Naomi to make any more unauthorized transmissions."

"What's going on, Colonel?"

"Naomi's been removed from this operation."

"What happened to her?" Snake shouted. "What did she mean when she said that FoxDie was part of this operation? Colonel, let me talk to her!"

"I won't. She's under arrest."

Snake was livid. "Colonel, you double-crossed me!"

"Snake, there's no time to explain! It's not what you think. Right now your job is to stop Metal Gear! Do you hear me?"

"Yeah, I hear you loud and clear, Colonel. I'm gonna do that *right now!"*

Snake shut off the transmission just as he entered the maintenance lab. Without bothering to check for the presence of guards, he scrambled up the mech, jumped to the catwalk, and went back inside the observation room.

The three laptops still sat on the workstation, awaiting the third and final code entry. Snake took the heated PAL key card from his belt and inserted it into the machine on the right.

"PAL code number three confirmed," the voice announced. "PAL code entry complete. Detonation code activated. Ready to launch."

"*What?*" Snake shouted. "No! Why? I deactivated it!" He took the laptop with both hands and shook it. "*What did you say??*"

A security door slid closed, replacing the blown-off one, and the sound of the slam reverberated loudly in the room. And then the lights snapped on inside the maintenance lab.

Metal Gear was awakening.

23

THE CODEC BEEPED. Master Miller was on the line. "Thank you, Snake! Now the detonation code is completed. Nothing can stop Metal Gear now."

Snake wasn't sure he had heard his former trainer correctly. "Master, what's going on?"

"You found the key and even activated the warhead for us, too. I really must express my gratitude. Sorry to have involved you in that silly shape memory alloy business."

"*What are you talking about?*"

"We weren't able to learn the DARPA chief's code. Even with Mantis's psychic powers, he couldn't read the chief's mind. Then Ocelot accidentally killed him during the interrogation. In other words, we weren't able to launch the nuclear device, and we were all getting a little worried. Without the threat of a nuclear strike, our demands would never be met."

Snake shook his head. Was he dreaming? Was he in a nightmare? This was *Master Miller* talking!

"*What do you mean?*" Snake shouted at the Codec.

"Without the detonation codes, we had to find some other way. That's when I realized *you* might prove useful."

"*What?*"

"First I thought that you already had the information and that we might get it from you, Snake, so I had Decoy Octopus disguise himself as the DARPA chief. Unfortunately, Octopus didn't survive the encounter . . . thanks to FoxDie."

Snake was livid. "You mean you had this planned from the beginning? Just to get me to input the detonation code?"

"You didn't think you made it this far by yourself, did you? I admit Vulcan Raven and Sniper Wolf tried to *kill* you—they had initiative I couldn't control."

Snake gritted his teeth. This guy wasn't Master Miller. "Who the hell are you?"

"In any case, the launch preparations are complete. Once the world glimpses the power of this weapon, the White House will have no choice but to surrender the FoxDie vaccine to me. Their ace in the hole is useless now."

"Ace in the hole?"

"The Pentagon's plan to use you was already successful . . . in the torture room." Miller laughed. "Snake, you're the only one who doesn't know. Poor fool."

"Who are you, anyway?"

"I'll tell you everything you want to know. If you come to where I am, that is."

"Where are you?"

"Very close by."

Colonel Campbell cut into the conversation. "Snake, that's not Master Miller!"

The man on the line replied, "You're too late, Campbell!"

The colonel continued. "Snake, Master Miller's body was

just discovered at his home. He's been dead since last night. I didn't know because my Codec link with Master Miller was cut off. We'd been trying to locate him, and I couldn't figure out how he was contacting you. Then Mei Ling said his transmission signal was coming from inside the base!"

"So who is it?" Snake asked.

"Snake, you've been talking to—"

"*Me*, dear brother," Liquid Snake announced, dropping the electronic enhancer that had disguised his voice.

"Liquid! How the—"

"You've served your purpose. You may die now!"

Snake looked through the observation window and saw that Liquid was inside Metal Gear's cockpit. The man waved and beckoned Snake to come down.

Anger and frustration took over. Snake drew the SOCOM and fired at the glass, but the bullets bounced off.

"Snake!" It was Otacon on the Codec. "That's bulletproof glass. You can't break it with an ordinary weapon!"

Snake ran to the door and punched every button he could find. Liquid had sealed off the room earlier. "Can't you open the security lock here?"

"I'll try. Just hold on a second."

Snake looked out the window again. The mech was plodding along the platform as Liquid attempted to get used to the controls. The man was an expert pilot, so it wouldn't be long before he mastered the beast.

"Hurry up, Otacon! I'm running out of time!"

"Just a little longer . . . !"

Damn!

Snake slammed his fist against the metal wall. It didn't hurt a bit.

"I'm hacking into security . . . !"

Liquid's bone-chilling laugh was transmitted through REX's audio system and echoed through the maintenance lab.

"Come on, Otacon!" Snake shouted.

"Almost there . . . almost . . . *there!*"

The door slid open. Snake rushed out onto the demolished catwalk, sidestepped the hole, and looked down at Liquid and his dangerous new toy.

"Solid Snake, *come on down!*" the FOXHOUND operative called in a mocking game-show-host voice.

Snake wondered how he *was* going to get down since the top of Metal Gear was no longer within jumping distance. Then, to answer his unasked question, a section of the platform began to rise. Liquid was able to control it from inside the cockpit. Snake had been unaware that such a hydraulic lift existed, but it made sense.

When the dais was high enough, Snake stepped onto it. Liquid then reversed the hydraulics to bring the lift down. As it moved slowly, Liquid held up a pair of sunglasses, the ones he had used to disguise himself as Master Miller on the Codec's monitor.

"How did you like them, Snake? Worked pretty well, I must say." Snake drew the SOCOM. "Oh, you'd point a weapon at your own brother?"

"*You* had Master Miller killed!" Snake spat.

"So I could manipulate you more easily. You performed quite well." The lift completed the trip to the floor. Snake stepped off as Liquid added, "Although the boys at the Pentagon are probably saying the same thing."

Snake was steaming. "What the hell are you talking about?"

Liquid shook his head and said, "*Tsk, tsk, tsk.* Following orders blindly with no questions asked. You've lost your warrior's pride and become nothing more than a pawn, Snake."

"What?"

"Stopping the nuclear launch, rescuing the hostages . . . it was all just a diversion!"

"A diversion?" Snake stood thirty feet away from REX. The hulking mech stopped moving and faced him.

"The Pentagon only needed for you to come into contact with us. That's what killed the ArmsTech president and Decoy Octopus."

"You don't mean—"

"That's right! You were sent here to kill us so they could retrieve Metal Gear undamaged along with bodies of the genome soldiers. From the beginning, the Pentagon was just using you as a vector to spread FoxDie!"

"That can't be true!" Snake shouted. "Are you telling me Naomi was working with the Pentagon?"

"They thought she was. But it seems that Doctor Naomi Hunter couldn't be controlled so easily."

"Explain!"

"We've got a spy working in the Pentagon. He reported that Doctor Hunter altered FoxDie's program just before the operation. But I must admit, no one knows how or why."

Snake wondered if that was why she was arrested. Perhaps Campbell was trying to find out the answer to that question.

"I had no idea she was motivated by such petty revenge," Liquid said. "We still don't know what changes she made to FoxDie. But it doesn't matter. I've already added the vaccine to my list of White House demands."

Snake lowered his gun a bit. "There's a vaccine?"

"Surely there is. There has to be! But that woman is the only one who really knows. At any rate, it might prove to be unnecessary."

"Why is that?"

"You were successful in coming into contact with all of us,

so we must have all been exposed to the virus. It's true that the ArmsTech president and Decoy Octopus were killed by FoxDie, but Ocelot, myself, and you, the carrier, were apparently unaffected."

Could it be a bug in the virus's programming?

"In any case, if it doesn't kill *you*, then I'm not worried, either. After all, our genetic code is identical."

"So it's true? You and I . . . are . . . ?"

"Yes, Big Boss was my father, too. We're twins. But not ordinary twins. We're twins linked by cursed genes. *Les Enfants Terribles. You* are fine. You got all the old man's dominant genes. I got all the flawed, recessive genes. Everything was done so that you would be the greatest of his children. The only reason I exist is so they could create you."

That revelation almost made Snake laugh. "I was the favorite, huh?"

"That's right! I'm just the leftovers of what they used to make you. Can you understand what it's like to know you're garbage since the day you were born?"

Snake had no answer to that. He simply stared at the man in the cockpit, trying to digest everything he'd just heard.

"*But*," Liquid said, raising his index finger. "I'm the one Father chose."

"So that's why you're so obsessed with Big Boss. Some warped kind of *love*?"

"Love? It's *hate*! He always told me I was inferior, and now I'll have my revenge! You should understand me, brother. You killed our father with your own hands! You stole *my* chance for revenge! Now I'll finish the work that Father began. I will surpass him. I will *destroy* him!"

Snake snarled, "You're just like Naomi."

"Well, I'm not like *you*," Liquid said. "Unlike you, I'm proud of the destiny that is encoded into my genes."

"Encode *this*, you bastard!"

Snake raised the SOCOM and spray-fired, but the cockpit lid fell into place with the speed of a blink and the bullets ricocheted off the bulletproof glass. Again, Liquid's laugh resounded throughout the lab.

"That was your last chance, Snake! Your blood will be the first to be spilled by this glorious new weapon! Consider it an honor . . . a gift from your brother! Behold, Snake . . . the power of the weapon that will lead us into the future!"

With that, Metal Gear emitted an earsplitting roar as if it were a dinosaur from a long-lost world!

My God! Snake thought. *They even gave the thing sound effects!*

And then the 12.7-mm machine guns let loose with a hail of bullets in Snake's direction. Luckily for him, Snake had been anticipating the attack. Every nemesis he had ever encountered loved to gloat and make a grand speech just before pulling the trigger. The only question was when the talking would end and the fighting begin. Snake's training incorporated reading the telltale signs in an opponent's eyes and voice inflection. The talkers were almost always the easiest foes to stay a step ahead of, but that applied only to enemies who weren't sitting in the most highly advanced war weapon ever devised.

Nevertheless, Snake somehow knew when Liquid would cease sermonizing and start brawling. Just as Liquid's fingers gripped the triggers, he was performing a cartwheel out of harm's way. At the edge of the platform, he jumped, did a somersault in the air, and landed on the other side of the sludge moat.

As Snake ran along the lab perimeter, Metal Gear turned, bellowed again, and took three steps forward. The high-intensity laser shot forth from the mech's underbelly and blasted a pile of crates to bits. Snake stopped running just in time, doubled back, and leaped back over the moat to the platform. By that time he'd been able to slip his hand into the pouch and remove a frag grenade. He pulled the pin and threw it at the cockpit, but the detonation failed to crack the glass cover. Snake then dug out two chaff grenades, pulled the pins, and threw them at the machine. At the very least, they would do some damage to the beast's targeting sensors and radar.

Liquid's response was to fire a Phalanga-F antitroop missile at Snake. Snake leaped forward to escape the worst effects of the blast, but its force propelled him directly between the walking behemoth's legs. Momentarily stunned, Snake realized he was lying on the floor, looking up at REX. From that perspective, the Metal Gear was awesome; it was either a magnificent, terrifying creation of which mankind could be proud—or it was the demon that would damn them forever.

How the hell am I going to stop this thing?

Snake shook away the cobwebs clouding his mind just as Metal Gear's enormous foot rose and prepared to stomp down and crush the operative to a pulp. Snake rolled out of the way as the heavy elephantlike appendage slammed onto the platform. The room trembled as if a minor earthquake had struck.

The Stinger! It's the only way!

He managed to get to his feet and move around the mech. The Stinger case was on the other side of the lab, across the platform. Snake knew he'd be wide open and susceptible to attack, but the only thing he could do was make a dash for it. Without a second thought, he started running as if he were competing for Olympic gold. The machine guns shot at him, but Liquid intentionally missed. Instead, the bullets prevented Snake from running in a straight line. And as soon as Snake changed directions in an attempt to zigzag across the platform, Liquid fired the guns and tore up the floor just inches away from his prey. When Snake was nearly halfway to his goal, a barrage of bullets halted his momentum. He was forced to leap to the floor and roll, and that left him dangerously vulnerable.

Liquid laughed, directed Metal Gear to look up at the ceiling, and launched another Phalanga missile. The rocket exploded on the metal roof, causing large pieces of heavy debris to fall onto the platform. Snake had to roll toward the sludge moat to avoid being crushed by the wreckage. Of course, the ceiling rubble was like confetti to the Metal Gear.

He looked at the moat and realized that he had to do it again. It was the only way to get to the Stinger.

Snake held his breath, closed his eyes—no time to fish out his goggles—and slipped into the sludge like a salamander. He struggled as hard as possible to swim through the muck quickly, turn a corner, and emerge on the side of the room where he had stored the weapon. Snake gasped for breath and crawled out just as Metal Gear's laser cut through the air above his head and obliterated the wall in front of him. He jerked his head down to evade the chunks of metal and brick that bombarded him but still felt as if he were being beaten by a hundred fists. As Liquid's laugh and REX's dreadful roar filled the room, Snake crawled to the pile of cartons and crates and placed his hands on the Stinger case. He opened it quickly, picked up the launcher, set it on the floor, and carefully loaded one of the three rockets into it. He then stood and faced the Metal Gear, which was standing amid the rubble on the platform.

Where to strike? The radome was the dish on top of the mech that controlled many of the radar sensors, the targeting, and the movement. That was the thing's Achilles' heel.

Make Master Miller proud, Snake told himself. *This one's for you, my friend.*

Snake squeezed the trigger, and the Stinger shot out of the launcher. The violent recoil against his shoulder was gratifying, for the missile struck its target dead-on. The explosion was immense, and for a moment the mech staggered. But the radome remained intact and functional. It was definitely damaged, but not nearly enough.

He had two more missiles and was going to need both of them to do the job. But before he could move back to the case to retrieve a second Stinger, Metal Gear fired a rocket at the grouping of crates. Snake leaped aside and rolled into the tunnel connecting the lab with the warehouse, which provided him with sufficient cover to protect him from the blast. The entire building rocked with the explosion.

"Come out of there, Snake!" Liquid shouted. "You're not a mouse! Come out of your hole!"

What was he going to do? If he went back inside to grab the Stinger case, REX would blow him to bits. There had to be some way to distract Liquid and get him to—

"Get away."

The voice came from behind him. Snake whirled around to behold the cyborg ninja standing a few feet away. The samurai sword was safely in its sheath, but the man formerly known as Frank Jaegar held a portable Vulcan cannon in his right hand.

"Gray Fox!"

The red light on the ninja's face covering glowed brightly for a second. "A name . . . from long ago. It sounds better than . . . Deepthroat."

Snake blinked. "*You're* Deepthroat?"

"You look terrible, Snake. You haven't aged well." The ninja walked forward, but Snake felt that he was no longer a threat.

"Fox, why? What do you want from me?"

"I'm a prisoner of death. Only you can free me."

The Metal Gear roared loudly outside the tunnel.

"Fox, stay out of this," Snake said. "What about Naomi? She's hell-bent on taking revenge for you."

The name evoked a reaction. The ninja paused and lightly touched his face. "Naomi . . ."

"You're the only one who can stop her."

"No . . . I can't."

"Why?"

"Because I'm the one who killed her parents."

Snake had no response to that revelation. He waited for the ninja to continue.

"I was young then and couldn't bring myself to kill her, too. I felt so bad that I decided to take her with me. I raised her like she was my own blood to soothe my guilty conscience. Even now she thinks of me as her brother."

Snake reached out to his old friend and said, "Fox . . ." but the ninja moved so that he couldn't be touched.

"From the outside, we might have seemed like a happy brother and sister. But every time I looked at her, I saw her parents' eyes staring back at me." Gray Fox stepped closer and touched Snake on the shoulder. "You must tell her for me. Tell her I was the one who did it."

"Fox . . ."

"We're just about out of time. Here's a final present from Deepthroat."

Before Snake could stop him, the ninja rushed out of the tunnel and into the arena to face the beast.

"Well, look here!" Liquid taunted. "In the Middle East, we don't hunt *foxes*. We hunt jackals. Instead of foxhounds, we use royal harriers! How strong is that exoskeleton of yours? Snake, are you just going to sit by and watch him die?"

Gray Fox shouted to the cockpit, "A cornered fox is more dangerous than a jackal!" And then the ninja lifted the Vulcan cannon and fired a succession of shots at the cockpit, producing considerably more damage than Snake's ineffective grenades had. Metal Gear returned fire with the machine guns, striking the ninja with dozens of rounds, but the exoskeleton succeeded in deflecting them. Gray Fox leaped sideways and darted to another part of the lab with lightning speed.

"Hold still, you bastard!" Liquid demanded.

Snake eyed the Stinger case that lay just a few yards away. This was his chance, for Fox had diverted Liquid's attention. The operative dashed to the case, removed the second missile, and loaded it on the launcher. He then performed a broad jump over the moat and walked to the center of the platform. Metal Gear's back was to him, but the radome was in plain sight. Snake shouldered the weapon, targeted the dish, and pressed the trigger.

This time, the explosion nearly knocked the radome off Metal Gear's body. The mech reacted as if it actually felt pain by bellowing with the volume of a thousand elephants. Metal Gear wobbled on its feet, almost as if Snake had blinded the thing. The rail arm groped about as Liquid struggled to regain control of REX's appendages.

Snake took the third and final missile out of the case and loaded it as Gray Fox crouched in front of the walking weapon. The ninja fired the cannon again, this time concentrating on the radome area. But the heavy rail arm swung, knocked the cyborg down, and held him prone. Gray Fox struggled to pull himself out from under the machinery, but it was no use. And then Snake watched in horror as Metal Gear's right foot lifted and poised over the ninja's helpless body.

It happened simultaneously. Liquid lifted the rail arm out of the way so that he could stomp on Gray Fox with the foot. But that action gave the cyborg the opening he needed to fire one last volley from the Vulcan. Metal Gear's foot fell just as the ordnance struck the radome at its epicenter. Flames erupted from the top of the mech as the gigantic dish crumpled and slipped to the floor. But the ninja's exoskeleton radiated a powerful electrical charge as Frank Jaegar was crushed by the tonnage.

"Impressive!" Liquid announced. "He was indeed worthy of the code name Fox. But now he's finished!"

But the destruction caused by the Stinger and the cannon fire had taken a far more serious toll on the mech than Liquid had expected. The entire top of Metal Gear burst into a blazing concoction of fire and electricity as several pieces of the structure broke away. Even the cockpit's cover separated from the nose and crashed to the ground, exposing Liquid. For the first time since the battle had begun, the FOXHOUND terrorist appeared concerned. Metal Gear was stumbling around the platform, out of control and crying like a wounded animal. A foot splashed into the moat and nearly tripped the mech, but Metal Gear merely lifted the foot out of the sludge, bringing a section of the platform with it.

Snake rushed over to where Gray Fox's broken body lay and knelt beside his friend. The red light was weak, and there were sounds of measured, shallow breathing. The exoskeleton had been crushed, and the ninja obviously had suffered severe trauma. Snake examined the helmet and found the latches that held on the face mask. He quickly loosened them and removed the plate, revealing the scarred, beaten face of Frank Jaegar.

The man whispered, "Now . . . in front of you . . . I can finally die."

"No, Fox. I'll get you out of here! I'll get you help!"

Gray Fox ignored his friend. He knew it was too late. "After Zanzibarland, I was taken from the battle. Neither truly alive nor truly dead . . . an undying shadow in a world of light. But soon . . . soon it will finally end . . . Snake, we're not tools of the government or anyone else! Fighting . . . was the only thing . . .

the only thing I was good at, but . . . at least I always fought for what I believed in. Farewell . . . Snake."

"Fox! No!"

But his friend expired with a final exhalation of breath.

"He prayed for death, and it found him!" Liquid gloated through Metal Gear's speakers. He had managed to gain control of REX's steering mechanism, but the behemoth still wobbled unsteadily on its feet.

Snake remained kneeling by his friend but slowly grasped the grip on the Stinger launcher.

"You see? You can't protect *anyone*! Not even yourself! Now . . . *die!*"

With split-second timing, Snake twisted his body, placed the launcher on his shoulder, aimed at the open cockpit, and fired. There was a tremendous explosion caused not only by the Stinger but also by the destruction of Metal Gear's central computers and power source, which was located behind the nose. Liquid screamed as flames engulfed REX's entire shoulder area. Snake covered his head but watched through the gap between his arms as Metal Gear quivered violently and went down on its knees. Then, with the weight and force of a falling building, the world's most dangerous weapon toppled over and crashed onto the floor.

The room jolted violently, knocking Snake over and into a blanket of darkness.

24

THE HAZE SLOWLY dissipated. Snake opened his eyes to see a dark room highlighted by bits of flame and smoldering brick and steel. He was lying on something hard that was somehow familiar.

His sneaking suit had been removed. He was bare-chested, wearing only his skintight pants.

"Sleeping late as usual, Snake?"

Snake's eyes rolled toward the voice. Liquid stood twenty feet away. He, too, was dressed only in tight pants.

"Liquid," Snake groaned. "You're still alive?"

"I won't die . . . as long as *you* live," his nemesis announced.

Snake rose and supported himself on an elbow. There seemed to be no serious damage to his scarred and bruised body, but he felt as if a gigantic sledgehammer had just pummeled him for a couple of days.

"Too bad," he said. "It looks like your revolution was a failure."

"Just because you've destroyed Metal Gear doesn't mean I'm done fighting."

Snake sat up. "Fighting? What are you really after?"

"A world where warriors like us are honored as we once were. As we should be."

"That was Big Boss's fantasy."

"It was his dying wish! When he was young, during the Cold War, the world needed men like us. We were valued then. We were desired. But things are different now. With all the liars and hypocrites running the world, war isn't what it used to be. We're losing our place in a world that no longer needs us, a world that now spurns our very existence. You should know that as well as I."

It was then that Snake realized where he was. Both he and Liquid were on top of the collapsed body of Metal Gear. Liquid must have dragged him unconscious to what was now the highest point in the maintenance lab.

Liquid indicated the fallen REX. "After I get our billion dollars, we'll be able to bring chaos and honor back to this world gone soft. Conflict will breed conflict; new hatreds will arise. Then we'll steadily expand our sphere of influence."

Snake sighed at the man's deranged viewpoint. "But as long as there are people, there will always be war."

"But the problem is *balance*. Father knew what type of balance was best."

"Is that the only reason?"

"Isn't it reason enough? For warriors such as us?"

Snake got to his feet. He had expected to be unsteady, but he seemed to be in full control of his faculties. He had a feeling he was going to need to be. "I don't want that kind of world!" he spat.

"Ha! You lie! So why are you here, then? Why do you continue to follow your orders while your superiors betray you?

Why did you come here? I'll tell you! You *enjoy* the killing, that's why!"

"What?"

"Are you denying it? Haven't you already killed most of my comrades?"

"That was self—"

"I watched your face when you did it!" Liquid laughed. "It was filled with the joy of battle."

Snake shook his head. "You're wrong."

"There's a killer inside you. You don't have to deny it! We were created to be that way."

"Created?"

"*Les Enfants Terribles!* The terrible children! That's what the project was called. It started in the early seventies. Their plan was to artificially create the most powerful soldier possible. The person they chose as the model was the man known then as the greatest living soldier in the world!"

"Big Boss . . ."

Liquid was enjoying this. He took a step closer, illustrating his story with hand gestures. "But . . . Father was wounded in combat and already in a coma when they brought him in. So they created us from his cells, with a combination of twentieth-century analog cloning and the Super Baby Method."

What was this guy talking about?

"Super Baby Method?"

"They fertilized an egg with one of Father's cells and then let it divide into eight clone babies. Then they transferred the clones to someone's uterus and later intentionally aborted six of the fetuses to encourage strong fetal growth. You and I were originally octuplets!"

As Liquid spoke, Snake felt his rage returning. As much as he wanted to believe that the man was lying, he *knew* that Liquid spoke the truth.

"The other six of our brothers were sacrificed to make us. We were accomplices in murder before the day we were born!" Liquid smiled. "So it was you and I. Two fertilized eggs with exactly the same DNA. But . . . they weren't finished yet." Liquid's smile vanished and was replaced by a snarl. "They used *me* as a guinea pig! To create a phenotype in which all the dominant genes were expressed . . . to create *you*. I got all the recessive genes! You took everything from me before I was even born!"

Snake didn't know what to say. He clenched his fists and waited for Liquid to continue.

"But . . . you and I aren't his only children."

"What?"

"The genome soldiers. They, too, are his progeny, carrying on his genetic legacy. But they're different. They're digital. With the completion of the Human Genome Project, the mysteries of humanity were laid bare. Thanks to Father's DNA, they were able to identify more than sixty soldier genes responsible for everything from strategic thinking to the proverbial killer instinct. Those soldier genes were transplanted, using gene therapy, into the members of the Next Generation Special Forces. That's how they became the genome soldiers. That's right, Snake! The troopers you've been killing right and left are our brothers, with the same genes as ours! They are our brothers, created artificially through the alignment of nucleotides to mimic our father's genes. They, too, are the product of numerous sacrifices."

"Sacrifices?"

"Human experiments. It was 1991 . . . the Gulf War. The military secretly injected soldiers with the soldier genes. The Gulf War syndrome that hundreds of thousands of returning soldiers complained about was a side effect of it."

Snake interrupted. "No. Everyone knows that Gulf War syndrome was caused by exposure to depleted uranium used in antitank rounds."

Liquid laughed. "That was just a cover story issued by the Pentagon! First they tried to say it was post-traumatic stress disorder, then chemical or biological weapons. The poison gas detection units and the antisarin injections—they were all just to cover up the secret genetic experiments."

"So, then the so-called Gulf War babies that have been reported by Gulf War veterans are—"

"Yes. They, too, are our brothers and sisters."

"Then the existence of the genome soldiers means that the experiments were a success?"

"Success? Don't be a fool! They're a complete failure! We're on the verge of extinction!"

"What?"

"Have you ever heard of the asymmetry theory? Nature tends to favor asymmetry. Those species which have gone extinct all show signs of symmetry. The genome soldiers suffer from the same problem—signs of symmetry. So do I, as do you. That's right. We are all on the verge of death at the genetic level. We don't know when or what type of disease will occur. That's why we need the old man's genetic information."

Snake replied sarcastically, "You want Big Boss's DNA so you can save your *family*? That's very touching."

"In nature, family members don't mate with each other. And yet they help each other survive. Do you know why? It increases the chance that their genes will be passed on to a new generation. Altruism among blood relatives is a response to natural selection. It's called the selfish gene theory."

"You're telling me that your genes are *ordering* you to save the genome soldiers?"

Liquid ignored the dig. "You can't fight your genes. It's fate.

All living things are born for the sole purpose of passing on their parents' genes. That's why I'll follow what my genes tell me. And then I'm going to go beyond. In order to break the curse of my heritage." Liquid paused and then added quietly, "And to do that . . . first I will kill you. Look behind you, Snake."

Warily, Snake turned to see a body lying on top of the Rail Gun. Red hair. Feminine body.

"Meryl! Is she alive?"

"I think so. She was alive a few hours ago. Poor girl kept calling your name. Stupid woman. Falling in love with a man who doesn't even have a name."

"I have a name!"

"No! We have no past, no future. And even if we did, it wouldn't be truly ours. You and I are just copies of our father, Big Boss."

"Let Meryl go!"

"As soon as we've finished our business. We're almost out of time."

"You're talking about FoxDie?"

"No. It seems now that the Pentagon knows Metal Gear was destroyed. They've arrived at a decision. They won't even need a battle damage assessment. If you want the details, why don't you ask your precious Colonel Campbell?"

Snake didn't want to do it, but he punched the transmitter on the Codec. "Colonel, can you hear me?"

"Yes," the man said. "I'm listening."

"What is the Pentagon trying to do? Answer me, Colonel!"

"Secretary of Defense Houseman has taken over active control of this operation. He's on his way here by AWACS."

"What for?"

"To bomb the facility."

"What?"

"Not only that. B-2 bombers just lifted off from Galena Air Force Base. They're carrying B61-13 surface-piercing tactical nuclear bombs."

"But Metal Gear is destroyed! Tell Houseman! Tell him!"

"Houseman heard that Naomi double-crossed us, and he's worried about FoxDie. Now that there's no more danger of a nuclear strike from Metal Gear, he's going to do whatever's necessary to cover up the truth of what really happened."

"He's going to drop a nuclear bomb to vaporize all the evidence, along with everyone who knows anything . . . ?"

"Don't worry, Snake! I'll stop the nuclear strike."

"How?"

"I may only be a figurehead here, but I'm still officially in command of this mission. If I issue an order to delay the strike, it'll confuse the chain of command and at least buy you some time. It'll give you a chance to escape!"

"But Colonel, if you do that—"

"It's okay, Snake. The truth is that FOXHOUND was already the subject of an undercover investigation. Meryl was transferred to the base just before the terrorist attack as a way of *manipulating* me."

"Those bastards!"

Campbell sighed. "I'm sorry. They forced me to cooperate in exchange for her life. You'd better get out of there, Snake."

"Are you sure? It'll be bad for you."

"Don't worry. It's the least I can do for you after all the lies."

"Colonel . . ."

"I'm ordering them to cancel the bombing run. After that there's no turning back. And th—*hey*! What are you—"

The Codec's monitor suddenly went offline. Snake shook it and cursed. After a moment, Mei Ling's distressed face appeared on the screen.

"Snake!"

"Mei Ling! What happened to the colonel?"

"I don't believe it!"

"What happened?"

"Snake, the colonel—"

The monitor went blank again from signal interference. Snake cursed a second time and tried to reestablish the frequency. But this time a new face appeared on the Codec.

Secretary of Defense Jim Houseman.

"Roy Campbell has been relieved of duty," the man announced. "This is Secretary of Def—"

"*I know who you are!* Put the colonel back on!"

"He's been placed under arrest for leaking top-secret information and for the crime of high treason."

"Ridiculous!"

"Yes, he's a ridiculous man. He truly believed that he was in command of this operation."

"You bastard!"

Houseman nearly smiled. Snake could sense that the guy was *enjoying* this. "There won't be a speck of evidence left. I'm sure the president would want the same thing."

"The president ordered this?" Snake demanded.

"The president is a busy man. I have complete authority here."

"How do you plan on explaining a nuclear attack on Alaska to the media?"

"Oh, we've prepared a very convincing cover story. We'll simply say that the terrorists exploded a nuclear device by accident."

"You'll be murdering everyone here. The scientists, the genome army, everyone . . ."

"Donald Anderson, the DARPA chief, is already dead . . ."

"So you didn't mean to kill him after all?"

"He was my friend."

"And you could care less about what happens to everybody else, huh?"

"Well, if you give me the optic disk, I might consider saving them."

"What are you talking about?"

"Metal Gear's test data! Anderson was supposed to bring it back. Baker had it."

"I don't have it!"

Houseman squinted. He wasn't sure if Snake was telling the truth. "Fine. Never mind. You and your *brother* are an embarrassment from the 1970s. Our country's dirty little secret. You can't be allowed to live. Alas. The bombs will be dropping soon, and I'm sure you two have a lot of catching up to do. Farewell."

With that, the Codec went dead. Snake looked up at Liquid, whose expression indicated that he had expected everything that had been said.

"There's no way out for us," Liquid remarked. "Let's finish this before the air strike." He pointed a finger at Snake and shouted, "You stole everything from me! Only your death can satisfy me. Only your death can return to me what is rightly mine!" He indicated Meryl and continued, "She'll make a beautiful sacrifice for our final battle. Do you see what's next to her?"

Snake turned again. This time he noticed the black box with the wires leading from it and wrapped around her chest. The device was obviously on a timer.

"That's the time limit for our final battle!" Liquid announced. "If you win, you might be able to save her. You could enjoy one brief moment of love before the end." He then gestured toward the edge of the platform on which they were standing. "And if you cross this line, you'll fall. At this height, it'll kill even you."

Snake inched toward the edge and looked down. Metal

Gear wasn't on its feet, but the height was still considerable. He could easily break his back if he fell.

Liquid lifted his fists and assumed an antagonistic position. "Let's go, brother. The bell has rung, and it's time to enter the ring."

Snake lifted his fists as well. So it was to be hand-to-hand combat. Snake was unaware of Liquid's abilities in that regard, but Liquid also didn't know that Snake had been Master Miller's top pupil in the hand-to-hand class.

The two men circled with their eyes locked on each other's. As they were both trained to blot out extraneous noises and distractions, they no longer were standing on top of the broken mech—they were in a boxing ring. The only differences were that there was no audience, and instead of rope barriers there was nothing—only a step off to certain doom.

Liquid took the offensive by moving in and rapidly striking Snake in the face. The man was so fast that Snake barely had time to attempt a block. He did that, but Liquid's fist still connected with his jaw. Snake retreated a step and let Liquid advance, a ploy he used to turn defense into offense. As Liquid leaned in for the punch, Snake kicked out his right leg and slammed it into his sternum. The FOXHOUND renegade felt the blow and stumbled backward. Snake didn't stop there. He continued to advance, utilizing his trademark one-two-three punch-punch-kick combination. But Liquid had a few moves of his own that surprised Snake. The man had a nasty underpunch that Snake couldn't manage to block.

They continued to spar for several minutes, delivering and accepting punishment in what seemed to be an essentially even match. It wasn't long before both opponents could anticipate what the other man would do. The fight was evidently a draw.

Snake knew he had to get Meryl and Otacon and get the

hell out of there before the bombers arrived. There was no time
to waste. He aggressively moved forward, spun his body, and attempted a roundhouse kick, but Liquid grabbed his ankle,
twisted it, and threw Snake to the platform. Before Snake could
roll out of the way, Liquid was on him, kicking him in the ribs.
The pain was immense, particularly after everything else Snake
had endured, but he forced himself to ignore it and grasp Liquid's calf to stop the kicking. Liquid pulled hard to free himself,
but Snake held on tightly. Finally, Liquid lost his balance and
fell, allowing Snake to jump on top of him. He pummeled his
brother with a succession of right-left power punches that would
knock out an ordinary man after the first blow. But Liquid lay
there and took it. Only when Snake paused to determine the
level of damage he was inflicting did Liquid expertly throw
Snake off him. Snake tumbled to the edge of REX's platform,
tried to stop himself from sliding, and slipped off the edge.

He grabbed whatever he could, which was the lip of the
platform that served as REX's flat head. Snake hung there, holding on for dear life as he tried to swing his legs back up to safety.

Liquid stood and appeared over him. "Good-bye, brother,"
he said as he lifted a foot and pressed it on Snake's right hand.
He began to grind the ball of his foot into Snake's fingers, producing an excruciating wave of torment that escalated up the
arm. Snake had to let go.

Snake hung by one hand, desperately searching for a hand-
hold beneath the lip. Then Liquid shifted his foot to Snake's left
hand and began to press.

With his free right hand, Snake stretched and grabbed Liquid's lower calf. He then pushed his thumb as hard as possible
into the soft, sensitive area below Liquid's bony ankle, the
Achilles' heel. The tissue there was aptly named, for Liquid
screamed in pain and released his foot. Snake then was able to

use both hands to pull himself up and back onto the top of the mech.

"Damn you!" Liquid shouted. He rushed at his opponent, but Snake sidestepped him, held both fists together, and smashed them into Liquid's lower back. The *oompf!* that Liquid uttered informed Snake that the blow had been painful and might have damaged the man's kidneys. Liquid staggered forward, trying to stabilize the agony, but Snake raised a knee hard into his throat. He then grabbed Liquid's long golden hair and pulled up the man's head.

Snake made a fist, drew it back, and drove it fiercely into his brother's face.

Liquid staggered backward to the edge of the platform. His feet caught on the lip, and his eyes grew wide. He waved his arms in that awkward, ridiculous gesture of people who lose their balance and then opened his mouth to scream. His eyes found Snake's and pleaded silently for help.

Snake had a sudden inclination to reach out and save his brother but at the last second chose not to do so.

Liquid cried out as gravity took over and the FOXHOUND terrorist toppled over the side. The heavy thud from below indicated that no protruding ledge on REX had broken the fall. Snake approached the edge and looked down. Like a rag doll, Liquid's body lay motionless on the lab floor.

Snake then turned his attention to Meryl. He ran to her side and examined the time bomb that was strapped to her body.

"Meryl?" He lightly touched her face and gave it a gentle slap. "Meryl! Wake up!"

She moaned and moved. *She was alive!*

"Meryl!"

"Uhhhh . . . Snake . . . ?" Her voice was hoarse. Her eyes flicked open and tried to focus on him. "Snake?"

"Meryl!"

"Snake! You're alive . . . ! Thank God . . . !"

"Don't move. I have to get this off you."

She gasped when she felt the wires.

"Stay perfectly still." Snake punched the Codec. "Nastasha? Are you there?"

Romanenko answered. "Yes, Snake."

Snake held his wrist so that an image of the bomb could be transmitted over the Codec. "Do you see that?"

"Yes."

"How do I get it off her?"

"It appears to be a timed explosive. Is there digital readout? How much time do you have?"

"I don't know," Snake said. "There's no LED."

"All right, I recognize the type of fuse. Listen closely. You see four colored wires, yes? The image on the Codec is not clear, so I can't tell what colors they are."

Snake pointed. "This one's red, this one's blue, these are green and yellow."

"Okay. Don't touch the blue one. I want you to gently re-move the green wire from the connector on the box. Try not to let the end touch any of the other wires."

Snake did so.

"Now you need to short out the box. Do you have a chaff grenade?"

"Yes."

"You'll need to explode it right there. Tell Meryl to cover her face. There's no detonation, but some of the particles from the grenade could hurt her eyes."

"Did you hear that?" he asked Meryl.

"Uh-huh."

Snake looked around the platform and noticed for the first

time that his sneaking suit had been discarded near her body. He grabbed it and wrapped it around her head.

He opened his pouch, removed a chaff grenade, and set it next to the bomb. "Are you sure this will do it, Nastasha?"

"Trust me, Snake. If you had left the green wire attached, it would have set off the bomb. But now the chaff grenade will disarm the bomb's sensory system. Like it does on cameras."

"If you say so."

He pulled the pin and stepped back several feet. The thing went off noisily, and Meryl yelped. Snake quickly moved back to her and pulled the garment off her face.

"Hi," she said.

"Thanks, Nastasha!" Snake ended the transmission and then leaned in to kiss Meryl, but he only gave her a peck on the lips. In response, she enveloped his head with her arms and held him there. Snake had to push himself off.

"Meryl, there's no time for that. Let me get these wires off you."

As he did so, he could hear the faint sound of airplanes. Since they were underground, there was no way to tell how close they were.

Then there was a distant explosion.

"Damn, the bombing's started!" He helped Meryl to her feet. The gunshot wounds had been treated and bandaged expertly, but she was in no shape to fight or run. "Meryl, are you okay?"

"*Are you okay?* Is that all you can say?"

He pursed his lips and then said, "Meryl, it must have been terrible."

"It wasn't that bad. I didn't give in to the torture."

"You were tortured?"

"And things worse than that." She put a hand to his mouth

to keep him from speaking. "But I was fighting, too. Just like you."

He shook his head. "You're a strong woman."

"Fighting them made me feel . . . closer to you. I felt like you were there with me. It gave me the strength to go on. But . . . I was scared."

"I'm sorry, Meryl."

"Don't say that."

"I tried to—"

"But it made me realize something. During all the pain and shame there was one thing I was sure of . . . a single hope that I held on to . . . and that hope . . . kept me alive." Tears welled in her eyes as she continued, "Snake, I wanted to see you again."

"Meryl . . ."

The Codec beeped. It was Otacon.

"Snake! It looks like you stopped REX!"

"Otacon, good news . . . Meryl's okay!"

"All right!"

"But I got some bad news, too. We're about to be bombed."

"I can hear it. I guess we're considered expendable."

"Is there a way out of here?"

"A way out? Uh, yeah. You can take the loading tunnel to the surface. There's a parking garage right next to you. The tunnel leads from there to the surface."

Snake looked down from the mech and studied the wreckage around the lab. "You mean the door in front?"

"No. It's a small entrance to the west of that door."

"How about security?"

"I just unlocked it. Who do you think you're talking to?"

"What are you going to do?"

"Me? I'll . . . I'll stay here."

"Otacon, this is a hardened shelter. They're going to use a surface-piercing nuclear bomb. It won't hold."

"I'm through regretting my past . . . Life isn't all about loss, you know . . . !"

"Otacon, don't be an idiot!"

There was a pause before Dr. Emmerich continued. "Okay, Snake, I'm a complete person now. I've found a reason to live. I'll meet you at the underground bunker. It's just next to the loading tunnel's entrance on the surface. At least we can try to set the hostages free."

"Can you make it there on your own?"

"I can sure try. Good luck!"

"Thanks."

"Thanks? Wow, that sounds kinda nice!"

He signed off.

"What's he doing?" Meryl asked.

"He's fighting right now . . . with his old self . . . to be the man he wants to be."

"He's fighting for us, too?"

"Yeah. And I don't want it to be in vain."

There was another explosion, this time closer. "It looks like we don't have time for a love scene," he said.

"Too bad. We have to go, huh?"

He took Meryl's hand and helped her down the pile of rubble once known as Metal Gear. Snake stopped momentarily to gaze upon the body of his brother. Liquid lay in a puddle of blood, showing no signs of life. The guy *did* resemble him. They shared distinctive physical characteristics, such as the cruel, snarling mouth that women found irresistible.

"Shouldn't we go?" Meryl asked.

"Yeah," Snake muttered.

They turned and left the terrible evidence of what Snake had suspected and feared his entire life. Even when as a child, he had acknowledged the fact that he was different from others his age. He was already sufficiently distinguished from his contemporaries in that he did not know his parents and had grown up with and been educated by a variety of foster "teachers." And he'd been training to be a soldier since early childhood. But none of that had bothered Snake. It was something else.

He never felt *normal*.

It was as if he was some kind of alien in a world full of human beings.

Now he knew why.

25

THEY WENT THROUGH the door that Otacon had remotely unlocked for them and entered an underground parking garage.
The place appeared to have been the scene of a skirmish, for
two civilian automobiles were overturned and burned. There
were several military-issued Overland Jeep MBs parked in a row
near the entrance, but otherwise the garage was hauntingly
empty.

"Oh, yeah," Meryl said. "See those overturned cars?"

"Uh-huh."

"Some of the civilian workers tried to escape the day of the
takeover. The guards stopped them."

"What happened to the rest of the employees' vehicles?"

"I don't know. They could have been scrapped for metal.
The terrorists use those jeeps, though. I'll see if I can find one
with the keys in it."

She limped toward the row of jeeps before Snake could stop
her—he had seen the surveillance camera just before she

stepped into its line of sight. Of course, an alarm rang. She froze like a deer in headlights.

"We're gonna have company!" Snake shouted. "Take cover!"

As she crawled inside a jeep, Snake moved quickly to the wall next to the door. A stack of petrol barrels provided sufficient cover, and so he crouched behind them and waited. Sure enough, three FAMAS-armed genome troopers entered the garage. One man barked orders at the other two and then pulled back to search the area where Snake was hiding. The other two separated and went for the vehicles.

It was perfect. The leader carefully walked back toward the barrels, giving Snake the opportunity to circle around the stack and sneak up behind the man. A decisive stranglehold dispatched the guard silently and efficiently. Snake laid the man down, picked up the FAMAS, and then stepped out from behind the barrels.

"Hey!" he called to the other two guards.

Two short bursts from the assault rifle was all it took.

"Meryl?" Snake called.

"Over here! There're keys in this one!"

Before running to her, he stripped the fur coat off the dead trooper leader so that he could give it to Meryl; she was dressed in skimpy clothes and would need it. She was in the driver's seat and already had turned the ignition when he got to the jeep. "I picked one with a toy in it." She indicated the belt-fed .30-caliber machine gun sitting in the back.

"Good work. You okay to drive?" he asked, throwing her coat.

"Never better. And you're a better shot, so get in!" She put the coat on and said, "Thanks! I'm not much of a fur person, but considering the circumstances, I'll wear it *just this once.*"

Snake leaped over the side of the jeep and checked out the gun as Meryl backed out of the space. Then, right on cue, a dozen troopers poured out of the garage door, spotted them, and began to fire indiscriminately.

"Floor it!" Snake shouted.

She burned rubber and headed for the tunnel, a long underground road that reminded Snake of the Lincoln and Holland tunnels in New York.

Meanwhile, Snake made sure that the ammo belt was fed into the gun properly as the guards' bullets flew over their heads. He grasped the holds and with both hands directed fire at the soldiers.

BOOM!!

The bombs were dropping closer. The entire structure shook as if a massive earthquake had struck. Many of the soldiers lost their balance and fell, and the others were mowed down by Snake's gunfire. The tremor subsided, and Meryl guided the jeep straight into the tunnel.

"We're not out of the woods yet!" Snake shouted over the noise of the jeep, which echoed loudly in the tunnel.

"I don't see the end of the road!" Meryl called. "Do you know how far it is?"

"No! Just keep driving!" She pushed the speed up to eighty.

After a half minute, they could see a barricade blocking the road ahead. Movement around it indicated that there were at least a few guards on duty.

"Snake!"

"I see them. I want you to drive straight through the barricade. They're just sawhorses."

He turned the gun around, aimed for the obstacle, and let loose with a barrage. The guards ran for cover, and three of them fell. The jeep burst through the blockade with a crash. The vehicle skidded for a couple of seconds, and then Meryl regained control. She increased the speed, and they continued their escape.

Another bomb fell and rattled the tunnel. Snake saw small pieces of plaster fall from the ceiling. For a moment he was afraid they might not make it out before the tunnel collapsed. He looked at the Codec and tried to contact Otacon, but all frequencies were disrupted.

"Snake, there's someone behind us!"

He looked back and saw two headlights rapidly gaining on them. It was another jeep. From that distance it was difficult to see how many men were inside, but it appeared that there was just a single driver. Could it be Otacon?

The flurry of machine-gun bullets striking the back of their jeep answered that question.

"Step on it, Meryl!"

"I'm on the floor as it is! Something's wrong with the transmission. It won't go into fourth gear!"

Damage from gunfire, most likely.

That meant the pursuing jeep eventually would reach them. Snake aimed the machine gun back toward the rear and fired. As the jeep gained ground, Snake recognized the long, flowing golden hair.

"Liquid! He's alive!"

"It's not over yet, Snake!" his brother shouted. More bullets sprayed the back of the jeep, and Snake was forced to duck. Liquid's jeep swerved back and forth, since its driver was trying to shoot and drive at the same time. Snake grasped the machine gun again and then noticed that there wasn't much ammunition left. The last of the belt was feeding into the weapon.

Make these count!

He fired and blew out the pursuing jeep's headlights. The windshield broke away, but Liquid had ducked below the dash. His vehicle swerved dangerously close to the tunnel wall and then got back on track.

Snake was out of bullets. He drew his SOCOM, but Liquid

rammed the back of their jeep hard. Meryl screamed, and Snake fumbled with the gun before he had a good grip on it. It dropped to the floor of the jeep, and he had to scramble down to retrieve it.

"I see sunlight!" Meryl called.

The end of the tunnel was a quarter mile ahead.

Liquid rammed the jeep again, causing Meryl to skid next to the wall. The jeep struck it, but the vehicle's speed worked in their favor as the jeep deflected off the surface and sped back to the center of the road.

The daylight was blinding.

The jeep practically flew out of the tunnel onto the icy, snow-covered road, hit it at a great speed, and began to skid and slide uncontrollably. Liquid's jeep did exactly the same thing as it exited the tunnel. The two vehicles spun wildly and eventually collided with each other with tremendous force. Both Snake and Meryl were thrown, but they landed in a large snowdrift that cushioned the impact. Still, Meryl cried out in pain, mostly from the trauma to her previous wounds.

Time stopped for a couple of minutes. Then Snake opened his eyes and crawled toward his companion.

"Meryl, are you okay?"

"Yeah." She winced when she tried to sit up. "Just a little shook up."

"Can you move?"

"Give me a minute. Right now I can't."

Snake studied their surroundings. Both jeeps were totaled. One was upside down and stuck in a snowbank; the other was aflame and on its side in the middle of the road. Liquid was nowhere in sight.

"What happened to Liquid?" she asked.

"I don't know. Wait . . ."

The bare-chested figure stood unsteadily on the other side

of the road. Liquid looked as if he had just taken a shower in blood.

"Snaaake!" he shouted. He pointed a finger and stumbled forward.

Snake rose to his feet, prepared to have another go at hand-to-hand combat with his nemesis. From the looks of his opponent, though, he didn't think it would last very long.

But then something happened. Liquid's face suddenly registered surprise and shock. He clutched his chest and gasped.

Heart attack?

Liquid's eyes bulged, and he dropped to his knees.

No . . . it's . . .

"Fox . . ." Liquid managed to say.

". . . Die," Snake finished for him.

Liquid fell forward onto the ice. Snake cautiously moved to him and knelt. He took the man's wrist and felt for a pulse.

Snake looked at Meryl and shook his head.

She was getting slowly to her feet. Snake returned to her to help. She leaned on him, and they walked onto the road.

"Where to now?" she asked.

"We have to find Otacon. He's supposed to meet us."

"Snake!"

The familiar voice came from around a large snowbank. They could see the tall, lanky young man in the lab coat waving at them.

"Over here!"

"Can you make it?" Snake asked Meryl.

"Yeah. As long as we don't have to run."

"I have a feeling the running is over. Hey, I just realized something. Where are the stealth bombers?"

She looked up. "You're right. The bombing stopped. What happened?"

"I don't know, but I'm gonna find out."

Otacon ran to them through the snow. He was carrying a large bag over his shoulder.

"Man, am I glad to see you two!" he said, shivering. "And man, it's *cold* out here!"

Snake wished he'd grabbed another coat, but he hadn't thought of it at the time. He indicated the bag. "What have you got there?"

"A bunch of C4. We'll need it to free the hostages."

"Where are they?"

Dr. Emmerich pointed to a smokestack protruding from the snow. "That's their ventilation. You see that snowbank a few yards from there, going down into that valley?"

"Yeah."

"That's the entrance. It's covered in snow."

"Okay, let's do it."

Snake and Otacon spent the next several minutes digging through the snow until they felt the hard cold metal of the bunker entrance. Otacon banged hard on it until they heard voices behind the door.

"Stay back from the door!" Snake shouted. "We're going to blow it!"

There was a muffled acknowledgment, and he nodded to Otacon. "Okay. Let's set 'em."

Otacon dug out three C4 explosives, and Snake placed them one at a time on the metal door. He set each one to detonate simultaneously by remote with his Codec. He banged on the door again and shouted, "We're ready! Get back now!"

They ran back to where Meryl was standing and took cover behind another snowdrift. Snake put his finger on the Codec button and said, "Here goes something."

The blast was big and noisy, and it seemed that a ton of snow catapulted out of the target area. Thick black smoke billowed out of the hole for a couple of minutes until it finally dissipated.

Then, a few at a time, people appeared. They were men and women of various ages, all dressed in civilian clothes and wearing winter coats. Otacon jumped up and ran to them. He greeted one of the men warmly, and they embraced.

"Aww, that's touching," Meryl said.

"I hope they have an extra coat for him."

Meryl stood and surveyed the barren white horizon. "Now the big question is, how do we get out of here?"

26

THE CODEC BEEPED. Snake was surprised and overjoyed to see that it was Colonel Campbell calling.

"Snake, can you hear me?"

"Colonel!"

"Are you okay?"

"Colonel, what happened? The bombing stopped. And . . . you're back!"

Campbell laughed. "I'm pleased to see you're happy about it. The secretary of defense has been arrested. Early retirement."

"Arrested?"

"I was able to get into contact with the president. Metal Gear, the training exercise . . . all of it . . . it was all Houseman acting alone."

"That figures. What happened to the air raid and nuclear strike?"

"The orders were rescinded. The F-117's and B-2 Spirits have returned to base. Once again, I have complete authority over this operation."

"I see. That's . . . that's great!"

"Washington isn't stupid enough to use nukes to cover up a few secrets. In any case, the danger's over. Thanks, Snake."

"Oh, Colonel . . . you can rest easy. Meryl's fine. She's here with me."

Snake had never seen Campbell so overcome with emotion. "Really? My Lord. That's . . . Snake, thank you. Thank you!"

"You're welcome."

"Snake . . . she's my daughter."

"What?"

"Meryl's my daughter. I didn't find out until recently. I got a letter from her mother . . . my dead brother's wife. I was going to tell her after this operation was over. I guess that's another secret I kept from you. And her."

Snake looked at Meryl, and she mouthed "What?" He shook his head and replied to the colonel, "Colonel, that's . . ." He had to laugh rather than finish his sentence.

"It's okay, Snake." Campbell laughed, too, and then said in all seriousness, "Snake, I'm sorry I kept a lot of things from you."

"It's okay, Colonel."

"Snake, I'm not a colonel anymore, remember?"

"Oh, right."

"I've got a present for you. Mei Ling just saw a snowmobile on the satellite photos. It's real close to you. This time of year the glaciers are pretty calm. You should be able to ride right out of there. I'll bet the boys at the DIA and the NSA never expected you to come home alive."

"Me neither. I better not show my face around there for a while."

"No danger of that. You officially died after your jeep sank into the ocean."

Snake said wryly, "That's not too far from the truth."

"There'll be a helicopter waiting for you on Fox Island."

"Listen, Colonel—I mean Roy—I mean, *hell*, Colonel, you'll always be the damned *colonel* to me! Anyway, we rescued all the civilian hostages. They're at the bunker near the loading tunnel entrance. Dr. Emmerich is with them."

"That's even better news, Snake. Mei Ling has already spotted them. We'll send a transport to pick them up."

Meryl limped over to where Otacon was standing. He had retrieved a coat, and the two conversed while Snake continued talking to Campbell.

"You gonna be okay, Colonel?" he asked.

"Don't worry. I've got an insurance policy: A hard copy of all Mei Ling's data. As long as I've got that, you, me, and Mei Ling will be fine."

. Snake checked the time on the Codec. "The battery on these nanomachines will run out soon. They won't be able to follow us."

"I guess we won't meet again."

"Don't worry. I'll pay you a visit sometime."

"Really? I look forward to that."

"Roy, just tell me one thing."

"What?"

"About FoxDie."

"Well, Meryl will be fine. She wasn't included in its programming."

"What about me? It killed Liquid."

"Naomi said she wants to talk to you face-to-face about that."

"Hmm. How is she?"

"Don't worry. Mei Ling's with her right now. I'll switch you over. Hold on."

Snake waited a few seconds, and then Naomi Hunter's face appeared on the monitor.

"Snake, it's me."

"Naomi . . ."

"I heard . . . about my brother . . ."

"I'm sorry. But he had one last message he wanted to give to you," Snake said. He quickly realized he shouldn't tell her the whole truth. It would make things worse for her. "He told me to tell you to forget about him and go on with your own life."

Tears appeared in Dr. Hunter's eyes. "Frankie said that?"

"Yeah. He also said he'll always love you. Naomi, your brother saved you, me, and the whole world. He fought with every ounce of strength in his body."

"Maybe . . . maybe now he's found some peace. He wasn't really my brother anymore . . . Ever since he fought you in Zanzibarland, he's been like a ghost. A ghost looking for a place to die." She sobbed and turned away.

Snake knew he had to ask the question straight out. "Naomi, Liquid died from FoxDie. What about me? When am I gonna go?"

Naomi sniffed and wiped her eyes. "That's up to you."

"What do you mean?"

"Everybody dies when their time's up."

"Yeah, so when is mine up?"

"It's up to you how you use the time left. Live, Snake. That's all I can say to you. You'll just have to trust me on this. You *do* have time, but even I can't say how much. Snake, each person is born with their fate written into their own genetic code . . . It's unchangeable, immutable . . . But that's not all there is to life. I finally realized that. I told you before, the reason I was interested in genes and DNA was that I wanted to know who I was, where I came from. I thought that if I analyzed my DNA, I could find out who I was, who my parents were. And I thought that if I knew that, then I'd know what path I should take in life. But I was wrong. I didn't find anything. I didn't learn anything. Just like with the genome soldiers . . . You can input all the genetic information, but that doesn't make them into the strongest soldiers. The most we can say about DNA is that it governs a person's potential strengths . . . potential destiny. You mustn't allow yourself to be chained to fate or be ruled by your genes. Humans can choose the type of life they want to live. Snake, whether or not you're in the FoxDie program isn't important. The important thing is that you choose life . . . and then *live*! It's what I'm going to do. Until today, I've always looked for a reason to live. But from now on, I'm going to stop looking and just live. Genes exist to pass down our hopes and dreams for the future through our children. Living is a link to the future. That's how all life works. Loving each other, teaching each other . . . that's how we change the world. It's the true meaning of life, and I just realized it. So thank you, Snake."

"You're welcome, Naomi."

"Good-bye, Snake."

The Codec transmission ended.

Meryl approached him and said, "Doctor Emmerich's staying with the hostages. He says for us to go on and find the snowmobile."

Snake looked up and saw the scientist waving. He waved back.

"Thanks, Snake!" Otacon called.

"Thank *you*!" Snake hollered back.

He then took Meryl's arm and followed the map that showed up on the Codec. It was slow going down a hill and over an icy outcrop of large rocks, but after a half hour they made it to the bottom of a cliff. Inside a small cave there was a ZR2500 Arctic Fox snowmobile. The keys were in the ignition.

Snake pushed it out of the cave and sat at the controls. Meryl got on behind him. He turned it on to let it warm up a bit. She held out her palm and showed him a bandana.

"I found this in the snow," she said.

"Let's keep it. As a reminder."

"Of what? A reminder of a successful mission or a reminder of the first time we met?"

"A reminder of how to live. Until today, I've lived only for myself. Survival has been the only thing I cared about."

"That's not just you. That's how everyone is."

"I only felt truly alive when I was staring death in the face. I don't know; maybe it's written in my genes."

"What about now? What do your *genes* say about your future now?"

"Maybe it's time I lived for someone else."

Meryl hesitated. "Someone else?"

"Yeah." He turned back to look at her. She'd never looked more beautiful. "Someone like you. Maybe that's the real way to live."

She smiled. Not knowing what else to say, she ventured, "So . . . where to?"

"David. My name is David."

Her eyes widened. "David? Really?" She laughed. "Okay, so where to, Dave?"

"Hmm. I think it's time we look for a new path in life."

"A new path?"

"A new purpose."

"Will we find it?"

"We'll find it. I know we'll find it."

"What are those?" She pointed at some four-legged animals in the distance. They had antlers and were as big as a moose.

"Caribou. For the Aleutians, the caribou is a symbol of life. It'll be spring here soon."

She whispered in his ear, "For us, too!" She placed her hands on his shoulders. He reached back and set his left hand on her right.

"Yeah. Spring brings new life to everything. It's a time for hope." He looked up at the clear sky. "I've lived here a long time, but Alaska has never looked so beautiful. The sky . . . the sea . . . the caribou . . . and most of all . . . you."

She giggled like a schoolgirl. "I think I'm gonna like this new life."

"Come on," he said, revving the snowmobile's engine. "Let's enjoy it."

With that, he accelerated and pulled out into the clean, virgin snow. The caribou ignored them as the snowmobile trekked across the whiteness toward new chapters in their destinies.

EPILOGUE

REVOLVER OCELOT LISTENED to the other man on the line and then spoke.

"Yes, sir. The entire unit was wiped out. Yes . . . yes, sir. Thanks to the vaccine, I'm okay. Yes, those two are still alive. The vector? Yes, sir. FoxDie should become activated soon. Right on schedule. Yes, sir, I recovered it all. REX's dummy warhead data is right there with everything else. No. There are no other records. They've all been deleted from the base's computer. No, sir, my cover is intact. Nobody knows who I really am. Yes, the DARPA chief knew my identity, but he's dead now. Yes. Yes, Liquid is dead. The inferior one was the winner after all. That's right. Yes, sir, until the very end. Liquid thought *he* was the inferior one. Of course, the other one thinks that, too. Yes, sir, I agree completely. It takes a well-balanced individual such as yourself to rule the world. Yes. Yes, sir. No, sir. No one knows that you were the third one . . . Solidus Snake. Right. So what should I do about the woman? All right. I'll keep her under surveillance. Yes. Yes. Thank you. Good-bye . . . Mister President."

Between 1996 and 2002, RAYMOND BENSON was commissioned by the James Bond literary copyright holders to take over writing the 007 novels. In total he penned and published worldwide six original 007 novels (including *Zero Minus Ten, Never Dream of Dying,* and *The Man with the Red Tattoo*), three film novelizations, and three short stories. His book *The James Bond Bedside Companion,* an encyclopedic work on the 007 phenomenon, was first published in 1984 and was nominated for an Edgar Allan Poe Award by Mystery Writers of America for Best Biographical/Critical Work. Benson has also written non-Bond novels: *Face Blind* (2003), *Evil Hours* (2004), and *Sweetie's Diamonds* (2006). *The Pocket Essentials Guide to Jethro Tull* was published in 2002. Using the pseudonym "David Michaels," Benson is also the author of the *New York Times* bestselling books *Tom Clancy's Splinter Cell* (2004) and its sequel *Tom Clancy's Splinter Cell: Operation Barracuda* (2005). Benson's latest original novel is *A Hard Day's Death,* published in April 2008. Visit the author at his website, www.raymondbenson.com.